GRAND NATIONAL

By the same Author

FRED ARCHER: HIS LIFE AND TIMES
NECK OR NOTHING: THE EXTRAORDINARY LIFE AND
TIMES OF BOB SIEVIER
THE CHELTENHAM GOLD CUP: THE STORY OF A GREAT
STEEPLECHASE
THE SPORTING EMPRESS: THE LOVE STORY OF ELIZABETH
OF AUSTRIA AND BAY MIDDLETON
A LIGHT-HEARTED GUIDE TO BRITISH RACING

Novels
RUN FOR COVER
STOP AT NOTHING
BEWARE OF MIDNIGHT
HARD TO HANDLE
WANTED FOR KILLING
HELL IS WHERE YOU FIND IT
ON THE STRETCH
GO FOR BROKE

John Welcome

GRAND NATIONAL

HAMISH HAMILTON

LONDON

First published in Great Britain 1976
by Hamish Hamilton Ltd
90 Great Russell Street London WC1B 3PT

Copyright © 1976 by John Welcome

SBN 241 89338 0

Photoset, printed and bound
in Great Britain by
REDWOOD BURN LIMITED
Trowbridge & Esher

To my daughter Pam
who made me write it

PART ONE

AUTUMN

1

Myles Aylward stopped the hired Cortina and looked at the map. The narrow, tarmacadam road curled bewilderingly through valleys and dingles but he thought that he must be near the place he was seeking. To his left ran a line of cliffs. Beyond them the September sun sparkled on a sea that was as blue and translucent as the Mediterranean.

From the ordnance sheet he identified a Martello tower on a headland in front of him. He looked at the map again. There was a cove below the headland and a rise of ground on the land-ward side. The road on which his car was halted turned and twisted through the gap between hill and headland. Beyond the gap a turn to his right should take him in a mile or so to Bartho-lomew Moriarty's training establishment, which was his desti-nation.

It was a strange, out-of-the-way place in which to train stee-plechasers, he thought. For the past fifteen minutes he had met no one at all. Even the patchwork of little fields on either side of the road had been empty save for a few sheep and a solitary donkey grazing. There was a small whitewashed farmhouse some distance away inland from whose chimney a thin spiral of smoke rose and drifted away on the light breeze. Save for these the whole landscape seemed quite deserted. A silence possibly unique in the countries of Western Europe lay over it all, dis-turbed only now and then as he neared the sea by the shrill cry of gulls.

Folding the map again he replaced it in the glove pocket and smiled slightly. Perhaps, after all, Mr Moriarty had chosen well when he selected this remote place for his training stables. He would have few labour troubles here and the men of West Cork were used to keeping their own counsel about those things that concerned only themselves and their employers. That, he thought, would be most important, for Mr Moriarty, from what he had heard, was a man who appreciated seclusion for himself and his horses. Down here he was a long, long way from Dublin and the eyes and ears of the stewards of the Irish National Hunt Steeplechase Committee.

Myles started the car and drove on. His thoughts were now full of the horse he had come to see and whether he would be justified in buying him, for there were special reasons why this purchase, if it came off, was an important one for him.

Myles Aylward was a racing journalist and a good one. He had two columns at his disposal for comment and criticism in one of the quality Sundays; four days a week he wrote as he liked for a Daily. There was, as well, a general racing article for a glossy weekly. He earned ten thousand pounds a year and was worth every penny of it.

Possessed of a fertile mind and a ready pen he could always find something fresh to write about or a new way of looking at old and famous occasions. Each year his descriptions of the great traditional meetings, such as Cheltenham, Aintree and Ascot, were eagerly sought for by his public. No respecter of persons he nevertheless prided himself on his fairness; but he spared neither horse nor man when he felt the occasion demanded it or he desired to say something which he knew needed saying. This had made him unpopular in certain quarters, not all of them august. He liked to champion those who he thought had had a raw deal in racing through no fault of their own. Those jockeys whom fashion and success had unfairly passed by, or trainers who suffered at the hands of authority or the whims of intransigent owners could always look to help from him.

Myles was very much a man of his age. The success which had come to him in journalism, though it was balm to his spirit, was not really what he had wanted from life. Ever since he had been a schoolboy he had nursed the ambition to be a successful steeplechase rider. He had been brought up in racing and he wanted nothing else. The leading jockeys were his heroes. Standing with his father by the parade ring, or inside it sometimes when one of their own was up, he would watch them mount and then swing down to the post, their big horses

4

moving with easy precision beneath them. Then, his breath catching at every stride, he would wait for them to come cracking into the last and, whips flying or holding tired horses together, battle for victory up the straight to the post.

From his father he had absorbed racing lore and knowledge of horses and their mastership. Always a reader, too, and a lover of books, he had devoured everything remotely connected with the sport upon which he could lay his hands. Almost as soon as he could read and write he had kept scrapbooks of racing photographs and reports culled from the papers.

At an early age he had been put up to ride work on his father's horses. Even as a boy he was introspective and soul-searching. Very soon doubts about himself and his own abilities began to creep into his mind. Horses took off with him all too easily; and, worse still, they did not seem to go for him as and when he wanted. During schooling, although he could sit tight and was seldom dislodged from the saddle, he had to admit that he was hopelessly bad at settling a young horse or persuading him to jump. He saw, or fancied he saw, the other lads looking at him and criticising his performances. Later he began to think they were laughing at him. 'He'll never make a horseman,' he had heard the head lad say one morning to his father when they did not know he was just behind them. His father, an easy-going man, said nothing to him, but Myles fancied he caught a look of sympathy or pity on his face as he watched his efforts.

This had all been in Ireland where they had lived long ago and where his father had trained a few horses and farmed two hundred acres, though farming had always come a bad second to racing in his father's scheme of things.

Then, when Myles was still at school, his father had died suddenly. His mother, an Englishwoman who had disliked Ireland, horses and racing in more or less that order, had stayed with her husband only because of the affection and physical attraction which sometimes exists between opposites. As soon as probate had been granted of her husband's will she had sold farm, horses and stock and moved to a small house at Putney, taking Myles with her. There, far away from the heady and dangerous world of horse-racing, she had settled down to a cosy routine of coffee, bridge and tea parties and had endeavoured to bring up her son to forget the enticements of the racecourse and to contemplate as his future a steady job in industry.

5

The endeavour failed. Though the horses had gone nothing could take away the fever they had engendered in Myles's blood. Nor could his mother prevent him reading the racing pages of the newspapers and anything he could find connected with the sport.

Then, a year or so after their return, a close friend at school had broken a collar-bone at the beginning of one Easter holidays. His father had bought a horse for him to point-to-point but his injury put that out of the question. Remembering Myles's enthusiasm and that he had ridden work in Ireland, the friend had written to know if he would come to stay for the holidays and take over the rides on the horse.

The friend's father was a rich industrialist. Myles's mother had been pleased and gratified by the invitation, the true intent of which had been carefully concealed from her, for she thought it might be helpful to her son's future. Truth to tell she found Myles rather a nuisance round the house during the holidays. His constant searching of the television programmes for racing and yet more racing was a reminder of a life she preferred to forget and a minor irritation as well.

When he arrived at Branston Manor, his friend's home, Myles had been far from fit, but he rode the horse out for a week before his first race. Soon his muscles and the all-but-forgotten grip and swing began to come back along with the exhilaration that came from the thud of hooves on the ground and the feel of wind past his ears in a gallop.

In the parade ring before the race he was almost physically sick with nerves. This was his chance, his opportunity to make a start, to commence the fulfilling of a dream. He kept telling himself that he must not make a mess of it, at the same time assuring himself that he would.

In the event he need not have worried. The father had bought well for the son. The horse had been carefully made and schooled and, moreover, he had been round before and knew exactly what he was doing. It was a confined hunt race; the other riders were even more unfit and inexperienced than he was, save for one elderly gentleman who had ridden dozens of winners twenty years before and who confided to Myles on the way to the start that he was just having a bump around for old times' sake.

Two fences out, Myles knew he was galloping over the rest of

6

them and that if he did not fall off or make some other sort of an ass of himself he had his race won. Muttering to himself, 'God, let me do this right, I must, I *must*,' he let the horse go between the last two fences. Jumping the last cleanly, he won pulling up by ten lengths. Two more victories on the trot followed and he returned to school something of a hero.

The next season his friend remembered him and asked him down again. A shortened and bowdlerised version of last season's successes had been given to his mother and, having acquiesced once, she could scarcely object to the second invitation. Others remembered him, too, for his friend's father had been lavish in his praises, and offers of outside rides came in.

But now he was not so successful. These rides were not all on patent safeties; it was necessary to do something more than just sit on them. Falls came, too, and riding three or four races in an afternoon he began to find the strain telling. It was more mental than physical; a nagging suspicion that his nerve might not be able to stand the constant wear and tear of the life he thought he wanted above all others began to creep into his mind. Always a self-doubter, he would go over and over his races in his mind, analysing what he had done and why he had failed, finding mistakes no one else saw, and blaming himself for losing races no one else expected him to win. As with the lads in the stable long ago, he fancied people were beginning to talk about him and to say that the promise of last season was not being fulfilled.

Then, ten days before he was due to go back to school, he had a double and some of his self-confidence began to return. Staying in the house was another friend, an Irish boy, who that night propounded a plan. His local point-to-point was due to take place, he said, in a few days' time. It included a race to be run over banks, probably one of the last, since the change to bush fences was then under way. He had a horse which he hunted and which he thought might win it. He himself, however, was too big and heavy to ride. Would Myles come over with him and ride the horse instead?

It was after dinner and the boys had been allowed to sit over the port. Myles was unaccustomed to alcohol which was seldom served in his mother's house, and he had enjoyed the taste of vintage port from a rich man's cellar. He had accepted immediately. Next morning doubts began to creep in. He had never ridden a race over banks, indeed never jumped one except on his cob out hunting in his father's time. The rosy glow of vintage port had long since disappeared. It all seemed a harebrained scheme but it was too late to back out.

The boy's father appeared to share some of the doubts when they arrived in Ireland a day or so later, and the proposition was put to him. However, he, too, felt he could scarcely refuse to put Myles up since he had been brought over expressly on the promise of a ride, and, after all, he had ridden winners in England.

In the parade ring before getting up, Myles noticed two hard-faced characters standing a few yards away both in racing jerseys. They were talking together earnestly and every now and then they looked across at him. The boy's father noticed them, too. 'The Gerahty brothers,' he said to his son. 'I didn't know they were going in this race?'

'I was dead sure they were in the Maiden,' the son replied. He, too, looked rather uncomfortable, Myles thought.

The father turned to Myles. 'Watch out for those two,' he said. 'Keep away from them if you can. This horse stays and he can jump. You might be wise to get out in front and keep there. Remember it doesn't matter a bit if you don't win. Just get round safely. That's all we want.'

These were not very reassuring instructions to receive on a first ride in a strange country. Myles glanced over at the two men. They looked tough, hard, competent and ruthless. As he watched, the taller of the two's mount was led over. It was a big, rangy, raking brute, just the sort of horse such a man should ride. He put his hands on the withers and vaulted into the saddle. He met Myles's glance with a look that was utterly expressionless. Then his lips twitched into a brief scowl. The next moment he was riding out of the paddock gate into the crowd.

Myles's mouth went dry. He wished h⁄ had never come. He wished the next ten minutes were over.

'They're being backed, I see, too,' the son said.

'Which one?'

'Phelim's. Mighty Rover. He's just gone out.'

There were only six runners so that it would not be easy to avoid the brothers if they did intend to devote their attentions to him. Myles lined up as far from them as he could. It did not avail him much.

At the first the tall brother jumped alongside him. He felt a

8

bang as they reached the top of the bank and an elbow drove painfully into his ribs. He rocked in the saddle and almost fell off. But he held on by the reins, jabbing the horse in the mouth as he came off the bank. The horse staggered, slithered, pecked and somehow recovered with Myles still on top. They had lost a good three lengths and the rest of the field were ahead. Myles decided the safest place now was at the back. But this tactic proved unavailing also. Going into the next fence the other brother, materialising out of nowhere, came upsides with him.

Thoroughly scared, Myles took a chance. He kicked the horse hard into the fence. As a result it stood back, flicked back at the bank and landed well out into the next field. Taken by surprise, the other Gerahty had been unable to indulge in any further tricks to put Myles out of the race. Myles then decided to take the father's advice to get out in front and stay there. He kicked on.

He was still in front approaching the third from last. It was a high narrow bank which he had noted as being a brute when he had walked the course. Ten lengths away from it he heard the thud of hooves behind him. Before he had time to think, the brothers had ranged up, one on either side. In another two strides they were closing in on him, squeezing him to blind his take-off.

Nothing in Myles's limited experience had prepared him for this. In the instant during which he had to make up his mind it seemed that there was only one chance to take and he took it. Again he kicked on, trying to burst through, out of trouble. But this time the horse, distracted by the attentions of the brothers, took off far too soon. He met the bank a foot from the top and they turned over into the next field.

Myles's one attribute as a horseman, his security in the saddle, made a bad fall into a worse one. He was still there when they hit the ground and the horse came over on top of him.

When the primitive ambulance services reached him he was unconscious. In hospital they found he had a broken right thigh, crushed vertebrae, concussion and a suspected fracture of the skull.

'Can I ride again?' he asked the surgeon when he was well enough to think of anything.

'Not if you want to go on living,' was the brief and brutal reply.

Myles's first feeling was one of relief—or he thought it was—and it added to his self-loathing. He was a failure before he started at the one thing that he had wanted to do, and he knew that the failure came from within, that he would never have made the grade anyway because of deficiencies in ability and temperament. A sense of inadequacy was to remain with him for the rest of his life.

Returning to school, he had succeeded in getting his A levels but he did not pass into Oxford as his mother had hoped. His back injury had precluded him from playing football so that, at school, there had been plenty of time for reading. Although he could not ride he was determined somehow to stay in racing and gradually a new ambition was born. He would become a racing journalist. During one holidays he taught himself to type and then, putting to use all the racing lore and history he had accumulated, he tried his hand at articles for racing magazines. Many of them came back though some contained encouraging slips from editors, but, to his delight, one or two were accepted. By the time he left school he was fully determined on the course his life would take.

Carefully concealing his moves from his mother, who was in any event beginning to take less and less interest in him, through an old friend of his father's he had secured an introduction to the sports editor of a great daily newspaper.

The sports editor, when Myles was sent up to see him, was both over-worked and out of sorts. Perhaps because he had had two more lunchtime gins in El Vino's than he had intended or were good for him, he had determined to give Myles short shrift and a maximum of ten minutes of his time. As Myles entered the office he grunted, belched slightly and motioned him to a chair. 'So you want to join a paper and write about racing. Why?' he demanded gruffly.

'I love racing and I love writing. I broke myself up in a point-to-point two years ago and I'm not allowed to ride.'

'How many A levels have you got?'

'Four. One in English.'

Despite himself the sports editor found he was becoming interested. He had always taken a pride in his instinct for the itch to write and his appointments had mostly proved him correct. He thought he detected it here in this rather fragile-looking boy who sat before him.

'Hm. Ever written anything?'

'Yes, sir. I've had three articles published. One in *Racing and Racehorses* and two in *Turf and Turnstile*. I've brought along photostats, if you'd like—'

'In a moment. What won the Derby in 1948?'

'The Aga Khan's My Love. By Vatellor out of For My Love, by—'

'All right, all right. I don't want the whole stud-book recited at me, boy. Now show me those articles.'

He glanced quickly through them, then leant forward and spoke into an internal telephone. 'Andrew? You're there. Good. I've got a young fellow here who thinks he can write about racing.'

'Not another?' The voice sounded unutterably bored.

'Yes. Still, I think you might see him.'

There was a sigh and then the tired tones said, 'Oh, very well. Send him along.'

'That is Andrew Mostyn, our chief racing correspondent. You've heard of him, I expect.'

'Yes, sir.'

The sports editor spoke into the telephone again: 'Send a messenger in.' Then, turning to Myles, he handed him the photostats. 'You can have these back. I've seen worse. The boy will take you up.'

There had been a fashion for Old Etonian racing correspondents when Andrew Mostyn joined the *Morning World*, and he was one of the languid ones. At Myles's entrance he yawned and extended a long, thin hand. 'I'd like to see those photostats,' he said. When Myles gave them to him he lay back in his swivel chair and hoisted his feet to the desk-top, displaying a pair of elegant yellow silk socks and beautifully polished brown brogues. But he read the articles closely and with care, giving them much more attention than had the sports editor. Then he yawned again and put his hands behind his head. 'Let me see,' he said as if the whole subject bored him intensely. 'Where is the racing today?'

'Newcastle, Nottingham and Perth,' Myles answered promptly.

'So it is. Come to think of it they are being covered by our people. That's why I'm here today, my lucky lad. Let's have a look at them.' He uncoiled himself from behind the desk and

11

crossed to a television set.

Together they watched a handicap from Nottingham and then a Maiden two-year-old race at Perth.

Mostyn turned off the set. 'Can you type?' he asked.

'Yes.'

'There's a machine somewhere about. Where is it, now? Oh, yes, by the window. Do me five hundred words on those two races, will you?'

'How long have I got?'

'Twenty minutes should be enough, I should think, wouldn't you?' Mostyn went out quickly and closed the door behind him.

Myles sat down at the typewriter. It almost seemed like that first point-to-point all over again. 'I mustn't, *mustn't* lose this chance,' he told himself, adding miserably, 'But I probably will.' And then his mind went blank.

For fully four minutes he sat staring at the typewriter in dumb panic. Then he caught hold of himself and concentrated. Looking at the empty face of the television, he willed the events of the past few minutes to return to the screen. He had memorised the names of the first three horses and the prices in each of the races, which was at least something. But precious time was flying by. Then, suddenly, his mind came back to life. He began to strike the keys.

On the stroke of twenty minutes Mostyn was back. Myles was just finishing the last line of his report. He pulled the paper from the typewriter and handed it over. Mostyn glanced at it. 'Your typing could do with some sprucing up, young man,' he said. 'Did Midsummer Day start at that price? Wait here, will you? There's a *Sporting Life* on my desk.' He left the room again.

Myles did not pick up the *Sporting Life*. He stared out of the window at Fleet Street, sick apprehension clawing at his stomach. Was it or was it not a good omen that Mostyn had gone off with his stuff? The time before his return seemed the longest Myles had ever spent, longer even that waiting to be put up before a race. At last the door opened and Mostyn came in. 'You can start on Monday on a month's trial,' he said.

After that Myles never looked back. Since he had failed once in a chosen career he was more than ever determined to succeed now. The drive to success combined with fear of failure made him a dedicated professional. He never missed a

12

deadline and his mistakes were so few as to be unnoticed. His natural diffidence was no help in the hurly-burly of racing journalism, but somehow he forced himself to overcome it when questioning trainers or riders and to shrug off with a laugh the rough replies he often received. He could keep a confidence, he was always ready to stand in for a colleague, he was never vindictive, and his style was knowledgeable and distinctive.

These characteristics all combined to draw attention to him. When, five years after he had joined the *World*, another daily, the *Post*, decided to open a second racing column of reportage and comment with less emphasis on betting and more on the whole spectrum of racing, he was offered the position.

Mostyn, who had proved a real friend to him and behind whose languid manner lay a shrewd brain, when consulted advised him to accept. There was little chance, Mostyn pointed out, since he himself was comparatively young, of Myles occupying his chair in the immediate future, and anyway the job seemed cut out for Myles's talents. He had made the move and had been given his own by-line, 'Myles Aylward', without any camouflaging under the name of some famous racehorse as had been the fashion and tradition in racing journalism.

He had held the job now with increasing success for six years. Gradually, too, he had become a bloodstock consultant. If his father had been unable to bequeath him his horseman's hands, he had passed on that gift of judgment and flair that can only be born in one and which is known as an eye for a horse. At first, his advice had been casually asked. When his recommendations had turned out well and it became known that such and such a winner had been bought on his suggestion more and more purchasers sought him out. His greatest successes had been with steeplechasers, for steeplechasing had been and remained his first and greatest love.

It was on behalf of Julius Marker, one of his earliest and most faithful clients, that he had made this expedition to Ireland and was now turning into the tarmac drive which led to the living quarters of Mr Bartholomew Moriarty's training establishment.

2

The drive led to a modern ranch-style bungalow. It was long and low with picture windows and was set on the top of a slight slope. Myles got out of the car and pressed the bell under the porch. The door opened almost immediately. A small man with a round face and two very alive brown eyes stood just inside the threshold. He wore a hacking jacket and jodhpurs. A silk scarf was wound round his neck.

'You'll be Mr Aylward, sir,' he said, extending his hand. 'Come along and have a drink after your journey. You'll have come from Cork?'

Myles had no intention of revealing where he had come from or indeed where he was going. Ireland, as he had long ago discovered, was a small country. People had connections and acquaintances everywhere. A chance word dropped in a bar could reveal your intentions to some listener who would be only too ready to pass them on. It was best to keep one's mouth shut and one's intentions to oneself.

The room they entered was as long and low as the house. There were deep comfortable chairs and sofas. The picture window disclosed a prospect of coast and headland and sea.

'Beautiful view you have from here, Mr Moriarty,' Myles said non-committally.

'Yes, indeed, sir, everyone who comes here says that about the view. Mr Macallister was here the other day and he was admiring it too. You know him, I suppose?'

'Yes, I know Tom Macallister.' Myles wondered just why the name of the big Scottish dealer and spotter had been introduced into the conversation. No doubt he would soon learn. From what he had heard of Mr Moriarty he had a motive behind all he did.

'Now, what will you have to drink, Mr Aylward? A gin and tonic?'

'Thank you, yes.' Myles watched whil a slice of lemon slid into the glass, followed by ice and a full four fingers of gin. It was a far cry, he thought, from his father's day when on similar occasions one would be brought into a parlour opened only for this visit or others like it and dank from disuse. There, one would be offered port wine or raw Irish whiskey served undiluted in a tot glass. 'Fill it right up, please,' Myles said as Moriarty reached for the tonic. He had no intention of allowing himself to be bemused by Mr Moriarty's morning hospitality. 'I like a lot.' He refused a second drink.

'It's Alexander, I think you said you'd like to see,' Moriarty said as they placed their empty glasses on the tray.

'Yes. I hope I'm not too early.'

'Not a bit of it, sir. Just the right time. Both lots are in. Anyway I always say any time is the right time to see a horse.' He opened a French door and led the way down a short flagged path to the yard.

Here again Myles was struck by the contrast with what would have met his eyes when he was growing up. Then there would have been tumbledown buildings, yards ankle-deep in manure and a National winner, one hoped, lurking at the back of a makeshift box whose walls might have been anything from an old iron bedstead to a row of empty orange boxes. Now there was a trim modern yard with a tarmacadam surface, clean, tidy and well swept. Airy boxes with freshly painted doors from which sleek thoroughbred heads protruded bordered three sides of the yard. On the fourth was a hay barn and a tackroom. A passage-way between two boxes led to another yard where Myles could see a further row of boxes. Mr Moriarty, he reckoned, must have at least twenty-five horses in at the moment.

A boy with a brush in his hand was called up. He had a mass of red hair and a grinning, freckled face. 'This is Mr Aylward, Tomasheen,' Mr Moriarty said. 'He'll be seeing Alexander.'

Myles followed them to a box about half-way down the right-hand side of the yard. The door was opened and he went in.

Alexander was a big horse. That much he could see immediately. He could see, too, that the straw was crisp and deep, the box bright and airy, the boy interested and willing. Mr

Moriarty, whatever else he was and did, ran a good yard.

The horse had a massive set of limbs under him. That much, too, Myles's first quick glance told him. The boy grinned as the horse nuzzled him and he stroked his shining neck.

'We'll have the sheet off him now, Tomasheen,' Mr Moriarty said. The boy undid the buckle and expertly slipped the sheet over the quarters.

Despite himself Myles almost drew in his breath when he saw the horse stripped. He had come along not quite sure of what would be offered for his inspection and fully expecting to be disappointed. A friend had seen Alexander running in Ireland and had mentioned him to Myles, saying that he might just suit Julius and that horses of his sort weren't easily come by nowadays. Indeed they were not as Myles well knew for they had gone out of fashion since they had sloped the National fences and put aprons in front of them. Nowadays it was more like a bigger edition of a park course. You could jump around on the forehand and get away with it, and no one much wanted these great battle-cruisers of horses who got back on their hocks, clouted the old ferocious fences and still stood up. The fact that small Irish breeders had mostly stopped breeding chasers had helped to alter things too. But here, if ever he saw one, was one of these old 'Aintree types' and, just possibly, a very good one.

'Monolithic monster' was the derisive phrase applied to this sort of horse by one of Myles's contemporaries. There was some truth in his contemptuous dismissal of them, for of the few who had come to the fore recently most had not possessed the speed to lie up in a modern National. It was little use being powerful enough to take Bechers by the roots if you also took about twenty minutes to complete the course.

But Julius Marker loved them and in his unceasing search for a National winner had given Myles instructions to buy if he could find one that was at all likely to fulfil his expectations and ambitions. Julius had commenced his career with horses in showing and it was to this, Myles always believed, that he owed his excessive, indeed almost obsessive, preoccupation with big horses. Also he never cared to admit that he might be wrong and, to prove that he was right, he went on buying them. Myles privately considered that the new school of thought regarding the National was producing more and more evidence to justify

16

its theories as year succeeded year. But he had to admit, as he stared in silence at the big horse before him, running his eye over the massive frame, the mighty backside and the great second thighs, that here might just be the one Julius was looking for, who could win him the great race.

For there was something about this horse that, despite his size, gave Myles the impression that he could go a bit if he was asked to. He ran over the breeding again in his mind. Alexander was out of a famous chasing female line, both his dam and his granddam had been winners and bred winners. But, more important for Myles's purposes and Julius's theories, he was by Archimedes who had been bred in the purple and had run fifth in the Derby. After the Derby, when being prepared for Ascot, he had fractured a seisamoid and been sold to a small stud in Ireland. There, at a time when there were far too many stallions about, he had failed to get high class mares and had passed through several hands, ending up as a country stallion at a fee of fifty guineas. Myles knew the trainer who had had him before the Derby and a few days earlier he had spoken to him. 'Archimedes,' had been the reply. 'Good Lord, yes, of course I remember him. He was one of the unlucky ones. He was stopped in his work before the Derby or he'd been certain to have been placed. And I'd have won the St James's Palace at Ascot with him if he hadn't gone wrong. In Ireland at fifty quid, is he? Just goes to show, doesn't it? He'd have won a classic with a bit of luck.'

'You'd like to see him out?' Mr Moriarty's voice broke into his thoughts. It was more a statement than a question. Myles nodded and they left the box.

As the boy walked the big horse away from them Myles scanned him critically. He went dead straight; that was the first thing. The latent power in his propulsion, too, was inherent in every stride he took. And when the boy trotted him Myles once more almost drew in his breath. For all his size his action was as light and flowing as that of a dancer in a ballet.

The boy paused beside him panting a little from his run with the horse. 'This fellow, sir,' he said. 'He could trot across eggs and not break one of them!'

Myles felt excitement mounting within him. Every instinct allied to his judgment told him that he must have this horse. He felt it in his bones that he was just the one Julius had spent half a

17

lifetime looking for.

'And the price?' he said quietly to Mr Moriarty as he watched the boy lead Alexander back to his box.

The trainer hesitated for a moment while Myles turned to stare idly out at the view between the gable of the house and where the yard began. The patchwork of green fields ran down to the cliffs. Beyond them the sea, utterly still, sparkled in the sun like a burnished shield. In a shaft of white a gannet suddenly wheeled and plummeted after its prey. A school of them gathered and one after another they turned and plunged and fell out of the sky. There must be mackerel there, Myles thought, collecting at the head of the little bay, making themselves all unknowing a killing ground for the birds.

Afterwards he would remember the whole scene, the green and silver of fields and sea, the gannets white against the blinding sun, but, consciously, he scarcely took it in for he was gripped in the tension of the moment. He wanted this horse as much, even more perhaps, than he had ever wanted one in all his years of dealing. And he was pretty certain he was not going to get him. Or not today at any rate.

Julius had, unusually for him, given Myles a limit and a strict one. A company of his had run into liquidity problems and Julius had been forced to inject a considerable amount of his own money to shore it up, for above all Julius hated failure. He had then sacked the managing director, the manager and most of the executives and demanded and obtained boardroom resignations. He had then been satisfied for the moment that matters were under control and immediate bankruptcy at least averted. Thereupon he had departed for his villa on Cap d'Ail in a thoroughly bad temper, convinced like many rich men in similar situations that he was going to lose half his fortune to save his face and all because of management incompetency. Before he went he had listened with half an ear to Myles's description of the Irish horse he was going to see. 'All right, then, if you like him, buy him,' he had said. 'But remember, ten thousand and not a penny more and that's final.'

Myles did not think ten thousand pounds was going to buy this horse.

Mr Moriarty also appeared to be lost in reverie. He stared at the sea, he looked upwards to the sky, he allowed his gaze to wander slowly round the yard. Finally his eyes came to rest,

a point somewhere around Myles's feet. 'What would
 ٰo fifteen thousand pounds?' he said softly, almost reve-
 ٫, as if such a sum should only be whispered between
 ٫ends.

Myles's heart sank. This was the figure he had mentally
assessed to be the one he would be asked. 'I would say, I'm
afraid, that that would be too much,' he said.

'But,' Mr Moriarty expostulated, the sing-song of his native
West Cork breaking strongly into his voice as he grew enthusiastic. 'Dis is a good horse, Mr Aylward. Dis might be a great
horse! Dis might be anything! Dis might be another Arkle!'

Myles smiled. 'Hardly that, I think, Mr Moriarty,' he said.
'On what he's done.'

'And what did Arkle do, will you be telling me, when he was
dis age, before dey started going on with him? He's done all
we've asked of him except dat time in England when dey
brought him down. Dis horse, Mr Aylward, is worth every
penny of what I'm askin' ye.'

'I wouldn't dream of crabbing your horse, Mr Moriarty, but
you know he's a bit unfashionably built for these days.'

'Ah, bejesus, Mr Aylward, don't say dat. Sure dis fellow he'd
gallop the Derby winner himself into de ground!'

'Maybe. Well, there it is. I have one or two others to see.'

They walked together to the car. As Myles opened the door
Mr Moriarty said to him: 'What had ye in mind then, Mr Aylward?'

It was the opening Myles wanted. He was known in his world
as a man who liked quick deals, who did not haggle but who
had a price and stuck to it. Once he had acquired the reputation
this, in fact, had once or twice enabled him to buy good horses
at lower prices than those who employed other methods. Sellers
knew that he acted for rich men with money behind them and
were therefore often reluctant to let him go once he named his
price. Although he had never dealt with Mr Moriarty before he
was quite sure the trainer would have found out all about him
and his methods before he arrived. He had a fair idea, too, that
the horse could be bought at the divide of the money, for what
he had said about him was true. He was unfashionably built to
many modern eyes and his sire was virtually unknown. He
would have bought him there and then save for the unusually
explicit nature of Julius's instructions. But he could now, he

19

felt, afford to drop a hint as to his intentions. 'If I don'
what I want I might be back,' he said.

'Well now I wouldn't wait too long, Mr Aylward. Mr M
lister said he might be back, too. And there's a gentlema
coming to look at him this very afternoon.'

'I'm sure there is, Mr Moriarty. However I must be getting
on. Good day to you.'

'And a very good day to you, too, sir.'

Two miles from Moriarty's, Myles turned inland to pick up
the main road to Cork. Once on it he soon found a lay-by and
pulled into it to eat his lunch. He unwrapped the sandwiches
the hotel had given him and poured out coffee from the
thermos.

Myles really loved thoroughbred horses and especially steeplechasers. He delighted in looking for them and at them when
he had found them. Now excitement over Alexander still consumed him. Everything he knew, everything experience had
taught him and instinct told him, convinced Myles that this
horse was something exceptional. He was not particularly worried about the threat of Macallister's return. Alexander was not
at all Macallister's type of horse. Macallister had been brought
up amongst flat racers and dealt mostly with them. The horses
he did buy for chasing were generally more bloodlike and flashy
types. Privately, Myles had little opinion of Macallister's judgment, and 'the gentleman who was coming in the afternoon'
was the oldest ploy in dealing. Just the same, he was now quite
determined to persuade Julius to buy the horse, and so convinced was he that Alexander was the right one that he did not
intend to lose any time in contacting him.

To Myles everything was right about this horse apart, at the
moment, from the price. For his form, too, as perhaps was to be
expected from an occupant of Mr Moriarty's stable, read
rather better than it looked at first sight.

The form books were in the briefcase beside Myles. As he
drank his coffee and ate his sandwiches he went over the entries once again to see if he could have missed anything or,
having seen the horse, if he could put a different interpretation
on the results he read.

It was Alexander's form the previous year which really interested him. In September he had won the Kerry National at

20

Listowel on firm going which, Myles thought, might not have been expected to suit so big a horse. It evidently had, however, since the form book said: *Tk lead 2nd last, never challenged, impressive.* He had run moderately next time out in a $2\frac{1}{2}$ mile handicap chase at Naas. Then Mr Moriarty had put him into the Troytown Chase at Navan. This was a high-class £1,000 race. The going had been returned as yielding. Alexander had not been backed with any significance, he had finished fifth and as a result Mr Moriarty had paid a visit to the stewards' room.

The Irish Racing Calendar had recently taken to reporting more fully the details and results of stewards' enquiries. Myles could not help smiling as he read once more the photostat of the calendar entry which he had before him. When asked to explain the riding and running of his horse, Mr Moriarty had been both voluble and expansive. The horse, he said, had had a touch of colic after Listowel. The $2\frac{1}{2}$ mile chase had been too short for him, he had run him there because he wanted a race for him before Navan, and he needed to know, too, if he was fully recovered from his colic. In the Troytown he had been doing his best but the jockey told him he hated the ground. He now thought he had made a mistake running him and that traces of the colic must still be in him. He intended to call in his vet. Cantillon, the jockey, said the horse was never going right. At the last he had been a dead horse under him. That was why he had decided not to punish him and had not ridden him out. Cantillon was Mr Moriarty's stable jockey. The stewards accepted the explanations and took no further action.

Mr Moriarty had then sent Alexander to England for the Great Yorkshire Chase at Doncaster. He had been thrown into the handicap with ten stone and had been the medium of a good old-fashioned gamble. Opening at 20 to 1 he had been backed down to 2 to 1 favourite. He must have seemed a certainty to Mr Moriarty and his friends and Myles could only guess at how heavily they had plunged on him. Certainties in racing, however, have a way of coming unstuck. He was going easily on the heels of the leaders at the second last when a horse had fallen in front and brought him down. After that Mr Moriarty had switched him back to hurdling.

What interested Myles in Alexander's hurdle races was that in his second he had had the speed to finish third beaten a head and a neck to a useful horse who had gone on to win the Spa

Hurdle at Cheltenham. And now, first time out for the season, he had just been fourth in a three mile chase at Tralee. And fourth was a very handy position to occupy if you wanted to win your next race with no questions asked or answers ready if they were, as both Myles and Mr Moriarty knew only too well.

Myles drummed his fingers on the steering wheel and gazed out across the rolling Cork countryside below the lay-by. Everything about Alexander was still etched in his mind, the way he moved, the carriage of his head, the bold eager look with which he regarded the world. He was determined to have him, but caution and experience dictated that he should look for further snags. One immediately occurred to him.

If he was right and the horse was as good as he looked, he was poised to run up a series of victories in England. For one thing the English handicappers would not have begun to catch up with him and he would, at the outset at any rate, be running under weights which would be almost derisory for a horse of such size and scope. Julius ran his horses straight so that there would be no question of his being dropped out or stopped. This might result in him figuring high in the handicap when the Grand National weights came out in February, and the Grand National would, of course, be Julius's objective.

On the other hand Myles was all but sure that last year's National winner, Rob Roy, was going to run again; the trainer of the winner of the Gold Cup of two years ago had also told him that he thought he would have a go at the National since the old horse had not the turn of foot for the championship. That ought to take care of the top half of the handicap so, even with a string of victories, Alexander ought to be fairly well in and, in any event, he consoled himself, Alexander was big enough to carry weight. That worry could look after itself. The other might be more serious.

Julius Marker had three ambitions, to win the Grand National, to be elected to the Jockey Club, and to see his daughter win at Badminton. There were a considerable number of people in racing who would have been prepared to offer long odds against his fulfilling any one of them, especially the second, and it was of the second that Myles was thinking now.

Mr Moriarty sailed pretty close to the wind in the running of his horses. He could do almost anything with horses and what he could do he did. He knew racing through and through and

22

he always had his answers ready and they were good ones. He had been into the stewards' room often enough but he had never, so far as Myles could find out, been sent on to the senior stewards. Could it be, though, that a horse with Alexander's background who, if he was good, would certainly win races pretty quickly in England, would prejudice the attainment of Julius's second ambition? Was it, Myles wondered, likely or even possible that Julius's enemies would use this as an excuse to blacken him with those who governed the elections to the Jockey Club, the august establishment of English racing? If that were so, Myles for personal and other reasons had no wish to be at the receiving end of Julius's wrath, should he find out. Julius's wrath could be extremely frightening at times, as was the ruthlessness with which he used the power his money gave him. Myles himself was sailing rather too close to the wind in a private matter where Julius was concerned, and he did not wish that wind to be turned into a storm.

But he still wanted the horse and he knew it could well take Julius five years or indeed forever to find another like him. He sighed, put away the form books, screwed the cap on the thermos and started the car. The business about the handicapper did not really matter, he thought. The other just might. And then he remembered someone whom he could consult, whom he knew he could trust and who would give him an honest and informed opinion. After he had spoken to him he would ring Julius in the South of France. He started the car and drove as quickly as he could to Cork. The empty Irish roads helped him and he made good time. He parked and locked his car, took out his briefcase and went up to his room. Once there he reached for the telephone.

While he was waiting for the call to come through he picked up the timeform ratings for Doncaster of the previous year when the Great Yorkshire had been run. Turning the pages he found the entry for Alexander.

ALEXANDER (Archimedes—Persian Battle), Irish gelding, winner over fences at Listowel this season, led three out 2½ mile chase Gowran Park when 6th of 10 to Royal Register. Appeared to be running on when fifth to Outside Half Troytown Chase Navan in yielding going last time out November. Probably stays three miles. May be unsuited to soft surface.

140 p.

The small p after the rating indicated that the writer thought Alexander likely to improve. So did Myles, but he was glad to have this expert encouragement.

The telephone beside him rang and he picked up the receiver. 'Mr Aylward? Your call to England.' He was lucky. The man he wanted was at home.

'Arthur?'

'Yes, Myles. If you're in Ireland, I suppose you've found a horse. It's not on as far as I'm concerned. I haven't room for any more.'

Myles laughed. 'It's not that, Arthur. It's something different this time. I have found a horse as it happens but I'm not trying to stick him into you—' And then Myles paused. What he was about to say might well seem supremely silly. Perhaps he had been too hasty in ringing Arthur without thinking it through. Julius's ambitions were well known, perhaps too well known for his own hopes of their fulfilment, for he could at times be both outspoken and indiscreet. But was Myles being wise in proclaiming this one so openly even to an old friend like Arthur Malcolm?

Arthur Malcolm trained a string of about thirty steeple-chasers at his home in Hampshire. He had been a friend of Myles's father and it was he who had given Myles the original introduction to the *Morning World*. He had taken an interest in him and helped him through the opening stages of his career in journalism when acquaintance with a man on the very inside of racing meant a great deal. And he had steadfastly remained on call for aid and assistance ever since.

Arthur was an establishment man as were most of his class and generation, who had grown up in an era of privilege and fought in a war that finished it. The list of his owners read almost like a roll call of the National Hunt members of the Jockey Club. Many of them were personal friends whom he had ridden with and against in the great days of amateur riding before the war. Had he not been a trainer he would undoubtedly have been elected a member of the Jockey Club long before and might well have been a steward by now. He was a man of simple certainties. One of the factors that had moved him to help Myles was his sympathy for the abrupt ending of Myles's

24

career in the saddle. Never in a million years could he have divined or understood the feeling of relief which the surgeon's verdict had brought to Myles or the deep buried shame for it that Myles carried with him always.

In his quiet way Arthur stood high in the counsels of the great in steeplechasing and he knew through conversations over the port and confidences which were never betrayed almost every step that was taken along the corridors of horse-power. Myles again began to wonder if he was wise in putting this call through at all. However, he was into it now. 'Look, Arthur,' he said. 'I've found a horse for Julius Marker. You know who I mean?'

'The fellow who trains with Chris Rokeby down in Dorset? He's had all these big horses he says he's going to win the National with?'

'He has another ambition, too, Arthur.'

'What's that?'

'He thinks he might be elected to the Jockey Club sometime.'

'Does he, b'God.'

'Would winning the National help him?'

'I suppose it might. They elected Jimmy Rank in the end though he never won it. Wait a bit, now I come to think of it he is a big supporter of National Hunt Racing. I wonder . . . What is this all about, young Myles?'

'The horse I've found is just the sort Julius likes. He's built like one of those old Aintree types but there's a touch of something else about him that makes me think he might be able to go a bit.'

'Are you going to buy him?'

'Yes, if I can, but there's one thing. Listen, Arthur. Moriarty has him. Do you know anything about him?'

'Moriarty? He's had a couple of damn good horses through his hands. He had that novice Silverine that Paul Cantrey did so well with.'

'I know that but it seems to me he's been in and out of the stewards' room almost ever since he took out a licence. And he's been in over this one already.'

'He's never been off, has he?'

'No.'

'Has he ever been sent on?'

'Not that I know of. No, I don't think he has.'

'Well, what are you worrying about then?'

'It looks to me as if this horse has been readied up for a bet. He's well down in the handicap, too. If I buy him he'll get in at the bottom here—'

'What you're trying to say is that this horse may beat the handicapper and clean up. People may say you or Marker or Moriarty has been cheating with him and it may rub off on Marker's chances such as they are of being elected.'

'That's about it.'

'I've been thinking while we've been talking. Things are changing in racing, especially since amalgamation of the Jockey Club and the National Hunt committee. As I said, Marker is a big supporter and as far as I know his horses are run straight. If he won the National it would help all right and, I suppose, given the right support—'

'Yes, but—'

'I wish you wouldn't interrupt just when I'm trying to think things out. As to Moriarty there's nothing against him here and precious little in Ireland from what you say. Nothing's ever been proved anyway. Perhaps some steward's secretary has his knife into him. That has happened, you know. This used to be a sport. I'm damned if I know what it is now except that it seems to me it's getting more like big business every day. And there are too many people in it who've never put a bridle on a horse in their lives—which goes for some gentlemen in authority too. I don't know. In my day we hadn't any of these bloody stipes snooping about and we got on all right.'

'Yes, Arthur, and most of the local stewards were blind or deaf or daft or all three and everyone knew everyone else and you all got away with murder, but times have changed.'

'I know, but racing was never intended to be a Sunday school treat. Whatever you say there's too much fiddling about, too much—what is the word?'

Myles grinned to himself. Arthur was well away on one of his hobbyhorses. It crossed his mind to think that it was, of course, the older establishment with whom Arthur had grown up. He and they might not much care for the younger men with their boardroom approach. In fact it was pretty clear that he didn't.

'Pecksniffery?' he suggested.

'I expect that's it. Never heard of it before but it sounds a good sort of word. One of those bloody young stipes had the effrontery to ask me at Warwick last week—oh, well, it doesn't matter. Anyway you go and buy that horse for your Mr Marker and win the National with him. I'll tell you this, young Myles, I'd a damn sight rather win the National than be elected to the Jockey Club and so would he if he's any good!'

Myles sat down and rubbed his chin. He wondered if Arthur might not be getting old-fashioned and out of touch. The club-like, old boy attitude of pre-war steeplechasing had, after all, gone forever even if it still was not quite such a business as the flat. But something of a business it had to be with the sums of money presently involved and the financial problems which faced all racing. He then began to consider whether if, for those personal reasons of his, he was not over-reacting to the whole situation. Anyway to some extent the conversation had cleared his mind for him. To win the National was indeed better than being elected to the Jockey Club, but one might help the other. He hoped Julius would see it that way. He hoped it might not all go wrong on them. Picking up the telephone he asked the operator to put through a call to France.

While he was waiting he turned on the radio to get the racing results. Listening to them was always an anxious ten minutes. Whilst the terms of his contract ensured that he did little tipping compared with other racing reporters, he was still required to make certain selections and a weekly nap. Since his column was widely read these had a following and when they went wrong there followed the usual spate of abusive letters to which he had never become quite hardened. His nap selection

as they were called. 'Three-thirty Uttoxeter. Brisbane, Eleven to two, Favourite,' said the announcer. That was it. He had napped Brisbane. It stopped a losing run of four and he breathed a sigh of relief. Presumably the flow of abuse would stop for a bit, too. Perhaps it was a good omen for his visit.

After he had noted the last result he took a leisurely bath. Then he went downstairs to the bar. As he entered it a voice almost beside him said, 'Hello, stranger.'

He turned. Sitting at a table just inside the door, a gin and tonic in front of her, was Evelyn Marker.

Myles stood for a moment looking down at her. 'And just what are you doing here?' he said after a pause.

'I smashed up Jimmy at Burghley,' she said in her direct way.

'God, Evelyn, I'm sorry. I didn't know.'

'That's just it. You never do know, do you? It's all this damned racing and jobbing. You never think of anything else.'

'It is time-consuming. I've been over here for the past few days looking at horses. What happened?'

'It was at the coffin. I was going too fast as usual. He hit it and turned over. He was dead lame when he got up. The X-ray showed he'd broken a bone in his knee. I had to put him down.' Suddenly her eyes filled with tears.

'I am sorry, Evelyn.' He said the futile words again. Then he leant across and briefly his hand brushed hers. They were not given to facile fondlings especially in public.

'I'm being a fool. Sorry. Get me another drink, will you, Myles.'

He beckoned the boy. 'Do you want a double? The doubles over here are quadruples to us.'

'Is that what it is? I wondered. The gin seems strange, too. You remember Jimmy, don't you?'

'Yes, I remember Jimmy.' Indeed he did, very well. All too well, perhaps. For that was how it had all begun.

He had been staying with friends in the Cotswolds and they had taken him to a One Day Event to be held in the park of some local magnate. It was a world of which he knew little and most of those who peopled it were names to him and no more. His hosts, however, were much involved with it, for they had a son and a niece riding. At lunch, dispensed from the back of a Range Rover, there were drinks with other friends and all the bustle, preoccupation and anticipation which precede any equestrian undertaking. After lunch, feeling slightly out of it, Myles had wandered off on his own.

The park was set on the top of a hill with a breath-taking view of the sweep and swell of the Cotswold countryside. He set out to walk the course, surveying with interest the unusual obstacles and wondering if he could ever have had either the nerve or skill to ride over them. Then he had selected a place where he could watch three fences. One was a fairly simple rail on the top of a bank taken on the way out into the country. The other two were in effect a combination which set the rider a difficult problem. The first, which was met after a galloping

28

descent through a beech avenue, was a slatted set of rails, high and stiff and leaning away from the approach. Once over this the rider had to turn sharply to the left and take on an in-and-out built of tar-barrels and old tyres.

Myles leant against the trunk of one of the beeches and watched several riders safely over the obstacles though one or two had difficulty with the slatted rails. He was gazing out at the stretch of country below him, telling himself that this was what used to be known as 'the cream of the vale' and wondering where and how a fox would make his point if he crossed it, when the thud of hooves brought his attention back to the immediate present.

A rider was coming down between the beeches. She was a fair-haired girl on a big, raking, hard-pulling chestnut and she was going very fast indeed. She passed him so close that he could almost have touched her. Her features were glowing and her eyes were alive with the excitement and ecstasy of the big horse's splendid speed and stride.

But that fence was neither to be trifled with nor taken out of a steeplechase gallop. 'Too fast, too fast,' Myles murmured as he watched her. Even if she got over it at that speed she would never make the turn but would almost certainly end up in the trees of the coppice twenty yards beyond.

Neither horse nor rider checked for an instant. The chestnut stood back and reached for it out of his stride. He hit the top slat hard. It did not stop him but it checked him and the drop beyond was enough to plunder his chances. Together the two of them turned over in the most crucifying fall.

Myles looked round. He was alone. Whatever spectators had been there had gone on to other fences. The girl was lying beside the horse. The fence judge, an elderly lady in tweeds, was gazing open-mouthed at the débâcle. Myles ran forward.

As he reached the girl she got shakily to her feet. Her eyes looked blankly at him for a moment and then they cleared. The horse, too, was scrambling up.

'Come on,' she said to him. 'Give me a leg. Quick. I must finish now.'

But Myles had seen what she had not. The horse was dripping blood from a cut on his near fore where he had struck into himself. He was also dead lame.

'You can't,' he said. 'That horse—'

'Can't I? And who the hell do you think you are? Get out of my damn way and I'll—oh.' She had taken up the reins and her hand was on the saddle, but then she saw the blood. 'Oh, Jimmy, Jimmy, what have I done to you?' she said. 'Are you all right? Oh, Jimmy—'

The tweed-clad lady had recovered her wits and her composure by now. Myles looked up to find her standing beside him. 'Get that gel and her horse off the course immediately,' she commanded. 'Don't you realise there's another competitor on his way?'

'Madam,' he said. 'I've only met this girl this minute. But from what I've seen and heard in that time, if you can tell her what to do and get away with it you're a better man than I am.'

At that moment another girl in jeans and a sweater ran out from between the trees. She took the horse gently by the head and moved him away a few paces. 'Evelyn, how awful,' Myles heard her say. 'Is he all right? What happened?'

It was on the tip of Myles's tongue to say that he did not think the cut was as bad as it looked at first sight, but this was obviously the girl groom. He did not think his interference would be welcomed and he moved away.

The picture of the girl going into the fence, everything about her alive and lovely remained with him however. She was the sort of girl he would not mind meeting again. He looked for her number on the card. *Miss Evelyn Marker*, he read. Marker! Surely she could not be old Julius's daughter? If so he had kept damn quiet about her. And then he remembered that he really knew very little about Julius. He bought horses for him, advised him when asked, sometimes met him racing or at his London flat, and that was about all.

He searched for her again amongst the throng when the results were given out but could not find her. Then he said goodbye to his hosts, found his car and drove down the narrow road to the village at the bottom of the hill. Round the corner was a stone-built pub with an inn-sign advertising THE DUKE OF DENVER swaying creakily in the slight breeze. Parked in front of the pub a little to the right of the door was a lone Lotus Elite. Something about the way it stood there slightly askew attracted his attention. Then he saw that the girl behind the wheel was the same Evelyn Marker who had fallen in front of him and had occupied his thoughts for the rest of the afternoon.

30

From the glimpse he had as he passed she seemed to be staring fixedly at nothing or rather at the blank cut-stone wall of the pub.

On impulse he braked, reversed and swung the Aston-Martin into the car-park beside her. Immediately he saw that her face was no longer full of fire and life as it had been in the instant of action up amongst the trees. Instead it was pale and drawn, the lips were tightly compressed and her fingers were clenched around the wheel.

'Are you all right?' he said.

She turned her head slowly towards him. 'Of course I'm all right,' she said. 'And who the—oh, it's you, is it. Who the hell are you, anyway?'

'Nobody very much. There's something wrong, isn't there? Was it that fall?'

'I can look after myself. It's none of your damn business. I wish you'd go away.'

'You may think you're all right but you look like all hell.'

'That's a come-on sort of thing to say to a girl I must—oh.' A spasm of pain shot across her features and she gave an involuntary gasp.

'I thought so. It *was* that fall. Where'd you get it? I've had them too if it's any consolation. I broke my back years ago in a point-to-point.'

It may have been that which engendered a fellow-feeling or it may have been that she was, temporarily, at the end of her tether, but she lowered her guard at least a little.

'It's my side,' she said. 'It hurts like hell. I think he must have hit me somehow when we fell. I pulled in here. I thought I'd get a drink—'

Ribs, probably, Myles thought. 'I'll get it,' he said. 'Don't try to move.'

The pub was almost empty and he was back in a moment with a double brandy. 'Sip it slowly,' he said handing it through the window. 'Now, where are you going?'

'Churchill. I'm staying with friends.'

'I'll take you there. They can get you to a doctor.'

'No. I'll be all right when I've drunk this.'

'You won't, you know. And you'll be a sitting duck for any officious copper if the car starts to wander on you and you pass out.'

She thought about that for a moment. 'You might just be right,' she said slowly. 'Who are you, by the way?'

'My name is Myles Aylward. I think I know your father.'

'The journalist? I've heard him talk about you. You buy those big carthorses for him he imagines he's going to win the National with.'

'That's one way of putting it. You must be feeling better.'

She laughed suddenly at that and then put her hand to her side. 'Don't make me laugh,' she said. 'It hurts.'

'We'll go in my car.' He opened the door and reached in to help her.

'Don't touch me,' she said fiercely. 'I'll manage.'

Manage somehow she did though her face twisted with pain as she struggled to get to her feet from the low-slung driving position of the Elite. He drove slowly and carefully to her friends' house, a cut-stone converted farmhouse set in a fold of the hills.

'Will you have dinner with me next week?' he asked her as he left.

'No. I don't know. Why should I?'

He had already guessed that directness was the best way of dealing with her. 'Because I want to see you again, of course. Anyway I'm more or less a friend of the family.'

'Put it that way and I suppose I might. Where?'

'The Mirabelle?'

'You do tempt a girl, don't you. All right, ring Daddy's secretary. Mostly she knows where I am. And if she doesn't it's just too bad, isn't it?' It was a declaration of independence of a sort. But she had dined with him, all the same, and a week later they were sleeping together.

It was an association which had to be kept concealed from her father. Julius Marker, though far from an ascetic himself, applied the double standard with Victorian rigidity and demanded of his daughter that she remained chaste. The mores of a permissive society were not for him. But as their association grew and their intimacy deepened Myles often wondered if Julius's innocence regarding his daughter's private life was as profound as she suggested. Rich and doting fathers were, Myles knew, capable of convincing themselves, sometimes until it was much too late, that the conventions of a louche society were applied to everyone's daughters save their own. But Julius was not given to self-deception. Perhaps, however, this was his blind spot, and, if she wanted it that way Myles was prepared to go along with her.

In fact their relationship was neither a complete nor an easy ne. She was wayward, fiercely independent, reckless in some things such as her riding, yet cautious and secretive about others as in the dealings she had with the men in her life. Above all she was determined not to be possessed. Sometimes they did not see one another for weeks on end and Myles suspected, though he did his best to put away such suspicions and the jealous torture they brought with them, that there were others whom she did see. Latterly these suspicions had been hardening into something approaching certainty and were centred on one person. Now he wondered what motives, mixed or otherwise, had brought her here.

'So you see,' her voice broke into his thoughts, 'I have to look for a replacement. Daddy told me you were over in Cork searching for something for him. What better person could I come to than the best judge of a young horse in England?' She gave him a little bow and a mocking smile as she raised her glass. Her eyes were bright again now. The tears had gone as quickly as they had come.

'Oh, I say. That's coming it a bit.'

'Daddy says so, anyway.'

'Does he? I didn't know that.'

'Do you remember that horse you bought out of a field for him to win the Champion Hurdle when he had ideas about going hurdling?'

'Nutcracker? That was a bit of luck. He'd have won it, too, if he hadn't been cast in his box the night before. He was only beaten a head and a neck.'

'Well, then, find something for me.'

'Does Julius know you're here?'

'Daddy? Of course not. He's in the South of France with some tart.'

'A tart? That's not his usual form.'

'Whatever sort of female flesh he amuses himself with then. Why doesn't he get married again? Those masseuses that come round make me sick.'

'We all have to have some outlet. He's not as young as he was. I don't think he wants a permanent relationship.'

33

'Have you seen anything?'

'For you? No, but then I wasn't looking.'

At that moment the tannoy in the ceiling crackled. 'A call for Mr Aylward. A call for Mr Aylward.'

'That's Julius now about this horse.' Myles got to his feet. 'I won't be long—I hope.'

Telling the switchboard to put the call through to his room he went up in the lift. The phone was ringing as he entered. He picked up the receiver. The line was clear and the reception perfect. 'Julius?' he said.

'Yes, Myles. Have you found me a horse?'

Julius Marker was lying on his face on a day-bed in the sun-room of his villa on Cap d'Ail. The sun had faded now. The curtains had been drawn and the heating switched on. He was naked save for a pair of brief swimming trunks. A nubile young woman from the agency in Monte Carlo was bending over him. His back glistened from the mixture of oils and unguents she was kneading into him.

'I've found him all right, Julius.'

'Do you like him?'

Myles drew a deep breath. 'As much, I think, as I've ever liked anything.'

'And you want me to buy him?'

'That's it, Julius. But you're not going to buy him for ten thousand pounds.'

'What are they asking?'

'Fifteen. He'll be bought a bit less, I imagine.'

Julius turned to smile at the girl. Her long blonde tresses brushed his naked back as she bent over him. He felt relaxed, soothed and, for him, remarkably at peace with things and his surroundings. He had really come out of that Papermix Ltd business far better than he had hoped. Those interests in Kuwait, too, carefully camouflaged of course and managed by that Parsee chap, looked like going a bomb now. Provided that the Parsee—what the devil was his name?—didn't get either too clever or too greedy. Still, the first pay-off must be very near. That would cover the initial investment including the required bribery and baksheesh. Then the profits should begin to flow. He had arranged it as he had tried to arrange everything throughout his business career, which had had its beginnings in a shady solicitor's office in Whitechapel. Cover your investments, get in quick profits for a starter and then, even if the bubble burst, or in this case if the Arabs got wise, you were at least safe with something. And if the deal ran right he was in for millions. He applied much the same principle to his purchase of horses. He did so now.

'Do you think he'll win something for us before the National?'

'He ought to. At least he'll be handicapped right unless the computer has a fit.'

'Then buy him, my boy, buy him.'

Julius put down the phone. He looked into the girl's eyes. They were very close to his as she bent over him, hands busy. 'I've just bought a horse, my dear,' he said.

'Comment?'

'A racehorse. Un cheval de course.' Julius rolled over on to his back. 'A creature in his own way as lovely and as useless—and as doomed—as you are.'

'Comment?' The stroking hands persisted.

'Ah—ah. Lower, my dear. Lower.'

This time she understood.

Myles rejoined Evelyn in the bar and they had another drink. 'How is he?' she said.

'He seems in better form.'

'That means he's making money.'

'I imagine that company reorganisation thing he was at must have come right. Or he pulled his chestnuts out of the fire, or whatever.'

'It's all right for him but what about the poor devils he sacked? They're not working people, Myles, who can draw their social security and be just as well off if they don't work. They're poor brutes with mortgages and school fees to pay. They're the new poor.'

'Perhaps, but isn't it a risk every salary-earner including myself has to take? Anyway I don't think he bothers about people much. They're pawns in his games. We all are. I wonder what would happen if—'

'If he found out about us? He has the same sort of mind as those French kings who sent their randy girls to convents or walled them up or something. If he found out that's what he'd like to do to me—if he could. Is there any way he could get at

35

you?'

'I don't know. He's on nodding terms anyway with Lord Beckwood, the owner of the paper. The Old Lord we call him. He might be able to put the screws on him I suppose. Anyway, you're here. He's in the South of France, and I'm to buy the horse. Let's forget him, shall we?'

'And you'll look for one for me?'

'Of course. To win at Badminton. His third ambition.'

'You're not buying it for him, Myles,' she said fiercely. 'You're buying it for me.'

Later they dined in the big, impersonal dining-room characteristic of modern Irish hotels and ate impersonal food and drank a moderate and very expensive bottle of wine. Over dinner he told her about the horse and how he had fallen for it and also of Mr Bartholomew Moriarty, his set-up and his shrewdness that was camouflaged by charm. 'They've all got it,' he said. 'Every one of them. They'd charm you into thinking them the finest fellows in the world who couldn't harm a deaf and dumb old lady crossing a road and they'll have the last penny out of your pockets at the same time. Lucky I'm half Irish. It helps to keep my feet on the ground.'

'Sometimes I wonder if you haven't got something of it in yourself, Myles. You can switch on and off like an electric fire, warm one minute, gone cold and dark the next. And you're the only man I know who has Daddy where you want him.'

'That's a relief. I'd hate to see you being walled up.'

'I wouldn't be much use to you if I was, would I?'

Later they drank brandy and watched the news on colour television. As they left the television room to go to the lift Myles said softly to her: 'Are you going to leave your door on the latch?'

She smiled slightly. 'Don't you think you'll have to try that to see?'

She was sitting up in bed, naked, reading a paperback, her fair hair spread like an oriflamme over the pillows when, half an hour later, he gently pushed open the door of her room. As always her loveliness caught him by the throat. 'It's been a long time,' he said.

'Three weeks?'

'Three years it's seemed like. Oh, Evelyn.'

She moved over in the bed. He dropped his dressing-gown to the ground and slid in beside her.

'I think,' she said, 'this is just what they did wall girls up for.'

'Gels, not girls. Do you remember that day at Daintree Park? That awful horsefaced tweedy creature.'

'She'd hardly get herself walled up.'

Is it worth it?'

'Walling up? Mm, oh, Myles. Yes, it *has* been a long time.'

Much later, the light out, they sat up drowsily and lighted cigarettes. And that was when the trouble began between them.

'Where were you?' he asked. 'I tried every day.'

'Did you? You promised you wouldn't. We were to keep ourselves separate, remember. No holds, no claims, no hard words.'

'It's easy to promise, especially at the beginning,' he said. 'If you only knew how much I've longed. You were back on Jimmy Rossiter's yacht, weren't you?'

She turned on him fiercely. 'You're spying on me?'

'I'm not. I swear to you I'm not. I can't help hearing gossip. Besides you were in Hector Mallinson's column. It's true, isn't it?'

Myles knew that he was being a fool, that this was the worst possible approach, the surest way of alienating her and of building a wall between them, yet he could not help himself. Jealousy and suspicion drove him on still further. Even as he said the words which he knew might well end this treasured happiness forever, he hated himself for doing it. But he was in the grip of an emotion he was powerless to control which compelled him to probe, to find out, to end the uncertainty which had been gnawing at him since he had first heard the stories that were circulating. 'Pat Colby was on the yacht, that first cruise when you went to Corsica before the season opened?'

'What if he was?'

'He was back on it again last week-end at the Hamble River and he was with you at Burghley.'

'What's wrong with that? You didn't come to Burghley. You'd have known about Jimmy if you had. You're so damn busy with your racing and your writing—and horse-coping.'

'Pat Colby's in racing too or hadn't you noticed? Goes a great gallop with the girls as well, or so I'm told.'

'Very clever. You are a clever man, aren't you, Myles? The

best racing writer in the United Kingdom, the best judge of a young horse—got a lot going for you, haven't you?'

'Pat Colby's got something going for him too, hasn't he? The best amateur seen since the war. "As good as the greats of the twenties and thirties and one of the very select few who can hold his own against the leading professionals." I wrote that myself.'

'He may have to turn. He's lost all his money. And if he does he'll need all the help he can get.'

'And I suppose he now knows where he can get it. Leading amateur last year—Champion Jockey this one.'

'That's more than you were ever likely to be anyway.'

'Christ!' She had really flicked him on the raw. He got out of bed and began to search for his dressing-gown.

She snapped on the light. 'What are you doing?'

'I'm getting out of here.'

She was sitting up in bed now, her lips parted, her face flushed with anger, unconscious of the bed-clothes thrown aside. She looked tousled, lovely and enticing.

'God, look at you,' he said. 'And you despise your father's tarts. At least they're honest. How often have you slept with him? Do you know how many other women he's had?'

'When I want your advice on my bedding arrangements I'll ask for it. Are you afraid that after him you won't rank much good in the hay?'

'So he's as good in the hay as on a horse, is he? Well, let me tell you this you can have your bloody Pat Colby and welcome to him.'

'You don't own me, Myles. I told you that long ago.'

'Who does then—Pat Colby?'

Then he was out in the corridor groping his way blindly towards hiw own room.

38

3

Myles Aylward did not sleep much during the remainder of the night. He turned and threshed around in the bed, his mind churning. Mostly he was blaming himself for the things he had said and cursing himself for the pent-up jealousy which had made him say them. It was, he knew, the deep and traumatic insecurity that lay inside him which had created that jealousy. Who was he to match himself against the glamour and success of such as Pat Colby?

From the very beginning, while filled with wonderment and gratitude that Evelyn had given herself to him, he had felt that she was not really for him and that he could never hold her. Passionate, wilful, wayward and spoilt she was all the things that he was not. Introspective as he was, he had known from the start that she spelt danger, and at the outset he had never intended to become so deeply involved with her. Yet he had been unable to help himself. There was a fire about her which fascinated him and, physically, he was utterly in her thrall. The thought of other hands on her body was like a knife in his guts.

That bastard Colby. There must be something serious between them for up to now she had been meticulous in her discretion where her men were concerned, and cautious to a fault to keep any whisper of a liaison away from her father. Yet she seemed to be flaunting Colby, or so the gossips said. Some of the gossip prevalent in a small closed society such as the racing world could be discounted but not all of it. Besides, she had appeared in Mallinson's column, her name linked with Colby's.

Hector Mallinson was a racing columnist on one of the steamier tabloids. He was a hard-hitting, muck-raking journalist and an able one. Once a week his column was devoted to hints, 'revelations', innuendo and disclosure about the private lives of racing people prominent or otherwise. It was said that this weekly dish of scandal put thousands on to the circulation of his paper the day it appeared. This was an exaggeration but it was at least true that almost everyone in racing bought it on that day, some to see who were currently coming under the lash, others to search for their names either with trepidation or expectation. No one knew just what were his sources of information but even his worst enemies—and they were many—had to admit that they were almost always accurate.

Myles continued to toss and turn. He had handled the whole thing desperately badly. He had been so drunk with the delight of seeing her and making love to her again that jealousy when it came had seemed to take possession of him almost like an evil spirit speaking its words not his. The trouble was, he told himself, that Colby was everything he was not. Colby and she were kindred in a way. Both of them were brave, reckless and unpredictable, people who expressed themselves superbly through action, as he had wanted and tried to do but failed. But, then, why had she come here? Perhaps to test him, to see how he measured up to Colby, perhaps even to say goodbye. Perhaps, perhaps. Groaning, he sat up in bed to greet the early sun streaming through the window.

Sleep was done with for the night, that was sure. But it was still too early to order breakfast. Getting out of bed he took his form books, notes and comparative tables out of his briefcase and began tentatively to rough out his next week's selections. The figures jumped and jumbled before his eyes. He could not concentrate. Her face and her body, the way she moved, the way she had looked in bed last night when they had been having the row, the expression on her face as he had left her, came constantly between him and the page. He abandoned the effort and turned instead to making notes for the general article he did for the glossy weekly.

Half an hour later he gave that up, too. Reading what he had written he decided it was lousy beyond belief. Picking up the sheets of paper, figures, article and all, he tore them into small pieces and threw them into the waste-paper basket.

He ordered breakfast, but he had very little appetite. He would, he thought, get the hell out of this hotel as soon as he could and make his way by easy stages to Mr Moriarty's training establishment. It would be just how his luck was running at the moment if, by a chance in a million, the mythical man who was coming to see the horse had materialised into fact and bought him. But cold logic told him that was extremely unlikely.

Before leaving the room he looked at the telephone, hesitated, and then picked up the receiver. Cursing himself for his weakness, he gave the number of Evelyn's room and asked to be put through to her. He had no very clear idea of what he was going to say when she answered. All he knew was that he must in some way try to mend the fences he had broken last night, to re-establish some communication and to postpone, if he could, at least for a little, the losing of her.

The switchboard told him that Miss Marker did not answer.

Outside Cork, passing under the viaduct on the Bandon Road, he wrenched his thoughts away from Evelyn and his own problems to concentrate them on Mr Moriarty and his proposed purchase of Alexander.

What Arthur had said to him on the telephone last night had to a great extent clarified his mind about Mr Moriarty and made him think more kindly of the trainer. After all, a trainer's job was to win races for his owners, which was a bloody difficult thing to do at the best of times and becoming more difficult every day. Moriarty won races and lots of them. If in the process he had a brush or two with the authorities, well, as Arthur had said, racing was never intended to be a Sunday school treat. And anyway they had never caught him out.

That list of appearances before the local stewards might well be the result of suspicion engendered by success or an over-zealous interpretation of the rules of racing by a steward's secretary. Again Arthur had been right when he said there were people coming into authority in racing who'd never sat on a horse let alone tried to compete with the multiple problems of training one. That new chap they'd made a steward, for instance, Myles could not for the life of him understand that appointment. He certainly couldn't put a saddle on a horse and Myles privately doubted if he knew which way the saddle faced when it was on. It was said that he was an acute businessman and would be useful on committees. Myles scarcely thought that would qualify him for adjudicating upon the careers and ambitions of men who rode over fences six times a racing day and whose problems, fears, and ambitions he had never faced. It suddenly occurred to him that here was the subject for his next article for the glossy magazine to replace the one he had torn to shreds. *Stewards New and Old* would do very nicely, he thought, for a title. The first sentence came immediately to his mind. 'It used to be said that the three qualifications for a steward were to be rich, deaf and blind, and of those the last two were the most important. . . .' Stopping the car, he took out his pocket tape recorder and got down the meat of a few more paragraphs. That was one problem solved, anyway.

The other immediate one was Mr Moriarty, but Myles had few doubts about dealing with him now. He had over-reacted to the whole thing because of his close association with Julius and his daughter. Anyway, Julius was more than a bit of a brigand himself even if he now tried to wear a respectable face. Maybe he and Mr Moriarty would get on very well together.

In Innishannon, Myles bought a paper and went into a pub. He ordered himself a large gin and tonic and turned immediately to the racing page. His nap had won convincingly and one of his other selections for the week had also come up. That wasn't too bad, he thought. As he read and sipped, the gin slowly permeated his joints and made him feel more human. He was even able to note with some semblance of equanimity that Pat Colby had had a double at Plumpton yesterday. A small paragraph underneath the results told him that Rob Roy was due to make his seasonal debut at Cheltenham on Saturday. He had noticed the name of the winner of the previous year's National in the list of entries and wondered if he would run. Rob Roy was a horse that had captured the imagination of the public and he had determined to watch his first run of the season and write on it. Trainers were certainly bringing out their good horses earlier and earlier, he thought. It made it easier for him, whose first and greatest love had always been chasing, to turn his attentions away from the boring back-end on the flat to the rival attractions of the sister sport. And the fact that they had chosen Cheltenham, an important name in chasing, made it simpler, too, for him to go there rather than to Ascot with which it clashed. But he had better confirm these arrangements with Vic Oldroyd, his fellow racing writer on the *Post* as soon as he got back.

Finishing his drink, he asked if he could telephone and was directed to a dark little room behind the bar where he put a call through to Mr Moriarty. The trainer was still out with the first lot, a female voice told him in the sing-song lilt of West Cork, but she'd give him the message and she was sure he'd make it his business to wait for Mr Aylward, sir.

Feeling slightly better, Myles went back to the car and drove on towards the coast. The weather held. The sun poured down on the empty roads and the green fields. Myles took his time and tried to keep his thoughts away from Evelyn.

Mr Moriarty, full of bounce and bonhomie, was waiting for him. They discussed the weather for the time of year, the harvest and yesterday's racing results. Ten minutes later, rather to his surprise, Mr Moriarty had sold Alexander to Myles for £12,500. 'Come in now and wet the deal,' he said looking at Myles in a manner that combined puzzlement, a slight suspicion that he had sold too cheap, and reluctant admiration.

'Just a second,' Myles said on impulse. 'You wouldn't have anything likely to make an event horse, would you?'

Mr Moriarty stroked his chin. Then he stared first at the ground and then at the sky in a manner Myles remembered from the previous afternoon and was beginning to recognise as a prelude to a prospective deal. 'Well now,' he said. 'Well now, I might at that. I just might now. Tomasheen!' He ended the sentence with a sudden roar and the red-headed boy appeared from nowhere.

Mr Moriarty, Myles reflected, probably had in his yard a horse that would answer anyone's request or, if it didn't, would be made to appear to do so. 'Mr Aylward would like to look at Merlin's Pride,' he said to the boy. 'Come along with us now.'

Merlin's Pride proved to be a handsome, strapping chestnut standing about sixteen hands. There is a sixth sense in horse-dealing. Good-looking and well-made though Merlin's Pride was, some indefinable quality about him hinted to Myles that he would not make a racehorse. That, however, would in no way hinder his prospects as an eventer. It might, in fact, actually enhance them. 'How old is he?' he asked. 'And how is he bred?'

'Seven off. He's by Avalon out of Princess Pat.'

'And what has he done?'

'He was hunted and ran in a couple of point-to-points last

43

year. This year he's been fifth in a bumper and we've given him a couple of runs over hurdles.'

'How many times did you run him in bumpers?'

Mr Moriarty hesitated fractionally before he answered. 'Four,' he said. 'He took a bit of time to come to hand.'

'I bet he did,' Myles said to himself. It was clear that he had not won a bumper, the name given to amateur flat races that figure in almost every jumping card in Ireland, for if he had Mr Moriarty would have said so. These races are also a great medium for a bet and the fact that Mr Moriarty had switched him to hurdling was an indication that he did not think he was ever going to be good enough to win one. The couple of runs over hurdles might mean anything. But he was a nice horse. 'Perhaps we could see him out,' Myles said.

Mr Moriarty, who had all the quick-wittedness and perception of his race, had summed Myles up pretty well by now; besides, he had, of course, as Myles had guessed, taken the precaution of finding out his ways of doing business. He had divined that the best method of encouraging Myles's interest was to take him into his confidence or at least to appear to do so. As they left the box, he laid his hand on Myles's arm. 'I'll tell you what it is, Mr Aylward, sir,' he said, with a great air of confidentiality. 'He's not going to win anything, and that's the truth. Except, perhaps,' he murmured almost to himself looking up at the sky again, 'a little race at somewhere like Wexford in the summer. Yes, perhaps a little race at Wexford in the summer. As it is, Mr Aylward, I'm just about sending him home, now. But jump! Holy God, Mr Aylward, sir, he'd jump Carrantuohill!'

That was all very well, Myles thought, but it meant that in racing parlance Merlin's Pride couldn't win an argument and his jumping would have to be taken on trust, unless, of course, Tomasheen, or someone else in the stables, put him over a few fences, for Myles had no intention of sitting up himself. He was turning these thoughts over in his mind and staring at Merlin's Pride in the silent, intimidating manner adopted by those who deal in horses, when a movement by the path leading to the house caught his eye. Someone was coming down it towards them. He turned to see who it was. Evelyn Marker was walking across the yard.

She was wearing jeans and jodhpur boots, a red and white

shirt and a loose jacket. Sudden joy and relief flowed over him in a way that was almost tangible. Just to look at her walking through the sunlight towards them was a pleasure.

'They told me in the house that you were here,' she said. 'That's not the horse you bought for Daddy, surely?'

'No. I asked Mr Moriarty if he had an event horse. You asked me—'

'I remember,' she said and smiled.

'I rang your room,' Myles said. 'They told me there was no answer.'

'I was out buying an ordnance map to find my way to this place.'

'Then—' he said and stopped, as he saw her toss her hair back in a gesture he knew so well. Last night was forgotten as if it had never happened. They were starting again. That was her way. Her moods changed like clouds crossing the sun. So, the sun was out again and he was in its warmth. Or was it, a voice inside him whispered insidiously, because she was not yet ready to let him go? Anyway, she was here, she was happy and the day was bright again.

Beside them Mr Moriarty was silently taking in the little scene and wondering wherein the chances of profit and advantage for him lay. He coughed.

'This is Miss Marker, Mr Moriarty,' Myles said. 'Actually it was for her I was enquiring about an event horse.'

'Pleased to meet you, miss,' Mr Moriarty said, sweeping off his cap and holding out his hand. 'He's as quiet as a lamb. Would you like to ride him, miss.' His eyes, which missed little, had taken in the jeans and jodhpur boots.

'I'd love to,' Evelyn said, immediately.

'Put a saddle on him, Tomasheen, and be quick about it, now.'

In a few minutes Tomasheen was back. There was a comfortable-looking hunting saddle on Merlin's Pride. Mr Moriarty ran a finger under the girths and Myles gave Evelyn a leg up.

They went through to the lower yard where a gate led out into a paddock. She trotted the horse for a little and then put him into a canter. Myles liked the way he moved with a long, swinging, easy stride. There were two schooling hurdles down one side of the paddock. She set him at these and he popped over them fluently.

45

'The young lady can ride,' Mr Moriarty said.

Yes, Myles thought, the young lady can ride all right. It wasn't lack of ability that would stop her getting to the top. She was too reckless, too enamoured of risk and excitement—which might partly explain why she was here at this moment—too quick to substitute dash for calculation. Myles believed, too, that she lacked the patience really to work at her horses out of season, getting them ready by hard, dedicated practice. Also he knew that, as might be expected, she hated dressage and that it was her weakest point. He watched her now as she turned round the top of the field, the horse going sweetly for her under her light hands, horse and rider at one in balance and movement.

Towards the far corner was an old-time steeplechase bank. It must at some period have been used for schooling but had long been abandoned. Its face was crumbling and eaten away, its wings broken and rotting.

As they watched, Evelyn swung Merlin's Pride out into a half-circle, turned him and cantered towards the bank.

'Christ!' Myles exclaimed. 'Can he jump a bank?'

'Be aisy, be aisy,' Mr Moriarty said. 'Sure, didn't I tell you he'd been hunted and that he'd lep—' But he leant forward a trifle anxiously, Myles thought, as the horse neared the fence.

Evelyn kicked him once. He pricked his ears, sailed effortlessly on to the top of the bank, changed his feet and sprang out into the farther field.

'It's not his jumping that stops him, I'm telling ye,' Mr Moriarty said, but it seemed to Myles that he accompanied the statement with a faint sigh of relief. 'It's a good long time since he jumped a bank,' he said. 'But he's not forgotten it.'

Evelyn was by now circling the farther field. 'There's a gap down below there, miss,' Mr Moriarty called to her.

She paid him no heed but sent Merlin's Pride at the bank again to jump it in reverse. Once more he did it without the semblance of a mistake. There was no doubt whatever, Myles thought, about the precision and fluency of his jumping.

She pulled up beside them and slid to the ground. 'Buy him for me,' she hissed in Myles's ear.

'Are you sure?' Myles murmured to her. 'He can jump all right, but it looks from what he's done that he's got a fit of the slows.'

46

'He'll gallop all right for eventing. Buy him.'

Within half an hour they were back in Mr Moriarty's sitting-room. He had had a profitable morning for he had sold two horses at good if not fancy prices. He was opening the gin bottle once again.

'Your health, miss,' he said as he handed Evelyn a cut-glass Waterford tumbler that held at least three parts gin to one of tonic. 'And good luck to ye both and to the horses now. Ye'll run the big horse in the National, I suppose, sir?'

'I don't quite know, yet,' Myles said cautiously. 'It depends on the owner, Mr Moriarty.'

'And don't be calling me Mr Moriarty, sir. Barty I am to me friends and all the world and to you, sir, and the young lady, God bless ye both.'

Mr Moriarty had been pouring himself portions of Irish whiskey—'A drop of the craythur,' was how he described it— on much the same scale as the gins he had been handing out to them. Myles thought that this flowery speech owed at least some of its contents to the whiskey bottle. But Evelyn, for all her hard-headedness, loved it, and it was at Evelyn, Myles guessed, that it was chiefly aimed.

'What a sweet thing to say Mr—Barty,' she said. 'And what a lovely place to live. Look at that view—' she gazed entranced out of the picture window.

'Once you come to West Cork, miss, you never forget it. They do say, you know, that it lays its hands on your heart.'

'Warm hands, Barty, I hope.'

'As warm as your smile, Miss Marker.'

More of Moriarty's gin flowed and there was now no need for Myles to treat the size of the drinks with caution and respect as he had done yesterday. Moreover Mr Moriarty turned out to be, like many of his countrymen, a plausible and persuasive raconteur. He kept them laughing with his tall stories until at length they all trooped out into the sunshine, smiling together and more than a little drunk.

'Leave your car here,' Myles said to Evelyn. 'You can pick it up later. Let's have a picnic.'

'Oh, Myles, what a fabulous idea. What a lovely horse, and what a lovely man! What a wonderful, wonderful day!'

They drove to Skibbereen and bought pâté and cold tongue and a bottle of unknown white wine, and rolls and butter and biscuits, and beer in case the wine proved too poisonous. Then they turned the car towards the sea.

On the map Myles located two dotted lines leading to a cleft in the coastline. The tourists had gone, the countryside lay in the sun, a green and gold patchwork of living colour, but empty and deserted. Barely a breath of wind disturbed the stillness.

The two lines indicated an unfinished road and they had to walk the last quarter of a mile to the sea. The cove when they came to it was a tiny inlet with a patch of silver sand at its head. In the very centre of this piece of sand, running a little way out into the water, was a clump of rocks.

Here, in the shadow of the rocks, Myles unpacked the bag. As well as the food there were all sorts of odds and ends he had thrown into it—the tape recorder, a camera, pencils, a pocket knife and a jar of barley sugar sweets. 'For energy,' he said to Evelyn as he held up the jar for her to see, and they both laughed.

The wine was better than it looked. After they had eaten and drunk they lay somnolent on the hot sand, occasionally touching each other, their fingers interlocking and loosening as if to reassure themselves of the other's presence.

The sea lapped gently at their feet. It was of an even more striking blue than on the day before, and the sun sparkled off it. The birds wheeled, the crowding cliffs contained the heat and the sand absorbed it. Altogether it was a languorous, sensuous and very private place.

Suddenly Evelyn sprang to her feet. 'Come on,' she said, 'I'm going in.' Already she was pulling her shirt over her head.

'It's very bad for you to bathe immediately after a meal,' Myles said drowsily, looking at her standing nude and admiring what he saw.

'I'll risk it. I'm not waiting then.' She went into the water like a white shaft and swam out towards the head of the cove.

Getting to his feet Myles pulled off his clothes and followed her. The water was as clear as glass. About ten yards out the sand ended and he could look down through fifteen feet of translucence to the rocks and fronds below. But it was surprisingly cold. After a few minutes Myles called to her: 'I've had enough. I'm going in.'

As he lay on the sand letting the sun soak into him and dry him he noticed the camera. Idly he picked it up. There was a

48

colour film in it, he remembered, and this was a day for colour if ever there was one. He photgraphed the rock and the remnants of their picnic and the cove itself.

When he looked up she was coming out, wading through the shallows. The water was glistening on her body. Caught there by the sun with the vivid background of cliff and sky behind her, she looked like some lively naiad emerging from the sea. On an impulse, driven by a desire to preserve for himself something of her that would be his own for ever, he lifted the camera and pressed the button.

In a moment she was kneeling beside him. She had not noticed him taking the photograph for she had been looking up at the head of the cliffs, nor would she have cared if she had. 'Myles, Myles,' she said. 'I do terrible things to you, don't I? And you buy me horses and bring me to wonderful places like this. Love me, Myles, make love to me here in the sun on this lovely, wonderful day!'

They spent that night at a guest house in a village by the sea, in a vast double Victorian brass bed, the stillness of an Irish autumn all about them. It was one of the happiest times they had spent together.

Next morning they flew from Cork to Heathrow. Myles drove her to her flat in Knightsbridge. She had been silent for most of the journey, withdrawn, almost watchful, as if contemplating a return to reality, to something for which she did not much care.

As she got out of the car she turned to him. 'Dear Myles. I'm not really worth it, you know. But it's how I am.' She ran a finger along his cheek. 'You must love me or leave me. Don't ever leave me, Myles.'

He drove slowly back to his flat in Eaton Place and parked his Aston-Martin outside. There was a pile of correspondence waiting for him and he knew the answering service would be crammed with messages.

At the moment he could not bring himself to deal with them. He wanted still to preserve something of that enchanted twenty-four hours. He took the camera out of the bag, unwound the spool and dropped the cassette into the little tin container. This done, he looked at it as it lay on his hand. There was no one he could trust to develop the reel with the picture of Evelyn on it and he had not the ability or knowledge to process it himself. The wise thing would be to destroy it. But, for the moment at any rate, he could not bring himself to this. Taking a roll of sellotape he wound it round the container. As he finished, the telephone rang. There was a china tobacco jar on the mantelpiece which he used for storing various odds and ends. Lifting the lid he dropped in the container and turned to pick up the telephone.

It was Vic Oldroyd to discuss their work and movements for the coming week. But what he had to say first drove everything else out of Myles's mind.

Pat Colby had taken out a licence to ride as a professional.

4

Robert, tenth Marquess of Warminster, was losing money at cards, a not uncommon proceeding. Behind him, watching the game, sat Arthur Malcolm, hating every minute of it and wishing profoundly that he was somewhere else, preferably in bed.

It was a new gaming club in Berkeley Street which had sprung up and suddenly become fashionable. Huge replicas of court cards covered the walls from floor to ceiling and the faces simpered down at the players or stared arrogantly at each other over their heads. The lighting was garish save directly above the tables where heavy shades muted it. The haze of tobacco smoke was everywhere.

Arthur Malcolm hated cards, late nights and smoke-filled rooms. He loved his wife, David his son—though he had to admit to a certain lack of communication there—his horses and his home where he trained them. But Robert Warminster and he had been at school together, they had fought together in a Lancer regiment in Tunisia, through the Kasserine Pass and up the toe of Italy. According to Arthur Malcolm's simple code, when a close friend said he wanted to see you to discuss a matter of importance, then you dropped what you were doing and came along. He glanced at his watch, sighed and yawned. He would not be back in time to go out with the first lot, that was certain. He had left explicit instructions with his head lad who had been with him for twenty years and who could be relied upon utterly, but he still disliked not seeing with his own eyes what his horses were doing. Two of them were running on Saturday at Cheltenham and one, Watchmaker, he had particularly wanted to observe in his work. The other, a novice hurdler, did not matter quite so much but there was a bit of a problem there too. He wanted the hurdler schooled and in Rendall, who rode for him, he had in his opinion the best schooling jockey in the game. But Rendall had rung to say that his wife was not well and he himself had a 'flue cold, and could they re-arrange the schooling? They could, of course, but he would have liked to have been there himself.

Of the two horses Watchmaker was the one to give him most worry. His owner, also an old Army friend, had recently been talking about cutting down. Watchmaker had been something of a problem last season, yet Arthur sensed that there was scope for improvement in him. If the axe were to fall it was almost certain that Watchmaker would be one of those to go but, because of what he felt about him and thought he saw, Arthur did not want to lose him. That was why he had been anxious to see him work and to make an assessment as to how he was likely to run at Cheltenham. It was always a tricky business running chasers early in the season especially as the good ones were now coming out in the first months, unlike the old days when they were kept in wraps until Christmas or later.

He sighed again and looked at his friend's features as they bent over the green baize. Robert Warminster wore the controlled expression of the true gambler in which excitement and concentration were inextricably mixed. But he was beginning to acquire that florid look, Arthur thought. Too much good living and too little exercise were painting their picture on his cheeks.

They had dined in White's where, in addition to sharing a bottle of burgundy, Arthur had drunk two glasses of vintage port. Then they had gone to Annabel's where Robert had ordered champagne, and finally they had ended up here. Arthur had consumed far more than his accustomed ration of alcohol and was regretting it. A large whisky and water stood untouched beside him. To make matters worse, in Annabel's they had somehow picked up Tommy Pereira and brought him along with them.

Tommy Pereira was an amateur rider and in Arthur's opinion a damn bad one. In fact, for Arthur Malcolm, Tommy Pereira represented a great deal of what was wrong with the world today. He had inherited a business fortune, something to do with jute, or so Arthur had been told, and he had spent lavishly buying horses to ride. At least he had the guts to sit up on them himself instead of getting someone else to do it; Arthur, reluctantly, gave him that. But he appeared to do most of his training in Annabel's or in gambling clubs. How then could he possibly perfect his art? For art, to Arthur and his like, it was. And nowadays these young men entirely lacked the dedication which in their prime consumed Arthur and his contemporaries. Then they rode out six days a week and spent the rest of their time schooling or hunting. And tried in every spare moment to better their skills by such ways as sitting for hours on a chair reversed with a racing whip in their hands practising endlessly getting it from the carry to the action position. Tommy Pereira, Arthur knew from observation, could not use a whip nor would he ever learn to. Arthur remembered seeing him ridden right out of it from the last in the National Hunt Chase by a young fellow who had lived in a stable for the past three years learning his job. The young chap had sat down and scrubbed his horse home like a pro while Tommy, upright in the saddle, 'like a bloody mounted policeman'. Arthur had commented to himself, had rolled around ineffectually, waving his whip and totally unbalancing his horse. And on the form he should have had a stone in hand.

'That chap would have won on either of them,' a grizzled bowler-hatted veteran of his own vintage had said to Arthur as they watched the winner unsaddling. 'Trains on pot, I suppose,' he had added as Tommy, blowing harder than his horse, passed them carrying his saddle.

'Smokes it anyway, I expect,' Arthur said looking with distaste at the long fair hair curling under Tommy's racing cap. In this at least he was right, for Tommy, on occasions, did.

The extraordinary thing was, Arthur's thoughts ran on, that Tommy Pereira was rather a friend of his son's. He could not understand the relationship but then there were a lot of things about his son he could not understand.

He looked again at the green baize table. He really had very little comprehension of how chemin de fer was played, but he gathered that Robert was, as usual, losing, and Tommy Pereira, equally as usual or so he had been told, winning.

He felt himself falling asleep and took a gulp from the glass of whisky in an effort to keep his eyes open. As if sensing his predicament his friend suddenly turned from the table and smiled. 'Keeping you out of bed, old Arthur,' he said. 'Won't be much

53

longer now.' Beside him Tommy Pereira also turned, looked at Arthur and laughed. To Arthur that laugh seemed to contain all the contempt of one who is spendthrift of his youth for another who is husbanding his years, and it did not increase his liking for Tommy.

To relieve the boredom and tedium that was encompassing him he tried to concentrate on the game. Over Robert's shoulder he could see the kidney-shaped table with the croupier sitting in its inner curve, the ebony *palette* in front of him. As he watched the bank passed and the polished walnut and silver shoe slid along the table to a gaunt, henna-haired woman with prominent teeth and avaricious hands.

'*Banco,*' Robert called from beside him. The hennaed woman slid the cards face down across the table. Robert examined his two, replaced them, and said 'Pass.' The banker turned up her cards. They were a five of hearts and a three of spades. Robert sighed slightly and sat back in his chair. The croupier's *palette* flicked out and swept away the chips in front of him. Pushing back his chair he turned to Arthur again. 'Now we'll go home— at last,' he said.

They took their coats and went down the ornate stairway. The commissionaire saluted and waved a white-gloved hand. Robert's black Rolls glided to the kerb.

'How much are you down?' Arthur asked as they settled themselves on the back seat.

'I don't know,' was the careless reply. 'Somewhere around four thousand, I suppose.'

Beyond stating that it was about the stud he wished to see him Arthur knew nothing of why he had been summoned, nor had Robert mentioned the subject during the evening. But that was his way. The discussion would come now, no doubt, over whisky and sandwiches and too damn late for common-sense, Arthur thought, with an instant bitterness which he immediately suppressed.

When David had shown neither inclination nor interest in riding horses fast over fences, Robert had given him a job in the stud and there, away from parental influence or what he would no doubt have called interference, he seemed, Arthur had to admit, to be displaying both application and an eagerness to learn which he had never shown at home. Perhaps, Arthur thought, he had expected too much of him and demanded too

54

high a standard. It was, he had been told, a mistake parents often made. At all events he was now too heavy ever to have made a successful amateur rider. In his formative years his build had turned into something like a forward in rugby football, a game incidentally, Arthur understood, he played very well. His mother was a big woman. It must have come from her.

Warminster House had long since gone the way of the other great London town houses and Robert now lived in Belgravia in a tall, bay-windowed stucco house looking out on to Chester Street. In the library, as Arthur had expected, were sandwiches wrapped in a napkin, a thermos of coffee and decanters of whisky and brandy.

'Help yourself,' Robert said, throwing himself into a leather armchair and putting his feet up on another.

Arthur poured coffee into a cup. At this hour it would probably preclude sleep but at least it was better than consuming more alcohol. He also suddenly realised that he was hungry. Turning back the napkin he took a chicken sandwich.

'It's about the stud, Arthur,' Robert said abruptly as he poured himself a whisky. Just how much alcohol had he got through in the course of the evening, Arthur wondered. It didn't seem to have made the least difference to him. But he never understood how these chaps kept it up.

'It's not going right,' Robert was continuing. 'I've put off doing anything about it for far too long. Too bloody idle, I suppose. Has your boy said anything?'

'Very little,' Arthur replied cautiously. 'You know he wouldn't betray confidences. But—'

'Yes?'

'Well, the plain fact of the matter is, Robert, your blood has gone thin.'

'I know that. Or rather I can see that, now. But these are general terms. Did the boy ever mention anything specific?'

'Well—' David had been most reluctant to speak at all at that lunch they had had together at the Red Hart two days ago. Under Arthur's relentless questioning he had, however, given something away.

The Clayhampton Stud, where the Warminsters had bred horses for centuries, had seen great days. Five Derby and countless other classic winners had been bred there. But recently it had gone into a decline and Robert's inattention since he had inherited had not helped matters. Nevertheless there was more to it than that. David had let slip something.

'He's puzzled you let Bloodstone go to Japan,' he said.

'Bradbury said he was too slow with his mares.'

'I know.' Arthur's mind was muddled with whisky, tobacco smoke and sleeplessness but he tried to choose his words carefully. He must not damage the boy but at the same time he owed it to Robert to tell him something of what he guessed was going on. 'Did you cash him well?'

'I forget. No, dammit, we din't. The Japs said they were taking the hell of a risk. He might prove infertile there with his history.'

'You're importing American stallions, too, I see.' Arthur refrained from saying that in his opinion it was in the mares that the real weakness lay. Bradbury was the stud manager. It looked a classic case of someone getting a monumental rake-off. But he had no evidence at all beyond what David had unwittingly implied, and he could not say this. 'Those two, Charlie the King and The Lariat, must have cost you a packet.'

'They did. There was the sale of another stallion some years back, too, that always puzzled me.'

'What was that?'

'Malifico. He went to Chile. I forget what Bradbury said about him. I thought he might have made the grade but I suppose he was useless.'

'How was he bred?'

'Dammit, Arthur, you don't expect me to remember that, do you?'

Arthur laughed. 'You'd better buy yourself a chaser, Robert,' he said.

'My father would turn in his grave. He used to say it was worse than dog racin'.'

'Your great-uncle was second in the National.'

'Yes, and lost every penny he had to the books and my father had to keep him in Cannes in the luxury to which he was unaccustomed. But to get back to the stud. Bradbury said these Americans were just what we wanted—fresh blood and quick returns.'

'He may well be right.' David had said something he hadn't meant to say about Bradbury and Arthur was beginning to realise how Lt-Colonel Bradbury, late of the R.A.V.C., was running the stud in the absence of interest from its owner; but he felt he had said enough.

'Bradbury's been with us since my father's time,' Robert said reflectively. 'I always thought him a good man.'

'I'm sure he is.' He changed the subject. 'Ever hear of Julius Marker, Robert?'

'Can't say I—Oh, yes, he's the financier chap, with the good-looking daughter, isn't he? Owns a few chasers. Why?'

'He's a big supporter of chasing. Is he ever likely to be elected to the Jockey Club?'

'Shouldn't think so. National Hunt Committee if anything. Oh, of course we're all one now. I keep forgetting. I suppose he just might, sometime. Wait a bit now, I believe I did hear his name mentioned. That was why, when I heard you say it, it rang some sort of a bell.'

Robert and his father and his father before him had been elected members of the Jockey Club almost as soon as they had reached their majorities. The list of members would have seemed incomplete without a Warminster in it, but Robert, in his casual way, took little part in its councils. 'Too bloody much of a business nowadays,' he had once remarked to Arthur. 'Let the chaps with business brains get on with it.' Even as he had agreed with him, the disturbing thought had crossed Arthur's mind that this in some way which he only dimly comprrehended was an abrogation of power and a misuse of privilege, another symptom of the malaise which had seized the country in its grip. It was the recollection of this which prompted his next remark. 'He's a businessman,' he said. 'He might be a help.'

'I know. But I think it was something to do with that which someone had against him. I forget who it was now. I suppose they crossed each other's paths sometime. You know that mightn't be such a bad idea of yours about having a chaser. What's the market like? Could I have a bet?'

'The market has gone to blazes since the betting tax but, yes, you could have a bet, especially on the National.'

'What would a National horse cost me?'

'That depends. Anything, say, from six or seven thousand up. In other words only a fraction of what you'd pay for a yearling at Newmarket if you bought there, which you don't.'

'It mightn't be a bad thing if I did the way things are going at

57

Clayhampton.'

'If you really are interested, come to lunch on Sunday and talk it over.'

'I'll ring you. Good God, I suppose I've kept you up far too late. Will you want an early call? Leave a note on the pad. Maxwell will bring you something in your room.'

For a moment Arthur contemplated abandoning bed altogether and driving home to Hampshire through the night to be in time to see the first lot out. Almost as soon as the thought came he put it to one side. He was far from drunk but he was dreadfully tired, sleep was rolling over him in waves and there was probably well over the legal limit of alcohol in his blood. He murmured his good night and clambered up the stairs to his room.

When he had gone Robert Warminster poured himself another whisky. Despite the penal taxation of recent years, his lavish way of life and lust for play, he had few financial worries. The Warminster fortune, much of it founded on revenue from coal discovered on their Midland estates in the nineteenth century, was quite secure. There was the huge income from ground rents in London and Birmingham, and the sale at just the right time of the West Indies property, annexed by some plundering ancestor in the reign of George I, had recently swelled the coffers still more. All of it was administered by a team of accountants who looked after a pyramid of companies and interlocking trusts. Robert had never concerned himself to understand any of it. His ex-wives, both of them, were provided for, as was his present one with whom he lived on terms of casual amity.

But . e was worried about t . e stud and its faadure and the performances of the horses that ran in the famous purple jacket and yellow cap. It was not so much that they never won a classic as that they never won a race of any sort. In his father's time there had been a private trainer. That had been changed and now the horses went either to Crankshaw at Newmarket or Bird at Epsom. They couldn't both be duds or crooks, he thought. In fact he knew from what they said or rather more from what they didn't say that both of them thought the material they were getting from the stud was useless. What was particularly galling was that Crankshaw had hinted only the other day that he'd be better off without them. A public trainer refusing yearlings from the Clayhampton Stud—twenty years ago, even ten, it

58

would have been unthinkable.

It all made the idea of running a steeplechaser the more attractive. If he were, for instance, to buy one and win or even run well in the National it would do something to restore the Warminster name in racing circles. But, far more important, it would help his own name. For he was becoming all too conscious of whispers and glances behind his back in flat-racing circles and that people were talking of him as the man who had betrayed the blood. Perhaps that was far too melodramatic a way of putting it. But if he were to buy and run a chaser and that chaser won races for him it would be as a result of his own efforts, he would owe nothing to Bradbury, the stud or anyone else and, besides, he repeated to himself, he could have the added enjoyment of a gamble.

He put down his glass. Bradbury, he thought, Bradbury. Old Arthur had hinted though he had said very little, that he didn't think much of Bradbury's buying policies and he was probably right that Bradbury was up to something. He supposed he ought to look further into it and find out just what was going on. The trouble was Bradbury had been there so long he had become a sort of mixture of institution and dictator. Secretly Robert was slightly afraid of Bradbury. Anyway the idea of owning a chaser, no, a National horse, was much more amusing and new and exciting. He went to bed.

Three hours later Arthur Malcolm woke. His head was aching, his eyes were hot, everything about him seemed to be impregnated with stale tobacco smoke. He groaned and sat up in bed.

A manservant in a black coat brought him a tray on which were coffee and a boiled egg in an egg-muff, toast and marmalade. As he shaved and dressed he drank two cups of the scalding coffee and ate the egg. Downstairs he wrote his name in the open visitor's book while the man packed his bag. When it came down he went out to the car.

It was sufficiently early for there to be little traffic on the road and the farther he left London behind him his head became clearer and his spirits rose.

Arthur trained his horses at Farhaven, his family home in Hampshire. He was fortunate in that all his gallops and his schooling grounds were on his own land so that he could use them as and when he liked without risk of the clashes of time, argument and ill-feeling which sometimes arise at training centres where gallops are shared. His father had trained his own horses there and laid down many of the gallops. When Arthur had become a public trainer he had increased and extended them.

Now he drove directly to the stableyard which lay behind the house. The yards, too, had been extended by Arthur. A new, modern yard had been built below the older one where his father had housed his horses. It was to the upper yard that the first lot would return and they were just entering when Arthur stepped out of the car. Dick Martin, his head lad, was leading them.

'Well?' he said interrogatively to Martin as he slid to the ground.

'All right, sir. No problems. Everything went just as you wanted.'

'And Watchmaker?'

'Didn't blow at all. He'll be all right for Saturday.'

Both of them crossed to Watchmaker's box. Already he was beginning to pull at the hay in the net which had been left for his return.

'He went great, sir,' the lad who did him said. He was standing by the horse's head and he gave his neck an affectionate pat.

'Good.' Arthur stood watching as the second feed of oats mixed with bran and chaff was brought. Watchmaker was a bay horse slightly lacking in quality and with a head that was rather too big for him. He was a great jumper but he lacked speed on the flat. Arthur, nevertheless, always had had the feeling that he might be better than he looked. This year, at eight, he could just be coming to himself. Even so, Arthur knew very well that he was never going to be Gold Cup class or anything like it. 'I'm afraid,' he said to the head lad, 'that Mr D'arcy is getting impatient. I think he wants to get out of him.'

'Perhaps he'll run well at Cheltenham,' the head lad said. 'He did need time. And it's a course that suits his type. He'll stay forever.'

'Well, we'll see. Did Rendall ring up?'

'Yes. His cold is better. He'll be over tomorrow to school.'

'Good. I want him to ride Harnessed Lad, Miss Meredith's hurdler. He runs at Cheltenham, too.'

60

Arthur went down the rest of the boxes talking to the lads about the horses in their care. He paid particular attention to Harnessed Lad, Meg Meredith's young hurdler. He, too, had worked well and he was eating up. Meg had bought Harnessed Lad herself at the Ascot sales and paid, Arthur thought, rather too much for him, that is if anyone could ever estimate what a horse was worth. Flat race-bred like most hurdlers these days there was no jumping in his pedigree at all. Arthur had not been happy about his initial efforts on the schooling ground and he always liked, somewhere in the back pedigree of any horse that was to hurdle ob steeplechase, at least an indication that his predecessors could leave the ground. He had been in two minds whether or not to run Harnessed Lad next week-end but old Meg had been insistent. Unlike some trainers he was never dictatorial with his owners who were mostly sporting people anyway—his wife said he was far too easy-going—and he had consented. But he badly wanted Rendall to ride a school on him before he ran and the news that his jockey had recovered from his 'flu was reassuring. He wondered what had been wrong with Rendall's wife. They were a quiet, devoted couple. Arthur made a mental note to ask about her when Rendall came over tomorrow.

Unless he wanted to observe a particular horse Arthur seldom went out with the second lot. He discussed briefly with the head lad the horses that were going in it and what they would do. Then he walked up the gravelled path to the house.

Farhaven had been built by Arthur's great-grandfather a hundred years before. Having amassed a sizeable fortune in the city he had, after the manner of his times, bought an estate and set himself up as a country gentleman. It was a fair-sized, mock Tudor manor house which had adapted itself surprisingly well to modern conditions.

Arthur's father had come out of the hell and the stench and the misery and heroism of the First World War with an M.C. and bar and an all but useless right arm from a sniper's bullet at Givenchy. He had brought with him an unquenchable determination to enjoy to the full the life that lay so unexpectedly in front of him.

There had been servants, motor-cars, hunters and house-guests at Farhaven in profusion then—and racehorses. Most of all there had been racehorses, an endless succession of hurdlers

61

and steeplechasers ridden first by himself despite his arm and afterwards by his son and his son's friends in those heady club-bable days of chasing between the wars. 'Lt-Colonel Malcolm M.C. had not cared much whether he won or lost races as long as he enjoyed himself, and he entirely lacked the dedication necessary to make a successful trainer. All that concerned him was that everyone connected with Farhaven and his horses should have fun. He had an equally carefree approach to the management of his money and when he died much of his father's fortune had gone. Death duties, for which he had made no provision, took a sizeable slice of what was left.

Arthur found himself far from rich but still possessed of private means. To supplement them, keep the place going and to stay in the sport he loved, he had taken out a trainer's licence. There was enough of his father in him to lack the ultimate driving ambition that sends men to the very top. But he was honest, hard-working and dedicated and he knew both men and horses. Also he was lucky in that his father's friends formed the nucleus of his stable and had given him a start. Modest success had come his way from the first and had been followed gradually by greater things. Though he had never trained either a National or a Gold Cup winner he had picked up one or two of the big handicaps and sponsored races, and he was always to be found somewhere in the middle of the list of leading trainers. He was fortunate, too, in that the family atmosphere of the stable had persisted. Mostly he trained for friends or friends of friends few of whom were betting owners. His critics said that he was slow and old-fashioned and many of the younger men laughed at him, but a gratifying and consistent flow of winners came from Farhaven each year just the same.

He let himself into the house by a side door. His wife was in the modern kitchen which they had made by knocking the former gun-room and butler's pantry into one. She was a big comfortable woman with a smooth unlined face. She had worn well, Arthur thought, as he kissed her. It was always a warming pleasure to come back to her.

'Well,' she said as she greeted him. 'How did that go? I'm making coffee. I expect you could do with some.'

Arthur pulled a chair from under the formica-covered kitchen table and sat down. 'I could indeed,' he said. 'We didn't get to bed until after three. I don't know how Robert sticks it.'

'I don't suppose he gets up until lunch-time. What did he say about the stud?'

'He's worried about it.'

'Is there anything wrong? Will it affect David?'

'It won't affect David. At least I shouldn't think so. As to there being anything wrong, I don't know. If David knows he's too loyal to say it. But I don't think I'd trust Bradbury very far. He's had too much power there for too long.'

'Because Robert is too idle to do anything.'

'There's something in that. But the real trouble as I told him is that their blood has gone thin.'

'If you ask me, Arthur, more than the blood in the stud has gone thin. The Warminster blood in Robert has gone thin, too.'

Arthur sighed. 'Yes, perhaps you're right. But he's a very old friend, you know, my dear. And he was the hell of a good soldier.'

'The war is over more than thirty years, Arthur.'

'Yes. Funny, isn't it. One can hardly realise it. It seems only yesterday. Anyway he's talking about buying a steeplechaser.'

'That'll be a change for the Warminsters, won't it?'

'It will, to be sure. I'd like to see the Dowager's face when she hears the news. Anyway I've asked him to lunch on Sunday.'

'Do you want anyone with him?'

'No. I don't think so. If he's serious about buying a National horse I imagine he'll send him to me to train and I'd like to discuss it with him.'

Arthur finished his coffee and went along the passage that led to his office and the secretary's room where the telex was. This was the part of the job he really hated, the paperwork, and there was more and more of it every day.

Arthur's office was purely functional. It contained a big, very tidily kept mahogany desk, with an office chair in front of it, ttwo banks of filing cabinets, a large card index and a safe. Bookshelves round the walls held bound volumes of the *Racing Calendar*, the stud book, form books and the *Bloodstock Breeder's Review*. It looked out over Mary's rose-garden and a sweep of woodland beyond it. On his desk were two large ledgers. They were the entry book and the day book. A communicating door led into the secretary's office.

Arthur sat down at the desk, put on his half-spectacles and pulled the entry book towards him. It contained all the current

63

entries for the horses in the stable. He checked over those for Watchmaker and Harnessed Lad with special reference to their races at Cheltenham, a three mile handicap chase and a two mile novice hurdle for three year olds.

There was no necessity for him to refer to the day book which was written up by the head lad and contained day to day details of each horse, illnesses minor and major, injuries, work done, and remarks as to general condition and as to whether certain horses had eaten up, or the like. Arthur had checked the entries for the previous day before leaving for London and the current ones would not yet have been made.

Then he turned to the card index. This contained the case history of every horse in the stable. Harnessed Lad did not concern him very much at this stage. He had only run once and his veterinary sheet was clean, for he had needed no attention beyond rudimentary wormings and other routine dosages since coming to the stable. Watchmaker was rather a different matter.

Arthur often wondered whether the work involved in keeping up these cards was worth-while for he had most of the information about his horses in his head. On the other hand reading through the entries did help to concentrate his thoughts. Now he took out Watchmaker's card and pondered it.

WATCHMAKER. B.G. *Clock Tower—Craft Mistress.*

Bought in Ireland, 3 yrs old. £2500. Unraced, he read. His eyes went rapidly down the card noting the novice performances and the few early ailments and then concentrating on the past season's record.

Watchmaker had run unplaced in his first two outings. He had won third time out, perhaps luckily for the horse that had been upsides with him at the last and going, Arthur felt, a shade better had fallen there. His next race had been in rather better company. He had finished fifth and while he had not really disappointed him, Arthur had hoped that he would run better than he did. After that race Arthur thought he had discerned faint signs of heat in the horse's off fore leg. Ever careful he had immediately stopped working him. By the time he was satisfied with the leg the ground had hardened up. He had advised his owner to put him by for the season and they had roughed him off.

He was eight years old now. This was the season which would show whether he had come to himself or not. Horses did sometimes improve immeasurably between seven and eight, when they reached their full maturity. There was no doubt that he could jump and Arthur was pretty sure he could stay though the coming three mile chase would tell them more about that. He should win races all right but whether he would win the sort of races his owner wanted him to was another matter.

Arthur put the card away and drew the entry book towards him again. He looked through it, searching for the names of those horses for whom four day declarations should have been made. Runners must be declared by their trainers four days before the day on which they run so as to enable executives to make up accurate racecards, and press and public to be informed with reasonable certainty of the probable runners. Seeing that these were sent off in time without omission or error where several different courses with meetings on the same day were concerned was a continual nightmare.

Taking the entry book from the desk Arthur opened the door to his secretary's room. There were banks of filing cabinets here, too, together with ledgers for owners' accounts, cashbooks for the day to day entries concerning the stable expenditure and the general cost of running it, which grew more frightening every week that passed, wages books, P.A.Y.E. and Social Security registers, all the paraphernalia, in fact, of a modern trainer's establishment.

Sitting at a desk facing the door was his secretary, Ruth Haymer. She was a distant cousin of Mary's, well into middle age, who had come to him from industry. For ten years now she had been at Farhaven devoting her entire life to the stable's interests. She lived in one of the estate houses in the village and worked six days a week, twelve months in the year. She was invaluable and Arthur did not think he could have carried on without her. Looking at a pile of bills she was entering into a ledger in her neat handwriting, he was sure of it.

'Good morning, Arthur,' she greeted him. 'How did you enjoy London?'

'I hated it.' Arthur sat heavily down in a Windsor chair in front of her desk. 'It's a terrible life those fellows live. Anything I should see?'

'Well—there's this. I've been going through the accounts.

65

Charles d'Arcy hasn't paid for four months.'

'Oh, Lord,' Arthur said. This was definitely not one of his mornings. Charles d'Arcy was Watchmaker's owner. 'That mare of his is useless, too. I've told him so and that he'd be better to take her home. But he bred her and he's determined to get a bracket for the stud. It costs as much to keep a bad horse as it does a good one but some chaps will never learn. If he's going badly I suppose he'll want to get out of Watchmaker.'

'What will I do? Write him a stiffish letter?'

'No, no, don't do that. Poor old Charles, he's hit a bad patch. He'll pay up in the end, I'm sure.'

'Look, Arthur, you can't go on playing fairy godmother to your friends forever. The feed bill has gone up three hundred per cent in the last six months. I've been doing some costings. Here are the figures. Just look at them.' She picked up a slip of paper and began reading from it. 'Jackson's for oats, six hundred . . .'

Arthur groaned. 'Not today, Ruth, not today,' he said.

'And that's not all,' Ruth went on relentlessly. 'The lads have had two rises in that period as well. I was talking to May Soames who does for Jack Humphry at Crambourne. She tells me anyone whose bill is three months behind gets a solicitor's letter. Four months and they sue.'

'Solicitors' letters! Suing! God God, what is the world coming to? Anyway, look, Ruth, I'll have a word with Charles about it myself. I'm sure to see him at Cheltenham.' He avoided meeting her eyes as he said this since both of them knew very well that having a word with Charles at Cheltenham over his bill was the last thing he would do. 'Anyway,' he went on, picking up the entry book. 'These entries and declarations . . .' Together they checked them over. When they had finished she ran down the list she had made. 'I'll put them on the telex straightaway,' she said.

Arthur's eyes went to the battleship-grey instrument which stood in one corner of the room. He did not understand it, he certainly could not have operated it himself, and he was sure he had not been able to afford it. But Ruth, who guarded his interests and finances so carefully, had persuaded him to install it and now the damn thing, which looked like the bastard offspring of a typewriter and a harmonium, gave him a direct line to Weatherby's at Wellingborough, the nerve centre of racing's administration.

Telexes and computers, he thought to himself as he made his way to the main part of the house, they were all part of this modern world of rush and go and the fast buck which he both disliked and did not understand. They were even handicapping by computer now. He wondered what his father and his friends would have thought of *that*.

In his study where he and Mary sat when they were alone he poured himself a king-sized gin and tonic. Sipping it he picked up the *Daily Post* to read what young Myles Aylward was writing about. He was half-way through the column when Mary came in to say that lunch was ready.

'Did Ruth have anything to say?' she asked as they ate their chops.

'Charles d'Arcy is behind with his bill. She thinks we ought to sue him. It's coming into fashion apparently.'

'I expect you ought to, dear, but you won't,' Mary said amiably. 'Why does he keep on with that mare?'

'Because he's too stubborn to admit she's no good. Do you know, dearest, training would be comparatively easy if it wasn't for owners.'

Mary smiled again. 'I seem to have heard that before,' she said.

After lunch Arthur started again on Myles's article and promptly fell asleep in his armchair. He awoke just in time for evening stables. After swallowing a cup of scalding tea and eating a slice of fruit cake, he made his way down to the yard.

The contact with his horses and the men who looked after them, together with watching the results of their labours on the racecourse, was what made training worthwhile for Arthur. He went down the boxes examining each horse with an eye tempered by years of experience, discussing with the lad, sometimes in the minutest detail, how each one was, how he had eaten or, if he was off-colour, how he was responding to treatment.

Horses vary as much as humans. They are highly-strung, placid, idle, brave and cowardly, though the latter had no place in Arthur's yard. As to the others they were docketed in his mind together with their failings and characteristics and the changes the years wrought in them.

When he had finished he went into the head lad's office.

There, taking a slotted board from the wall he slid into the various positions the names of the horses and the lads who would ride each in work tomorrow. Once or twice he paused to consult the head lad. Both of them knew each other and their horses so well that the whole operation did not take more than a few minutes. The head lad took the board which he would later hang in the archway between the yards. Then, as always, Arthur stayed for a chat.

'I see Mr Colby has taken out a licence,' Martin said. 'Going to ride for Mr Rokeby, too. He should do well.'

'Yes,' answered Arthur shortly. He was not one of Pat Colby's more dedicated admirers though he was the first to admit the skill and polish with which he rode.

'They've got one in Watchmaker's race at Cheltenham on Saturday,' went on the head lad.

'Oh, what's that?'

'Pirate Gold. You remember him. Chancy devil he was last year. All over the place at his fences. But he could go when he wanted to. They may have got him steadier this year. I doubt it, though. He fell at Nottingham last time out.'

'Yes, I do remember him now. Not an amateur's ride I should have thought but then I suppose Colby isn't one any more.' And never was for the past two seasons, he added to himself, though he did not say so.

Arthur went back to the house and poured himself another large gin. He permitted himself two before dinner and no more. The one at lunchtime today had been a rare dispensation occasioned by his late night. As he drank it a vague idea about Watchmaker began to form in his mind. Whether the idea ever came to fruition at all depended on how the horse ran on Saturday.

5

'Daddy' Rendall was all but certain the horse was going to fall. In so far as he could spare a thought for anything else as they came between the wings of the second last, which was a fence he hated anyway, he thought to himself that they all did it sometimes.

For Daddy's money Watchmaker was the safest jumper in the yard. He'd ridden him now for two seasons and he had not fallen since his novice days. It had rained heavily the night before. The ground was on the soft side which Watchmaker did not much care about. All the same this time he'd given Daddy a better feel than ever before so that he thought the horse really was coming to himself at last. Moreover four out he was going so well Daddy thought he was going to win. 'Watch that bugger in front,' Tim Hanway had called to him there. It was that checky young sod Pat Colby on that tearaway thing of Rokeby's.

Pirate Gold had run up the fourth to the right but he'd been clear enough not to do any damage. Daddy had been inside him at the last open ditch and had thought himself safe. Then the mad bugger had tried to duck out to the left and as near as dammit put Daddy and Watchmaker over the rails.

Pirate Gold had been nearly down there and so had Watchmaker. Unused to making mistakes or having them made for him, Watchmaker, knocked clean out of his stride, had been thoroughly upset. Daddy let him go along for a bit to recover but Tim Hanway had come to him and gone past and then someone else came up on his outside. He was aware the Guv'nor wanted to win this one. If he was going to have any chance at all he had to get back into the race. He picked

Watchmaker up again. As they came into the fence he realised he was in trouble. They were going to meet it so wrong that it would be a miracle if they survived. He tried to make Watchmaker stand back and failed. Watchmaker wasn't even damn well looking at the fence. Daddy sat still, waited for it and damned Pat Colby's soul.

The miracle did not happen. To make matters worse Watchmaker slipped taking off. He hit the fence half-way up. There was a smash of birch and he turned over.

It was a small field. Just the same Daddy lay curled up into a tight ball until he knew they had all gone. Then he got to his feet. He was quite unhurt. With his usual common sense Watchmaker had refused to career after the others. He was standing placidly a few yards away, the broken reins trailing the ground beside him.

Daddy walked over to him. 'You are a silly bastard, you are,' he said. Then he remounted and began to ride back to the stands.

Daddy Rendall was about as far removed from the hell-raising image of the steeplechase jockey as he well could be. He was a stocky man of medium height. He was thirty-seven years of age, which is old for a steeplechase jockey. During his years of riding he had acquired the ridge of muscle across his shoulders and the barrel chest which come to most of those who mill over fences for any length of time. His face was square, battered and good-natured with a nose set slightly awry from a badly-mended break received so long ago he had almost forgotten the fall that had caused it. A kindly and easy-going man in a tough and sometimes ruthless profession he had never been known to lose his temper or do a dirty trick. Always he had been ready to lend a helping hand or often, more materially, hard cash, to those who were down and out or slipping from the ladder of success, out of the frame and into oblivion. He was fatherly, too, to frightened youngsters commencing their racing career, ready with a quiet word of advice or encouragement at the start or in the changing room. As a result, many of them came to him nowadays with their troubles and listened to his counsel. All this had earned him the sobriquet of 'Daddy', by which name he was universally known all over steeplechasing England. Arthur Malcolm was one of the few who could not bring himself to use it and still, after ten years' close association, addressed him

70

firmly by his surname.

Daddy was above all a horseman, and he was a superb schooling jockey. He had hands, sympathy and understanding; horses of all sizes, sorts and descriptions went well for him. He had come to race riding from a farming family, point-to-pointing and a year or two in a chasing stable where he graduated from work-rider to the racecourse proper. He had not had the advantage of an apprenticeship on the flat to help him master the art of riding a finish. His finishes were at best workmanlike and at worst distinctly untidy. They were the weakest of all his skills and earned him criticism both from the crowd and from some owners and trainers. Like his employer, too, he lacked the ultimate drive for success that might have taken him to the very top.

But Daddy loved horses and riding them in races and dreaded the time when he would have to give up. The dread was not entirely concerned with the wrench of leaving a sport he loved, for there was the money aspect, too. He had little or nothing put away. His years with Arthur had been happy ones and, no one, he always told himself, could have asked for a better Guv'nor. But the money was scarcely munificent. Arthur paid him a retainer of £1,000 a year. Although retainers in steeplechasing were rare enough and were, even when offered, almost derisory when compared with the flat, this was not really sufficient by present-day standards. But it had been agreed some time ago and when Miss Haymer typed each year's agreement from the last one and presented it to him to sign before filing it at Weatherby's, he had never been able to bring himself to ask for more. Arthur's owners were generous with their presents according to their lights but they were, almost to a man or woman, non-betters, with the exception of Miss Meredith whose betting was so eccentric that it scarcely counted. There was, therefore, seldom anything above the standard ten per cent of the stake coming to him and there had been no really big wins like the National which would have brought a sum sufficient to be put away as a nest egg for the future.

Millie, his wife, was always at him to do something about the money or to retire and get a steady job. But then Millie had hated his racing ever since their marriage. At the beginning she had come with him and tried to share the interests and excitements of a jockey's life. But the constant strain of watching each fence thinking it would be his last, coupled with the dreadful moments of suspense when waiting to see if he got to his feet after a fall, had all proved too much for her. Nor had it improved his riding to feel her anxious presence there in the stands watching him, all the time on the brink of hysteria, her hands shaking so that she could hardly hold the glasses. Then, ceasing to watch, she had come along to help with the driving and had sat in the car park reading a book. That had not worked either as the roar of the crowd and the tension building up in her before his reappearance had proved almost as much a strain as the actual watching. Now she remained at home, sending him off with the fatuous injunction, 'Do be careful today, dear,' which would have driven a less placid man into a fury but which he had managed to turn into a joke, coming home to her, chucking her under the chin and saying, 'I had a very careful day today, Millie, I won two races.' Sometimes, now, she would look at his races on television and, if he fell, he would try to get up as quickly as was consistent with safety. Then he would give a wave in the hope that it would catch the camera and show her he was all right. Mostly, however, she busied herself about the house and looked after the two boys.

Millie, he supposed now, was perhaps right in a way. Maybe he was pushing his luck too far in going on so long. So far he had been fortunate in the matter of injuries. Apart from the usual collar-bones, an arm some years ago, a cracked shin bone last season and a few ribs from time to time, he had escaped major physical damage. And he had loved every minute of it. Moreover there was nothing else, really, he could do, certainly without losing his independence. The thought of becoming someone else's travelling head lad and caring for the horses on the racecourse without riding them was anathema to him. He had not the capital to set up as a trainer and in any event did not much want to. He had seen enough of the worries and responsibilities of a trainer's life not to have any desire to take them on, and Millie would hate that too. To buy a farm where he could keep and school hunters and racehorses who had proved recalcitrant and would not go for others, that might be something—if he had the capital. Well, perhaps they'd win the National this time. That was the big one, that was the race every jockey wanted to win, and it carried the greatest money rewards too. He hoped he had remembered to wave to Millie after that fall but his thoughts had been so full of ideas about Watchmaker and the feel he had given him and the National that maybe he hadn't. Well, she probably wasn't watching, anyway.

Back in their little house on the outskirts of Wolverhampton his wife turned off the television set with a click. He had got to his feet. That meant he was all right, even if he had not waved. Nowadays he was more and more prone to forget. She supposed it meant that he didn't care so much or maybe he just thought she was not interesred any more. At all events another race was over. And his next ride was a hurdle. That was not so dangerous.

She looked fondly at her two boys aged seven and five now engaged in fighting over the construction of a Lego ship. They wouldn't be jockeys. Not if she had anything to do with it. Then quickly, she put her hand to her side. She wished the pain there would go away. It flickered like, sort of, as she had told the doctor, a kind of lightning inside her. The doctor had been harried and over-worked with a mass of other patients to see in his surgery and a hard day of calls behind him. He had not seemed to be either very interested or impressed. Housewives, he had said, were having a bad time of it nowadays, and he had given her some pills. She had not told Bill—she, too, resolutely refused to call him by his racing nickname—any of this. The other day, when it was worse, she had pretended it was an upset stomach. Vallium, someone had told her the pills were. They seemed to relieve the pain a bit anyway. Crossing to the sideboard she opened a drawer, took out the plastic vial, opened it and swallowed one.

Arthur Malcolm was waiting for Daddy as he came in. 'What happened?' he said.

'Young Colby nearly had me over the wing.' Daddy slid to the ground and began to undo the girths.

'Thought as much. Can't keep his bloody horse straight.'

'It wasn't his fault. I don't think anyone could keep that Pirate Gold straight, the way he was today. This old fellow was going great until then. I thought he'd win it. What did win it?'

'Colby.'

'Did he? What was the distance?'

'Four lengths. He was clear at the last. Made a mess of it and

73

then came on. He'll be a useful horse all right if they can ever get him to settle.'

'Look, sir, I've been thinking. You can forget that fall. This fellow is a far better horse than last year. He gave me a real good feel this time. He might be a National horse.'

'I'm glad to hear you say that. I had much the same idea myself.'

At that moment the owner came up. Charles d'Arcy was a round, bustling little man in a covert coat and a polka-dot scarf. Daddy had the saddle over his arm now. He passed him with a smile and a finger to his cap.

'Well, Arthur, that wasn't very good, was it?' Charles said.

'No, Charles, it wasn't. It may not have been as bad as it looked, though. Rendall says he is a different horse from last year. He thinks he might make a National horse.'

'Too far away and too many chances involved for me. I wish I had a Gold Cup horse.'

'He'll certainly never be that.'

'I'm a bit short of readies just now. Can you cash him for me, Arthur?'

'I might be able to. You've no objection if he stays with me, have you? I must tell you, Charles, I still believe he could make up into something. But if you're determined to get out of him I have someone in mind who might take a chance with him.'

'Of course I don't mind. I'll be glad to see the end of him.'

'You ought to get out of that mare, too, Charles.'

'Produce a bracket for me for the stud and I'll have her home damn quick.'

Neither gentleman thought of mentioning the question of the overdue training bill.

Arthur watched the lad lead Watchmaker away. He wished the horse had stood up though he doubted very much whether he would have beaten Pirate Gold even if he had. Colby's horse had come up the hill like a champion and young Colby, he had to admit, had ridden him like one too. He made his way to the weighing-room to collect the saddle and weight-cloth for Meg Meredith's hurdler. As he did so he recollected with a sinking heart that old Meg had her betting boots on.

Meg Meredith's betting boots were as famous in racing as she was. They were a pair of hideous, high-sided yellow button boots which came half-way up her legs. She had first worn them

74

so many years ago that everyone including herself had forgotten the exact occasion. But she maintained that they had then brought her luck and an enormous return from the tote on one of her own outsiders. Ever afterwards she put on those boots whenever she had decided that one of her horses was due to win. In arriving at this conclusion she did not consult the form book, her trainer or any of the accepted oracles. Instead she had a mysterious 'Book of Stars' which was about the size of Burke's Peerage. It went everywhere with her but no one save herself and Joseph, her general factotum and man about the place, was allowed to open it. This, her dreams—exclusively occupied by horses, so she said—and some advice from Joseph, was what she relied upon to determine her betting days.

Meg Meredith was one of the last of racing's real eccentrics. She was a tall gaunt woman with the face of an amiable horse. She lived in a castle in Yorkshire apparently quite alone save for Joseph but no one could confirm or deny this since no guest had passed its portals within the memory of anyone in racing, including Arthur Malcolm who had trained some of her horses for the past twenty years.

From this northern keep she set out periodically to make raids on the racecourses of England, only, however, when her own horse was running. Her conveyance was an elderly Daimler resembling a cross between a conservatory and a railway carriage and said by legend to be one of those originally used by King George V and his consort on state occasions. In this, chauffeured by Joseph, she trundled round England stopping when required at chosen hotels she had patronised for years and where, advised by Joseph in advance, a suite was always ready for her. Here, too, she maintained complete seclusion and was waited upon only by Joseph who was popularly said to valet her amongst his other activities.

The sole places where she was available for consultation or interview by her trainers or those few others to whom she might wish to give instructions regarding veterinary or other matters were the parade ring, where in defiance of all stewards' orders and instructions if she wished to see anyone at all she did so, and the back of the Daimler after racing. Here, assisted by every conceivable accoutrement in the way of decanters, cocktail sets, sandwich cases, coffee percolators and even an antique spirit lamp, she dispensed hospitality chiefly based on home-brewed sloe gin, gave orders and listened to such advice as she was prepared to accept, which was precious little.

Arthur met her in the parade ring. 'The horse looks well, Arthur,' she said to him. 'The stars are right. Two nights ago I dreamt I'd have a winner this week. I saw it quite clearly. The only thing that's wrong,' she added seriously, 'is that in my dream the horse was a chestnut and the jockey was wearing different colours. But I'm having a bet today.'

'Look, Meg, this is only his second time out. Last time he flattened every hurdle. Rendall has him jumping pretty well now. But I don't think you'll win it.'

'Rubbish, Arthur. The book says so and the book has been having a great run lately.'

The form book doesn't though, Arthur thought despairingly. Aloud he said: 'Who are you betting with now?' for Meg changed her bookmaker almost as often as she changed her mind.

'Larry Buckner. Lays me a point over the odds, he does.'

And a lot of other people too, Arthur thought. Buckner was on the rails having taken over his father's pitch but the son did not have his father's flair, or so Arthur had been told. If some of the stories were true he wondered how long Buckner would last in the present era of cramped odds and restricted betting. Well, it didn't matter much to him except that he had liked and respected old Joe Buckner the father, as had most people in racing. On the rare occasions that Arthur had a bet, his maximum was a tenner and that was only about twice a year. He turned his attention to more immediate concerns.

Rendall was now standing beside him raising his whip to the peak of his cap to salute old Meg. Rendall and he knew each other and their horses so well there was rarely any need for explicit instructions to pass between them. 'Miss Meredith has had a bet,' he said quietly. 'You'll have to put him in with a chance somewhere.'

'He has a fair turn of foot,' Daddy said.

'Yes. Get him settled and jumping nicely and then you'll know yourself when to send him on.'

The bell went, the boy turned the horse in towards them. Arthur stripped off the rug, put his hand under Daddy's ankle and whisked him into the saddle.

Arthur watched them leave the parade ring and then walked

76

out through the tunnel underneath the stands on to the lawn.

The whole incomparable sweep of Prestbury Park was spread before him. The heights of Cleeve Hill were a vivid backdrop behind the green of the turf, the white rails and stark black fences. Arthur had seen it all too often before for him consciously to consider the beauty of his surroundings. Besides, his thoughts were on other things.

This might be a nice young horse of Meg's, he thought, if only he was allowed to give him time. He hadn't wanted to run Harnessed Lad here at all, but, as always, if she was riding one of her hobby-horses then nothing anyone could say or do would influence her. She divided her horses, quite arbitrarily, between him and a young nephew who was said to be her heir at least at the moment or until she changed her mind. And it was typical of her that Arthur, who was better with chasers, mostly ended up with her hurdlers while young Alastair Bragdon, who was better with hurdlers, got most of the chasers. They were said to have had a young horse last year which was to be a likely National hope later on. He had not been out yet and Arthur wondered what had happened to him. Probably, he reflected, still filling himself with good Yorkshire grass at Warwork Castle because the stars had not yet told Meg the time was right to bring him in.

Raising his glasses he watched Harnessed Lad going down to the start. He was a damn nice mover whatever else, Arthur thought. If only he had had more time and more schooling at home—owners! he thought for the millionth time, owners!

In fact Harnessed Lad ran much better than he had feared and every bit as well as he had dared to hope. Daddy gave him plenty of time to see the first few hurdles and under his tender hands he jumped them perfectly. Coming round the last bend he was fourth and moving up to challenge. But Pat Colby on a big, rangy, overgrown brute of Rokeby's on whom he had hugged the rails all the way was second and going ominously well. Three horses, Harnessed Lad, the leader Larousse, ridden by Tim Hanway, the reigning champion, and Pat Colby's mount, rose at the last almost together.

But now Harnessed Lad was being asked to jump under pressure for the first time in his life. He made a woeful hash of his attempt, scarcely rising at the hurdle at all. The other two came on and the big youngster, driven right out by Colby up the hill, got his head in front and just held it there at the post. It was the hell of a finish for an ex-amateur to have ridden, especially against the champion who could hold his own with the best on the flat. But whilst giving Colby all credit for it Arthur told himself that he did not think the big horse would forget his introduction to racing in a hurry.

Daddy, wisely accepting defeat, dropped his hands halfway up the hill and was caught and passed for fourth place. That meant, Arthur considered, that at least no irretrievable harm had been done to Harnessed Lad. It crossed his mind that in these changed times the stewards might have something to say to Rendall for not riding his horse right out. Well, if they did, he would certainly have something to say to them. It would be just the sort of thing that new businessman chap would do. He glanced at the front of his racecard to see the names of the stewards. Two of them were old friends, the third he hardly knew. The new man's name, what was it? Bennett? Beverley? Barkley, that was it, did not appear. Then Arthur remembered that of course it wouldn't. Barkley had been given accelerated promotion to the ranks of senior stewards and could not act at meetings.

Meg seemed to have retired to the Daimler and he had no intention of seeking her out. He had a word with Rendall who was pleased with the running of Harnessed Lad. Then, after he had had a look at the horses with the travelling head lad and satisfied himself that there were no cuts or injuries, he began to make his way towards the car park.

As he approached the stairs leading to the club buildings through which he would pass, a young man came up to him. He was a very smartly turned out young man in a covert coat, cavalry twill trousers, a trilby hat and a Tenth Hussars tie. Arthur recognised him as one of the younger of the stewards' secretaries. 'Excuse me, Major Malcolm,' the young man said. 'I—er-that is to say—'

Arthur stopped, turned and stared at the young man with steely eye. 'Yes?' he said, unhelpfully.

The young man swallowed. He was not enjoying this, moreover Arthur's general countenance reminded him all too strongly of a certain interview he had had with his adjutant regarding lateness on parade after a night out. 'Well, er—' he went on fingering his tie. 'Mr Barkley asked me to say to you and this is—er—quite unofficial of course but—er—he thinks you should know that he is not happy that Rendall persevered sufficiently with your horse from the last hurdle.'

Arthur stared at the young man in silence for several moments, giving him ample opportunity to realise that the look in his eye was really remarkably like that of his adjutant's on the other occasion.

'Mr Barkley is here, I suppose,' he said at length.

'Oh, yes. He comes racing a lot now, sir.'

'Does he, indeed. Well, you may convey my compliments to Mr Barkley and tell him that when and if he wishes to question the riding of my horses I am at his disposal at any time but that I suggest he does so through the proper channels. You may further tell him—and this is also quite unofficial of course—that when you or he has trained and ridden as many horses as I have I will consider your qualifications to assess the actions of myself and my jockey. Do I make myself quite clear?'

This was proving even worse than the young man had expected. 'Oh, yes, indeed, sir. I hope you understand—'

'I understand perfectly. And you—what's your name? Raynham, isn't it?'

'Yes, sir.'

Arthur's lips twitched slightly. 'You can further convey my compliments to Mr Barkley,' he said. 'And tell him that the next time he contemplates doing anything like this he should think twice about sending a boy on a man's errand. Good day to you.'

Arthur was still angry as he drove home through the traffic. That damned whippersnapper Barkley, he thought. He'd never even damn well sat on a horse to his knowledge. What the hell did they think they were doing when they elected him in the first place? They'd have been a damn sight better with old Julius Marker whatever they thought of him. At least he'd been in racing for years and was an ardent supporter. The thought of Julius Marker brought his mind back to Robert Warminster and in turn to a curious conversation he had heard behind him when Pirate Gold was being led in.

'That doesn't look like a Burglar Alarm horse to me,' a voice had said. 'They're mostly common brutes. He looks more like a Malifico. Wasn't Burglar Alarm at Clayhampton for a bit?'

'I believe so. He didn't fit in there. Bradbury has him himself

79

now. He's getting winners, too. You're dead right, Ted, Pirate Gold looks far more like a Malifico horse. Come to think of it there were others about his time, too, that didn't look like Burglar Alarm.'

Arthur had looked down at his racecard to check Pirate Gold's breeding. *Burglar Alarm—Double Doubloon*, he had read. Then he had turned to try to locate the speakers but they had melted into the crowd. Thinking over what Robert had said about Malifico and the area of speculation this conversation opened up drove all recollections of Barkley and the young stewards' secretary out of his mind.

Back at Prestbury Park Myles Aylward was watching the Cleeve Hill Steeplechase from the Press Stand. This was the race which had been chosen for the re-introduction of last year's National winner, Rob Roy, to racing and it had to be admitted that at the moment he was running deplorably. He had top weight, of course, and he would not be anything like wound up, but to Myles's eyes these factors neither explained nor excused the manner of his running. He had, so far, never really been in the race at all. He had made a bad mistake at the fence in front of the stands and as Myles watched he clouted the last open ditch so hard he was almost brought to a standstill.

But Rob Roy had been a National winner and a good one and two things good Grand National winners must have in abundance are heart and courage. Down the hill he suddenly caught hold of his bit and commenced to run on. Once into his stride he sailed through a flock of beaten horses and was with the leaders at the last. Those mistakes, however, and the effort of carrying 12st 7lb through testing ground were too much for him. He weakened on the hill and Pat Colby on a novice of Rokeby's, who was just coming into handicap class and was getting nearly two stone, drew away to win by a length and a half, thus giving his rider a treble on his first appearance as a professional.

'What a marvellous way to start,' the man from the *Globe* said to Myles as they left the stand.

'Yes, isn't it,' Myles agreed though the words were bile in his mouth. He wondered if Evelyn was here to watch it. He had not seen her but then he had been working all the afternoon. With the other man he walked to the winner's enclosure to hear what

Rob Roy's trainer had to say about his horse's performance and future plans.

Val Errington, who trained Rob Roy, was a permit holder, a tough cheerful extrovert who farmed a bit and jobbed in horses and who knew himself to be lucky indeed to have bred and owned this one good horse after half a lifetime spent with selling platers and moderate handicappers. He was his usual ebullient self with the press when they gathered round him.

'Well, boys,' he said. 'I suppose I was a bloody fool to run him here. The distance was too short and the ground was wrong. But I had to bring him out somewhere, hadn't I—eh?'

But when questioned about his horse's jumping he evaded a direct answer. 'Yes, I saw those mistakes,' he said. 'But did you see the way he ran on again? This is one hell of a horse, lads. He's all heart, that's what he is. You mark my words he'll win again at Aintree whatever weight they give him. We're not discouraged—we never are!'

After that Myles made his way to the press room. He knew already what his column was going to be about. He had always prided himself on his fairness and objectivity and the fact that he hated Pat Colby's guts had nothing to do with what he was about to write. Sitting down, he began to transcribe his notes.

If ever I saw a champion jockey in the making, I saw one today. On his first day as a professional Pat Colby rode three races to land three winners and displayed a virtuosity in the saddle I have not seen since the days of Fred Winter and Bryan Marshall.

Mr Derek Power's Pirate Gold is no armchair ride and it would not be unfair to say that he scarcely jumped a single fence here today without raising the blood pressure of his connections. In addition he made an unholy mess of the last with the race apparently at his mercy. Yet Colby sat him like rock; he had him on his feet and balanced in a couple of strides and won going away up the hill.

On Mrs Ellan's Recovery in the Novice Hurdle he had to play an entirely different tune. Recovery is a big horse and still largely unfurnished. Colby had him on the rails all the way. Throughout the race he did not give an inch of ground, finally producing Recovery at the last to beat Tim Hanway a neck in a hectic finish—and beating Tim Hanway a neck, as

81

his fellow riders know only too well, takes some doing. To cap a wonderful afternoon Colby won the Cleeve Hill Chase on Maxim Gun from Chris Rokeby's stable to which he is now attached. Rob Roy, giving away lumps of weight, was never going really well but was running on at the end to finish third.

Pirate Gold may well turn out a champion if they can ever get him to settle. Colby looks one already and even with the **35**   start the others have got on him since the beginning of the season, if you can get him at anything better than prohibitive odds for the championship I, for one, suggest you take them.

When Myles had telephoned this in he felt in considerable need of a drink. Although he would dearly have liked to slant his article away from Colby he knew that, had there been no personal feelings involved, that was how he would have written it. Therefore that was the way it had to be. He was a professional and there was no more to be said. But he still needed that drink. Going down the steps he walked over to the bar.

Drinking when racing was one of the habits his original mentor, Andrew Mostyn, had warned him against. 'If they see you there and they spot any mistakes at all they'll say you are watching your races from the bar,' he had said. 'And *that* won't do you any good.' Now that he was established it didn't make so much difference, he supposed, but the old habit held, and he seldom entered a bar on a racing day.

Almost the first person he saw was Chris Rokeby. Julius's trainer was a tall, thin man with a weatherbeaten face which owed its crimson colour in equal parts to fresh air and whisky. He had ridden as a professional many years before without much success but when he had taken out a licence to train he had showed almost immediately that he had the flair and understanding as well as dedication and horse management which are essential for the training of steeplechasers. Two Gold Cups, a Champion Hurdle and, some twelve years ago, a Grand National, had already come his way. He was rude, aggressive and outspoken, but he knew his job and, as in other walks of life, it was the successes that counted.

'Congratulations,' Myles said to him.

'Thanks. Have a drink. What'll it be? Whisky?' Rokeby paid for the drink and pushed the glass into Myles's hand. Then, as if suddenly remembering something, he said: 'Hey, you, Myles, what's this bloody animal you've sent me for Julius?'

'Alexander, do you mean? The Irish horse?'

'Yes, that's his bloody name. Only he's not a horse. He's a fucking hippopotamus!' This was said at the top of Rokeby's not inconsiderable voice. The whole bar could hear him and indeed faces were already being turned towards them. Down at the end Myles could see the purple cheeks and baby face of Hector Mallinson buried in a large whisky but quite obviously taking in everything that was said. Myles felt his spirits dropping and his anger rising. He had had just about all that he could take that day, he reckoned. He wondered just what use Mallinson could make of all this. He'd fit the conversation in somewhere at the back of that lousy mind of his and bring it out when and where it was best designed to hurt, of that Myles was certain. And worse was to come.

'That daughter of his was down looking at him yesterday,' Chris went on.

Myles wondered if Pat Colby had been with her. Almost certainly, he supposed, in view of the stable connection. 'What did she say?'

'She said you must have been out of your tiny mind.'

'Have you done anything with him?'

'I've cantered him.'

'Who rode him?' He had a pretty good idea but he might as well know.

'Pat rode him. Says he wouldn't win an argument.'

'I see.' Myles put down his glass and walked out of the bar.

'Now, what's got into him?' Rokeby asked his companion.

'You were a bit rough with him, weren't you?'

'Rough? He should know by now that when I say those sort of things they are meant as a compliment!'

'He didn't act as if he did. It was Myles Aylward the journalist, wasn't it? I thought I heard there was a sort of a thing going between him and Marker's daughter. Is that right?'

'If it is I didn't know about it.' Rokeby, suddenly subdued, and thinking his own thoughts, buried his nose in his glass.

Outside the bar Myles almost ran into Andrew Mostyn.

'Hullo, Myles. What did you think of Rob Roy?' the older man said.

'Rob Roy? Hard to tell, isn't it? I doubt if that race means anything. I didn't like those mistakes, though. He can't do that at Liverpool.'

'No. He's a spring horse, of course. He was probably just being bloody careless and idle first time out. I don't think he goes all that well for young Phillips, either. Manton was claimed elsewhere. I hear, by the way, that you're getting a new boss.'

'What?'

'Good Lord, Myles, you should know better than I. But you never did bother about office politics, did you?'

'I haven't been near the place for days, I must admit. I usually go in only to claim my expenses!'

'Well you do know that Reeling, your sports editor, has had a couple of coronaries already?'

'Of course. That's common knowledge.'

'He had another at the beginning of the week. He'll never work again. They're drafting in a new man immediately.'

'You certainly know far more than I do, Andrew. Who is the new man?'

'Featherstone from the *Globe* or so I'm told.'

'Good Lord, but he's a sort of all tough talk and tits man.'

'Yes, it does seem a strange sort of choice for the *Post*, if it's true, but things are changing on the street like everywhere else, Myles. Anyway I believe he's all right to work with even if he does have ideas of his own.'

Myles went on towards the car park. He did not suppose that the new sports editor on the *Post* would make much difference to his job even though Featherstone did seem rather a strange choice for the conservative and slightly sedate *Post*. What concerned him far more was what Rokeby had said about Alexander. Could he conceivably have been wrong in his judgment when he bought him? He doubted it. If ever his flair and experience had told him here was a racehorse it was in the case of Alexander. And, anyway, Chris was famous for always trying to double-bluff the press. If he publicly decried a horse it very often meant that he really thought the world of him. The reverse applied too as several unwary racing scribes had found to their cost.

But, as always, with Myles, a niggling doubt gnawed at him. In any event there was nothing he could do but wait and see how the horse went on. But what had Rokeby meant by

84

Evelyn's remark if indeed she had made it at all? He thought of trying to find her and discussing it with her. Perhaps he could ring her when he got back. Then it came to him that she might be with Colby. They must have been together at Rokeby's. Perhaps he was with her now. He simply could not face getting in touch with her and finding Colby there. Today had been a day of glory for Colby. They could well be celebrating it. This led to other thoughts and images of what might happen between them later on if they were. He cursed his imagination and trod on the accelerator.

6

Pat Colby was not with Evelyn. Pat Colby was at a party and Pat Colby was having a ball. To ride three winners in an afternoon is a rare enough event in the life of any professional jockey but to start with a treble was a triumph and he knew it. Congratulations were showered upon him from every side. Drinks were thrust into his hand and dolly birds were practically climbing all over him. He was the centre of attention and loving every moment of it.

The party was being given by an owner friend of Tommy Pereira's. Tommy and Pat were friends of long standing. In fact Pat lived rent free in a cottage on Tommy's farm in Gloucestershire. That day they had, as they often did, gone racing together.

Pat had changed from champagne to brandy and was feeling, as he would have expressed it himself, superfine. With a glass at his lips he let his eyes roam over the party. The dolly birds were beginning to bore him and he was avid for further prey. His glance alighted on a figure that had just entered the room and was standing by the doorway. 'Wow,' he said and whistled slightly through his lips. 'Who's that?' he nudged Tommy in the ribs, and Tommy followed his gaze to where a tall statuesque blonde was just taking a drink from a tray. She was wearing a mutation mink coat belted at the waist. Beneath it were a pair of long shapely legs. She stood out amongst the dolly birds like a peacock amongst pigeons.

'Why is she wearing that coat?' Pat said.

'At a guess I'd say because she has nothing on underneath. Lay off that one, Pat.'

'Why? Who is she?'

'Don't you know? No, I suppose you wouldn't, they haven't been all that long in racing. She's Miriam Barkley, the wife of that chap they've just made a steward.'

'Him? He's not a steward, he's a joke. He doesn't know which end a horse farts from!'

'That doesn't make it any—' He was speaking to the empty air for Pat had left him.

In a moment Pat was beside her. 'Hi,' he said.

She turned to look at him. 'Hi to you,' she said lazily over a very brown whisky.

She had, he noticed, eyes of a striking shade of blue which were now tinged with a faint haze whether from drinks, drugs, desire or some other additive or emotion it was impossible to say. Those eyes now moved over him slowly from head to toe exactly, he thought, as he himself would judge a horse—or a sire. A prickle of excitement ran up his spine.

'You're Colby, aren't you?' she said with studied insolence. 'Are you any good?'

'I'm never good.'

'That's not exactly what I meant.' She swallowed a deep draught of the big whisky. Then she swayed slightly and her hand went to the top button of her coat. 'Christ, it's hot in here,' she said.

The coat opened under Pat's fascinated and concentrated gaze. Tommy had been right. There was nothing underneath in the way of clothes that he could see, and he could see pretty far. But what was there looked good—and ripe for the picking. His hand went out towards her. 'Let me help you with the next one,' he said.

Suddenly Tommy was back at his side. Although Tommy Pereira deserved all Arthur's strictures as an amateur rider he was a kindly man and a loyal friend. He had watched the action between the two from across the room. He did not want to see Pat not only ruin a wonderful start but also lay up for himself what would almosd certainly be a pack of troubles later on. Seducing—if in this instance you could call it that—a steward's wife was not the best way for a professional jockey to start his career. 'There's someone over here who wants to meet you,' he said desperately to Pat. It was not much of an extraction gambit as he well knew but it was the best he could think of in a hurry. He doubted if it would work and he was right.

87

Her eyes switched to look at him. 'Tommy Pereira,' she said. 'I might have guessed. Fuck off, you horrible little man.' Then, for an instant, she allowed her gaze to move around the room. 'Christ!' she said at the top of her voice. 'What a middle-class lot you've got here. Let's revv things up a bit.' With that she threw her glass into the fireplace. It made a satisfactory and resounding smash.

Conversation stopped as if cut off with a knife. All attention was centred on the little group by the fire. She stood for a moment with her arm out, poised.

'Nice shooting,' Pat said. 'I couldn't have done it better myself. Every time a coconut or a good cigar. Try another.' He handed her his glass.

'Thanks, friend.' Suddenly her eyes glazed completely. She sighed, leant back and passed out cold.

By this time all the buttons were open and the coat flew wide. Both Pat and Tommy were able to confirm from the evidence of their eyes that their guesses were true. 'Can I carry her?' said Pat delightedly, stepping forward.

Tommy grabbed his arm. 'No you don't,' he said. In the confusion he began pushing his friend towards the door. 'You've had a bloody good day. Don't go and murder it all now, you reckless devil. She's bad business. I'll tell you why when we get out of here. Come on.'

'Dammit, Tommy, you're not my nurse.'

'Sometimes I think you need one.'

'Let me have another drink, then.'

'All right, but remember it's not going out of fashion—yet.'

Pat picked a glass of brandy from the tray of a passing waiter who was staring transfixed at the spreadeagled delights of Miriam Barkley revealed before him. He swallowed it in one gulp.

Outside they found Pat's Double Twelve Jaguar in the forecourt. 'I'll drive,' Tommy said. He had drunk very little during the party for drinking was not one of his indulgences.

'No, you damn well won't. Haven't you done enough bossing around already?'

Tommy knew his friend sufficiently well to realise that in getting him away from the party he had in fact done enough. By pushing him any further he might only create in Pat a state of complete bloody-mindedness which, compounded by success and alcohol, would compel him to go back in to the party, and then heaven only knew what would happen. Besides, Pat's voice was clear and his gait was steady. He had not, in fact, drunk a great deal, but he had been wasting and had eaten little for twenty-four hours. 'Very well then,' Tommy said resignedly.

Pat opened the door and slid behind the wheel. He started the big car without any fumbling and swung her on to the drive. There was a considerable amount of wheel-spin and engine-roar as they took off but that was his natural way of driving. 'What a dish. You are an old shit, Tommy, taking me away. God, I thought the gateway was wider than that.'

'You didn't miss the pillar by more than an inch, and it's wide enough—usually,' Tommy said grimly.

Pat had in fact been fit to drive or very nearly so when they had set out. But the last large brandy was now beginning to percolate into his bloodstream. On the open road the big car gathered speed with the rush of a rising lift. Fortunately there was not much traffic about but Tommy noticed that their changes of direction when required were not as controlled as they might have been. A light rain was falling, too, and the wipers were on, presenting an additional hazard. He was about to make a muted protest when Pat began to sing.

'Martin McGluskie loved whisky and gin,
Martin McGluskie loved wild, wild women,
Martin McGluskie had whores by the score
Martin McGluskie kept askin' for more—'

'Pat—'

'Martin McGluskie loved whisky and gin,
And horses and gamblin' and wild, wild—Christ!'

For it was then that the roundabout came up. The Double Twelve Jaguar is no child's toy and the roundabout was coming up very quickly indeed. It is not getting up speed in a fast car that presents the difficulty, it is getting rid of it. Pat's reflexes were honed to a fine edge by his fitness and his riding but alcohol had dulled and disturbed them. Too late he realised that the speed was not coming off quickly enough and he went for the brake. He almost got away with it.

The off-side front wheel touched the concrete kerb of the

89

roundabout's centre. The tail of the Jaguar swung violently. Pat caught her as she did so but he was a shade too late. Even then had it not been for the greasy surface of the road he might have held her. As it was the tail broke away. They slid sideways across the exit road. Pat swung the wheel in an effort to point her into it. He over-corrected. She straightened, swung, hit the roadside edge, mounted the grass verge and ploughed to a standstill.

The two young men sat quite still for a moment. Then: 'I think I hear angels' wings beating somewhere,' Tommy said. 'Thank God for safety belts. Are you all right?'

'Just about. They shouldn't put those bloody roundabouts in the way.' His speech was now becoming definitely slurred. Then he began to sing again, this time at the top of his voice: 'Martin McGluskie loved whisky and gin, and horses and courses and wild, wild—'

At which point the police car appeared. It passed them and slowed to a halt just beyond the Jaguar. A door opened and a constable got out. He had a torch in his hand.

'Fucking fuzz,' observed Pat. 'Let's get the hell out of this.'

Several things then happened all at once and far too quickly for Tommy to do anything about them.

Pat opened the driver's door evidently with some muddled idea of making a break for it. The policeman, now beside the car, took the edge of it on his shin. Pat started to run. Then, seeing the policeman swaying into his path, took a drunken swing at him, stumbled and fell.

'Can't you young hooligans bloody well grow up,' growled the constable, switching on his torch. Then, suddenly, as the beam hit Pat's features: 'Good God, it's Pat Colby, isn't it?' He put out a hand and pulled Pat, none too gently, to his feet.

'Yes, officer, it's Pat Colby all right,' Tommy said coming round the car. 'Why?'

'He brought up a Canadian for me today at Cheltenham. That's why. I suppose I owe him something—'

'What's going on? Do you want any help?' the other policeman had left the car and was coming towards them.

'It's all right. I'll handle it,' the first one said. But by this time the other man was beside them.

'Fucking fuzz,' observed Pat thickly.

'What?'

'It's nothing, officer. He's had a bit of a shock,' Tommy put in.

'I see. Have either of you two gentlemen been drinking?'

'Well—'

'Perhaps you'd be good enough to blow into this. Is this the one who was driving? We'll have him first, please. Did I see him trying to strike you, Jack?'

'No. He just stumbled getting out of the car.'

'Stumbled—staggered I'd say by the look of him.'

The next steps were inevitable, and the routine tests and charges followed. Pat had sobered up by the time they reached the station though it was obvious that his blood count was going to be in excess of the legal limit. But for once he appeared to take to heart Tommy's whispered injunctions to behave himself, and beyond a few further muttered imprecations which Tommy did his best to cover up, he did so. The Jaguar was found to be perfectly drivable and, after two hours, with Tommy at the wheel, they were allowed to go.

By the time they arrived at Pat's cottage it was late. Tommy cooked scrambled eggs and made black coffee for them both. Neither of them talked very much. Pat was still slightly fuddled; he was muttering about his luck and cursing the fuzz. When he had finished his coffee he went to bed.

Tommy washed up the cups and plates. He was by now very tired. He debated about driving the Jag up to the house and then remembered that Pat had said something about going down to Rokeby's to lunch to discuss Pirate Gold and other plans. That would mean an early start and he would want the car. The couple who looked after him up at the house were used to his being absent without warning. They would not worry if he did not turn up. Tommy went upstairs, found a pair of Pat's pyjamas in the airing cupboard and the spare bed made up. He put on the pyjamas, switched on the electric blanket, turned back the covers and climbed in. He was asleep in two minutes.

If Pat had a hangover the next morning he did not show it. He was cooking breakfast when Tommy came down, and he grinned at him. 'Two eggs or one?' he asked. 'Bacon? Kippers? Kidneys? You say it, we have 'em. That was quite a night.' His eye was as clear and his hand as steady as if he had never touched a drink. Tommy, who, despite his abstention, had a

91

slight headache, spared a moment to envy his friend his constitution. 'Bloody fuzz.' Pat went on. 'I suppose I'm for it.'

'Looks like it. You were a bit unlucky. You brought up a Canadian yesterday for that first chap. I think he might just have let us away with it if I'd said I'd drive. Then the other one came along and started getting officious.'

'Just what did happen? I'm a bit hazy.'

'I'm not surprised.'

'What about that blonde?'

'Leave her alone, Pat.'

'You getting morals or something?'

'Listen, Barkley may be a joke steward. Actually I doubt if he is. He's a damn good administrator and he's out to learn and he's learning fast, too fast, perhaps. Apart from that I know chaps who had deals with him in the City and they told me to look out if you crossed him. She's a near-lush and a near-nympho and the rest if you want it and twenty years at least younger than he is. He's blind crazy about her and he wants her all for himself.'

'Selfish bugger.'

'You can put it that way.'

'She's still quite a dish.'

'Maybe, but there's poison in it for you.'

'What'll I do about this drunk in charge?'

'Get a good barrister and pray if you know how to which I doubt.'

'You'll do that for me, Tommy boy, won't you? I mean the barrister bit.'

Tommy sighed. 'Yes,' he said. 'I suppose I will. Are you going down to Chris's today?'

'Yes. Lunching with him. I reckon he might run Pirate Gold in the Gold Cup.'

'I should get that wheel checked. If you take it up to the house Johnson will have a look at it for you before you go. Where are you riding on Monday?'

'Plumpton. Chris has three runners. Are you coming?'

'No. I've things to do in London.'

'London? Why don't you stick to the job more? Ride out. Buy yourself a few more decent horses. You'll never get anywhere the way you're going on now.'

'I'm not sure that I want to. I'm not one of your death or glory boys. I just like riding round. I think I'll run old Cummerbund in the National though.' Tommy picked up the *Sunday Post* and opened it at the racing page. 'I see Myles Aylward says you're the next champion,' he said.

'Does he? That creep.'

'Is he a creep? I thought he was rather a nice chap.'

Just then the telephone rang. Pat picked up the receiver. 'Yes, speaking,' he said. Then: 'Just a minute, I want to look.' He reached for a red-bound engagement book and opened it. 'What did you say the name of the horse was again? General Buller, I see.' His hand was reaching for the form book when he changed its direction and placed it over the mouthpiece. 'Biggs-Swaffham wants me to ride General Buller at Nottingham for him,' he said to Tommy. 'He's a permit holder somewhere, isn't he? You know most of these chaps. What's he like?'

'Never schools his horses. What's it in?'

'A novice chase.'

'He'll bury you,' Tommy said, spreading marmalade.

'I thought as much. Bloody cheek asking me.' Pat took his hand from the mouthpiece. 'No,' he said. 'I'm afraid I can't. I've just checked my book.'

Hardly had he replaced the receiver when it rang again. 'Yes,' he said. 'Yes,' and now Tommy noticed the eagerness in his voice. 'I'm sure I can.' He flipped the pages of his book. 'That's quite okay. Thanks. I'll be glad to. Wednesday. See you.' Putting back the instrument he turned to Tommy. 'Paul Cantrey wants me to ride Kingfisher for him at Windsor on Wednesday.'

'Cantrey—the leading trainer. My, my, we are coming on, aren't we? What's happened to Tim Hanway?'

'Hurt a shoulder in the last yesterday, apparently.' Pat swallowed his coffee. 'Well, I've a long drive before me. I'd better be off.'

'Drop me at the house first and better get that wheel looked at.'

When they reached the house Tommy got out and Pat pushed the Jaguar into gear. 'What about the wheel?' Tommy said.

'Bugger the wheel. It stood up all right last night, didn't it?' Pat grinned his reckless grin, let in the clutch with a bang and was gone in an instant down the drive, leaving two tyre marks on the tarmac and a faint smell of burning rubber behind him.

Tommy, watching him go, caught the whiff and shook his head. 'The demon king,' he said to himself softly and went into the house.

7

'Well now, what about this National horse you were to find for me, Arthur?' Robert Warminster, a cigar in one hand and a glass of brandy in the other, sat in Arthur's study with his feet stretched out to the fire.

'I have one in mind, but he'll be a gamble, Robert.'

'I like gambles. What is he?'

'Watchmaker. He's qualified to run so there's no need to worry about that.'

'Qualify? I didn't know you had to qualify for the National.'

'According to the present conditions, and I don't suppose they'll change them, you must either be placed in a chase at Aintree or have won a race value a thousand pounds on with eight hundred pounds added to the stakes. That race he won at Newbury last year lets him in.'

'I see.'

'He's coming eight. We know he can jump. He's never fallen except once as a novice and yesterday when young Colby nearly knocked him down. Rendall tells me he was giving him a great feel until then and that he's a far stronger horse than he was last year.'

'Who owns him and why is he selling?'

'Charles d'Arcy. He's not interested in the National. He wants a Gold Cup horse.'

'What does he want for him?'

'I should think about £5,000 would buy him.'

Robert puffed reflectively at his cigar for a few seconds. 'You know,' he said. 'I've been thinking about what you said the other night. It is quite correct that the price is only a fraction of what we'd pay for a top yearling if we were buying one.'

'You must remember, of course, that there is no end product in a chaser. If he breaks down badly or goes wrong he's only worth what you can get for his hide. With a yearling you have at least possible stud value or a sale abroad.'

'Still, I think it's a risk worth taking and you say I can have a bet.'

'You can have that all right. But, mind you, Robert, all I'm saying at this stage is that I think he'll make up into a National horse if he stays sound.'

'Cautious old devil, you are. All right, buy him for me.'

'Do you want to see him?'

'Who? The horse? Good God, no. I'm far too comfortable here. Cold and smelly places racin' stables, I've always thought, especially in winter. I'll take your word for him, Arthur.'

'Very well. Pour yourself some more brandy.'

'Thanks, I will.' Robert reached for the decanter on the table beside him and re-charged his balloon glass. 'By the way,' he went on, 'your Mr Julius Marker—I ran into Dick Roicey in White's yesterday and he happened to bring his name up. Dick is one of the stewards at that new place—Wrayfield Park. Marker, as I expect you know, is in it, too. He acts as a steward there with Dick. Dick tells me he has been most generous and helpful to them. Last year he presented a challenge bowl for a three mile chase. Cost him about a thousand apparently. Now he's talking of sponsoring a National Trial Chase. Dick is seriously thinking of putting his name forward for the Jockey Club. Says he'd be an addition.'

'That's a damn sight more than you can say for some of them,' Arthur said with feeling. 'By the way, Robert, did you ever have anything to do with a horse called Burglar Alarm?'

'Yes. I won him in a raffle.'

'You did *what*?'

'The villagers at Clayhampton have a raffle each year. They got hold of this fellow somewhere, don't ask me where. I always tell the secretary chap down there to buy up blocks of tickets to help the fund. And then, damme, if I didn't go and win the brute. I tried to give him back but no one'd have him.'

'So what did you do?'

'I told Bradbury to keep him and try him. I forget how he was bred but it was nothing much and of course he didn't get any mares. Finally I got fed up and gave him to Bradbury. Told him he could have him for himself if he wanted. He took him to his own place. Oddly enough he got a few winners for him and now he's getting chasing winners or so I'm told.'

'He's got what might be a very good one at this moment. Pirate Gold. If they get him to settle, and they probably will for Rokeby knows what he's about, he could be a Gold Cup horse.'

'Good luck to them, then. Though now you mention it I seem to remember when I had him someone told me his stock couldn't gallop fast enough to warm themselves.'

'Anyway it was Pirate Gold who nearly knocked us down yesterday.'

'Did he? Nearly knocked over by the get of one of my own horses. That's a sort of omen, isn't it? I'll have to buy him now.'

All gamblers are suspicious, reflected Arthur, but for the life of him he could not see how Robert had conjured an omen out of this incident. Anyway it confirmed that he was going to keep Watchmaker and he was pleased. He had always taken a special interest in this horse, sensing that there was in him a latent potential for unexpected improvement. Now his judgment appeared to be about to be borne out for Rendall's remarks after the race were confirmation of it. Watchmaker, he felt, could develop into a live National hope such as he had not had in his stable for some years.

'You'll stay for tea?' he said to Robert.

'No. Thank you for the lunch, Arthur, but I must get back to Town. When will you run this horse next?'

'He's in a three mile chase at Towcester and another at Southwell. I'll run him in one of those if all goes well, but I want Rendall to school him first to get his confidence back after that fall. You know, Robert, when horses that aren't accustomed to falling do come down it shakes them. Anyway, Rendall will put him right again. He's the best schooling jockey I know. I'm lucky to have him.'

'Getting on a bit though, isn't he, or so I seem to have heard?'

'I don't agree. In my opinion he's still better than most of them.' Arthur was always fiercely loyal to his employees.

When Robert had gone Arthur and Mary had a quiet cup of tea together and discussed yesterday's racing and today's prospective purchase of Watchmaker. Then Arthur did his evening stables and came back to the office. Ruth, as always, was there,

working on the books. 'Did you see Charles d'Arcy at Cheltenham?' were her first words as Arthur entered.

'Yes. He's selling Watchmaker.'

'Good. Then he can pay his bill out of the proceeds. Did you
tell him?'

'No. Of course not. I told him that mare was no good. I wish
he'd take her home.'

'Arthur, you're impossible. He'll have to pay up. Look at this
farriery bill—'

'I know. It's the very devil. But, listen, Ruth, I think Lord
Warminster is going to buy Watchmaker. I want to check his
entries.' He was in the act of opening the book when the tele-
phone rang. Ruth picked up the receiver and listened. Then:
'Miss Meredith,' she said, and handed the instrument to
Arthur.

Arthur took it with a sinking heart. Meg seldom telephoned.
When she did it usually spelt trouble. This was no exception.
She came straight to the point. 'Arthur,' she said. 'I'm not at all
pleased with the ride Rendall gave my horse yesterday. I looked
for you after the race to discuss it with you. I would have
expected you to wait for me.'

'I'm sorry, Meg. I had to get back.'

'I'll tell you now what I would have said then. You both knew
I had a bet. That horse had every chance if he'd been ridden
right out—'

'I'm not quite sure what you are saying, Meg,' Arthur said,
dangerously, into the receiver. Anything affecting the running
and riding of his horses always raised his hackles and this from
one of his owners coming after yesterday's interview with the
young stewards' secretary touched him on a raw spot. 'Are you
suggesting your horse was stopped?'

Meg shied away from that one. 'What I'm saying is that Rendall isn't a jockey any more. Now if young Colby had been on
my horse—'

'If young Colby had been on your horse he would probably
never win another race, Meg, and you've been in racing long
enough to know that. Your horse needs time. It was only his
second hurdle. I thought he ran very well and that Rendall rode
him admirably.'

'When I back my horses I expect to see them really trying'.

'That's a serious accusation to make, Meg, and I'm afraid I

won't stand for it. He did try. He was well beaten at the last and couldn't have won. That race will have brought him on.'

'What do you mean you won't stand for it, Arthur? You're my trainer, aren't you? All I want you to do is to get rid of Rendall and put Colby up the next time he runs. Then he might win.'

'As from about two minutes ago I'm not your trainer any more, Meg. My stable jockey is my stable jockey and rides my horses. How soon can you get your horses out of my yard?'

Meg had gone considerably further than she had intended. She enjoyed needling people, especially men, and she had felt aggrieved that Arthur had not waited to discuss the race with her. He was becoming altogether too independent lately in her opinion and needed what she described to herself as 'a rap over the knuckles'. But now the ruler seemed to have rebounded on her. At the back of it all she both liked and trusted Arthur. She was old enough to be set in her ways and she did not want to search for another trainer. Young Alastair Bragdon had enough of her horses and anyway she didn't really think very much of him. She had not yet made up her mind what she would do this season with Form Book, the young horse they had thought about as a National horse. But she hated apologising or admitting that she could have been in any way in the wrong.

'You shouldn't take me up so quickly, Arthur,' she said. 'There's no need for that at all. I was merely expressing a perfectly natural point of view. After all I'm entitled to that, aren't I?'

'Not if it entails accusations against me and my jockey.'

'Very well, if you think I made them I withdraw them, but of course I didn't make them at all.'

Arthur looked down at a sheet of paper Ruth had put on the table before him. On it was written: *Miss M pays her bills PROMPTLY.* He sighed. Damn modern life, he thought. Really he'd be well shot of Meg and her whims and tantrums. And, if it came to that, he could afford it, too. But there was something in Ruth's message and if inflation went on—anyway if he kept her he could presumably keep Charles d'Arcy too. 'In that case—' he said slowly.

'That's splendid, Arthur. We're friends again. Now, where will you run Harnessed Lad next?'

'I'll look up my book and let you know. But one thing must be clear, Meg. Rendall rides him.' Arthur put down the telephone and turned to Ruth. 'I suppose you're right,' he said. 'I'd better keep her. But she can be an old witch at times, you know. Now get me Rendall on the phone, Ruth, will you please, like a dear.'

Daddy Rendall had stayed in bed late that morning. He had brewed himself a cup of tea from the teamaker beside the bed. As he sipped it he read through slowly and with great care the racing pages of the three Sunday papers one of the boys had brought up to him. After he had finished the commentaries and articles he scanned the results one by one, analysing them as he went along and sometimes referring to the form book to check performances and compare weights. A photograph of Pat Colby stared up at him from beside Myles's column with the caption *Future Champion?* underneath it. Daddy smiled wryly to himself. If anything was certain in racing it was that no one was ever going to write that about him now. When he had finished the racing pages he turned to the football results. Having read those, he threw the papers aside and got out of bed.

As he shaved he felt an ache in his leg from his injury of last year and there was a twinge of something in his left shoulder. He thought, too, that he was more tired than he should have been and began to wonder again if he was going over the hill. It was not the riding, he reassured himself, and his nerve, he was certain, was as unshaken as ever. That being so, then it must be the travelling. There was no getting away from it, the travelling was the really damnable part of the job. Driving in all weathers often in the dark of the early mornings, and at this time of year always in the dark of the evenings, coming home with the lights and the heater on and the wipers going too as often as not, was a tax on everything, nerves and muscles and co-ordination. The motorways helped, of course, but even then you were likely to be dodging those infernal juggernauts most of the time. It all added up to the fact that the travelling was a far greater toll on your resources than the actual riding. And he was fortunate enough, for Wolverhampton was not a bad centre though it was too far really from Major Malcolm's stables. They had chosen it quite by chance when they were first married and were lucky to find anywhere to live. After that he'd never really thought about the house until recently. It had only been a dormitory for him, usually if he wasn't riding he was schooling and often he was doing both.

Thinking of schooling brought Watchmaker to mind. He'd want schooling after that fall just to make sure that he'd not lost his confidence. There was no doubt in Daddy's mind now that he was at least a stone better this year than the previous season. He could well be a National horse and a good one. He wondered whether they were going to keep him. It could mean a lot to him if they did for he might just be the horse he had always hoped for. To win the National would be a wonderful culmination to his career. He could hang up his boots then and buy that farm. He thought about what the Guv'nor was likely to do with Watchmaker next. Probably put him into a little race somewhere and hope to win it. Careful, that's what Major Malcolm was.

Downstairs Millie had cooked a Sunday joint. It was done to a turn and there were roast potatoes and cabbage and Yorkshire pudding to go with it. The boys tucked in but Daddy, though he had few weight problems, ate sparingly. What he did eat he enjoyed. Marvellous cook and housewife, Millie was, he told himself.

The boys chattered and argued between themselves, but he and Millie hardly spoke. They never discussed racing now for if they did it always appeared to end in an argument about his giving up. Besides, this morning his thoughts were still full of Watchmaker and the National. Again the prospect of a little farm where he could school and care for horses came to him. He thought this might be worth mentioning to Millie. 'I wonder,' he said, 'if we should think of moving from here?'

'Moving?' Millie said, sharply for her. 'Moving? Whatever for?'

'I thought if we could get a little place more in the country. The boys—'

'The boys? What do you mean by the boys? They're quite happy here. And it would mean taking them from the school. Anyway I don't want to start the business of trying to settle in somewhere else.'

'The country? Oh, Daddy, yes, let's!' Thomas, the elder of the two, who had been listening, spoke up. 'And, Daddy, could I have a pony? Johnny Lockson at school has a pony. Oh, Daddy, it'd be great!'

Daddy looked at his son and saw his own wide-apart grey eyes looking back at him. The boy's hands were on the table.

101

They were smaller replicas of his own, broad, capable horse-man's hands with short spatulate fingers. Daddy's eyes met Millie's across the cloth.

'There'll be no ponies in this house and no talk of them and that's final,' Millie said. 'We've had enough horses in this family for a lifetime with your father and his riding.' Suddenly her breath came in a little hiss and she put her hand to her side.

'Are you all right, dear?' Daddy said anxiously, getting quickly to his feet.

'Yes, yes, it's nothing, only a bit of a stitch.' Millie began to clear the table.

'Are you sure, old girl?' Daddy crossed to her and put his arm round her waist.

'Yes, yes, of course. Now come on, boys, fetch and carry. There's roly-poly pudding for you and me and fruit salad for Dad. Come on, bustle along now.'

After the meal Daddy had a look at his engagement book. Apart from his rides for Ardhur it was disconcertingly empty. Arthur's horses were not all that much this year either, he thought, apart from Watchmaker and that young hurdler of Miss Meredith's which might make up into something. The others could improve of course; it was early days yet. But his telephone seldom rang these days with offers of outside rides. It was just another sign, he supposed, that he was on the down-ward slope. He turned on the television and dozed the after-noon away in front of it and the electric fire.

At about five-thirty the telephone did ring. Thomas an-swered it. 'It's Major Malcolm, Dad,' he said.

'We seem to have kept Watchmaker,' were Arthur's first words.

'That's very good news, sir. It'd be a pity to lose him now.'

'Lord Warminster has bought him. Subject to the vet, of course, but I can't imagine there'll be much trouble there. Now, Rendall, look, I want him schooled after that fall. We're racing tomorrow. Tuesday then, I think. I want Miss Meredith's young horse schooled too. The others of course but those two particularly. I assume that's all right for you?'

'Yes, of course, sir.'

'Do you want a bed?'

'It would be easier if that's all right.'

'I'll tell Martin. Common Error runs on Tuesday. We can go

on together.'

'What have you in mind for Watchmaker?'

'He's in a three mile chase at Towchester on the 5th. I shouldn't think there'll be much else in it. If he's still all right I'll run him there and then we'll see.'

'What does his Lordship think about the National, sir?'

'He's very anxious to have a cut at it.'

'That's the best news I've heard for a long time. I'm sure he'll go well.'

'It's a long way away yet, you know,' Arthur said.

But Daddy, reassured and ultra-sanguine like all steeple-chase jockeys, went back to his armchair and fell fast asleep dreaming of his little farm.

Although it was Sunday Tommy Pereira spent the morning looking for his solicitor. This was not as strange as might at first appear for Michael Ordway practised in Cheltenham and lived about ten miles away. Moreover he was, like Tommy himself, between wives. He had given up the custody of his two children in the divorce settlement and, as a result, was living a lonely dis-organised sort of life, looked after spasmodically by two daily women. At week-ends to keep his mind occupied he brought home two briefcases stuffed with papers and spent long hours working on them with a tape-recorder for company. Tommy, whose divorce had been amicable but who knew something about the circumstances of the other's, frequently tried to al-leviate his loneliness by asking him over for a meal or a pre-lunch or -dinner drink and a chat.

At first there was no reply from Ordway's house but at the thrd try about 11.30 the solicitor himself answered. 'I'm sorry,' he said to Tommy's query. 'I don't have the telephone in the bedroom any more. I was working late last night and must have slept it out.'

'Could you come over and share a Bloody Mary and what-ever is going for lunch which won't be much, I should think? I must warn you though, Michael, that I want to talk shop.'

'That's all right. Yes, of course, I'd be delighted. Don't make the Bloody Marys too strong if you want to keep me sensible. Is this anything serious, Tommy?'

'Not for me. It may be for someone else.'

Tommy went off to mix the vodka and tomato juice, carefully

103

adding Worcester sauce and celery salt. In about an hour's time
Michael Ordway arrived. 'That looks good,' he said as Tommy
poured the drink. 'I never know why these things have such a
splendid effect on Sunday mornings. It must be the Worcester
sauce.'

'That's one of the understatements of the year.'

'Were you racing yesterday?'

'Yes, and thereby hangs a tale or rather the tale.' Quickly
Tommy outlined the events of the previous evening. 'Just how
bad is it and can you do anything about it?' he concluded.

'To answer the last question first, precious little, I'm afraid.
There is one chance, though. This chap, Colby, he'd just
turned pro you say. He'd ridden three winners that day and
he'd been to a smart party where things might have gone to his
head.'

'They certainly did that.'

'And he has the chance of being a great success?'

'Myles Aylward in the *Sunday Post* today is tipping him as a
future champion.'

'And his car is essential to him in his business.'

'Absolutely.'

'Under the Act, as you may or may not know, the magistrates
have power not to impose disqualification where there are
special reasons relating to the person's livelihood, but the reasons must be connected with the offence not the offender.'

'What does that mean in plain English?'

'It means that if you put this plea forward you've got to show,
or perhaps I ought to say should show, that the special reasons
are connected with the actual act of committing the offence.
The best way I can explain it is by giving an example and the
one most often used is that of an off-duty doctor having a few
drinks and then getting an urgent call he can't refuse to go to.'

'That's not the case here.'

'No. And I should tell you, too, that the courts are getting
much stricter in giving this dispensation.'

'So it's hoeless, is it?'

'Not quite. There's still a chance. It's a slim one but better
than nothing and I may add that every conceivable and indeed
inconceivable defence or defences have been put forward in
these cases and they are all listened to. What was the blood-
alcohol reading, do you know?'

'I'm not sure—about a hundred and fifty I think.'

'That's not too bad. It might make them sympathetic for a start.'

'You know he wasn't all that smashed. He'd been wasting and that and the winners and the general air of excitement did for him. Also at the best of times I think a little goes a long way with him.'

'I was hoping you'd say something like that. You see, a sympathetic bench can always bend the law a bit and sometimes in these cases they do. Given a fairly reasonable blood-alcohol content which should start us off well we can put in a hell of a plea about his youth and sudden success, smart party going to his head, unaccustomed to high life, car absolutely essential to him, championship at stake, future blighted, blah, blah, blah, you know the sort of thing.'

'I don't as a matter of fact, but I'm interested in the working of the legal mind.'

'Well, there it is. I'm not saying we'll get away with it but it's well worth trying.'

'What about the rest? He took a swing at that policeman, or at least I think he did, it looked like it.'

'Perhaps he only put out his arm to try to balance himself when he stumbled. Anyway the policeman didn't make anything out of it, you say. He even seems to have suggested it was a stumble.'

'Something like that. It seemed to me he was anxious enough to cover up for Pat. He might just have let us go if it hadn't been for the other chap. Pat's treble was part of the copper's Canadian.'

'What on earth's that?'

'It's a form of bet, you ignorant lawyer. And if you don't understand it it would take too long to explain it to you. Can they still bring charges of assault?'

'They can, I suppose, but I'd say it's most unlikely. They'd almost certainly have charged him then and there.'

'Well, then, what happens next?'

'Colby will have to turn up on remand at the next sitting of the court. They must have told you about this.'

'I think I did hear something about Wednesday. We were under a bit of pressure.'

'Can you see that he is there?'

'Yes, of course. Luckily I think it's a non-racing day. How soon will the case itself be heard?'

'That depends. At a guess say six weeks to two months.'

'I suppose you'll get counsel?'

'Yes, there's a very good chap called Seton who does our police work now. I'll instruct him unless you or Colby have any choice.'

'I'll leave it to you and Pat wouldn't know a barrister from a barnacle.'

'You say that the sympathetic copper was called Milligan. I'll do what I can to track him down and sound him about his general attitude to the case. One of our clerks drinks in a pub much frequented by the fuzz. It can be very useful. About the breath charge if we get a sympathetic bench—and Seton is very good with them, I may add—we just may, and I emphasize may, get away with a whopping fine.'

'What are the odds? I want to tell him. It's just possible it might bring him to about one half of his senses if he has any. He's the most reckless bugger I've ever known.'

'You really want the odds?'

'Yes.'

'About five to one on he loses his licence, if that's the correct racing parlance.'

'It's clear enough. Thanks, Michael, we'll be in touch.'

Later in the afternoon Tommy had another visitor, an unexpected one this time. David Malcolm dropped in on his way back from his parents. He had not, it seemed, stayed long with them. 'I don't know,' he said gloomily, burying his nose in a gin and tonic. 'I don't seem to be able to get along with them any more. Especially the old man. As far as I can see he's still fighting the battle of El Alamein or somewhere. I never know which is what in that old war.'

'Most of that generation are.'

'Bill Bradbury isn't. You can talk to him. He's just like one of ourselves.'

'From all I hear he's betting like a drunken sailor. How are things at Clayhampton, anyway?'

'All right. Why shouldn't they be? Don't you start getting on at me, Tommy. The old man was trying to pump me about the stud, too. If Bill's betting, why shouldn't he? It's his own money.'

106

'I hope so.'

'What do you mean?' Like his father David was intensely loyal and he flew to his boss's defence.

'Bill Bradbury, from all I hear, always likes to be one jump ahead. The trouble about that sort of chap is that when he falls he comes the hell of a one and the rest of the field gallops over him, quite apart from the fact that he is likely to bring others down too. Come to think of it, hasn't he got Burglar Alarm?'

'Yes. Why?'

'Pat Colby rode a thing for Chris yesterday called Pirate Gold. He's by Burglar Alarm and a bit more than useful, I'd say. He's a chancy bugger now but if they get him right and they will, I'm sure, he'll be a Gold Cup horse, or Pat thinks so anyway.'

'He had a treble, I see. You were racing. Anything else happen?'

Tommy Pereira had many good points, but he had one grievous fault. He could not hold his tongue or let a story go past him. The invitation to recount the events of the day before was far too good to refuse and he poured into David's attentive ears the whole saga including Pat's remarks about the joke steward and his wife.

When David arrived back at Clayhampton he found Colonel Bradbury returning from showing a party of visiting Argentinians round the stud, and was asked in for a drink. Bradbury had a bluff, hearty manner and David had spoken accurately when he said that his boss was at home with younger people whereas many of his generation were not. He had, too, a fund of anecdotes, most of them scatalogical or scandalous or both about India and the shires, and he told them well. To many of his contemporaries who saw through him he was both bogus and a bore, but to David and others like him he was a good companion of a slightly old-fashioned sort and a generous host. He had a way with employees, too, and his labour relations were excellent.

Soon David was laughing at his sallies. Then he for his part remembered Tommy's story and recounted it. '"Joke steward" did he say,' Bill Bradbury chuckled, smacking his thigh. 'By God, that's a good one. And by God, it's true, too. Did young Colby say anything else?'

'He said Barkley doesn't know which end a horse farts from.'

'He's about dead on there, too. Help yourself to a glass of gin, my boy. Did I ever tell you what Morrow-Bailey said to the stewards when they had him in after the Meerut Meeting in '35?'

'No,' David said, settling down to listen delightedly to another of his employer's reminiscences.

When David had gone Tommy Pereira made his way upstairs. In his dressing room he looked carefully at his hair in his three-piece mirror. It definitely needed attention. He had an appointment with André to see to it in London tomorrow. The wave at the bottom just where it met his neck badly required resetting, and he had rather neglected it lately. He liked it to come out just so beneath the bottom of a top-hat when he went hunting. Then its golden gleam showed up very well against the scarlet of his coat.

No one had ever in his hearing accused Tommy of either effeminacy or lack of heterosexual prowess, but he took a tremendous pride and interest in his appearance. If questioned about his hair as some of his elders had had the effrontery to do once or twice he took pains to point out that Rupert's cavaliers had worn theirs in ringlets, a style he had not himself adopted to date.

When he had finished his examination of his hair, deciding that the tint too required renewing, he entered his bedroom and crossed to a big wardrobe in the corner. Opening this he reached inside and pulled down one of the wooden hangers. A panel at the back slid open and Tommy passed through into another, smaller, room. It was, in fact, a portion of a dressing-room cut off from an adjoining master-bedroom.

The walls of this room were hung with silk panels cut and slashed with bizarre colours and designs. The furnishings were simple, a deep easy chair, a large electric fire which he switched on, a bookcase and a table on which stood a large round ceramic jar. Lifting the lid of this Tommy took from it a long thin cigarette. This he brought to the chair, lighted with care and then sat back inhaling deeply. Soon the acrid scent of marijuana filled the room.

Tommy drank practically nothing. He held himself entitled therefore to this indulgence. It soothed and relaxed him and gave him joyful visions. But he was going to take damn good

108

care no prowling copper found him out.

Myles passed the morning in his dressing-gown, reading and analysing the racing results and noting with interest that young Steve Barrett who had done Julius's horses at Rokeby's for the last couple of years had been promoted to riding and had been on Rokeby's other runners at Warwick yesterday. He wrote up his records, sketched out an article which had been commissioned by *Turf and Turnstile* and made up his piece for tomorrow's paper which was always the most difficult of the week since he had covered the actual racing fully for the Sunday.

Rokeby's remarks about Alexander still rankled, and in the afternoon he succeeded in getting in touch with Evelyn. When he rang she had just returned from the cottage in Sucsex which Julius had given her and where she kept her horses. They arranged to have dinner together at her flat.

She was in slacks and a sweater, drinking tea out of a mug, eating buttered toast and reading the *Sunday Post* when he arrived. 'I've read your article, Myles,' she said in her direct way. 'That was decent of you.'

'He deserved it,' Myles said. 'I'm a journalist and a professional or I try to be one. He's bloody good.' He was determined to avoid such a scene as his jealousy had provoked before. 'Look, Evelyn, have you seen Alexander—you know, the horse I bought in Ireland?'

'Yes. I was down with Chris on Friday.'

'Did you tell him he wasn't a horse, he was a fucking hippopotamus and that I must be out of my tiny mind to have bought him?'

'No. I said he was the hell of a hulk of a horse. I remember saying that because I'm not quite sure why I used those words, but I did and he is. You can translate them into fucking hippopotamus if you like. I never said anything about you being out of your tiny mind. What is this?'

'Chris was shouting the odds all over Cheltenham that he was no good. According to him, Pat rode him in a canter and said that he wouldn't win an argument. Did he?'

'Ride him in a canter? Yes, and I was there. But he didn't say he wouldn't win an argument. He said it was far too early to say but he gave him a feel as if he could go a bit.'

'That's more like what I thought.'

109

She went on as if she had not heard him. 'You'd better know this, Myles. I was with Pat. He told me he was going to ride out Julius's new horse. I wanted to see him. We drove down together.'

'I have no right to ask who you were with,' Myles said steadily.

'But you are asking, aren't you?'

'In a way, I suppose, but I did want to know about Chris and Alexander.'

'I'm not going to give him up, Myles.'

'I mustn't say why, must I?'

'"And I said I will list for a lancer,"' she hummed suddenly. '"Oh, who would not sleep with the brave!"' Then seeing the hurt on his face she crossed to him. 'I'm a pig, aren't I, poor Myles. And it's not that at all really. I heard that silly jingle on some old nostalgic film on the box and it stuck in my mind. It's just that, oh, I don't know, he's exciting and he's fun to be with. But Myles, look, dear Myles, I'm so fond of you and I do depend on you.'

'Well, that's something, I suppose.'

'I'll go and cook us a gorgeous dinner. Open the wine and help yourself to whisky.'

He found a bottle of Haut Brion in a corner cupboard. Drawing the cork with care he placed it in the hearth. Then he mixed himself an enormous whisky from her decanter.

In the candlelight of her dining alcove they drank the Haut Brion and ate the steak she had grilled. Their talk was of horses and racing and writing and eventing and the new horse he had bought her. They studiously avoided the name that lay between them.

Later they went to bed. For once she was gentle and undemanding. He for his part made love almost desperately for he now knew how much it would cost him to lose her.

Meg Meredith sat in her Gothic library at Warwork Castle staring at the flickering lights thrown out by the huge log fire that blazed in the great granite fireplace. Five terriers of all sorts, shapes, sizes and descriptions sprawled in various attitudes of abandon on the worn rug before her. When she had put down the telephone at the end of her conversation with Arthur she knew she had been worsted and she did not care for the knowledge.

Meg Meredith's body had never known the touch of man in his passion. In her youth she had been even more angular and heavy-faced than she was now when age and an imperious way of life had brought to her carriage and features a certain sort of grim distinction. Men, it is true, had in those early days pursued her for her money but Meg, who had never been sexually foolish and might well have been happier had she been, had recognised them for what they were. It was her tragedy that the ones she would have welcomed had stayed away. Those who had courted her she had mentally dubbed 'the predators'. Even when she realised that the years were flying by and that she would never have unleashed the passions she knew to be latent within her, an instinctive fastidiousness prevented her from yielding. Once she had been tempted almost beyond the point of no return. A gay, charming and utterly amoral gentleman ranker had come to pay and press his suit. He might have given her the short-lived happiness he had brought to countless other women before he spent her money and rode away, but, recognising him for what he was, she had dismissed him.

Now, in her late sixties, regrets had come to her for never having given herself at least to Blaise Calverly who had perished romantically in the Western Desert leading a hopeless charge of obsolete tanks against Rommel's panzers. Had she done so, she told herself, she would have had some sort of fulfilment and a memory to look back upon instead of a lifetime of dreamed-up eccentricities which had now become so real to her that she could not abandon them.

Although never attracted by her own sex she had become resentful of men and enjoyed needling them, upsetting their plans and exercising against them such power as her money gave her. It was a sort of vicarious revenge. In fact at sixty-eight, Meg was a thoroughly mischievous old woman. She considered ringing Arthur again and immediately dismissed the thought. She had pushed him far enough, almost too far for her own comfort in fact. She sought about in her mind for someone else to torment and to avenge herself upon for her defeat by Arthur. Suddenly she chuckled. Reaching out a hand she lifted the antique telephone receiver that stood on the ornate Victorian desk beside her.

'Yes, Madam,' came Joseph's voice almost immediately.

111

'Get me Mr Bragdon on the line, Joseph, will you,' she said.

Alastair Bragdon was pouring himself a large whisky and looking at his wife. He had just finished his evening stables and what he had found there had brought him no comfort. 'There's still heat in Racing Car's leg,' he said abruptly as he handed her a drink.

'Oh, Lord, Alastair, does that mean he's off for long?'

'I don't know what it means yet. It was there after he worked yesterday. It's either a sprain or he's hit himself. I thought it might have gone today but it hasn't.'

'It isn't the tendon, though, is it?'

'No, thank God. We'll just have to stop him in his work and wait. It may come right fairly quickly. You never know. But I wanted to run him in that chase at Stratford and I think he'd just about have won it. Why can't horses have tin legs?'

'Or be machines?'

'The funny thing is a motor-racing chap I used to know told me machines aren't machines either, if you know what I mean. They break down too.'

Just then the telephone went. Alastair picked it up, knowing only too well who it would be. 'Yes, Aunt Meg,' he said.

'Alastair,' Meg cooed into the telephone. 'How are you, my dear boy?'

'I'm very well, Aunt Meg,' her nephew replied, guardedly. He always distrusted his aunt when she was being affectionate. 'And you, too, I hope.'

'Getting older, my dear boy, getting older. I'm sending Form Book back to you tomorrow. You've room, I suppose?'

'There's always room for you, Aunt Meg. Have you done anything with him?'

'We've just brought him in. And, Alastair?'

'Yes, Aunt Meg.'

'I want you to win next year's National with him for me.'

'The National! But, Aunt Meg, he's a big horse. He's only six now. He wants time.'

'Time, ah, time, that's what we old people have too little of, Alastair. Besides, my stars tell me next year is the year.'

'Christ,' said Alastair under his breath.

'What did you say, dear boy?'

'Nothing, Aunt Meg, but, look, I know we discussed him as a long-term National hope, but he's not even qualified yet.'

'Then you'll qualify him for me, won't you, Alastair? Or don't you want him?' she added dangerously.

'Of course I want him, Aunt Meg, and I'll do as you say.'

'I was sure you would, Alastair. The book tells me, too, that I'm making the right decision—and Joseph agrees. So we'll win the National with him, won't we, Alastair?'

'I'll do my best, Aunt Meg.'

Meg put the receiver down and smiled at the fire. Then she gently rolled one of the terriers over with her foot. 'Little Alastair,' she said scratching his stomach, 'is going to have to put his thinking cap on.' She chuckled to herself again. This certainly made up for the brush with Arthur.

Alastair looked at the silent receiver, replaced it and finished his whisky at a gulp. 'Oh, God,' he said. 'That was Aunt Meg as you've probably guessed.'

'What's she up to now, the wicked old woman?'

'She's sending me Form Book back.'

'But that's good, isn't it? You said he was one of the nicest young horses you've had.'

'She says she wants me to win the National with him. He's six; he's not even qualified; he'll be as big as a bull and when I can even run him God only knows.'

'What's she up to? Why won't she give him time?'

'She says she hasn't much of that commodity left herself.'

'That's about the best news we've had for years.'

'But don't you see, unless I get this bloody horse at least up to the gate at Liverpool she'll as like as not disinherit me and leave everything to that wretched Joseph. Is that the *Calendar* beside you? Give it to me, will you? I'd better go and do the entries. Who'd be a racehorse trainer, for God's sake?'

In a room he had set apart as his 'racing room' high up in his half-timbered mansion situated in what is known as the Surrey stockbroker belt Martin Barkley sat studying video tapes.

Three walls of the room were lined with bookshelves. The fourth was taken up by a television set on which he was presently running the tapes. On the shelves was the racing library which he had acquired by the simple expedient of telling a sporting bookseller to buy him one. It had entailed considerable capital outlay to procure quickly complete sets of the

113

Racing Calendar, the *Irish Racing Calendar*, the *Bloodstock Breeder's Review*, the *Stud Book* and every known form book as well as the books of racing history and recollections which thronged the shelves. The other installation, a video recorder, had cost him a great deal more.

He had borrowed from the Jockey Club video tapes of certain races which he had either heard about, seen for himself or marked for further attention from a study of the form book. Most of them concerned two things—controversial finishes or cases of horses alleged not to be doing their best.

Martin Barkley was a thorough man. Although he had come late to racing he was determined to master its mysteries for he did not accept that the mystique of the sport was anything like so esoteric as its practitioners liked to pretend or would have him believe. Furthermore it was his opinion that a lot of nonsense was talked about the horses themselves, and that a racehorse was no more unique in its problems than any other performing animal. Anyway, to his thinking, the horses were the least of the matter. It was the public who must be catered for. To this end there were two problems with which he was determined to concern himself particularly, that of the disqualification rule for crossing from the last fence, and horses which were not trying or which had not been ridden out for a place.

It appeared to him that the English rule which gave the stewards liberty to interpret whether or not the actual interference robbed the other horse of a chance of winning was being much too loosely interpreted. Most of the local stewards had ridden themselves and in Martin's view they were too much inclined to give the benefit of the doubt to the horse which had crossed the line in front unless the interference was so flagrant that they had no other option. 'Well, he won anyway, didn't he?' one of them had said to him when, as a local steward before his promotion, he had argued over what he considered to have been a wrong decision. 'And anyway the other fellow was stopping every stride. As to that business of dropping your hands and looking appealingly at the stewards' stand I know all about that on a tired horse. Done it myself as a matter of fact.'

When Martin had pointed out that the French rule was mandatory and permitted the stewards no discretion he was met with the reply: 'I know, and the ruddy frogs can't even

114

apply their own rule properly. What about the Prix Robert
Papin last year? There was crossing there if ever I saw crossing
yet they allowed the result to stand.'

But Martin, studying the tapes, was more than ever convinced that he was right. Nor was he in any way deterred by the
entrenched attitudes of the older men. He was aware that here
again he was up against conservatism and prejudice based on
experience, both of which in this case were exemplified for him
by Arthur Malcolm. He was well aware, for he was shrewd
enough, that the message conveyed to him yesterday by the
young stewards' secretary had been considerably bowdlerised
by the time it arrived. Even in its revised and watered-down
form, however, he did not accept Arthur's explanation. He
resented the 'old boy' outlook of Arthur and his like. They still
thought of steeplechasing as a sport, as he supposed it had been
in their young days when they cheated each other with a happy
abandon and got away with it. It was not, however, Martin
held, a sport any longer. It was a branch of the entertainment
industry.

He switched off the recorder and looked at his watch. It was
time for tea. Miriam had gone off somewhere after lunch. He
supposed she would be back for dinner but with his mind full of
his coming afternoon with the tapes he had forgotten to ask.
Goodness, he thought, how lucky he was to have a lovely creature like Miriam consent to marry him. She was everything a
man could want, decorative and beautiful beside him on formal
occasions, warm, sensuous and vital in bed. He hoped she had
enjoyed the party last night and wished he had not had to rush
off and take those continental calls, leaving her to go on alone.
She had come back late, after he had gone to bed and was
asleep. She had joined him and woken him to a drowsy, languorous, wonderful coupling. After that and again in. the early
morning she had seemed even more passionate than usual.
Almost too passionate, he thought, for a man in his middle fif-
ties. He was feeling slightly old and faded after the events of the
night, exciting and delightful though they had been. His mind
filled suddenly with erotic images which he firmly pushed away
from him.

Crossing to a wall telephone he ordered tea to be sent up to
his racing room. Then he put on a tape of last year's Grand
National, switched on the recorder again and settled down to

115

watch.

The Grand National—now there was a race. To Martin it was the race of all races he would want to win. It would set a seal on his importance in steeplechasing. When last had a steward won it? He could not remember. Unfortunately he had not, as yet, a runner this year. Cabin Steward whom he had run last year had fallen at Valentine's and had subsequently broken down. Cost a pretty packet, too, Cabin Steward had. Eighteen thousand pounds as a promising five year old and his return in winnings and place money had been something under fifteen hundred. And now he was finished or so they said. His horses were with Paul Cantrey, the leading trainer. Always aim at the top had been his motto through life. When he had entered racing he had secured an introduction to Cantrey and had succeeded in persuading him to train for him. Now Cantrey had instructions to look for a replacement for Cabin Steward at almost unlimited money. But National horses or more exactly National horses with a chance do not exactly grow on trees as Cantrey kept telling him, and so far none had come to hand. But that he would have a runner this year and a good one Martin Barkley was determined.

As he watched on the screen before him the smash and thunder of the field crossing Becher's and the surge and effort as they turned for home, he wondered if his luck would hold and that this year might see him leading in the winner between the two traditional mounted policemen.

Pat Colby drove down to Somerset as if such things as breathalysers, prosecutions and assaults on the police never existed. But he was delayed on the way. The wheel held up all right. The tyre, however, had been damaged by the impact of the night before. It blew out at eighty miles an hour outside Exeter.

Pat held the ensuing slide without any trouble. Difficulties came when he set about changing the wheel, for strips of rubber had wrapped themselves round the hub. He arrived at Chris Rokeby's stables just as the pre-luncheon Sunday drinkers were leaving.

They had a quick lunch served by Chris's wife and then took their coffee along to Chris's littered study. Papers lay about everywhere—old, unused entry forms, bills, receipts, letters, accounts from Weatherby's, all were piled in apparent confusion on the desk, the chairs and the floor. Above the desk was a faded picture of Chris winning the Grand Sefton, his one win of any consequence as a jockey, and beside the window was an oil painting of his National winner. Chris only employed a part-time secretary. His wife doubled her domestic duties with those of book-keeper, accountant and general watch-dog on the secretarial side. Somehow between the three of them a sort of order came out of it all and few mistakes were made even with that constant trainer's nightmare of the four day declarations.

'Now,' Chris said sweeping a very dirty brown spaniel and two old copies of the *Racing Calendar* off a chair. 'Sit down. I want to talk to you about Pirate Gold. Well?'

'He could be a Gold Cup horse if we can get him to settle and stop running out, or trying to.'

'He is a Gold Cup horse and we are going to get him right. We'll have to school hell out of him. That's where you come in. A long-legged bugger like you is just made for the job. You ought to be able to wrap your legs around him. It'll be a change from wrapping them round something else—eh?'

'I'll school him all right.'

'I'll want you here a lot. If it's a hard winter, travelling down from where you are isn't going to be on. There's an empty cottage in the yard. You'd better move in.'

This did not suit Pat at all. In Chris's yard he would be under his direct surveillance and his private life would be private no longer. He could just imagine Chris's remarks if he saw dolly birds emerging from his cottage early in the morning, to say nothing of other prospects he had in mind. The fact that he was almost certainly about to lose his driving licence and that if he did living in his trainer's yard would make life far easier for both of them did not even occur to him. He had, too, no intention of telling Chris of the events of the previous night. He could just imagine Chris's language if he did. With luck he might never hear about it until it was over and, with luck, anything might happen.

'I don't think I can do that,' he said. 'I've taken a cottage from Tommy Pereira for three years.'

'Tommy won't mind. He's about the most slippery-arsed bugger that ever sat in a saddle but he's a good-natured sod. He'll let you off the hook.'

117

'I'll have to ask him.'

'You do that. Now, about Mr Marker's horse. He'll want to run him in the National, of course. He's a big, quality bugger. He might well be a bit more than a handicapper.'

'He has some form in Ireland too, if that means anything. What do you aim to do with him?'

'Keep him away from Pirate Gold, however good he is. The old bugger won't want to run him in the Gold Cup anyway. We'll aim Pirate Gold at the sponsored races and keep the other fellow for handicaps.'

The telephone rang. Chris picked it up and listened. Then he handed it to Pat. 'It's a bird,' he said. 'For you.'

'Pat Colby?' a voice he could not at first place said. 'We met last night—remember. Miriam Barkley.'

'Sure I remember.'

'I rang your house but there was no reply. I knew you rode for Rokeby so I thought I'd just try. I'll be visiting friends near you this evening. If you're coming back, what about a drink at that pub there, the Red Rose.'

'I'll be back all right. I have a better idea. What about coming to my place and having a drink there? It's just a mile or so up the road from the pub.'

'What time?'

'Say 6.30?'

'I'll be there.' The line went dead.

'Hum,' Chris said. 'I'm not interfering with your affairs, my lad. I may or may not have heard that voice before. Do you know how many a promising jockey has killed himself?'

'No.'

'By digging his grave with his tool. You look out, my lad.'

Pat drove back to Gloucestershire like the wind. When he arrived it was a few minutes after six. He lighted the fire, fluffed up the cushions on the sofa, pushed it nearer the fire and put out drinks.

At a quarter to seven a car's lights turned into his little drive. He opened the door and went out. As Miriam drew the car to a halt she wound down the window and looked up at him. 'Sorry I'm late,' she said. 'I think I must have got lost.'

'And now I've found you. Lucky old me. Come right on in.'

118

8

'Afraid of me! You must be joking!' Myles and Vic Oldroyd, his fellow racing reporter on the *Post*, were sitting in Jules Bar drinking pre-luncheon Bloody Marys. They were discussing their new sports editor, his aims, intentions and personality.

'He thinks,' Vic said with a grin, 'that you're a remote, independent figure with a big following and an establishment background. He's never met you. I knew him long ago when we were both cub reporters on the old *Globe*.'

'So he's sent you along to soften me up for this new idea of his. All right, Vic, what is it?'

Vic twirled his glass. 'Times are bad on the street, Myles. You must know that. The *Post* always held the middle ground. Middle-class, I suppose, if you care to call it that. There isn't really a middle class any more and those that are left haven't any money. We're catering to an all but nonexistent public. Circulation is dropping like hell. When did you last see one of those boxes on the front page proudly displaying ABC figures? And the old Lord has woken up to it at last.'

'What's he want? More nap selections? I hope to hell he's not going to make me go in for more tipping. If he does the circulation will really take a dive, let me tell you.'

'No. It's not that.'

'Just what is it, then?'

'Featherstone has told him that the sports pages, all of them, are old-fashioned and he's given Featherstone a free hand. For a start they're bringing in that ghastly fellow Dickinson to do a controversial football and cricket column. You know the sort of thing—when you're knocking, knock the lot, especially the establishment and the MCC, and win by all means just short of knives and knuckle-dusters.'

'Those, too, if you can get away with it. What does he want us to do? Knock the Jockey Club? That's old hat. Mallinson's doing it every day. I do it in my own time and when I want to. Incidentally I hear on the grape vine that that new chap, Barkley, is all on for adopting the French rule about crossing. He could just be right. I'm going to do something on it for *Turf and Turnstile* next month.'

'He's the wrong man to bring it forward, I should have thought. Too junior. They say Pat Colby is humping his wife. But then, who isn't. No, it's not the Jockey Club. He's got an investigative team together and he wants us to help them.'

'That's a new one, all right. Where does he propose to start?'

'With Larry Buckner.'

'Buckner—and what is he supposed to have been up to?' Myles was getting more sour every minute and the reference to Pat had not helped or cheered him. He wondered if Evelyn knew this bit of racing gossip. He ordered two more drinks.

'He's been leaning on people.'

'Who for instance?'

'Look, Myles, I know you hate it. It's not really part of our job, I agree. But Featherstone only wants us to help his team. We can make the sort of enquiries they couldn't, and that sort of thing.'

'And how does he suppose we can get the time for it when we're expected to be covering racing?'

'I don't like saying this but he knows you manage to find time to do a bit of horse-coping on the side.'

'Who doesn't?'

Vic sighed. 'Listen one second, Myles,' he said. 'Times are changing fast. No one is secure on this street any more. You know as well as I do that in real terms every paper in England is making a loss. In the next few years jobs won't be easy to come by. I shouldn't wonder if very soon racing is only covered by TV and the specialist papers.'

Myles was neither mollified nor persuaded. 'All I can say is,' he replied, 'that I was employed to write about racing and not as a bloody flat-foot, shamus, private eye or whatever. Besides, I wouldn't be any good at it. I haven't the mentality and I'm no hero either. If you say Buckner is leaning on people I don't want to be at the receiving end. Who has he been leaning on anyway?'

'Chris Rokeby for one.'

'Chris! He chose the wrong man there. I imagine Chris would be well able to lean back.'

Vic smiled. 'That's one of the reasons Featherstone wants our help. He sent down one of his team to make enquiries. You know the type, all long hair and trendiness. Chris found him hanging about the yard and didn't like either his looks or intentions. He dumped him in a feeding trough. He was in El Vino's the other day wearing a black eye and a new hair do and swearing about assault.'

'He'll be a bloody fool if he takes an action. Chris would love it and the West country magistrates would just laugh at him. But what about Chris and Buckner anyway?'

'Do you know a boy in Chris's yard called Steve Barrett?'

'Of course. He did two of Julius's horses. Now I see he's riding second to Pat.'

'Last year they ran Pirate Gold in the Sun Alliance Novice Chase at Cheltenham, if you remember. Apparently, then, they believed he went better for Steve than anyone else. Chris thought he'd win and they had a hell of a bet on him. The news got out and the whole countryside backed him—mostly with Buckner because that's where he operates and has his betting shops. Two days before the meeting Steve was driving back across the moor. He says he stopped to have a pee. When he turned round his car was hi-jacked and gone. Someone picked him up on the moor next morning with the hell of a bang on his head. His story was that he tripped trying to find his way in the dark and hit his head on a stone.'

'What happened to the car?'

'It turned up in Moretonhampstead the next day. It was a wet night. Steve got double pneumonia and was out of action for two months.'

'It's an unlikely story of Steve's all right. Pirate Gold ran out at the ditch. I forget who rode him. I suppose in reality Steve was beaten up because he wouldn't do what they wanted.'

'Or they just made sure he wouldn't ride.'

'There was no complaint to the police?'

'Not about Steve's knock on the head. Only about the theft of the car.'

'I can imagine. It's the sort of thing Chris would want to play

121

very close to the chest. Is there anything else?'

'Yes. Errington had Rob Roy in the Whitbread last year. He won the National very easily if you remember, but there were two Gold Cup horses in the Whitbread set to give him ten pounds, and he looked thrown into the handicap. Buckner had a diabolical book on the National because of Rob Roy and then, after it, there were all sorts of mixed doubles and whatever going forward on Rob Roy for the Whitbread. A week before the race Errington got a letter bomb.'

'That's going it a bit, isn't it? What happened?'

'Featherstone is still piecing it together from what the team have picked up. Apparently Errington smelled out the bomb in some way. Featherstone thinks there may have been a threat first and this put him on his guard. Anyway they defused it before it could do any harm. But Rob Roy, if you remember, didn't run in the Whitbread.'

'Very profitable for Mr Buckner. And the rest?'

'At the moment there's one other but they're handling it themselves. Briefly—a punter called Carton brought up a Yankee last year. He stood to win about £5,000 for a £5 stake. *He didn't get it.*'

'Why?'

'Buckner's office told him he hadn't made the bet and produced dockets to prove it. He was shouting his head off in a pub in Taunton calling Buckner a crook and everything else to anyone who would listen. Two days later he was knocked down by a hit and run driver who was never traced. Now he won't talk but they think his brother may. Anyway that one's the team's baby not ours.'

'So what are we to do with the other two?'

'It's you, I'm afraid, Myles. Featherstone knows you have a bit of an in with Chris through Julius Marker. He wants you to go down and find out just what did happen to Steve or at least to get a line on it.'

'And get dumped in a horse trough for my pains. And what about Errington?'

'The idea is that you pay him a visit telling him you want to interview him about the well-being and prospects of Rob Roy this season. Featherstone thinks you'll probably be able to find out something about the letter bomb on the side.'

Despite himself Myles found that he was becoming interested. Like almost everyone else in racing he had heard vague stories about Larry Buckner. He knew that Larry liked living it up, that he kept strange company and that he gambled himself. At the same time he felt uneasy about taking on the task. It was not really part of his job and he didn't much care about the element of risk involved.

'What if I refuse to play?' he said.

Vic hesitated, and then he said slowly, 'I don't know, Myles. Featherstone can be awfully tough and he seems to have set his heart on this.'

Myles got to his feet. 'I'll ring you later on,' he said.

It was a fine bright afternoon with a hint of frost in the air. Myles decided to walk back to Eaton Place. As he went he turned the matter over in his mind. He was happy on the *Post* and he did not want to leave. With his reputation it should be a simple matter to land another job if he had to go. But it might not be quite as easy as it would have been a year or so back. Things were bad on the street, Myles recognised the truth of Vic's remarks and he knew that at least one if not two dailies were confidently expected to be unable to survive the next few years. All of these had their own racing correspondents. The market could well become flooded before long. Despite his name and abilities there might just not be room for him if he were to leave the *Post* or be gently eased out by Featherstone. He hated the idea of free-lancing and it would almost certainly mean a big drop in income. At least, he consoled himself, he was a bachelor, unlike many of his contemporaries, and he did not have a wife and family or for that matter a mortgage to worry about.

That brought his thoughts suddenly back to Pat Colby. So he was having it off with Barkley's wife, was he? And how many others, too, he wondered, and again found himself speculating if Evelyn knew about Miriam Barkley. Even if she did not, it ill-behoved him to tell her and he knew her well enough to realise that it would not do his cause any good if he did. But he felt all the more strongly now, as he had felt all along, that the association with Pat Colby would bring unhappiness and possibly danger to her. But words and warnings would only be an encouragement to her reckless spirit. The chips would have to fall where they might. Perhaps he would be around to pick them up.

As it happened, the decision about seeing Chris Rokeby was all but taken out of his hands. When he entered the flat the telephone was ringing. It was Julius from the South of France. 'I'm held up here for a week or so,' he said. 'I'm having some sort of trouble with my back. What about this big Irish 'osse?' It was an affectation of his which Myles heartily disliked to refer always to horses as ' 'osses'.

'I know very little,' Myles answered. 'Beyond that he's arrived and they've started to work him.'

'I like the sound of that 'osse. I want to know if he'll win races for me before the National. And I can't get anything much out of Chris on the telephone. You know what he's like when you ring him. Go down there, will you, Myles, and find out about him for me? I want to know what Chris thinks and what he's going to do with him.'

'Chris may not take very kindly to that.'

'He'll take to it, all right. He'd better. He has six of my 'osses eating their heads off in his yard. I'll tell him you'll be down. Ring him and fix a time.'

Myles sat and stared at the silent telephone for a few minutes. Then he made up his mind. He rang Vic, told him of the conversation he had just had and of the opportunity it offered. He could see Errington on the same trip.

'I'm glad,' Vic said. 'Featherstone is really very keen.'

Later in the week, having picked a day on which there was no racing, Myles drove down to Somerset. He made an early start and soon found himself threading through the narrow cliff-like lanes that led to the village of Wintercombe above which Chris had his training stables. He was not in any way apprehensive about the coming interview. Julius was an important patron of Chris's stable and Julius had, he knew, sent prior warning of his arrival. It was true that, when confirming the time of his arrival with Myles on the telephone, Chris had been his usual gruff and grumpy self. Even so, during the conversation, Myles thought he had detected some slight unbending on the trainer's part. In his passion for security and the double bluff, Chris had gone much too far when he had engaged in that shouting match at Cheltenham, Myles thought, and now he was perhaps beginning to regret it.

But at first, when they met in his study, Chris showed little sign of altering his accustomed blustering and at times brutal approach to interviews and interviewers. He leant against the edge of his littered desk, a cigarette dangling from his lips, his hands thrust deep into the pockets of his jodhpurs. 'All right,' he said. 'Mr Marker sent you. I know all that. He phoned me. Why the hell isn't he here himself?'

'He's having some trouble with his back, I believe.'

'More like trouble with his front from what I hear of the goings on down there. What does he want to know about this horse, then?'

'The truth, chiefly. Look, Chris, it's no good your shouting the odds at me now like you did at Cheltenham. Julius has taken a fancy to this horse . . .'

'He hasn't seen him yet.'

'I know. It doesn't alter the fact that he likes what he's heard about him. He wants to know what you're going to do with him. If he's a National horse he wants to pick up his expenses on the way. You know how he is.'

'Are you his racing manager?'

'You know very well I'm not. Let's say for the moment I'm his racing adviser.'

'You're a pressman. I don't like the press. I never have. I've never trusted them. I've been done by the bastards too often.'

'We all know that. And so you lay false trails for them. I've a pretty good idea you were doing that at Cheltenham. But I'm wearing a different hat today. Julius isn't all that pleased about what you haven't told him. He's your biggest owner, isn't he?'

'I don't tell him much because I'm not happy about security from here on long distance calls.'

The mention of security, Myles noted with relief, was going to give the opening he wanted for the second part of the conversation. 'I see. But now I'm here as Julius's representative. You can tell me.'

Chris gave him a shrewd look and pulled on his cigarette. 'Clever bugger, aren't you,' he said. 'All right, then, but this is off the record—understood?'

'Yes. Agreed. Absolutely.'

'I said that at Cheltenham because that bastard Mallinson was in the bar. I hate him.'

'I thought it might be something like that. You didn't have to pin my ears back, though.'

Chris gave him a quick look. 'I'm telling you now, aren't I,' he said.

'Go right ahead.

'So far as I can see this is a bloody good horse. I worked him yesterday with Pirate Gold and there was damn little in it. He can go all right.'

'What are you going to do with Pirate Gold?'

'That's my business. You're here to talk about Alexander.'

'Let that one pass, then. So Alexander's good enough for a real tilt at the National.'

'He's all of that. In fact the big bugger might be a fraction better than that.'

Myles felt a flow of relief run over him. His judgment hadn't been so far out after all. 'Are you putting him into the Gold Cup?'

'I'll enter him, I think. But I don't suppose Mr Marker will want to run him. It's the National he wants and always has, isn't it? It would be madness nowadays to try to take the two.'

'It's the National, all right, that he's after. What's the plan then? You've levelled with me, Chris, and I'm grateful, and I'll tell Julius. But he'll still want to know.'

'He's in a little chase at Towcester next week. I'll run him there just to see how he goes. If he's what we think he is we could have a crack at the big Pattern sponsored races. But since the aim is the National I think the plan would be roughly the S.G.B. Chase at Ascot, the Great Yorkshire Chase and a run at Haydock or Wrayfield to see how he copes with the drops. He's a big horse and he takes the hell of a hold, they tell me.'

'If he picks up one or two of those, Julius ought to be satisfied.'

'Mind you, I'm making no fucking promises. How'll you tell him?'

'I'll ring him from London. The lines there will be safe enough.'

'Will they? Information straight from a stable. If it has to go through any exchange you can't be too sure. They ought to employ the bloody bookies to run M.I.5.'

'I hear you had a bit of trouble last year?'

'What do you mean?'

'Young Barrett getting knocked out.'

126

'What hat are you wearing now?'

'The press one, I suppose. Since you've levelled with me I'll do the same with you. My new boss is after Larry Buckner. There are stories going round. One is about young Steve Barrett being hi-jacked on the moor last year. We thought you might help.'

'Larry Buckner is a bad bastard. He comes from the next village, Brayton, over the hill. I don't know where he got it from. His father, old Joe Buckner, was a decent man. So, on breeding it must be the mother. She died young. Anyway that doesn't much matter. Young Steve was knocked on the head all right and got pneumonia out of it. If I can help to nail the bastards who did it, I will.'

'You won't sling me into a water-trough?'

Chris chuckled. 'I found that hairy monster poking about the yard asking questions and I supposed he was one of Buckner's boys. I put him into the trough before I thought much about it. One of the lads gave him the black eye. He was one of yours, was he?'

'Not exactly. Look, I'll tell you what we know.' Quickly Myles recounted what Vic had told him.

'That's not the whole story as you've guessed.'

'Of course.'

'We fancied Pirate Gold like hell for the Sun Alliance Chase at Cheltenham. Steve had been schooling him. He had come to racing from show-jumping and the little bugger has natural hands. I thought then he'd go best for him especially when he knew him. I've changed my mind now. I think he needs stronger handling. That's one of the reasons I've got Pat Colby, but that's another matter.'

'I know young Steve. He did a couple of Julius's.'

'He's going to be a bloody good little jockey, but he's not quite ready for the top yet. Anyway the whole West Country knew about Pirate Gold and were on him to a man—mostly with Buckner. As you know, two days before the meeting he was coming back across the moor at night.'

'We don't think the story put out was the right one.'

'Too true, it wasn't. What happened was this. A car was stopped near Calne Tor. It looked as if it had broken down and a man standing beside it with the bonnet open flagged Steve down. Like a bloody fool he stopped. Two toughs hauled him out and offered him five hundred in readies if he'd let Pirate Gold run out. He refused. As a result they roughed him up pretty thoroughly and went off with his car. You know the rest except that I couldn't get a decent rider at such short notice and had to put young Tailby up. He couldn't ride one side of him and he *did* run out. I don't know if they got at Tailby or not but I shouldn't think they needed to. Anyway we all lost our money.'

'You didn't tell the police this?'

'No. Only about the car. We didn't want the fuzz round the place upsetting everyone. It doesn't do a stable any good from any point of view to have those buggers smelling round. We thought we'd handle it ourselves. We got nowhere. There is one thing, though.'

'What's that?'

'Young Steve told me the two men who roughed him up had stockings over their faces. But the chap who flagged him down, naturally enough, hadn't. He turned away pretty quick when Steve stopped but he still thinks he saw enough of him to recognise him if he ever sees him again.'

'Can I see Steve?'

'Since we've gone so far, I suppose you can. Wait here and I'll get him. There's whisky in that cupboard, by the way.'

In a few minutes he was back, accompanied by a small neat boy in jodhpurs, a polo sweater and a green anorak.

'Now then, young Steve,' he said. 'Mr Aylward here thinks he can help us find who roughed you up on the moor last year. Tell him about the man who flagged you down.'

'You remember me,' Myles said.

'Yes, sir, very well. You used to come down with Mr Marker. And, sir, that new big horse you sent us, he can fairly fly!'

Chris paused in the act of pouring whisky. His eyes met Myles's and for once he laughed. 'Christ! stable security!' he said. 'Well, that's the way it is. Here, try this.' He handed Myles a glass and pushed a bottle towards him. 'You won't believe it, but a grateful owner gave me a case of this and it's supposed to be something special.'

'Could you describe the man by the car for me?' Myles asked Steve.

'I only had a glimpse of him, sir. He was by the bonnet with a torch in his hand, I remember. I think he waved it at me. Then as I pulled up I did get one good look at him in the lights.'

128

'What was he like?'

'He was medium-sized, wearing a hat and a tweed overcoat. The hat was pulled down over his eyes and he had a scarf round his neck. It hid his face pretty well but one thing did happen.'

'What was that?'

'When he moved away the scarf slipped down and I saw that he had a sort of pucker on his chin as if he'd been in an accident or something.'

'Scar tissue.'

'Is that what it's called? Anyway he pulled the scarf up again very quickly and then the two toughs were out of the back of the car and on to me.'

'Nothing else?' Myles said.

'No, sir. It's not much, I'm afraid.'

'I think you did very well. I see you're riding more now.'

'Yes, sir. The Guv'nor's been very good to me, putting me up.'

'Good luck to you.' The boy left the room and Myles turned to Chris. 'That's about it,' he said to him. 'Thanks, Chris, for your help.'

'I hope you nail the bastard,' the trainer said. 'And remember, damn you, Myles, anything I've said about Alexander is right off the record.'

'Including the fact that he'll win at Towcester?'

'He could pick 'em all up and carry 'em home. He's an absolute stone-cold fucking certainty—and that's off the record too.'

'I'll print it as it stands,' Myles said and finished his whisky.

Chris did not press Myles to stay for lunch. As usual, however, he had brought sandwiches with him and, pulling into the side of the moorland road, he ate these on his way to see Rob Roy's trainer. While he did so he wrote up his notes, dictated into his pocket recorder and gloried in the beauty of the moor. It was a crisp autumn day, the sun shone on the heather, and big, fleecy clouds sailed across a background of blue sky. For a few minutes he sat thinking over his present position. First he thanked his stars that he was doing a job he loved, and for the independence or at least semi-independence his success had given him. Definitely, he decided, even if he did not particularly care for this present assignment he was going to carry it out to the best of his ability, for nothing, nothing at all, would put his

129

second chosen profession in jeopardy. He had failed in the first; his success in this one meant far too much for him to risk another failure. The implied warnings behind Vic Oldroyd's words had gone home. Above all he did not want to be out in the street again, looking for another job, especially in the present economic climate. In his own time in journalism he had seen several careers wither and fade without the backing of a paper behind them.

Cloutsworthy, the village where Val Errington trained, lay a few miles from Linton, almost on the sea. It consisted of a single narrow street sloping down the side of a coombe. Through the open window of the car Myles could smell the salt tang of the estuary. It was out of season and there were few people about, but half-way down the street the stocky figure of the trainer stood on the pavement waiting for him.

Behind Errington was a broad archway above which hung a heart-shaped sign with GENUINE ANTIQUES displayed on it in olde Englishe writing. To his right was a diamond-paned bow window through which Myles could see a furniture display.

'"Genuine antiques",' Myles said, smiling, as the trainer crossed to the car. 'Are these the horses?'

Errington grinned. 'You could say that about some of 'em I've had,' he said. 'That's the missus's game—furniture. Don't know a thing about 'em myself. So long as I've got something to eat off and to put me sit-upon on in the evenin's that's enough for me.'

'I hope I'm not late. I've been with Chris Rokeby and I had lunch on the Moor. It was so lovely up there I sat on looking at it and trying to write up some notes.'

'Aye. It's a good place to live. One of the few of 'em left. No, you're not late. I usually wait here for those who haven't been before. It's easy enough to miss.'

The archway led to an open tarmac space where Errington told Myles to leave the car. A pair of wide wooden gates gave on to the yard. The whole place was, Myles noticed, spotless. The tarmac surface was brushed and clean and the loose-box doors all freshly painted in cream picked out with black.

'You'll want to see our hero, I expect. That's what the lads call him.' He bustled straightaway towards a corner box and Myles followed him.

130

Rob Roy was about as unlike Julius Marker's idea of a National winner as any horse could be. He looked what he was, a well-bred but well-nigh useless flat racehorse who had taken spectacularly to jumping. Hopeless on the flat he might have been, but Myles noticed that he had the broad, powerful second thighs of the true jumper, and he had, besides, big ears, a broad forehead and a wise kindly eye. He looked magnificent, big and bursting with health for, as Myles also noticed, Errington was not hurrying him and had left plenty to work on. Next spring was far away and that was when he'd really be required to be lean and rangy and ready to run for his life.

'Looks a picture, doesn't he, the old hero,' Errington said, slapping the horse affectionately on the neck. 'I know what you're thinking, Mr Aylward,' he went on, turning a shrewd eye on Myles. 'You're thinking he looks too bloody much a picture, aren't you?'

'Well . . .' Myles said non-committally.

'Come along then and we'll have a talk. That's what you've come for, after all, isn't it?'

At the far side of the yard the trainer opened a door and ushered Myles into a tack-room. It was, like the yard, spotless. The tack, hanging from hooks, gleamed and shone like old and polished mahogany. The pitch-pine lining the walls was cleaned and grained. A fire burned in a grate in one corner. Errington pulled two chairs up to this and motioned Myles to one of them. He tilted his own backwards, took a pipe from his pocket and commenced to fill it. Val Errington liked to talk and in Myles he felt, rightly, that he had someone who liked to listen. Half the art of the interviewer consists in listening and, when required, prompting at the right moment. But Errington required very little prompting.

'I've always said and I still say it,' he began. 'He's a spring horse. Most horses coming from the flat are just that if people would only realise it. These well-bred buggers, they don't like the cold and the wet and the wind. They want the sun on their backs and the smell of spring. Whether they're from the flat or not, though, most of my horses are spring horses. They have to be. I train 'em on the golf course. Did you know that?'

'I heard something of it,' Myles said. 'I wanted to ask you a bit more about that, as a matter of fact. The golf course. How . . .'

Errington chuckled. 'You're thinking it's all ups and downs and bunkers and things. It's not like that. I'll show it to you later if you like. There's a strip alongside the first few holes by the sea. I got permission to level what needed levelling, which wasn't much. Gave it to me for a nominal rent, they did. There's not much golf played on week-days here and anyway we've usually finished working by the time they come out. Summer before last the committee did begin to kick a bit but since the old hero won the National and put this place on the map there hasn't been a squeak out of them.'

'Is it because of the give in the ground then . . .?'

'That's it. That turf beside the sea, it never gets too hard or too soft. I can work my horses there when no one else can. But they get a bit to like it too well. The old hero, now, he loves it. That's why, whatever he looks like, he's a real Aintree specialist. The turf at Aintree is the best in England—a bit like what we've got here. It never really firms up. You could almost say you're galloping on a featherbed. Ever ridden over it, Mr Aylward?'

'No. I'm afraid my riding career was very moderate.'

'I was third on old Glenfiddich. Best horse I ever had until this fellow came along. But that would have been before your time. Barring accidents I'll win next year all right.'

'You'll go up in the handicap.'

'They'll give me twelve stone or eleven twelve anyway, I shouldn't wonder. But weight—that fellow will laugh at weight in the spring. And another thing—listen, Mr Aylward, this new National since they reduced the top weight to twelve stone and sloped the fences doesn't take half the winning it used to.'

'I'm with you there,' Myles said.

Errington went on as if he hadn't heard him. 'Nowadays, too, the really high-class horses, they keep away from it until they've passed their best. They go for the Gold Cup. I'm not saying I wouldn't beat most of 'em at Aintree now with the old hero for he really loves the place. They'd be giving me weight, too. I think I'd massacre 'em!'

'He does love Liverpool, does he?'

'He's a stone better there and he knows it. Some horses, they really enjoy those fences, and then it's all dead level and the ground is good. He has everything going for him there. On park courses nowadays maybe he's a bit too deliberate in his jumping, too slow at his leps as the Irish say. Take the Whitbread last year. Donizon, the Gold Cup winner, was set to give him ten pounds. He looked thrown into the handicap. He didn't run. Even so I'm not sure he'd have won it if he had.'

'I know he didn't run. What happened, Mr Errington? You got a letter bomb, didn't you?'

The trainer snorted. 'A letter bomb! The papers made a lot of fuss about it. But that wouldn't have stopped us!' he said. 'He didn't run because he had a dirty nose. He got a touch of the virus. Nothing much but it stopped us running him.'

'I suppose there was a lot of local money on him?'

'The whole West Country had him to win. That alone was why the bomb wouldn't have stopped me.'

'There have been one or two other cases. My paper is very interested in them. Can you tell me a bit more about what happened?'

'I'll tell you all I know which isn't much. About a week before the race I got a telephone call telling me to stop him. I told the caller what he could do with himself. He said something very unpleasant would happen if I didn't. He gave me two days to make up my mind and said he'd call again.'

'Did he?'

'Yes and got the same answer.'

'Can you remember anything about the voice or the call?'

'It was long distance and the voice wasn't a local one, I can tell you that. Come to think about it now, the voice was sort of educated if you see what I mean, and yes, on the high-pitched side.'

'Did you tell the police?'

'Not then. No one likes them hanging about the place and making a fuss, especially when you've lads and horses in the yard. Besides, I've had threats before and nothing ever happened. Most of 'em were hoaxes.'

'This one wasn't, it seems.'

'Not entirely, anyway. At breakfast a day or so later the missus got a flat parcel addressed to her. It looked a bit like a book. We don't read books much, the missus and I. She was just about to open it when, I dunno, something clicked in my mind. Letter bombs were in the news just now. I shouted at her not to touch it.'

133

'What happened then?'

'We looked at it. There was no print on the label or any identification. I felt a bit of a fool, Mr Aylward, I can tell you, but in the end I sent for the police.'

'And it was a bomb?'

'Yes, a small one, they said.'

'Was your wife frightened?'

'My old woman? She's tougher than I am!'

'Have you any idea who did it?'

'Idea? I'm damn well certain it was that bastard Larry Buckner. He held all the bets, didn't he?'

'Look, Mr Errington, my paper is anxious to get him if he's the man, or to uncover who's behind all this if he isn't. You're training the ante-post National favourite. It may happen again or something like it. The police got nowhere, I suppose?'

'No. They never traced it.'

'Well, we may. Will you tell us if anything new comes to light or anything fresh occurs?'

'I'll help you all I can. But if ever I get a chance to lay my hands on Larry Buckner when no one else is around, God help him!'

9

Both Arthur Malcolm and Chris Rokeby noticed that the other had a runner in the Autumn Handicap Chase at Towcester for five year olds and upwards but neither thought very much about it. Arthur's head lad had reported to him that Alexander was a big Irish horse recently come over and added that he had heard a whisper he could go a bit. He might, Arthur decided, be anything or nothing and dismissed him from his thoughts. Chris did not think much of Watchmaker's form of the previous year and, recalling that he had fallen in Pirate Gold's race at Cheltenham, put him out of his calculations. Both arrived independently at the conclusion that the danger was Alastair Bragdon's Ever Faithful, who had some apparently promising recent form and who would probably start favourite.

Robert Warminster was anxious to see his horse run before he departed abroad to winter in warmer climes. He demanded from Arthur explicit instructions about getting to the racecourse, about lunching and viewing facilities, and complained about the weather.

A few days before the race Julius telephoned Myles. He had just returned from Cap d'Ail, he said, and his back was still hurting him. He asked Myles to drive him down so that they could talk about the horse on the way. He also complained about the weather.

In fact the weather had suddenly changed very much for the worse. It was cold with a raw biting wind and a hint of rain and sleet in the air. A spatter of rain splashed on Myles's windscreen when he pulled up outside Julius's flat above his Mayfair offices in Brook Street.

The door opened almost immediately, for Julius prided

135

himself on his punctuality, and he came out followed by a man carrying a hamper.

'Put it in the boot,' Julius said, and then began to lever himself slowly into the low car. 'I'm still damn stiff,' he said in answer to Myles's query. 'They've put me on butazolidine. I thought you only gave that to 'osses. Not that it's doing me any damn good. All right, Parsons, is that stuff stowed away?'

'Yes, sir.'

'Very well. Put my hat and coat into the back if you can find any way of doing it. I don't know why you want to go about in an inverted sardine can,' he grumbled to Myles. 'Are they in? Let's get on, then.'

In appearance Julius slightly resembled the conventional idea of John Bull. He was of medium height, broadly built with a wide, strong, fresh-complexioned face. It was not until you looked a second time and saw the downward turn of the lips at the corners of the mouth, the strength of the big jutting nose and the hardness that lurked behind his eyes, that you realised the power that lay underneath the bluff facade. He was very smartly turned out in a bespoke tailored tweed suit. The coat which Parsons had placed on the occasional seat behind him was a covert coat, also bespoke tailored with a brown velvet collar, and his trilby hat came from Lock. 'Well now,' he said, taking a leather cigar case from an inside pocket and selecting one with care. 'Tell me about this 'oss. I hope he's as good as you say.'

'You'll like him, I'm sure. We'll have to wait until this afternoon to see how good he is,' Myles replied cautiously.

'What did Chris say?'

'You know what he's like. Young Steve Barrett, you remember him, he did your horses once, but he's getting more rides now, he says he can fairly fly.'

'Jockeys,' Julius said scornfully. 'I wouldn't pay much account to that. They can never tell you and they always think their geese are swans. I've heard too many of them cracking things up as world beaters that wouldn't win a selling plate.'

'Chris thinks he's useful. He should win today. In fact I suppose he must win today if he's half ready. He has nothing much to beat.'

'Colby rides him, I see. I didn't know Chris had taken him on. Just turned professional, hasn't he?' There was a noticeable

136

lack of enthusiasm in Julius's voice.

'He and Chris are having a great run,' Myles said non-committally. 'He had a winner too for Paul Cantrey last week.'

'Hm. Seen anything of my daughter recently?'

Myles hoped he suppressed his involuntary start. He had not anticipated the conversation taking this turn. What was the old boy getting at? Had he heard gossip? It was unlikely since he had only been back for so short a time, but with his resources and intelligence system you never really knew.

'I saw her racing last week. She's all right so far as I know.'

'She never writes to me,' Julius grumbled on. 'I rang the cottage last night and then the flat and there was no reply from either. Gadding about, I suppose. Why the devil won't she settle down?'

The question did not appear to require an answer, at least from him, and Myles concentrated on his driving. The wipers were going steadily now and rain was slashing against the windscreen.

After his interviews with Chris and Val Errington Myles had been summoned to see Featherstone. The new sports editor was a man with a slightly furtive air and a straggling moustache that appeared to represent a cross between mandarin and military. He had expressed himself very satisfied with the reports Myles had sent in, and had said rather vaguely that they appeared to be making progress. He had also been at pains to compliment Myles on his recent articles and a flukey piece of tipping that had come off. He had then added that a member of the Private File team would be at Towcester. This was one of the crime reporters whom Featherstone had switched to the Larry Buckner project. He knew, Featherstone said, a lot about crime but very little about racing. Myles had been instructed to meet him on the course and to show him the ropes, with especial reference to Larry Buckner.

The rain had ceased by the time they parked the car, but there was still a cold, biting east wind sweeping in across the Northamptonshire landscape. After lunching from the hamper they both separated to go their various ways. Under the number board, as arranged, Myles met the crime reporter, whose name was Malvey.

'I expect you've been briefed that I know bugger all about racing but lots about villains,' Malvey said.

'That's just what I've been told. What exactly do you want to know now?'

'How to find my way about. Then I want to hang around and find out just how Buckner operates.'

'Very well. Come on.'

Myles showed him the various divisions and component parts that go to make up a racecourse. After that they went down to the rails. Betting had not quite begun on the first race. Buckner was on his stand chatting to his clerk. As unostentatiously as he could, Myles pointed him out to Malvey. 'Will he spot you hanging about watching him?' he asked.

'Not on your life. I've done this sort of thing before. I'll keep out of the way. Anyway he'll be busy once the betting starts, won't he?'

'Yes, that's so.' But Myles, like Chris, had great respect for bookmakers' intelligence services. 'Anyway if you want me I'll be around the weighing room where the jockeys come in.'

It was in front of the weighing room that he met Julius again. 'I've seen the 'oss,' Julius said through clouds of cigar smoke. 'I like him. That's what I call an 'oss. That's a damn nice sort of an 'oss. That's the kind of 'oss I like to have.'

Myles devoutly hoped, though he did not say it, that Julius would be of the same opinion in two hours' time.

It was in front of the weighing room also that Arthur met Robert Warminster. Robert was muffled up to the ears in a huge leather sheepskin coat, a scarf, large woolly gloves and a tweed hat. 'Christ, what weather!' he said. 'Do you always have to go racin' in this? I'm beginning to regret it already. There doesn't seem to be anyone I know here, either. Come and have a cherry brandy. I've just had two to try and get warm.'

'Sorry, I haven't time. In case you're interested the horse is very well.'

'Shall I have a bet?'

'He must have some sort of a chance. A little each way perhaps, Robert.'

'Very well. I'll stuff a couple of monkeys on him. Might as well.'

Arthur swallowed. He was not used to betting owners, and disapproved of them on principle, but as he went off to get the saddle he reflected that a thousand pounds was, after all, only a fraction of what Robert was prepared to win or lose at the tables

138

each night.

The Autumn Steeplechase was the second race on the card. There were eight runners and Bragdon's Ever Faithful was favourite at three to one. Martin Barkley had a runner, too, a horse called Minor Patent which did not figure in the betting. He came into the ring hatless, wearing a yellow camel-hair coat and accompanied by his wife who was very smart in tweeds.

The fact that he never wore a hat was another affront to the old brigade who would almost have preferred to have been seen racing without their trousers as bareheaded.

In the ring they were standing talking to Cantrey and his jockey when Pat Colby passed. Miriam, looking up and seeing him, called out, 'Hullo, Pat,' and gave him her most flashing smile.

Pat Colby may have been and indeed was a reckless fool on his feet. On or near a horse, however, he was a wholly dedicated, committed and highly skilful jockey. All his thoughts were now concentrated upon the big horse he was going to ride, how he could win on him and add another winner to his ever-increasing tally. He had had a double at Wincanton the previous day and was now rapidly climbing the table of winning jockeys. His rise had caught the imagination of the racing press who, following Myles's lead, were writing him up as a coming champion and a very present threat to those at the top. He loved the limelight and intended to remain in it. Chris, he knew, was confident of winning this race and had had a bet. The owner was back from France to see Alexander run and during a telephone conversation he had had with her a day or so back Evelyn had told him she would also be there.

He, too, thought Alexander should win and he was planning his tactics in his mind. Alexander was a big, strong horse. He would require holding up, Pat thought, and then, on the long run in, he would need to time his moment to let him go. Though they had never of course tried him fully at home Alexander gave him the impression that he could accelerate, and his study of the form books, laconic though their comments were, had, in so far as they went, confirmed this. Chris never liked his jockeys to win their races by too wide a margin. It meant, he held, that they got unnecessarily clobbered by the handicapper. A length, he always said, was as good as a distance. It was the place in the frame on top of the others that counted.

With all these thoughts in his mind Pat barely saw Miriam. His first reaction was that some bloody racing bird was grinning at him. Anyway he always held that women were better in bed than on a racecourse where, in his opinion, they either *made trouble or got in the way. Then he suddenly realised who* it was. He smiled quickly, knowingly, raised the butt of his whip to his cap in a slight salute and passed on.

'Well!' thought Miriam to herself. 'Well!'

'I didn't realise you knew Pat Colby,' her husband said.

'I met him at a pardy, that party after Cheltenham you were too busy to go to.' It may have been the imagined snub of Pat's passing her by, she never quite knew, but something impelled her to add: 'He's very attractive.'

Her husband stared at the jockey's retreating back. He was suddenly very conscious of the gap in ages between him and Miriam. He had heard, too, as who in racing had not, stories of Pat's sexual adventures. The dread that was always with him that a time would come when someone younger would take her away from him came back now in full force. Simultaneously the first seeds of suspicion began to burgeon in his mind.

Beside Daddy, Arthur Malcolm stood surveying the runners as they went by him. 'That's Alexander, another of Marker's big 'uns,' he said, looking to where the lad was leading him round.

'Nice horse,' Daddy said. 'Real old National type with a dash of blood in him.'

'Nice girl,' Robert Warminster said, looking across the parade ring. 'That's the daughter, isn't it?'

Arthur followed his glance. 'Yes,' he said shortly. 'Looks clean-bred, doesn't she? I can't think where old Julius got her.'

The bell had rung by the time Evelyn joined the group of which her father was the commanding figure. 'Well,' he said seeing her. 'Where the devil have you been, then? I've been trying to get in touch with you since I came back.'

'I've been minding my own business and my own life and letting you do the same,' Evelyn said coolly.

'Very kind of you, I'm sure, but I want to talk to you, my girl. You'll have dinner with me tonight.'

'What if I said I've another engagement?'

'Break it.'

140

Father and daughter stared at each other for a long moment of mutual hostility. Then Evelyn took a deep breath. 'I haven't as a matter of fact,' she said slowly. 'I'll come, but I don't guarantee that I'll stay. Are you going to win this race?'

Julius grunted. 'Ask Chris,' he said.

The lads had turned their horses' heads towards the centre of the ring once the bell had sounded.

'Just allow him to settle. Then win if you can—but not by too much,' Chris said as he put Pat up.

Pat scarcely glanced at Evelyn. His entire attention was concentrated on the coming race. She knew this and appreciated it and liked him better for it. He nodded to Chris to show he had heard. Then he dug his feet into the irons and began knotting his reins as he joined the procession round the ring.

Alexander went down to the start, taking a nice firm hold and no more. Pat had little trouble settling him during the early stages of the race, so much so that he began to wonder if the big horse was not being too easy. He had taken a far firmer hold at home. Then all at once it came to him that he might well be riding something special. It was because he was interested that Alexander was not pulling his arms out. The reason he took such a hold at home was probably because he saw little sense in what he was doing and wanted to get it over and done with as soon as possible. Here he was enjoying himself. You could put him anywhere. He was, too, a bold, fluent jumper, meeting his fences just right and gaining yards in the air. Pat had him on the rails virtually all the way and at every stage in the race he seemed to be telling him that he was galloping all over the other horses, only waiting the word to go on and win.

Daddy was also pleased with his ride. He had been right about Watchmaker. He was a stone better this season. He was taking hold of his bit and wanting to go. Arthur had warned him that he might be a bit short of finishing speed, so he should, if possible, jump the last fence in front and make the best of his way home. He did just that and the long straight spread out in front of him.

As he caught up his horse on landing Daddy heard the thud and beat of hooves of another coming at him from behind. Daddy was far too old a hand to indulge in the modern vice of looking round. It would be that one of Rokeby's, Alexander, he thought. He had seemed to be going far the best of the others.

141

He kicked on for home.

Up on the stands Arthur and Chris were watching their horses with experienced and attentive eyes.

He'll go on now. He's got first run. He should hold him, Arthur thought.

He has his race won, Chris said to himself. He's only got to let the big fellow go. With his pull-out he'll go past him like a racing yacht.

But on top of Alexander Pat was suddenly feeling not so confident. Before they came into the last something had happened. Alexander had faltered and now, definitely, he was not lengthening his stride as he should. He would have to make his effort much earlier than he had intended. He let the big horse down to ride him out. But when he did so, the instant response he had expected was not there. He went for his whip.

But Daddy had indeed got first run and Daddy too had gone for his whip. The two horses came on together with Watchmaker holding on to his lead.

All sorts of thoughts raced through Chris's mind. His first reaction was that Pat had been over-cinfident and left it too late; his second and fairer one, that Alexander was not as good as they had thought.

Alexander ran on gamely enough under the whip. He came to Watchmaker's girths, stayed there but could get no further. Watchmaker, in fact, kept pulling out a little bit more. He passed the post a length to the good. Both Arthur and Chris hurried from the stand to the unsaddling enclosure.

'Well done, very nice, very nice indeed,' Arthur said to Daddy as the jockey undid the girths.

'I thought the big fellow was going to catch me,' Daddy said nodding towards where Alexander stood, blowing from his efforts in the space reserved for the second.

'But he didn't,' Robert Warminster was jubilant. 'That's excellent, Arthur. My first winner for over six months. And a nice touch too.'

'He's not right,' Pat hissed in Chris's ear as he slid to the ground. 'Something's wrong. He lost his action coming into the last. And he was never right after it.'

'I've seen it,' Chris said. 'Spread plate. And he's cut himself.'

A thin trickle of blood was running down Alexander's off fore where the knife edge of the thin racing shoe had sliced into him.

142

'Get him away as quick as you can,' he said to the lad. 'I want to have a good look at him.'

The sheets were thrown over them and the horses led away to their boxes. Robert, still jubilant, insisted on Arthur sharing a bottle of champagne with him.

Very soon the inquests, which are the inevitable consequence of every race, began.

Chris's was short and to the point. 'That's not a bad cut,' he said to Julius after he had examined Alexander. 'Provided there's no other damage done, and I don't think there is, I'll have him working in a week.'

Once he knew the reason for defeat and was satisfied that he had not been cheated or conned, Julius was a good loser. 'That's it then,' he said. 'We're lucky it's not a damn sight worse. Where do we go next?'

'The S.G.B. Chase at Ascot,' Chris said. 'I'll have the big bugger just about right for it if all goes well.'

'Win that then,' Julius said, 'and we'll start paying our expenses for Aintree. Come and have a drink, Chris. I could do with getting out of this wind. You too, Evelyn.'

Walking with him towards the bar Evelyn thought that there were moments when she almost admired her father.

Daddy did not have another ride that afternoon. He had changed when he met Arthur. 'That's a tough devil, that Watchmaker,' he said. 'He just kept on pulling something out. He'll run well at Liverpool. I thought that horse of Mr Rokeby's might beat us, though. He was going best all through.'

'Didn't quicken,' Arthur said. 'Spread a plate. I saw it as they came in. That's probably the reason. He could be very useful.'

'Is his Lordship pleased?'

'Oh, yes, delighted. He's going abroad next week. We'll have a free hand—provided we win the National for him!'

'It's a long way until March,' Daddy said soberly.

'I'm afraid it's no good. He's just not genuine, that's all there is to it,' Tim Hanway said to Alastair Bragdon as he pulled the saddle off Ever Faithful.

Alastair nodded. 'It's what I rather thought,' he said. 'That second last week at Wincanton was a flash in the pan, but I had to find out. I couldn't win an argument at the moment.'

Tim paused with the saddle over his arm, hesitated and then

said: 'Have you still got that good novice Miss Meredith had with you last year? He should win races for you.'

'That's just one of my problems. She sent him back to me last week. He's about as big as a house. God knows when I'll get him on to the racecourse.'

Tim Hanway grinned. 'She has ways of her own, Miss Meredith,' he said.

'You can say that again,' Alastair said with feeling as he watched the lad leading Ever Faithful away.

Minor Patent had run rather better than expected, finishing a fairly close fourth. 'We might win a little race at Market Rasen with him, I suppose,' Paul Cantrey said to Martin Barkley. 'But I should put any thoughts of the National out of your mind.'

'I want a runner. You know that.'

'I've got Boyle in Ireland keeping an eye out but he hasn't come up with anything yet. It seems to me we should watch the sales. Something likely is pretty sure to be entered between now and then at either Ascot or Doncaster. I'll go through the catalogues and let you know.'

Myles was making notes on the back of his racecard in his own personal racing shorthand when Malvey came up to him. Myles had been bitterly disappointed in Alexander's performance until he, too, had seen the spread plate. Now he realized that it was a set-back but far from a major one. Robert Warminster's successful entry into steeplechasing was the story most of his competitors seemed to be going for. From what he had heard it was probable that Robert's remark about it being his first winner for six months was likely to be headlined in some part of the racing press, which would not please his flat race trainers.

'Who is that chap standing there talking, the one on the left?' Malvey's voice broke into his thoughts.

Myles followed his glance. 'Bill Bradbury, do you mean?' he said. 'The other is Arthur Malcolm. He trains Lord Warminster's horse that won the first chase.'

'Bradbury. I see. What does he do?'

'He manages Lord Warminster's stud. Clayhampton.'

'What would he be doing with Buckner?'

'Betting, I imagine. They say he bets like hell.'

'It looked a bit more than that to me. They seemed to be having a couple of pretty close conversations. I couldn't get near enough to hear what they were saying.'

'Then perhaps you'd better try to listen in on what those two are talking about.'

The sarcasm was quite lost on Malvey. 'Good id:a. I'll do just that,' he said. He drifted off apparantly quite aimlessly. Under Myles's fascinated gaze he stopped a few yards away from the two men and then, while casually studying his race-card, slowly edged nearer and nearer to them.

In fact, however, the conversation between Arthur and Bradbury contained nothing of interest or assistance to Malvey.

'Congratulations, Arthur,' Bradbury said. 'Nice to see the Lord getting a winner again. I didn't know he was taking up this game. In fact I didn't believe it when I saw his name in *Sporting Life*. Thought it must be a misprint. When I found it wasn't I came along to see.'

'Thank you,' Arthur said. He had not failed to notice that Bradbury had walked up to him from the direction of the book-makers. That conversation he had chanced to hear about Pirate Gold and its implications had bothered him on and off ever since, as did the stories that were going round about Bradbury's betting. He had tried as tactfully as he could to sound David out about the stud and had run up against the blank wall of David's determination not to discuss it. He was beginning to doubt the wisdom of his having sent David to Clayhampton at all though it had seemed the right thing to do at the time.

'Is he here?' Bradbury asked.

'Who? Robert? I think he's just gone. Didn't care for the weather, he said.'

'We hardly ever see him now. Is he going abroad this year?'

'I believe so.'

'Do you know when?'

'Fairly soon. He has no more runners on the flat, he told me.'

'I suppose he'll be away all winter?'

'I imagine he will except that he'll be back in good time for the National.'

'Oh, I see. Wants to start with a bang? And your horse is his hope, I suppose? He never does anything by halves, does he?

Well, I'll wish you good luck for him then.' Bradbury gave his hearty laugh and passed on.

It did not occur to Arthur that he had been skilfully cross-examined about Robert's future movements but he felt vaguely uneasy as he always did after talking to Bradbury. There was some quality of falseness about the fellow which he found hard to pin down and which disturbed him.

Miriam Barkley smarted for the rest of the afternoon under the snub she imagined she had received from Pat in the parade ring. That one encounter in the cottage between them had been nothing like enough for her. She wanted him again and she wanted him badly. She and Martin were due to leave before the last race. At the car she made the excuse that she had a sudden call to the lavatory and hurried back towards the enclosures.

Luck favoured her. Pat had no ride in the last and was also leaving early. He was outside the weighing room with his bag in his hand when she met him.

'You weren't very sweet to me this afternoon,' she said.

'Sorry. I was busy.'

'Where are you going now?'

'Home.'

'Will you be there all the evening?'

'Probably. Why?'

'Martin's staying in town. I think I can manage to get away. Will you wait? I'll ring.'

Pat smiled. 'I'll wait all right,' he said. 'And I'll have something ready for you.'

In the car on the way home Miriam said: 'You're staying in the club tonight?'

'Yes. I have to see Jack and Dan about that Detroit loan. We'll be late, I'm afraid.'

'I hate being alone in the house at night.'

'I'm sorry, darling. I must do this, though, it's very important. If it goes through then I promise I won't leave you . . .'

'Don't ring. I'll go to bed early and take a sleeping pill. It's hell being wakened by the phone.'

When Martin had dropped her and driven away, Miriam took a slow, luxurious bath admiring herself as she did so. Her body was her most prized possession and the thought of giving it to someone whose sexual drive matched her own stirred and thrilled her. After leaving the bath she walked naked about the huge bedroom she shared at times with her husband, selecting with care the clothes she would wear for the coming encounter. A nice demure racing miss in twin set and pearls she would be tonight, she thought as she returned to her dressing-table and slowly began applying Chanel to her secret parts. What fun it would be taking that chaste outer covering off or having him take it off to discover again the uninhibited delights that lay beneath.

Downstairs, she poured herself a large brandy. As she sipped it, still savouring the joys of anticipation, she dialled Pat's number. He had just come in and he was free for the evening, quite free he said with something like a chuckle. She put down the receiver, poured herself another brandy which she drank very quickly, and then went out to the car.

Martin had given her a Jensen which she drove with some skill and almost always at an entirely illegal speed. As she fled down the M.4 towards Gloucestershire and the west, her thoughts were all of Pat Colby and his sexual prowess. As they rushed through her mind she wriggled on her seat. 'I'm like a bitch on heat,' she said to herself. The excitement he generated in her puzzled her and for a moment she paused to wonder why a woman of her experience should be behaving as she was. It was because Pat Colby made the blood race through her, she decided. He set her on fire and it was a long time since any man had done that.

'Come in if you're not busy,' Julius said to Myles when they reached London. 'I'd like a word about this 'oss. And don't bother about the parking meter, I've fixed the attendant.'

Julius's flat was as impersonal as an old-fashioned hotel suite. The furniture was mostly solid Victorian mahogany which gave the whole place an air of heaviness and gloom. The old wood, however, shone from polish lavishly applied and was free from the least speck or taint of dust, for both Julius and Parsons were particular, methodical men.

There was a small study off the living-room and it was to this that Julius led the way. A bookcase containing racing calendars, stud-books and works of reference filled one wall. A writing-desk set on ornately carved legs occupied the window

147

recess. In front of the fireplace was a club fender, with beside it two leather easy chairs. In a corner drinks were set out on a side table.

Julius placed his considerable rump on the fender and gestured towards the table. 'Help yourself,' he said. 'And pour me a whisky while you're at it. Water. No ice. Cigars in that box. You might give me one.'

'Well now,' Julius said, when he had the drink in his hand and the cigar going to his satisfaction, 'What did you think of that?'

'You couldn't expect any more with the spread plate,' Myles said. 'He did well to run on the way he did.'

'That thing of Malcolm's that beat us, Watchmaker, he isn't much, is he?'

'He might be a bit better than you think. I had a word with Daddy Rendall afterwards. He told me he's a vastly improved horse.'

Julius snorted. 'Jockeys again!' he said. 'Doesn't mean a damn thing.'

'Sometimes it does if it's about their own horses and Daddy's no fool even if he's getting on a bit.'

'He's over the hill or so they tell me. I can't think why Malcolm keeps him on. He's over the hill, too, I suppose. You satisfied with the ride Colby gave our fellow? They tell me he wants watching.'

Myles felt Julius's eyes boring in on him. 'Perfectly,' he said as steadily as he could. 'I thought he gave him a copybook ride. And as to his wanting watching they'll say that about anyone, especially when he's had a sudden run of success. If you ask me, he's far too ambitious to want to do anything oother than win.'

'Perhaps so. I've bin hearin' things. Now then, what about the future of this 'oss? Where do we go next?'

'Didn't Chris say something about the S.G.B. Chase?'

'That's in December, isn't it? What's it worth?'

'It's a sponsored chase with money added. Have you got the programmes book? All my stuff is in my bag in the car.'

'In the bookcase behind you. Third shelf up on the right. At least it should be. I have a standing order every year.'

Myles crossed the room. The yellow spine and white cover of *Programmes of Steeplechase and Hurdle Race Meetings Under Rules of Racing, Part I* was just where Julius said it would be. Myles took it down and leafed through it. 'Here we are,' he said. 'Ascot. Saturday, December 14. *The S.G.B. Handicap Steeplechase for five years old and upwards about three miles. £6,000 added to the stakes.* If I had last year's form book I'd be able to tell you the value to the winner then. I don't suppose there'll be much change.'

'Next shelf on the right.'

'Let me see. Who won it last year, Admiral of the Blue, wasn't it?' Myles looked at the index. 'Admiral of the Blue,' he read when he had turned up the entry. 'Took lead 17th. Never headed. Easily. Value to winner £3,233.'

'That'll do. Pay the expenses or some of 'em. What happened to him?'

'Who? Admiral of the Blue? Ran in the National last year and finished fifth. He hasn't been out yet, this season. I think I heard he was a partnership horse and there was some dispute between the owners. Chris will want to give Alexander a run before the Ascot race if that cut heals quickly and I'm sure it will. Did he tell you his engagements?'

'He muttered some of 'em. It's getting damn near the stage when I have to look in *Sporting Life* the morning of the race to see if my horse is running or not.' Julius took a pigskin Badminton diary from his pocket. 'He's got him in the Mackeson and the Hennessy.'

'He won't want to run him in those. He'll clash with Pirate Gold and anyway he thinks nowadays they're not a National horse's cup of tea. He's probably right, too. Anything else?'

'Kempton. October 25.'

'He won't be ready for that.'

'Ascot twice, Sandown, Cheltenham. Then Lingfield early December.'

'He has him entered all right. In case of hard weather, I suppose. I'm surprised he gave you so much information.'

'He didn't. I had practically to shake it out of him. Then he gabbled them off and said he'd have to look in his book to make sure.'

Myles laughed. 'Next time you talk to him he'll tell you he was thinking of some other horse. But my guess is that he'll go for the Kirk and Kirk at Ascot or more likely that Lingfield race. They're both stakes and good ones. They'll help to pay your way.'

'They'd better.' Julius sighed. 'I'm entertaining my daughter

149

to dinner,' he said. 'I wish I'd done more—oh, well, never mind, that's not your affair, my boy. Good night.'

Myles was dismissed. He finished his drink and left. As he stepped out of the lift he met Evelyn coming in.

'So you've been in the seat-box, too, have you?' she said. 'What sort of a mood is the old monster in?'

'All right. A bit in and out.'

'Is he disappointed about Alexander?'

'Not really. He's been in racing too long for that. Look, Evelyn, I know it's none of my business, but go a bit easy on him, will you, I think he's lonely.'

'And whose fault is that?' Evelyn asked sweetly as she pbessed the button for the second floor and the lift doors slid across.

Parsons showed Evelyn into the room Myles had just left. Julius was still sitting on the club fender sipping his second whisky and lighting his second cigar. 'Give my daughter a drink, Parsons,' he said. 'What do you want?'

'Whisky, please.'

'Soda and ice, Miss?'

'Yes, please, Parsons.'

'I don't like to see young girls drinking whisky,' Julius said when Parsons had left, thus choosing the worst possible way in which to open the conversation. 'We'll have dinner here,' he said. 'I don't feel like going across the way tonight. I've told Parsons to put something up.'

'Yes, father,' Evelyn said with a dangerous meekness pregnant in every syllable if Julius had only noticed it.

'That's a nice young feller,' Julius went on.

'Who? Myles Aylward, the journalist? I met him downstairs.'

'You know him?'

'Slightly. I suppose everyone who goes racing knows him slightly.'

'Why don't you settle down?' Julius said then. 'All this racketing around, it never did any girl any good. One day you'll wake up and find yourself old—where'll you be then?'

Despite her show of independence Evelyn remained in some awe of her father. On the way to keep the appointment for dinner she had found herself, much to her annoyance, keyed up and wondering uneasily what it was all going to be about. She

150

knew her father hated her drinking whisky and that alone had been an act of defiance inspired by nerves. And now for a moment she almost dissolved into nervous giggles. Was he really trying to throw Myles at her head? If he was, the situation was positively comic if it did not carry such serious undertones for them all. She decided she must head him off this perilous ground. 'Settle down,' she said scornfully. 'You ought to be in the ark. And anyway it's a bit late to come the heavy father with me.'

'What do you mean?'

'When mother died you never gave a thought to me. You pushed me away into some hidden corner in your life, if it was even that. You were too busy making money. Consolidating your fortune, I think you called it once, to spare a thought for me.'

'Your mother's death knocked me endways. I had to throw myself into something or go off my head.'

'That's no excuse for those ghastly schools you sent me to. You never came near me. And then those frightful finishing schools in Hertford and Paris with all those bitches. And that old butch that ran the Hertford place that I had to kick in the crotch to keep away from me. You never investigated that with your famous intelligence service, did you? Oh no, you accepted what they said about unruly conduct and packed me off to Vincennes to another one. You didn't care much about me then. Anything could happen provided I didn't get in the way.'

'Why didn't you tell me?'

'Tell you! I don't suppose my letter would have got past the first personal secretary. And if it had you'd only have sent someone to clear up the mess and do your dirty work for you. He'd have believed anything the old bitch told him . . .'

'Very well then. That's water under the bridge. What I'm saying to you now is for your own good.'

'Christ! After all these years! You must be joking!' Evelyn crossed to the drink table and poured herself another whisky.

Tempers on both sides were beginning to rise. 'I've told you before,' Julius said. 'I don't like young girls drinking whisky, and I don't like them swearing either.'

Evelyn swung round to face him, glass in hand, her eyes blazing. 'Don't you indeed! Then let me tell you there's quite a lot about your way of life I don't much care for. And I'm independent now in case you've forgotten. There's the flat and the cottage and the money you settled on me. But perhaps you have forgotten just as you conveniently forgot me altogether when I was growing up.'

'I haven't forgotten. You may not be as independent as you think.'

'What does that mean?'

'Never mind. What about this Colby feller?'

'So that's it, now, is it. Well, what about him?'

'He's a bloody good jockey, and that's all he is. I've learned about him, his women and his betting.'

'You made it your business to find out, I suppose?'

'Yes. I did. And about you, too. You were even in the gossip columns. Mallinson had it.'

'You don't believe that scum, do you?'

'Sometimes I do. At least he made it easy for me to find out the rest—or most of it.'

'Can't you leave anything or anyone alone?'

'Not where my daughter is concerned. Have you slept with him yet?'

'That's my business. And if your bloody intelligence service is so good why don't you know?'

'I'm asking you.'

'You're not going to get an answer. For a man who makes such use of masseuses you're very interested in morals all of a sudden, aren't you?'

A slow red flush suffused Julius's face. 'I'm an old man,' he said slowly. 'And a tired one. What I do with myself is my affair. You're young. You have a chance. I'm trying . . . .'

Evelyn scarcely heard him. 'You'll be talking about the double standard next,' she said furiously. 'Let me tell you one thing now. My life is my own and don't ever interfere again. And another—I'm not staying to dinner this or any other night.' She put down her glass with a bang, took her purse and scarf from one of the armchairs, and swept out of the flat.

Julius heard the front door slam. He finished his drink, told Parsons his daughter would not be staying, and went in to dinner alone.

He knew he had handled the interview badly to say the least. He was accustomed to dealing with white-collar associates, most of whom were terrified of him and all of whom he could

152

bully. He had found out too late that he could not bully his daughter. Now that he had found it out he could recognise something of his own steel in her. To frighten her, something tougher than threats was required. There was one weapon ready to hand but he immediately discarded any thought of using it at the moment. In fact as he sipped his claret and the level in the cut-glass jug beside him slowly diminished he found within himself a growing admiration for the way she had stood up to him during the clash of wills. He liked spirited people and his daughter had made it abundantly clear that she was one of them.

But he had lost her now, perhaps irretrievably, and he was lonely. The long wastes of the evening stretched before him. He did not want to watch television and there was unlikely to be congenial company at his club. His friends nowadays were few and those out of London, either living abroad or in retirement in the country. Self-pity, an emotion he rarely allowed himself to entertain, began to encroach upon his thoughts.

There was a discreet establishment in St John's Wood he knew about and sometimes used. Here loneliness could be assuaged temporarily and at a price. There were thick curtains, dim, discreet lights, vintage champagne and an interesting variety of decorative attendants. Mavis, the proprietress, always appeared to have a soft spot for him. Though he knew very well this was a trick of the trade, he permitted himself the luxury of being taken in by it. Telling Parsons he was going out and not to wait up, he put on his coat, went down to the street and hailed a taxi.

Arthur Malcolm's mind moved slowly but when something was occupying it he worried and worried away at it until he came to a conclusion. Now it was filled almost to the exclusion of his horses and their problems with the Clayhampton Stud, what was going on there and how it might affect his son's future. Over dinner that night he confided his fears to his wife. 'You see, my dear,' he said. 'I think Robert has been systematically swindled over the years. I hope I'm wrong but it looks uncommonly like it.'

'But how could he have been so foolish?'

'That's just it. A lot of it is due to his own carelessness. I'm sure, for instance, that when Bradbury got rid of those sires and

153

bought in American blood there was a huge rake-off in it for him. But that's really not the worst of it.' He told her of the conversation he had overheard at Cheltenham.

'You think he switched the progeny?'

'It looks very like it. It's the oldest trick in the world. You have two sires, one good, the other mediocre at best. You ascribe the foals of the mediocre one to the good one and sell them as such. He's just reversed it, that's all.'

'What do you mean, exactly?'

'Robert gave Bradbury that useless brute Burglar Alarm as a present. As he said himself, the progeny of the few mares he covered couldn't run fast enough to warm themselves. Originally they tried them on the flat and of course they were no good. Then Bradbury turned to breeding stores for chasing from him. I've been doing a bit of homework and I've looked up those early Burglar Alarms. All they could do was to stay and one or two of them did win small three mile chases.'

'But all this must have happened some time ago.'

'Yes. When Robert was younger he bothered even less about the stud than he does now, if that were possible. Bradbury had an absolutely free hand.'

'Then there's no possibility of David being involved?'

'I think you can set your mind at rest about that. But I don't much care about his being there if what I'm guessing is correct. Anyway, to go on, Robert had a pretty good sire there called Malifico. Do you remember him?'

'Wasn't he second in the St Leger?'

'He was. And won the Eclipse as a four-year-old, admittedly in a bad year. Well, with Malifico I believe Bradbury saw his chance. He covered the mares sent to his horse, Burglar Alarm, with Malifico and put them down as Burglar Alarms. Immediately afterwards a few Burglar Alarms ran on the flat, most of them from mares owned by Bradbury himself, and a fair proportion of them won. Then, of course, he began to get better mares for Burglar Alarm. But Malifico horses were flashy and temperamental, absolutely unlike the real Burglar Alarms. He must have seen the danger of comparisons if they went on running on the flat. So he stuck to producing steeplechasers a goodish proportion of which were of course really by Malifico. They did very well and as time went on he got better and better mares. But if you study the form you will see the difference in

154

the way the produce of the two different strains ran.'

'I can see that but wasn't he taking an awful risk?'

'He was and that's where it becomes really bad. Obviously with the two different ways of running someone was going to smell a rat sometime. Robert told me that night in London that even he had wondered about the sale of Malifico. Then that conversation I heard at Cheltenham—who the devil can it have been? I wish I'd seen them—set me really thinking to see if there was any way of proving I was right.'

'What did you do?'

'I found a photo of Malifico easily enough in an old copy of *Turf and Turnstile*, but I couldn't lay my hands anywhere on one of Bubglar Alarm. In the end I asked young Myles Aylward if he could dig one up for me. He did. In fact he got a couple and I compared the pictures of the two horses. They could be twins. One is a dead ringer for the other.'

'Good heavens! You mean he actually switched the sires and sold Burglar Alarm to South America?'

'That's just what I mean.'

'The old rogue. What cheek! If Robert wasn't a friend you could almost admire him for it. But how did he manage the passports for instance?'

'I don't think that would trouble him. He's a vet, remember. There would of course be some difference in the markings. Bound to be, but he could fake those pretty easily. Nowadays, you know, with the number of horses about, you do fairly often get genuine mistakes in passport markings. I asked Dick Davison, the senior Stewards' Secretary, about it and he told me they'd recently had a lot of trouble and had to call in passports for amendment. When they went into it they found the errors were all plain veterinary mistakes and there was no fraud about them.'

'But could he do all this himself? Wouldn't he have to have someone in the stud who was in the know and helping him? It'd be the stud-groom, I suppose. Thank God this was all before David's time.'

'It's usually the stud-groom in these matters. I asked Robert about the Clayhampton groom and if there had been any changes. The answer was that there had been. Henson, the stud-groom during those years, left a while back. It was something to do with his health, Robert said Bradbury told him.'

'Where did he go?'

'I asked that too. Robert said that he understood from Bradbury the poor chap had cancer and died soon after.'

'What are you going to do, Arthur?'

'I'm bound to do all I can to help Robert. It's mere supposition at the moment but I'm sure I'm right. I wonder if Henson is dead. He may have tried to blackmail Bradbury and Bradbury either bought or frightened him off. The latter, more likely.'

'But you can't do any detective work yourself, you haven't time.'

'That's so. I thought I'd ask Myles. I won't tell him the whole story. But he knows everyone and he might be able to find out where Henson is if he's alive. These journalists, you know, they can find out anything and everything if they put their minds to it.'

'You're sure it won't hurt David?'

'How can it? It'll be a shock to him, I suppose, when it all comes out. But that may not be any harm. It'd teach him that these flat-catchin' chaps like Bradbury aren't always the best to get mixed up with. I can't talk to him at all. He was impossible that evening he was here when I tried to discuss the stud with him.'

'He's very easily led, David. You remember that trouble we had with him at school?'

'He's also very friendly with that young Pereira who is the worst tailor on a horse I ever saw.' Arthur was utterly unconscious of the complete non-sequitur contained in his statement.

'But Tommy couldn't have anything to do with this or Bradbury surely? He wouldn't need to. He's very well off.'

'No. No. I'm not suggesting that for a moment. It's just that David will make the wrong friends.'

His wife sighed. 'Perhaps we all did at one time or another when we were young,' she said. 'I hope, Arthur, you are wise in getting yourself mixed up in this. After all, it's largely Robert's own fault. He's simply too idle and too careless to look after his own affairs. He's so useless—Robert. Honestly I begin to think I almost sympathise with Bill Bradbury.'

'I've given my word to Robert I'd try to help him find out what has gone wrong with the stud,' Arthur said with finality, pushing back his chair.

'You must do as you think right, dear,' Mary said. I only

156

hope, she added to herself as she began to collect the plates for the dish-washer, that it doesn't all end in tears.

PART TWO

WINTER

10

Tommy Pereira sat on a cramped bench at the back of the tiny courthouse at Little Chiddington and wriggled uneasily. The accommodation for the public was scarcely palatial, he reflected, as he stared at the embossed Royal Arms over the chairman's head. To make matters worse it was extremely cold for England was in the grip of a bitter frost which had lasted almost three weeks. It was now mid-January and Tommy had lost count of the number of racing days that had been lost. At least, he thought, the hard weather and absence of racing had deprived Pat of that excuse for not attending the court, and he had succeeded, though not without difficulty, in getting him up to this particular post. The question now was how he would behave having arrived there.

The loss of racing had put Pat, predictably, into one of his foulest tempers. Before the frost came he had been rapidly climbing up the jockey's table and was lying third, only twelve wins behind Tim Hanway, the leader. He had duly won the S.G.B. Chase on Alexander, cleverly by a length, to Chris's pleasure, grudgingly expressed, and no doubt profit, for they all had backed him. He had regarded himself as a certainty on Pirate Gold for the King George at Kempton on Boxing Day but the frost had killed those hopes. Inactivity and frustration had combined to make him both sour and savage. If he were to lose his driving licence—and he was now beginning to face the realisation that this was only too probable—it seemed likely to put an end to his ambition to head the table for this year at least. As a result he hated the law and lawyers with all the energy of a spoilt and wilful nature. So, hardly to Tommy's surprise, the first conference with Seton, the barrister, in his

161

chambers at Bristol, had not been a success.

Seton was a youngish man in his mid-thirties with a brisk, businesslike manner. He sat behind a big desk littered with law reports, books of reference and briefs bound with pink tape. There were more briefs spilled around on the floor beside him. Bookcases lined the walls. He was wearing the subfusc suit, white cutaway collar and dark tie of his trade.

Pat's casual swagger, his high-necked sweater, windcheater and jeans were out of place here as Seton's dress would have been at morning stables in a training establishment. Truth to tell, Pat felt himself at a disadvantage in these totally foreign surroundings and this increased his resentment against everyone and everything connected with the case.

'Well, Mr Colby,' Seton said, sensing some of this and trying to put him at his ease. 'What is going to win the Grand National this year?'

'I am,' Pat said flatly and with finality. Then he stared, glowering, out of the window.

Seton looked quickly at him. After a moment he turned his gaze towards Michael Ordway and Tommy who were seated on chairs in front of his desk and slightly raised his eyebrows. 'I see,' he said drily. 'I'm sure we all hope you will. Meanwhile, perhaps I'd better explain to you the defence we propose to put forward for you. First I should make it clear that your blood count is over the limit and thus, basically, there is no defence.'

'If you're trying to make out I was as smashed as a scrambled egg, I wasn't,' Pat said.

'I'm not trying to make out anything, Mr Colby. All I'm doing is explaining the defence we can make or endeavour to make. It is not going to be easy in view of the present strict interpretation of the Act by the justices. I'm instructed, however, that your licence is an absolute necessity to you in your career as a jockey. I want to try to keep it for you if I can. In these cases every known form of defence has been tried and will continue to be. I intend to attempt to make the Bench sympathise with you on the grounds that you were—er—wasting, I believe it's called.' He looked down quickly at his brief. 'And that a quite exceptional set of circumstances led to the offence. But I must have your cooperation as I hope you understand.'

Pat gave a surly nod.

162

'Very well then. I have the facts in your proof your instructing solicitor has sent me. I would like, however, to know more about this wasting. I understand that it amounts to starving yourself to do a weight at which you can ride a given horse in a handicap race. Is that correct?'

'Just about.'

'I believe also that sometimes this wasting process is assisted by pills which may have an effect on one's tolerance to drink. Do you ever use them?'

'Those things? I never touch them.'

'That line is out then. Do you waste habitually?'

'No. I don't have much trouble with my weight but in this instance Mr Rokeby wanted me to ride this horse and I had to get five pounds off to do ten stone. We thought he had a chance.'

'And did he?'

'Yes. We won.'

'Giving you three winners that day—a treble, I understand.'

Pat nodded.

'Can you tell me what you did have to eat in the twenty-four hours before the incident?'

'A dozen oysters and a glass of champagne the night before. A cup of tea for breakfast.'

'Is that all?'

'Yes.'

'And you rode in, let me see, six races—steeplechases—and won three of them. Good heavens, how do you do it?'

'I see what you're getting at,' Michael Ordway put in. 'Would it be a good idea to get the actual number of miles covered?'

'Three of them were hurdles,' Pat said looking at the ceiling.

'For the purpose of the mileage I don't think that matters,' the barrister said. 'We'll get the number of fences jumped later on, that might be useful, too. All this, taken with the lack of food, can be used to impress the Bench. What is the figure?' he looked at Michael.

'I have the card here. Just a moment.' The solicitor took out a pencil. 'Thirteen miles and about two hundred and fifty yards,' he said.

Seton made a note. 'What I'm getting at is the set of unusual circumstances surrounding the offence,' he said. 'Of course this is at best what I think you racing gentlemen would describe as a

163

long shot. A lot will depend on who we get as a Bench. Old Violet Wrenbury usually sits as chairman. She's a motherly old thing with a soft spot for the younger generation. If we get her we should be off to a good start. Then there's Tom Warriner. He's a constant racegoer, I believe, and knows a lot of racing people. Perhaps you know him, Mr Colby?'

'Never heard of him,' Pat said.

The solicitor concealed a smile. So much, he thought, for Tom Warriner, his horsey suits, saloon bar boasting and name-dropping of what this or that leading jockey had told him.

When the conference was over and Pat had left the room Seton motioned Tommy and Michael to remain behind for a moment. 'Look,' he said, 'we may have a fair chance of getting away with this especially before old Ma Wrenbury but that chap of yours, if he goes on the way he has today, he'll lose his own case.'

'It looks very like it,' Michael Ordway said and then, turning to Tommy, 'You'll have to do what you can with him.'

'He's a good-looking sort of chap,' Seton went on. 'He's only got to turn those baby-blue eyes of his on the old lady and blink them a couple of times and she'll be eating out of his hand.'

This was the message Tommy had tried to put across at dinner the night before the case was heard. Alternatively he had bullied and cajoled his friend in an attempt to persuade him to be on his best behaviour.

'I don't see why I should have to go at all,' Pat had said sulkily. 'Can't you write a letter for me or get me to swear an affidavit or whatever you call it?'

'That's not on. You'll have to turn up. And listen, Pat, for God's sake try to play them along. Seton says your only hope is to act the idiot boy or the innocent child or something. You don't want to throw away your chance of the championship, do you? And you won't be champion without a car.'

That shaft sank home.

'I suppose you're right,' Pat said after a pause for thought. 'What am I supposed to do? Touch my forelock?'

'Just look at Madam Chairman as if you were every mother's only son. It's a sort of con trick. So far as I can see that's what most court cases are. And another thing, believe it or not, Seton isn't against you. These bloody lawyers, I've had something to do with them, and when they're getting up a case they always

164

seem to give the impression that their client is in the wrong. But it doesn't stop them fighting for you like tiger cats once they get into court. By the way, has Chris said anything about the case to you?'

'He's never mentioned it. The other thing, remand or whatever you call it, wasn't in the papers. It looks as though he doesn't know anything about it.'

'You didn't tell him?'

'Not bloody likely. If we get away with it he may never know until it's all over. Anyway, what business of his is it?'

'Quite a bit I should have thought. You're his first jockey. If he does find out he'll mention it all right and in capital letters, what's more. Is there anything in your agreement with him about not being able to fulfil your duties giving him a right to cancel?'

For the first time Pat looked startled. 'No,' he said. 'At least I don't think so. I didn't read the thing. I just signed on the line where I was told to. As far as I remember it was the usual printed form. You don't mean—?'

'If you lose your licence I wouldn't put it past Chris to try to cancel whether it's in the form or not. He has Alexander fancied for the National and Pirate Gold for the Gold Cup in his yard, remember. He'll want a jockey who can get around and ride them.'

'Christ!' Pat stared in silence into the fire. Shortly afterwards he went to bed in an unwontedly chastened mood.

Tommy had not the least idea if what he had said about Chris's probable reaction to an adverse verdict had any foundation in fact, though he was pretty sure that whatever Chris did was likely to be explosive. His mentioning the possibility of Pat losing Chris's retainer had been a desperate measure to try to bring home the seriousness of his position to his friend. And, next morning, it seemed to have worked.

They had agreed that Tommy should drive them both over to the court at Little Chiddington. After breakfast Pat presented himself at Tommy's house in good time wearing his only dark suit, a covert coat and a brown trilby hat. He was also wearing an expression of almost angelic innocence on his features. Tommy wondered if he had been practising it in front of a looking-glass.

The second conference with Seton, which took place on the

165

pavement in front of the court, all three shivering with cold, had gone better, too.

'We've got the Bench I was hoping for,' Seton said. 'Old Ma Wrenburg, Tom Warriner and Dr Stanton. They'll be disposed to be sympathetic, I'm pretty sure. Old Ma, you know, she's a nice old biddy if you go along with her. Yes, ma'am, no, ma'am, three bags full, that sort of thing. And Tom, well, flatter him a bit if you can, when he asks questions about racing even if they're bloody silly. Okay?'

Pat smiled his sudden, charming, little-boy smile. 'I'll have a damn good go,' he said.

'Fine. Now there's another thing to look out for. Peter Robinson is prosecuting. He's a very able cross-examiner and he's an expert at putting the knife in. Answer him as briefly as you can. But above all don't lose your temper. He'll try to make you when he sees what we're up to. I'm quite certain of that especially if we're going well.'

'I'll be a good boy, just this once,' Pat said. 'You keep my licence for me, that's all.'

'There's another piece of luck, too. Your solicitor has found that the policeman, Milligan, will do all he can to help. Mind you, having said all this, I don't want to raise any false hopes. None of this may work. Especially if Tom Warriner has been out late last night playing poker with his chums and his liver is at him.'

'What odds do you give?'

'I'm not a racing man. I don't know how to quote odds. All I can say is that the law is dead against us. Our only chance is to try to make them bend it a bit.'

'So it's the riding that'll do it if anything does?'

'You can put it that way.' Seton glanced at his watch. 'I'd better go in. I have another case in the list.'

Hearing the minor cases being dealt with, no lights, speeding and the like, Tommy's thoughts drifted away. Inevitably they turned to racing and the events of the past months.

Pirate Gold had won the Mackeson Gold Cup convincingly enough and already was being quoted at a short price for the Great Prize at the National Hunt Meeting, the Cheltenham Gold Cup. Rob Roy, to everyone's surprise, had come out and won the Hennessy Gold Cup at Newbury, the other steeplechasing classic of the first part of the season. It had, Tommy thought, been a slightly sub-standard field, but it had made the horse a warm fancy to win his second Grand National. But a greater surprise, to the racing world and the public alike, had been the name of the man who rode him.

Val Errington, in common with most permit holders, had difficulty in engaging top jockeys to ride his horses. Mike Manton, who had ridden Rob Roy when he won last year's National, had been claimed elsewhere as had almost all the others in the top flight. Errington had been at Towcester and seen Daddy win on Watchmaker. The ride he had given Arthur's horse had stuck in his mind. He had rung Daddy and, finding him free for Arthur had nothing in the race, had booked him. The horse, still big and burly, had been given a tender ride by Daddy; the level, galloping course had suited him and a fall at the second last by Admiral of the Blue, who had been greatly fancied, had removed a possible threat. Rob Roy, ridden out by Daddy with his hands and heels, had stayed on to win by a length and a half. It was Daddy's biggest win for years and, Tommy thought, must have set his telephone ringing again for Daddy had had several outside rides before the frost set in.

Tommy himself had ridden his own National hope, Cummerbund, in a three mile chase at Plumpton and had ended up on the floor. The horse had hit himself in the process and was only just back in work when the frost came. Tommy did not know whether to be glad or sorry for he had a problem of his own on his hands. He thought he was losing his nerve.

It had crept up on him completely unawares. Although he knew it happened to others he never believed it would or could happen to him. He was unadventurous. He rode only his own horses, which he saw were well schooled before he sat on them, save on rare occasions when he was asked to ride for others. These requests were becoming fewer and fewer and, when they did come, were carefully scrutinised by Tommy before he accepted the ride. When he got up he hunted his horse round and won if the winning was there, for, as he said himself, he was never one to risk his neck by riding into the last fence as if it wasn't there. He had for years now enjoyed all this in his amiable and unambitious way. But he was not enjoying it any more. Before going out to ride in his last few races nerves had reduced him to a shaking jelly of fear and apprehension. Up till this season nerves had never bothered him.

167

In fact on one occasion when going out to ride in a hunter chase at Warwick a fellow amateur had asked him as he tied his racing scarf round his neck, 'Do you ever wonder, when you are putting that thing on, will someone else be taking it off?' No, Tommy had replied with truth, he didn't. But he did now. Worse still, the apprehension did not leave him once he was in the saddle. The fences looked bigger and bigger as he came into them and he had an uneasy feeling that it was his throwing himself back as they left the ground that day at Plumpton which had caused Cummerbund, normally the safest of jumpers, to fall at the open ditch.

What the hell was causing this, he wondered? It could not surely be his habit of smoking pot. All the clever chaps he knew in London assured him that it was far better for you than alcohol. It couldn't be too many women either for the plain fact was that he hadn't had a woman for well over a month since that actress walked out on him. Women might be the end of Pat but not of him. Of course the sensible thing now was to give up and either sell all his horses or put a pro on them. But Tommy, easygoing and unambitious as he was, had his pride. He had told his friends that he would ride Cummerbund in this year's National and he intended to do so. He was not going to give up before he had proved to himself that he could still ride over those fearsome fences. Having done so then he could perhaps hang up his boots without dishonour, if that was not too high-flown a way of putting it. At the same time he remembered that if the thaw came he was due to ride Cummerbund again at Leicester next week and he felt slightly sick at the thought.

The sound of Pat's name being called broke into his reverie. 'The Crown against Patrick Adrian Colby.' The clerk's voice came clearly across the little court. Pat walked with a firm step to the dock. Tommy sat up and looked around him. His first thought was that there seemed to be several familiar faces about. He began to take stock.

The bench reserved for the press was crowded. He immediately recognised Myles Aylward, another racing reporter from a London daily, two men whom he assumed to be agency reporters and, with a sinking heart, sitting at the extreme end of the bench, the figure of Hector Mallinson. There being no racing, he realised, the newshounds of course would gather here for what they could get. There was precious little hope of

168

keeping it from Chris now.

Hector Mallinson appeared to be staring fixedly at a point in the public benches somewhere to the right of Tommy. At the same time as he took this in, a waft of expensive scent rolled over him. He glanced sideways and what he saw almost made him gasp.

Miriam Barkley was sitting a few feet away.

God, thought Tommy, how bloody brazen can you get? As if Pat's career was not in enough jeopardy already, here was this bloody bitch putting another hazard into it. Her presence would be splashed all over Mallinson's column tomorrow and if Barkley didn't by now suspect what was going on he'd certainly know all about it the moment he opened the paper.

The damage was probably already done, Tommy thought, but still he might be just able to save a little out of the wreck. There was only one man between him and Miriam. Tommy turned to him. 'I wonder if you would mind changing places with me,' he said. 'I want to speak to the lady next to you.'

The man nodded and the exchange was made, not without a certain amount of clatter, which earned a frown from the Bench.

'Get out of here and quick,' Tommy hissed at her once he was seated. 'Do you know who is down there on the press benches? Hector Mallinson and he's spotted you!'

She turned her exquisitely coiffured head towards him and even Tommy, hating her, found time to think how bewitching she was. 'Go to hell,' she said, and turned back to survey the court.

By this time the police witness, Milligan, was in the box. After he had given his formal evidence Seton rose to cross-examine. 'You arrested him yourself, you say, and brought him to the station?'

'Yes, sir.'

'That took, I suppose, some little time, say half an hour?'

'I would think so, sir.' Milligan was standing staring straight in front of him, expressionless, after the manner of all police witnesses.

'And would it be correct to say that during this time he was entirely rational?'

Dear heavens, thought Tommy, remembering the events of the night, I hope he knows what he is about. But Seton, with the

169

knowledge gleaned from Michael Ordway, knew very well what he was doing. He had made a small initial gain. There was, indeed, a slight risk in pursuing the matter a little further, but a favourable answer to one more question could be an enormous help. He was all but certain that he would get it. He decided to take what risk there was. 'And throughout the entire period during which he was under your surveillance, he was co-operative?' he said.

'Yes, sir. Very co-operative.'

'Thank you, officer. Now, something happened to him when he stepped out of the car. The car, as we know, was off the road owing to a skid. The ground was rough or roughish where it was?'

'Yes, sir.'

'And it had been raining?'

'It was raining at the time, sir.'

'Quite so. Now I put it to you, officer, that what actually happened was that the accused stumbled on this rough and slippery ground.'

'That's what it appeared to be to me, sir.'

'A stumble?'

'Yes, sir.'

'Such as might indeed happen to anyone under these conditions?'

'I would think so, sir.'

'Thank you, officer.' And thank all the little Gods that be and Canadians and all other accumulative bets whoever and wherever and whatever they are, thought Seton as he sat down.

But when he put Pat into the box he was faced with a far more formidable task. It was true that Pat looked Madam Chairman straight in the eyes as he took the oath, and the expression of hapless innocence on his face would have melted the heart of a far less susceptible old lady than she. That, however, was only the beginning even if it was a good one.

Tom Warriner, a red-faced man in his middle forties, looked at Pat with interest. Dr Stanton, the third magistrate, picked up a pen and stared at the ceiling through steel-rimmed spectacles.

'Mr Colby,' Seton began. 'You are a professional jockey, are you not, and this is your first season as such?'

'Yes.'

'You are twenty-four years of age and this is your first season

170

as a professional? It would be fair to say, I think, that you have been almost uniquely successful?'

Pat nearly succeeded in blushing. He cast his eyes down to where his hands were gripping the edge of the box and then raised them to stare open-eyed at Madam Chairman. 'I don't really think I could say that at all,' he said. 'I've just been very lucky.'

It was exactly the sort of answer that Seton had hoped for. They were improving on their good start. He could see Ma Wrenbury almost simpering in sympathy already.

'Perhaps you are being too modest. At all events it is correct, is it not, that having only become a professional in September you are now third in the championship table?'

Here Tom Warriner interrupted. 'One of the jockeys in front of you,' he said, 'is Tim Hanway, who has been champion for the past two years?'

'Yes.'

'How many wins does he lead you by now?' Seton asked.

'Six.'

'So he has a good chance of catching him by the end of the season if he doesn't get knocked out,' Tom Warriner said to the court in general.

'Exactly, sir, and that, indeed, will be part of my submission,' Seton said gravely.

Then, turning to Pat again, he went on. 'Now, on the occasion in question you were returning from a party given by some racing people you did not know, I understand.'

'Yes. I was taken there by a friend.'

'It was a very sophisticated party?'

'What? Oh, well, yes, there was a lot of drink and things, yes, if that is what you mean.' Pat blinked his eyelids rapidly.

'Most of the people there would have been older than you?'

At this point Robinson got to his feet. 'I have no objection within limits to my friend leading the witness,' he said. 'But if we are now getting to the meat of the defence, such as it may be, as I rather suspect we are, then I think the witness should be allowed to speak for himself.'

'Very well,' Seton said. 'Be good enough then, Mr Colby, to tell us what happened.'

I hope to hell he has enough sense not to, Tommy thought grimly as, drenched in waves of Miriam's Chanel, he leant

171

forward to catch Pat's reply.

He need not have worried. Pat was beginning to enjoy himself. He was the centre of attention, which he loved. He had been given a part to play and was determined to play it up to the hilt. Besides, thinking the matter over last night, Tommy's comparison with the law as a game had appealed to him. And when he played games he played to win. 'Well, you see,' he said, 'I'd been wasting to ride this horse of Mr Rokeby's . . .'

'Wasting?' Ma Wrenbury said with her pen lifted. 'Wasting? What is that?'

'I'll explain, ma'am,' Tom Warriner put in quickly. 'Jockeys are given certain weights to ride in handicap races. Very often these are well below their natural weight. They have to starve themselves to do it.'

'Dear me. But surely that is very bad for these young boys? Don't you find it a great privation, young man?'

'Well, yes, ma'am. I do indeed.'

'When did you have your last meal before you went to the party?'

'I had a dozen oysters the night before, ma'am.'

At least he had enough sense, Tommy thought, to leave out the champagne.

'And you must do this for a living? You don't get paid unless you ride, I suppose. And it is a very dangerous occupation, too, it seems. I heard Mr Warriner say something about getting hurt.'

'There's always that risk, ma'am,' Pat said demurely.

'Dear me. Dear me.' She looked as if she was about to report the whole matter to the Society for the Prevention of Cruelty to Children.

Seton went on from there, quietly putting together before the Bench a picture of Pat's youth, his innocence, his vulnerability, his lack of food and the amount of physical exertion he had put in that day. 'Thirteen miles and in every one of them jumps with the risk of physical injury, even death, lurking on the other side.' He continued with the unforeseeable set of circumstances which had led Pat to the party, his lowered tolerance to alcohol through wasting and the absolute necessity to him of his car in his profession.

'Do you mean to say that this young man, apart from the other perils of his trade which he has outlined to me, must drive

172

forty or fifty thousand miles a year on our crowded roads in order to earn his living?' Ma Wrenbury said.

'That is so, ma'am,' Tom Warriner put in. 'And I've heard it said that the driving is almost as much a strain as the riding. Do you agree?' he asked Pat.

'It's a strain, yes, but we have to do it,' Pat said.

'I think I remember you had a fall that day,' Tom Warriner went on. 'I was there. Wasn't it in the hurdle?'

'That's quite right, sir. Half the field galloped over me.'

I hope he hasn't the form book with him, Tommy thought. It was a soft one at the ditch in the Novice Chase. Pat certainly believes in pushing his luck.

'I thought I remembered it,' Tom Warriner said with satisfaction.

'A fall! Half the field galloped over you! Goodness, gracious me!' Ma Wrenbury said faintly.

Tommy stole a look at the prosecuting solicitor. He was writing furiously but he did not show any signs of consulting the form book or other authority to check Pat's statement.

Truth to tell, Peter Robinson was far too concerned with the way the case was going to think of checking where the fall occurred even if he had known how to do it. He knew nothing of racing and would not have recognised the form book had it been thrust under his nose. But he knew his job and could appreciate very well what was happening to his case. He had not, in fact, given much thought or preparation to it. When he saw it on his list it had appeared to be a clear-cut breathalyser offence. He had scanned the analyst's certificate, noted the blood-alcohol content, assured himself that there must be a conviction, and had turned then to more difficult and important matters. And now here was Seton putting up this cockeyed defence and, what was more, showing every sign so far of getting away with it.

They'd appeal, of course, he reassured himself, and the Divisional Court would be certain to set the finding aside. Or he supposed it would, for one was never quite certain what would happen on appeal. One might find oneself in front of someone wanting to make new law or twist the old. The result of the case did not really make much difference to him personally but if they lost, and they looked very much like losing, then there were the costs of the appeal to be considered and questions might well be asked about that. His only hope now lay in cross-

173

examination and how the hell was he to cross-examine this young thug with the facts as stated and the Bench breast-high against him? Old Ma Wrenbury was always a sucker for a handsome face, especially a young one, and that fool Warriner was wanting, of course, to curry favour with a leading jockey and tell his chums all about it in the White Hart afterwards. There was the law as a last resort but much use the law was going to be to him with Ma Wrenbury and Tom Warriner fawning over this brat.

He had, however, he thought, just a chance if he could shake Colby in cross-examination. By doing so he would destroy all the sympathy Seton had built up for him. He turned the pages of his notes, searching for the weak point in the evidence-in-chief. It had gone so well for him with that copper, whom he now strongly suspected to be bent, that it was a well-nigh hopeless task. But this fellow could not possibly be the straight bat, steel-true *Boy's Own Paper* hero they were putting him forward to be. He decided on a policy of all-out attack.

'Now, Mr Colby,' he said. 'You are not quite the innocent your counsel is suggesting, are you?'

Pat opened his eyes wide and stared at him. 'I—I'm not quite sure what you mean,' he said.

'I mean that steeplechasing is a tough game, isn't it?'

'Well, yes, it is.'

'And you have to be tough to survive?'

'Fairly, I suppose.'

'And you've survived very well so far?'

'Pretty well. I've been very lucky, I think, as I said.'

'And you meet all sorts of people in it from the highest to the lowest?'

'You meet all sorts of people—yes.'

'So I suggest to you that what my friend has called a sophisticated party was not such a strange experience to you as you would have us believe?'

We're getting into a danger area here, all right, Tommy thought.

'I'm not very used to those parties and I had had a heavy day.'

'A heavy day? Three winners? Wasn't that something to celebrate?'

'Well, yes, if you put it like that.'

174

'And don't you usually celebrate such a day?'

'Oh, no, usually we go home to bed.'

Yes, but whose bed? The one belonging to this bitch beside me if he'd half a chance, Tommy thought, glancing at Miriam and noticing as he did so the sudden leer on Hector Mallinson's features.

'You say you're not used to starving yourself—what is described as wasting, I believe. Then why did you do it?'

'Mr Robinson,' Tom Warriner put in. 'I don't think you quite understand. Colby is first jockey to Christopher Rokeby, a leading jumping trainer. If the trainer wants him to waste to do the weight then he must do it. That is so, isn't it?' He turned to Pat.

'Yes. I had to,' Pat said looking appealingly at Ma Wrenbury.

'Mr Robinson,' Ma said severely to the solicitor. 'Surely you realise by now that the dangerous and arduous profession in which this young man is engaged exposes him to unusual perils and temptations quite apart from the risks entailed in itself. I must say I should not care for any son of mine to embark upon it.'

Robinson was now driven back on his line of last resort—the law on the matter. 'Yes, ma'am, but I must point out that the law as it stands states categorically that any reason for exception to the penalty imposed must move from the offence and not the offender. Here we are dealing solely with the offender.'

'Are we? I confess that from the evidence-in-chief given by this young man I gathered that the circumstances surrounding the offence were unusual to say the least.'

'I am trying to show they were not.'

'So I apprehend. Do you wish to continue with your cross-examination?'

He did but he was beating his head against a brick wall and he knew it.

At the close Seton made a speech ramming home in an impassioned appeal all the points he had brought out in evidence. Finally he read to the court the article which Myles had written about Pat's performance on the day in question. 'Will you ruin and reduce to ashes the promise of this young man's wonderful career?' he concluded. 'I am sure, your Worships, that you will not.'

Ma Wrenbury seemed on the point of tears. She and Tom Warriner conferred together, nodding their heads. Then she turned to Dr Stanton who had not opened his mouth during the hearing but had played with his pencil, staring alternatively at the ceiling or out of the window. He coughed. 'I must confess,' he said, 'that I believe Mr Robinson's point to be good in law and well taken.'

A thunderous frown appeared on Ma Wrenbury's forehead. 'The Bench will retire for further consideration,' she said.

When they had left their places Robinson turned to Seton. 'You old rogue,' he said. 'I should have suspected something like this. Do you think you've got away with it?'

'Up to two minutes ago I thought I was on a certainty. What's come over Stanton? I've never heard him open his mouth before.'

'His nephew lost his licence in a breathalyser case two months ago. That could be the reason.'

Tommy heard this last remark as he joined them. 'That'll shorten the odds a bit, won't it?' he said to Seton.

'These damn Magistrates, you never know where you are with them,' Seton said. 'Our only hope now is that old Ma will bully the wits out of him. She may, too, at that. Hullo, here they are.'

Ma Wrenbury looked stern and appeared to be breathing hard. Tommy's heart sank.

'Patrick Adrian Colby,' she said. 'We have considered this matter between us. We find you guilty of driving a Motor Vehicle with an excess of alcohol in your blood. On that count you will be convicted and fined the amount of one hundred pounds.'

Hell, thought Tommy, he's lost it.

But Ma Wrenbury was going on. 'In view, however, of what has been most ably urged on your behalf by your counsel and in exercise of the powers conferred on us by statute we find that there are circumstances moving from the offence'—here she stared meaningly at Robinson—'which would justify us in not suspending your driving licence. We therefore do not do so. We do, however, issue this warning, that should you ever be involved in a like or similar offence you can expect no such leniency to be extended to you. We hope you heed this warning. You may go.' She smiled at him, a rather sweet, sad, old smile, and Pat left the dock.

176

'Christ!' Pat said as he met Tommy in the passage outside the court. 'A hundred nicker. That's a bit rough, isn't it? When do I pay?'

'You don't know how lucky you are, chum,' Tommy said to him. 'And here's the man you can thank for it.' He nodded to where Seton, his arms full of papers, was approaching them.

'Did I do all right?' Pat asked as Seton joined them.

'I couldn't have asked for a better witness. You were first-class.'

'Thanks. So were you. That's what I said—it was the riding that did it. I was almost beginning to believe some of the things you said about me myself!'

'Don't get picked up for a motoring offence for a long time,' Seton said. 'You really will be for it if you do. Anyway I'm glad it went so well. I must get back to chambers and on to the tread-mill once more.'

'Clever chap, isn't he?' Pat said as they came out into the bright, hard winter sunshine. 'Hullo!'

Miriam Barkley was standing waiting for them. 'Come and celebrate, Pat,' she said. 'Lunch in Burford. Another winner. You win them all.'

Near them, by the kerb, a car was parked. Evelyn Marker was sitting behind the wheel. Pat hesitated and then went over to her.

'I came down,' she said, looking straight at him, 'because I thought you might need someone to drive you back. But you seem to have made other arrangements.'

'Come on, Pat,' Miriam called. 'I'm waiting.'

At that moment another car pulled into the kerb. 'He isn't going anywhere,' a voice said from behind the wheel. 'Except with me.' The passenger's door was flicked open. 'Get in,' Chris Rokeby said.

'It seems you'll have to make do with me,' Myles said to Evelyn.

'Why are you here? It's not like you to come and gloat.'

'I didn't. Pat's news these days. What with the frost and no racing we have to fill the sports pages somehow. Featherstone asked me to come down. Might get a human angle, he said. We're great on human angle on the paper nowadays.'

'You seem to have got something for your trouble in that case.' Evelyn looked along the street to where Miriam Barkley was getting into her scarlet Jensen.

'I'll leave her to Hector Mallinson. He's here, too. His page tomorrow should make interesting reading. Come and have lunch with me, Evelyn. Do, please. We can go to the Running Stream at Nun's Stopford. It's only a few miles away.'

Evelyn stared at the back of the Jensen disappearing at some pace down the street. 'All right,' she said after a moment or two. 'But someone wants you, I think.'

Myles looked up to see the long figure of Malvey standing at the door of the courthouse beckoning him. 'Looks like I've work to do,' he said. 'Anyway I won't be long with him. Meet me at the pub in half an hour.'

'Very well,' Evelyn let in the clutch and pulled away from the kerb.

'Time for a quick one?' Malvey asked Miles as he joined him.

'Yes, if it's very quick.'

They found a pub down the street and went into the saloon bar. It was a tiny place furnished with three high-backed oak settles. The tables in front of these formed alcoves giving some privacy. In one corner was a small semi-circular bar. Malvey went over to this and ordered Myles a gin and tonic, and a vodka and peppermint for himself. There was no one else in the bar save for an elderly man in a worn tweed coat drinking a pint of bitter and reading *Sporting Life*.

Malvey stared at his pale-green drink with some distaste. Then he lifted his glass and sipped it. 'Ulcers,' he said, wrinkling his long nose. 'Bloody ulcers, damn them. Whore's drink, that's what this is. But anything else sets them alight. That's not to say this doesn't, too, sometimes. Do they bet on it?'

Myles was startled. 'What? The case? I shouldn't think so.'

'No, no. The jockey's championship there was all that chat about in there.'

'You may be sure they do. And the market is getting bigger every year. Now with the frost and no racing it's about the only thing they've got to bet on. The dogs aren't enough by themselves to keep the mug punters going.'

'I thought so. One of Buckner's men was there. I saw him sprinting for the telephone.'

'If Pat lost his licence it would certainly make a difference to the odds. How's the investigation going?'

'We keep digging. It looks a bit now as if Buckner is only a front man. There's someone bigger behind him.'

'That makes sense. I never really thought that Larry Buckner had either the go or the guts to carry through the things you said he was up to.'

'He's in it all right. Up to the neck. Front men always are. But he's an amateur. Amateurs at this game invariably make mistakes, usually bloody silly ones. That's what I wanted to tell you.' Malvey stared lugubriously at his drink, picked up the glass and swallowed what was left in it.

'Do whores really drink that stuff?' Myles asked him.

'It purifies the breath, ducks, that's what they used to say. The ones I see on the game now seem different somehow. They must be, I suppose, when every little bit you meet is ready to open her legs for the price of a drink. I don't know. Sometimes I wonder if I know anything much about anything any more. But I know the likes of Mr Larry Buckner.' He stared at the empty glass in front of him and shook his head when Myles offered him another. Then he belched slightly and went on: 'Like I said, he's an amateur. If he feels the pressure on him he'll make a mistake. And when he does he'll make a big one and a bloody silly one. When racing starts again keep your eyes open, will

179

you?'

'But this isn't my scene at all. How will I know?'

'You'll know all right. It'll be under your nose.' Malvey stood up, thrust his hands into the pockets of his long, old-fashioned, slightly threadbare tweed overcoat, and walked with his sideways, almost drifting motion towards the door. He opened it a few inches and slid out, leaving Myles alone. His last words seemed to Myles to convey some sort of slight threat, as if he was going to be involved personally in all this. With a feeling of unease lingering at the back of his mind, he too finished his drink and went out to his car.

Evelyn was waiting for him in the lounge of the Running Stream, sitting in a chintz-covered armchair in front of a roaring log fire. A pile of illustrated papers was on a small table beside her and she was turning over the pages of the *Tatler*.

'That's a welcome sight,' Myles said, stretching out his hands to the flames. 'It's parky outside.'

'Just what happened, Myles? I found it awfully difficult to follow what was going on. I gather he can still drive. Is that right?'

'That barrister fellow rode a blinder for him. He got him off on the suspension and saved his licence. He was fined a hundred pounds.'

'He won't like that. Pat never has any money. But didn't the old girl say something at the end? She sounded a bit as if she was lecturing him like some of those old bitches used to lecture me at the finishing schools my dear father chose for me.'

'She warned him that if he was ever up again on a motoring offence he'd be in dead trouble. She was trying to put the fear of God into him in a motherly way, I imagine.'

'If so, she was wasting her breath.'

'That's what I thought too. But he will just the same.'

'As of this moment I should think he's catching hell from Chris. This damn frost. It sets everyone on edge and scratchy.'

'There's a thaw coming. Milder weather setting in from the west. I heard it on the radio coming over.'

'Will the hold-up have interfered with Alexander? Chris won't have been able to work him and time is getting on. He's a big horse.'

'Not much, I should think. Funnily enough, just before the

frost I ran into Barty Moriarty at Worcester. He had a runner there. He's the chap we bought Alexander from. Do you remember him?'

Evelyn smiled. 'How could I forget?'

'He told me that for a big horse Alexander required very little work. Some of them are like that. Chris will have found it out by now.'

They were at lunch then, a bottle of Niersteiner between them. The frost had kept most people at home. There were only two other tables occupied in the small, oval dining-room. A fire of logs blazed in the hearth. The intimacy, the soft glow of the wine, the feeling of isolation from the world produced by the frost outside and the warmth within combined to bring back to both of them that day in West Cork and the happiness they had had together there.

'And you, Myles,' Evelyn asked softly. 'How are things with you? Are you still playing detective?'

That night they had spent together in the flat, when they had seemed to be so at one and she in one of her gentler moods, he had told her something of what was happening on the paper and of his hopes and fears. Later he had worried lest he had said too much. Pillow talk, he had thought wryly, it always leads to trouble. But at least he had not named names and had only spoken in general terms. He still had, too, like an echo in the back of his mind, the last words Malvey had spoken to him in the pub at Little Chiddington. As much to head her off this dangerous ground as anything else he said: 'Funny thing about your mentioning playing detective, people seem to think journalists can find out anything. A while back Arthur Malcolm wanted me to try to trace a stud-groom who used to be at Clayhampton.'

'Why on earth would Arthur Malcolm want to find out about someone at Clayhampton?'

'Search me. His son is there. That might have something to do with it. Anyway Arthur thought this chap might be dead. I had someone search in Somerset House. He's not dead so far as we could find out. To tell you the truth I forgot all about it until a few days ago Arthur rang me to know if I had found out what had happened to the chap. Henson his name is. I imagine Arthur had forgotten, too, until the frost came along and gae him time to think. This damn frost has a lot to answer for.'

Evelyn leant across the table, her eyes alight with interest. 'It must be important or else Arthur wouldn't have bothered you,' she said. 'And aren't Arthur and Lord Warminster great friends?'

'I believe so, and now I come to think of it Warminster bought that horse of Charles d'Arcy's, Watchmaker, in Arthur's stable, to run in the National or so I heard. He's off in Kenya or somewhere now. He's an idle devil. Clayhampton is running down as you probably know, and he doesn't seem to give a damn.'

'He isn't in Kenya now. I saw him in Annabel's a few nights ago.'

'What?' Myles looked up, startled. 'I thought he always wintered abroad and didn't come back until the beginning of the flat. What on earth can have brought him back now and in the middle of this frost? Are you sure?'

'Absolutely. The people I was with said exactly the same thing as you. Perhaps it's something to do with Clayhampton. Could Arthur be making these enquiries for him?'

'He could, I suppose. If Arthur is really after something I ought to help, I think. I owe him a good turn. It was he who got me started in journalism, after all. And wait a bit. Before he asked me about Henson he had me dig out a photograph of a sire old Bill Bradbury the manager there has. Burglar Alarm. He's the sire of Pirate Gold, by the way.'

'Surely someone at the stud must remember Henson? If he ever went into pubs to have a drink, some old inhabitant would know something. And he or his wife must have done shopping. It should be easy enough to pick up some sort of trail. Couldn't you go down and ask around?'

'I could, I suppose, but I hate that sort of snooping and I'm no good at it. I'd be sure to make a mess of it and make myself too obvious. But I could ask Jim Malvey if he'd go down. It's the sort of thing he thrives on.'

'Jim Malvey? Who's he?'

'One of our crime staff. He was there today. He was the chap who wanted to see me after the court. He told me, by the way, that the bookies had runners there to check on whether Pat lost his licence or not. It'll make a difference to the betting on the championship.'

'Bookies—betting, it's all money, money, money now, isn't

182

it? No one seems to think of anything else. Except you, perhaps, Myles.'

'I'm lucky. I've got a good job. I'm paid for doing what I like.'

'So is Julius. And what he likes is making money, though heaven knows he's got enough of it. Even the horses have to pay. You know that.'

She had not spoken to her father since the row in her flat, nor had he made any attempt to seek her out or communicate with her. She did not regret what had happened, nor would she withdraw one word of what she had said, she told herself, for it had had to come to a showdown between them sooner or later. The flaunting of Pat Colby and their association had been her way of forcing the issue. She had become tired beyond measure of the constant surveillance exercised by her father and the subterfuges it forced her to adopt. Pat Colby had arrived in her life at an opportune time. She would never have allowed Myles to have been the instrument through which she and her father came to face one another. Myles was too vulnerable in himself and too open to reprisal in his job. Although she told herself it was a weakness in her character she felt protective towards Myles. Pat, on the other hand, was hard and tough and resilient. He could look after himself. These, in fact, were the qualities which she admired in him.

Martin Barkley breakfasted early and alone. Miriam had her orange juice and coffee brought to her much later in the bedroom.

The Rolls was calling for him at nine o'clock to take him to London. He had a directors' meeting at eleven and a meeting of the Stewards of the Jockey Club in the afternoon. Today, in fact, marked a watershed in Martin's life. The meeting in the morning was of the directors of Martin Barkley Ltd, the company he had founded and which which had made his fortune. Having secured the necessary solaces, such as keeping the Rolls and his driver and having his house run through the company funds, he was kicking himself upstairs into the chairman's seat. This would give him all the time he wanted to concentrate on the two things which now filled his life, his wife and the future—and, he hoped, better—administration of racing, both of which subjects he was finding every day increasingly fascinating.

Luncheon at his club, therefore, at which he would share a bottle with the new managing director, whom he had personally picked and whom he had been grooming for the job for the best part of a year, would mark the transition between one period of his life and the next.

It was this coming period to which he was now eagerly looking forward and which he was sure would be far richer, happier and altogether better than that which had gone before.

The letter summoning the Meeting of the Stewards, together with its agenda, lay before him on the table. It never failed to give him a little thrill to open the envelopes marked *Private and Confidential* and to find inside the letters bearing the heading 42 PORTMAN SQUARE. Then, again, it was still exciting to read: *Dear Sir, I beg to inform you that a meeting of the Stewards will be held . . .* and to know that these words were addressed to him not only as a member but as a steward of that august and self-elected body. Even if he sometimes felt like pinching himself for reassurance that it was the truth and not a dream, a steward he undoubtedly was and he intended to make his presence felt far more in the future. Glancing through the agenda, he decided that there was very little in it which should take up much of their time. If they got through the specific items on the agenda pretty quickly he intended to raise again under 'any other business' the matter of not riding a horse out for a place. A Steward's Instruction had been issued about this and it was minatory enough in its wording. He had the Rule Book beside him and to refresh his memory he opened it at the section headed RIDING in the *Instructions by the Stewards of the Jockey Club. The Stewards will not tolerate*, he read, *the practice amongst riders of easing horses out of places when they find they are unable to win.*

That was all very well but Martin was of the opinion that certain local stewards, not all of them but certain ones to his knowledge, were not interpreting this instruction as strictly as they should do. Some of the members, especially the older ones, regarded him, he knew, as a misguided nuisance. After one morning meeting of the Club he had heard Colonel Dick Roicey, one of his particular anathemas, confiding to a crony in the luncheon room after his third pink gin: 'If that feller had ever tried to hold a tired horse together coming up the hill at Cheltenham he might think different. I remember . . .' Remember, remember, that was half their trouble, Martin thought. The old men, they were always looking over their shoulders, backwards, never forward and into the future. Even the eighteenth-century title for the Secretary to the Jockey Club, 'Keeper of the Match Book', had an archaic ring about it and seemed somehow to typify their attitudes.

He suddenly remembered that it was Wednesday, the day on which Mallinson's gossip column appeared in the *Morning Echo*. His papers lay beside him in a little pile with *The Times* on top. Underneath were the *Financial Times*, which he put to one side to read in the car on the way to London, *Sporting Life* and the *Morning Echo*.

Martin's breakfast-time reading had become almost a ritual with him. As he drank his orange juice he opened his post and read such of it as did not consist of begging letters, circulars or bills. With his bacon, eggs and kidneys he glanced at the headlines in *The Times*, and then went quickly through the letters, the leaders and the obituaries. The financial pages he reserved until later unless there was some company in which he had a particular interest reporting. With his toast and marmalade he read *Sporting Life*. Since the frost still held, much of it this morning was devoted to greyhound racing and did not detain him long. The *Morning Echo* he reserved for his post-breakfast visit to the lavatory.

Finishing his coffee, he picked the paper up and made his way along the hall to the cloakroom. Comfortably seated he opened the pages and turned immediately to Mallinson's column. The first paragraph was headed LADIES RACE:

Racing personalities turned up in force at Little Chiddington yesterday for the case of The Crown against Patrick Adrian Colby, presently third contender for the champion jockey's crown. It was a mere matter of the said Patrick Adrian Colby having driven with an excess of alcohol in his blood. The offence occurred on the night of September 20th last when Patrick Adrian Colby was returning from a party, a not unknown occurrence in Patrick Adrian Colby's life, by the way. The defence called it a sophisticated party, a good name indeed for the goings on that night from all this scribe has heard. Pat Colby kept his licence by some legerdemain with the law this reporter is totally unable to account for save we know said Colby has a way with the ladies and Madam

185

Chairman seemed a very susceptible chairman indeed. Talking of ladies an interesting selection were there in attendance inside and outside the court. Amongst those present, as the best people say, was the daughter of the owner of a current National fancy and the wife of a new and active Jockey Club steward currently occupied in ruffling some Establishment feathers.

Who carried off the prize? Neither, oddly enough, though both were seen to try. Patrick Adrian Colby was last seen driving away in the company of Chris Rokeby, plain-speaking trainer and Colby's present employer, who arrived in time to prevent the claws coming out. Young Colby's odds in the jockey's championship will not shorten as a result of this case by the way. The odds in the battle of the sexes, or 'who gets Colby?', should not shorten either. Who wins this far more interesting contest is still anybody's guess.

Martin stared at the article as he had sometimes scanned the cold and forbidding print in a contract that had gone sour or a clause in a policy that captured him without hope of escape. He knew only too well that he was the steward referred to and Miriam the wife. All the recent vague suspicions about Miriam's behaviour which he had tried to write off as the distorted imaginings of an older man became suddenly crystallised and clarified. Fighting down an impulse to tear the offending article into shreds and stamp on them he read it slowly again.

Although he would have to check with his diary he was pretty sure that even the dates tallied. He remembered only too well her coming home from the party after Cheltenham and her devouring greed for sex that night. She must, he now deduced, have met Colby at the party and something had happened to prevent her fulfilling herself with him. And, since then, he had sensed a change in her. It was slight but, with his heightened perceptions where she was concerned, it was enough for him to notice it. She had been anxious enough for him to spend nights at his club, he now remembered with dismay, encouraging him so that he could, she said, get the winding up of his business affairs settled quickly and spend more time with her. And, at the same time, she had protested her loneliness. Lonely indeed! He recalled, too, that at times

186

recently she had been apart, distrait, as if wrapped in a private dream. All these were signs of a woman who, if she was not in love, was in the grip of a sexual infatuation. He knew Miriam well enough by now to know that love was not a word that loomed very large in her vocabulary. He recalled, too, the look that had passed like a bolt of lightning between her and Colby that day at Towcester and Colby's insolent grin.

He left the lavatory with the paper in his hand and made his way up to his study. There he opened a leatherbound desk diary and verified the dates. They corresponded all right. The dates of the party, Colby's arrest and the Cheltenham meeting were one and the same. There was no escape, he had to face the facts just as he had had to in business when the cold, unforgiving print stared up at him. His wife was betraying him, flagrantly, brazenly, so that her conduct was blazoned abroad in Mallinson's column. If this were so, it might not be for the first time. The husband, he told himself, in the words of the old cliché, was always the last to know. Well, he knew now.

What was he to do? He had rearranged his life so as to be with her. Even if he had not, it would be nothing without her. Just to look at her, to watch the way she moved, talked, bore herself in public and in private brought warmth to him. And the touch of her hands was like magic. He could not bear to lose her. And he knew her well enough to realise that if he taxed her with this he would lose her. Not only that but the accusation, were he to make it, would provoke scenes that would leave their scars on him forever. Where she was concerned he was a coward for she held him in thrall, a thrall that still existed whatever she had done, and he was satisfied that she knew her power and would use it without mercy. He recognised now, too, that somewhere at the back of his mind there had always been a lingering suspicion that she might and could be betraying him. His happiness had depended upon his ignoring this. He had pushed it from him as a man does who buries something in shifting sands. Mallinson's article had now swept those sands ruthlessly away to reveal the truth of that suspicion in all its ugliness. His dreams of a better, happier, fuller life with her were shattered.

And what of the Jockey Club meeting that afternoon? They would be laughing behind their hands at him now, if indeed they hadn't been doing this for some time. Mallinson's article

187

had brought it all out into the open. It would weaken his influence and strengthen the hands of those opposed to him. He wondered if he could face them. But, except where Miriam was concerned, Martin was no weakling. He had faced hostile boards before and had browbeaten angry shareholders into submission at company meetings. He could and would go on with his fight for reform even if much of the anticipated pleasure in carrying it through had gone from it.

He stared at the article again, cursing Mallinson for the ridicule he had brought on him but more especially for forcing him to face facts, and cursing himself for not knowing what to do. While all sorts of furies and fancies were racing through his brain the telephone beside him rang. It was Paul Cantrey, his trainer.

'Martin,' Cantrey said. 'Glad I got you before you left. Have you the Doncaster Sales catalogue?'

Martin turned to a shelf beside him and ran his finger along the spines of the books that filled it. Then he took down the fat, yellow-coloured volume that constituted the catalogue of the coming Doncaster sales. 'Yes,' he said. 'Why do you ask?'

'There's a horse coming up you might look at. Admiral of the Blue. Lot 109, page 775 of the catalogue. He was fifth in the National last year. Two young chaps own him in partnership. I didn't mention him before because I thought he might not come up. Now I'm told he won't be withdrawn under any circumstances. He's definitely to be sold.'

With an effort Martin's mind switched to racing. But his was a mind trained to grasp business problems and emergencies, to switch from grappling with disaster to conjuring with hope. He forced it to work now. 'I know the horse,' he said. 'He fell at Newbury. Has that anything to do with it?'

The trainer chuckled. 'It has everything to do with it from what I hear. Those two young chaps bet like drunken sailors. They had a bundle on him at Newbury. Now with the frost they've no way of getting it back. Anyway they've fallen out, or so I'm told. He'll be sold. He should run well in the National. But you'll have to pay for him.'

'Is he sound? Could that be why they're selling?'

'He's to come up with a clean, sound certificate. I don't think you need worry about that.'

'I'll come back to you, Paul. I've a lot on my mind at the

188

moment.'

'He's the only likely National horse to come on the market so far. I wouldn't let him go if you want a runner.'

'I'll ring you, Paul.' Martin put down the telephone. Once more he forced his thoughts away from his personal problems. He badly wanted a National runner. But would even a winner compensate for what he was losing? But would he lose her? Was there nothing he could do? Not against her, perhaps; but as he began to turn the matter over more rationally in his mind a cold and forbidding hatred against the man who had done this thing to him was born.

12

The man who sat facing his accountant across the long table in his library-cum-boardroom had his own reasons, like Pat Colby and others, for detesting the frost and hoping for a thaw.

The accountant, a thin man with a sharp nose on which sat a pair of steel-rimmed half-glasses, looked up from the papers which were spread out between them. 'It's going badly, Larry,' he said. 'You can't get away from it. There was a run of winning favourites right through to the stoppage. Pirate Gold in the Mackeson and Roy Roy in the Hennessy hit us really hard.'

'And with this damn frost there's no money coming in at all now.'

'Greyhounds. That's all, and it's chicken feed.'

Larry Buckner stared out of the window at the frost that lay white on the slope of the hill on which the house was built. He had no business to be living here, he told himself, and he should have realised it years ago. Even though he had transferred the house to the company and had converted most of it to offices for the company's use, it still didn't make sense.

Friarsford was his father's house, built on to and extended by him when the money first started to flow in back in the twenties during the gambling boom after the First World War. It had been stuffed with servants then, and horses and high-living. Old Joe Buckner had always wanted to live like a duke or how he imagined a duke should live, and he had maintained a standard of living that would have beggared most of those who then occupied the Dukeries. Larry still thought affectionately of his father, his bluff, boisterous manner, his loud suits, and his damn-your-eyes acceptance of himself and everyone else just as he found them, which had made him popular wherever he

190

went. But it had all been much easier then—with a wrench Larry pulled his thoughts back to the present. 'If this frost would only break,' he said. 'Then we could get on with it again. At least it would start the cash flow moving.'

'It's gone too far for a thaw to do much good,' the accountant said remorselessly. 'There'll be a flood of money for Pirate Gold in the Gold Cup and Rob Roy in the National. If they win you're finished, Larry.'

'If they win—if they win,' Larry said. 'They won't win. All right, Pirate Gold may win the Gold Cup, I give you that. Chris and young Colby seem to have done a job on him and got him settled. But the betting on the Gold Cup is only a fraction of that on the National. I don't have to tell you that.'

'No. You don't. And Rob Roy is going to start a short-priced favourite.'

'So much the better. He'll get twelve stone. He won't win it twice. He can't. All right, I know all about Reynoldstown and Red Rum. How many others have been tipped to win it twice and failed? And Reynoldstown wouldn't have won it the second time if Mildmay hadn't broken his reins and Davy Jones ran out. And Red Rum wouldn't either only for the miracle of his getting fast ground twice in succession. Miracles happen only once in a lifetime and we've had ours.'

'They say now Reynoldstown would have won it anyway. Davy Jones was tiring and Reynoldstown had the hell of a pull out.'

'He had twelve stone two on his back. More than they're allowed to carry nowadays. That long run-in would have stopped him. As I said Rob Roy will get twelve stone or near it and it'll stop him now.'

'He's a good horse,' the accountant said gloomily. 'Look how he won the Hennessy. How many National winners have done that? None. I wouldn't be surprised to see him win again. Even if he doesn't I doubt if it'll save you. Why don't you sell out? Both of the big chains have put out feelers.'

'No.' Larry stared out of the window again, his long, weak face taking on lines of determination. Like most weak and vacillating men, on the rare occasions when he did take a stand nothing would make him budge from it.

Larry Buckner had never wanted to be a crook. As with most things he did, he had drifted into knavery almost unbeknownst

191

to himself, and when he woke up to what he was embroiled in he was frightened.

It had all begun with his father, he told himself, and his obsession with proving that a bookmaker could be as great a gentleman as anyone. 'Gentleman Joe' they called him after a bit, and how he had loved it. He had owned racehorses himself and backed them in the grand manner. Finally, the ultimate extravagance, he had taken on the local pack of hounds and had mounted and turned out himself and his hunt servants in a way that the great spender of those times, Lord Lonsdale, the Yellow Earl, might have envied. He had shown sport, too, for, as Larry had to admit, he did everything with skill and success whenever he put his mind to it. But the business had been neglected. A succession of managers had cheated the old man left, right and centre. Larry, an only son, had been spoilt and cossetted. At Eton and Oxford, spending freely himself, he had been too young and ignorant to help. Nowadays, he thought, none of this would have happened. Men like his father possessed by *folie de grandeur* had long since disappeared. Nowadays no one wanted to prove he was as good as his betters. Instead the people upstairs broke their necks in their haste coming down to show they were no better than those downstairs.

When the old man had died there had been the devil to pay and also debts and, despite the debts, estate duty. Determined, foolishly he told himself now, but people saw things differently then, Larry had taken control of the business and had paid off the debts and the estate duty. In order to do so he had had to incur debts of his own and he had had to bet.

There was a seamier side to the old man's life. In his path to success he had met and done business with characters, some of them on the edge of the underworld and others well over that edge. Certain of these had approached Larry with offers of help and in desperation he had accepted them. As always they had demanded their price.

Larry still controlled the business—just. He held fifty-one per cent of the shares. The other forty-nine were divided between two holding companies whose labyrinthine shareholdings even Larry could not unweave though he knew or thought he knew who actually controlled them. He knew, too, that although in name he controlled the company, those who owned the holding companies in fact controlled him. His weakness, his taste for high-living, acquired, he wryly told himself, through his having been educated above his station, his disastrous start when the old man died, had all combined to put him in their power. Also, he had carried on the tradition by having a son at Eton and a daughter at Benenden and these, too, were hostages to fortune.

All this together with a sentimental refusal to let his father's name disappear and a weak man's horror of losing face had made him give a determined 'no' to any suggestion of a sale. He could not sell anyway, he told himself, without the permission of those or rather, he believed now, of him who controlled the holding companies.

On the face of it no one would have suspected that a person in the position that man held was likely to be mixed up in all this. Yet he was, and his apparent aimless affability hid a degree of ruthlessness Larry had seldom seen excelled. If only certain people knew! Yet he dare not divulge the name or the connection between them. Fear for himself and his family, if nothing else, dictated that.

But he had, he told himself, been able to exercise some restraining influence. It was he who had first pleaded and then insisted that the letter bomb sent to Errington had been sufficient to frighten but not lethal enough to maim. It was he who had made sure that one of his own men went along with the heavies who beat up young Barrett, to exercise restraint or try to. In the end of course they had used him as the decoy. Afterwards, when he heard this, Larry had feared that in some way through the decoy, it all could be traced back to him and that they had only consented to his use so as to cover themselves. He had spent hours in panic-stricken anxiety when he had heard that young Barrett was in hospital with pneumonia, dreading that the boy should die and his implication in the matter come to light. But Barrett had recovered, and nothing further had come of it all. It was almost a year ago now and he could breathe freely again.

Larry sighed, got to his feet and crossed to an ornamental armoire in a corner. Opening it he took out a bottle of brandy and poured a stiff measure. Why the hell did I ever allow myself to get into this? he asked himself for the thousandth time. I should have chucked it all up when the old man died and emigrated or got a job with someone else. I was always good at figures, or . . .

The sound of wheels on the gravel below interrupted his thoughts. He crossed to the window and looked out. A taxi from Taunton was pulling up by the grandiose front porch his father had built on to the house. Looking down, Larry, his thoughts still on the past, remembered hounds there congregating round the old man. He could see him now, glass in hand, sitting a huge, well-bred weight-carrying hunter bought for a cool thousand to carry him in front of the best. He would be exchanging jokes with the members of his field, the scarlet of his face almost matching that of his coat, and in a moment or two would move off, his hounds in front of him, a wide smile on his face, laughing at some sally and ready to ride for his life without a care in the world. Most of the field that had followed him were gone now, either killed in the war or crippled by taxes. Those were happier days and he fervently wished his father had never seen them.

The driver of the taxi opened the door and a man got out. At this moment he was the very last man in the world Larry wished to see.

If Larry hated being a crook the man who left the taxi and shortly afterwards entered the room loved every moment of it. He had been born with the instincts of a villain and the ability both to exploit and conceal them. He had prospered. People thought him a spendthrift, a fool, and a gambler. He encouraged them to do so though he was none of those things. It gave him pleasure to laugh at what the world thought of him and to rob the worldlings who put these thoughts into words.

'Well, Larry,' he said as he entered the room. 'You look like a man with a lot on your mind.'

'Travers, the accountant, has just been here.'

'I thought I passed him on the drive. I came down by train. I didn't want to risk the roads in this weather. Things are bad, are they?'

'According to Travers they couldn't be worse. And this damned frost . . .'

'Accountants always panic. And things are never so bad you can't do something about them. For a start there's a thaw coming.'

This news, mixed with the brandy, brought some cheer to Larry. 'Then we can get things going again. Travers is worried stiff about Rob Roy. I've told him he won't win another

194

National. Not with the weight he'll get. There'll be a flood of money for him from all over the West and we'll make a killing.'

'Travers wets his pants whenever a 6–4 favourite comes up at Wincanton. But it wasn't that I came to see you about.' He contemplated Larry for a moment, congratulating himself on his own cleverness. How wise he had been to get Joe Buckner Ltd into his grasp. It was true that Larry had the majority shareholding but since Larry was in his hands too that was really more of a protection than a liability. If anything went wrong Larry would catch what was coming in the way of obloquy, blame or, in that unlikely event, criminal proceedings. Larry was the ideal front man for a skilled manipulator like himself. It was all very amusing, really. 'You may be in different trouble than you think,' he said.

'What do you mean?'

'You remember those little jobs you had to do last year to level your book?'

Larry swallowed. 'You thought them up.'

'Just so. But that's all I did. As I recall, Larry, dear boy, you had certain connections with the Benn brothers from days gone by and you made use of them. The Benn brothers play things rough, sometimes rougher than you want, don't they, Larry? I only dropped hints in a receptive ear. You did the rest.'

'But—'

'Then there were those two beaten favourites at the beginning of this season at Devon and Exeter and Newton Abbott. Remember them? Got you off the hook and to a good start, didn't they, Larry? Young Victor Elliott rode one of them for Errington. He's never put him up again. Odd, isn't it?'

'You suggested giving him—'

'But I didn't give him the five hundred nicker, did I?'

'Just what are you getting at?'

The other man leant across the table. 'I'll tell you what I'm getting at, Larry. I was told that a man called Malvey, a crime reporter on the *Post*, was going racing which he'd never done before. It's not his job. Then I heard he'd been seen around with Myles Aylward and that they were hanging about your stand. I made enquiries, and I had a look myself.'

'And—'

'They've set up a new investigative team on the *Post's* sports page. Featherstone, the new sports editor, is behind it. It's a brainchild of his to try to get circulation going again. Private File, they call it. They've already uncovered some scandal in soccer. Now they're having a go at racing. They've been with Chris Rokeby and Val Errington.'

'What can they say?'

'Nothing much if you've covered your tracks properly. But it looks to me as if they're after your balls, boy. They've tried to get hold of Carton, that punter you squeezed over his big win. He's not talking but his brother is singing like a canary.'

'Christ!'

'They're unlikely to have uncovered any real stuff yet. Even that brother can't tell them much, so stiffen yourself, Larry. Have another brandy, it may put some fire into your belly. Anyway you're in it now and you can't get out.'

'What do you want me to do?'

'None of the others of that team know anything about racing. Myles Aylward must be the brains behind them. If he drops out the whole investigation may fall to pieces. You'll have to pressure him a bit.'

'But how do we know he's going to break if we do? It may make him step things up.'

'It won't. I've done a bit of homework on him. He started off trying to ride as an amateur. He gave up pretty quick. Couldn't take it.'

'I thought he broke his back in a point-to-point.'

'What if he did? Lots of people have broken their backs and gone on riding. Tim Hanway's done his twice.'

'But Myles is a respected figure. I know him slightly. I've always found him pretty decent to deal with.'

'The trouble with you, Larry, is that you've been trying to be a gentleman for so long you've almost become one.'

Larry flushed. 'I still don't see how . . .'

'Lean on him, Larry. Just lean on him a little, that's all.'

13

The cool clear air of an early morning on the Downs came to Alastair Bragdon as he sat his hack, watching his horses prepare to school. The magnificent, rolling sweep of open country stretched about him into vast misty distances. Far away he could just see another string working, strung out like dots along the skyline. The surroundings were far too familiar to him for him to give them any of his attention. All his thoughts were concentrated on his own string and, in particular, Meg Meredith's Form Book.

The thaw had come just in time to give Alastair a last chance to qualify Form Book for the National. To do this he had to run next week at Warwick in a three mile, thousand pound race, and he had to win. Form Book had been brilliant in his novice races winning three on the trot, his jumping quick and bold to the point of recklessness, annihilating his rivals. It was his jumping which was worrying Alastair now. He had run twice in handicaps, finishing second in one after a bad mistake at the ditch. He had fallen in the other. This was exactly the sort of thing that happened to brilliant, extravagant novice jumpers when they entered handicap class. They then came up against experienced horses who took them on, exposed their youthful limitations and brought them down. After that last fall he simply had to get a school and a good school into Form Book before he ran again.

Some trainers, such as Arthur Malcolm, who worked their horses over their own lands, had schooling grounds on them which they could use as they liked. Alastair shared this one with six others whose stables were grouped around the little village of Linsbury set in a fold of the Downs below him. That entailed fitting in his schooling with the times and in the periods laid down by the gallops manager.

He had been on edge all the morning knowing the importance of this school. The horses, too, after their enforced idleness on the straw had been above themselves, kicking, jumping and squealing and generally serving notice that they were likely to cause trouble later on. One of the lads had been unshipped in the yard and there had been a row, quickly quelled, between two others over a matter of missing tack. That was something he would have to sort out on his return. Just one more worry to add to his day, Alastair thought.

All this meant that they had been late arriving at the schooling ground and that Alastair, who lacked the quality of absolute imperturbability possessed by those who reach the top of the training profession, felt his nerves stretched almost to screaming point.

The tension had communicated itself to the lads who were always edgy, anyway, during the minutes before schooling began. Precariously perched in short leathers on horses' backs that seemed to be coiled under them like steel springs ready to fly, fingers cold and numbed, the harsh, high wind cutting through their anoraks and sweaters, many of them looked at the black forbidding fences and felt a secret dread at what the next hour would bring. The wind lifted the horses' rugs and ran like ice along their thin coats making them kick and fly-jump. Two of the lads, the same two who had been quarrelling over the tack, started to swear at each other as one of their horses plunged out of the circle, setting the other's alight. Alastair cursed them into silence.

A car was parked at the top of the lane leading to the schooling ground. As the horses filed into it a stocky figure got out and walked towards Alastair, his crash helmet swinging from his hand. 'Which one is it you want me to ride, sir?' he said.

'Form Book. He's over there. Young Davies has him.' Alastair beckoned and the lad brought the big novice over.

'Nice horse. I remember him.' Daddy Rendall buckled the strap of his helmet round his chin. The lad put a hand under his leg and whipped him into the saddle.

Like most trainers in a small way Alastair could not afford to take a retainer on one of the leading jockeys. He had some sort of tenuous third claim on Tim Hanway who had always been friendly towards him and who had helped him. But Tim did not care about schooling and only did it when the current Guv'nor who had first claim on him insisted. Most of Alastair's own lads were indifferent or inexperienced riders. One of them, young Davies, was showing promise and Tommy Duckham, who was close on sixty, rode well but his nerve was past schooling something like Form Book. It was a problem to get his horses, especially a brilliant one like Form Book, properly schooled.

During the frost Alastair had turned this problem over in his mind again and again. When the thaw came, it it ever did, he simply had to get a school into Form Book before he ran him. Then, at dinner with friends one night talking horses and racing to the exclusion of everything else as racing people do, someone mentioned the ride Daddy Rendall had given Rob Roy in the Hennessy. Someone else had remarked how under-rated as a jockey he was, and a third had said that Arthur Malcolm held him to be the best schooling jockey in the country. That had set Alastair thinking.

The next morning he had rung Arthur who had confirmed that this was indeed his opinion about Daddy. When the thaw had come Alastair had got in touch with Daddy to ask him to school Form Book for him. Then they had had to arrange a time that fitted in with Arthur's requirements and Daddy's other engagements. This had not been as easy as it would have been four months before, since Daddy's services were now much more in demand. Alastair would have liked to have given Form Book more work before he schooled him, but what with the rush to get horses out after the thaw and fitting in with Daddy's free mornings, this was the only day they both could manage.

'What do you want us to do?' Daddy's voice broke into his thoughts.

'Steady half pace, first time. I'll send two others along with you.'

'Anything about this horse, sir?'

'He has the hell of a jump in him. That's his trouble. He's too bold.' Alastair hesitated and then went on: 'He belongs to Miss Meredith. She has her mind set on running him at Aintree. The only chance I have to get him qualified is at Warwick next week. He fell in a handicap last time out.'

'I know Miss Meredith,' Daddy said. 'We have a couple of hers at Farhaven.'

'All right. Let's get on.' Alastair turned his horse, kicked him into a canter and pulled up at the open ditch.

The fences over which they were to school this morning were replicas of those they would meet on a racecourse save that they were about six inches smaller in height. They were, however, just as stiff, the birch of which they were made being as tightly packed as true racing fences, and a horse could not afford to take liberties with them. Schooling over these fences meant business; it was virtually the real thing.

Alastair turned to watch. The three horses wheeled into line abreast. Daddy was in the middle. Young Davies was on his near side and Tom Duckham outside him. They jumped off and came down towards the first fence. The drum of their hooves on the age-old turf of the Downs came to Alastair as they reached their gallop. This was always a moment of excitement however often you had experienced it. Alastair leant forward in his saddle.

They reached the first fence and cleared it. The ditch, where Alastair was standing, was the third. As they approached the second, Alastair swore under his breath. Young Davies, who had been in a thoroughly foul temper all the morning, was disobeying his instructions. It looked as if he had determined to show a thing or two to this elderly man who had been brought down to school their best horse. He was making a race of it. Worse still, Duckham's horse had caught the infection and was following him. Daddy had no option but to lie up. Even so, Alastair noticed, he had the big horse beautifully balanced. That was something.

They came over the second fence, their hooves a drumbeat on the firm turf. And then Alastair realised something else. Young Davies, the young fool, having set an over-fresh horse alight, was now being taken off with or very nearly. All three were going much too fast. Davies, never one to show fear, his face alive with the excitement and intoxication of the moment, decided that his only hope of surviving the ditch was to kick on still faster into it. By some dispensation of those gods who look after fools and fearlessness, his horse met it right and cleared it. Form Book, as an over-bold horse will in such a situation, stood right back and reached for it.

He hit the top with a crash and landed sprawling but still on his feet on the far side. Daddy never moved in the saddle.

Alastair, despite his mounting fury, had time to notice how his hands allowed the big horse just enough rein to recover, keeping the gentlest touch on his mouth yet without that jerk or pull which would have brought him down. Form Book staggered, but he stood up. Daddy pulled him together and schooled him quietly over the next two fences. Then he pulled him up and slid to the ground. He was looking anxiously at Form Book's off fore.

Alastair cantered over to him, scarcely able to control his fury with Davies and yet knowing that he must. Davies could wait; the horse had first claim on his attention.

'What is it?' he demanded.

'I thought for a moment he might have hit himself,' Daddy said. 'But he seems all right . . .'

'Move him along. Yes, he's sound. We'll do it again. And properly this time. You, Davies, do you hear me? I'll speak to you later.'

Daddy hesitated. Though he had no very high opinion of his abilities, he did not want to appear to seem to teach Alastair his business especially in front of the lads. Then he made up his mind. This was a good horse. He'd risk a rebuff. He'd had them often enough after all. 'I think, sir,' he said, 'that he'd go better with an old horse if you have one. He doesn't need leading, really. Just a chance to settle and get himself right.'

Alastair scratched his chin. 'There's Credibility,' he said. 'But he's an awful old plug. I'm trying to sharpen him up a bit.'

'He'll do, sir.'

This time it was better. Form Book, apparently none the worse for his mistake, came down the line of fences immaculately under Daddy's tender hands. But Daddy was frowning as he pulled him up. 'I wonder if he is feeling that leg a bit, sir,' he said.

Alastair had had enough advice for that morning. He was bothered, too, about what he was going to do with Davies and the other lad. He'd have to do something but if he didn't get it right they'd both ask for their cards and walk out. Davies was promising if he'd only learn to behave himself. And replacements were all but impossible to get especially at this time of year. All he'd find was throw-outs from somewhere else far worse than those two. 'Nonsense,' he said to Daddy. 'He's perfectly sound. Go down again.'

Again Form Book jumped impeccably, brilliantly even, with Daddy's hands alternatively coaxing and restraining him.

'Well?' Alastair asked.

'He has a great jump in him, just as you said.' Again Daddy hesitated to speak his mind. He'd already been rebuffed about the leg and he was still not quite happy that Form Book was not feeling it. But Daddy, unlike some jockeys, really loved good horses and hated to see them messed about. The trouble about these young gentlemen-trainers, he thought, was that they were always in too much of a hurry, and half of them never tried to understand the animals they were dealing with. They might just as well be bicycles or motor-cars for all they cared. And they had no patience. Part of it was due to the times they lived in and the people they dealt with, he supposed. But if it had been his own Guv'nor, now, who had Form Book, things would be very different. Major Malcolm, he wouldn't hurry that big horse, no matter who put the pressure on. Daddy felt he owed it to the horse to say something. 'He won't jump Liverpool this year,' he said. 'He's too bold. And he's still trying to hurdle some of his fences. You can't do that with Aintree fences even now.'

'He'll have to try. Miss Meredith has her heart set on it.'

'Could you not tell her, sir, she's likely to spoil a good horse?'

'Have you ever tried telling Miss Meredith anything? No, I don't suppose you have. Anyway, thanks for your help. Now you've been here, perhaps you'll come again.'

'Any time, sir, provided it fits in with Major Malcolm.'

'And will you ride him for me at Warwick?'

'I'd be glad to, sir, if I'm free. I'll have to look in my book and let you know. I'm not sure, too, what the Major runs next week.' It had been a long time since Daddy had been able to pick and choose his rides. That chance mount on Rob Roy had been indeed a turn of luck for him. 'Can I ring you, sir?'

'Yes, of course, but as soon as you can, will you? If you can't take the ride I'll have to look around for someone else.'

'Very well, sir. I'm going to the Major now and I'll know by tonight.' Daddy took off his helmet and walked over to his car.

As he drank his breakfast coffee Alastair turned over in his mind what Daddy had said. He knew that the advice he had been given was right. Time, he thought again, not giving them time had ruined more good horses, especially steeplechasers,

202

than any other single thing in training. But time was money. Apart from mad women like old Meg who had their own special requirements to be met, people in racing, with certain rare exceptions who never came to small trainers like him, wanted quick returns. He tried to give them what they wanted. In a way it suited him well enough for he lacked the patience to wait and bring on and bring out the latent ability in a horse. That was why he was more successful with hurdlers than chasers. You didn't have to wait so long with them. He wished he had the money to go over to the flat. There you hadn't to wait years for a horse to come to his maturity. You had them for two or three seasons and then you threw them away and started all over again. Maybe if Form Book, against the odds, ran well in the National old Meg would leave him enough to set up a stable on the flat. Where would he go? Newmarket? Not at the beginning—he sat up, closed his mind to daydreams and castles in the air and opened *Sporting Life*.

After he had glanced through the paper and checked his entries and declarations he went out to do his morning stables.

The head lad came up to him, a serious look on his face. Alastair's heart sank. More trouble. And he had not dealt with those lads yet.

'There's heat in that horse's leg,' the head lad said.

Alastair's heart sank still further. 'Which one? Not . . .'

'Yes, it's Form Book. They were saying something about old man Rendall mentioning it up there.' The head lad nodded over his shoulder in the general direction of the slope of the Downs behind him.

'Oh, God. How bad is it?'

'Bad enough.' The head lad had all the natural gloom of his kind. Together they made their way to Form Book's box.

Alastair ran his hand down the horse's foreleg. There was heat in the tendon. It was not as bad as it might have been or as the head lad gloomily suggested but it was quite sufficient to stop him in his work. He did a mental calculation. The race was at the end of next week—almost a fortnight away. If the heat went quickly he just might make it. Form Book would have to be put back into work in a hurry and it was not the right thing to do especially with a potentially top-class horse, but with Meg breathing down his neck he felt he had no option. 'It must have been that mistake,' he said. 'He struck into himself. Rendall was right after all. Very well. Cut his feed, bandage and poultice him.'

'He'll never run at Warwick now. Not with that leg.'

'It may come right quicker than we think.'

'It may. But they never do.'

Driving down to Hampshire, Daddy had every reason to be pleased with the way his professional life was going. When luck in racing turned, it certainly turned all the way, he thought. The success on Rob Roy had brought him back into the public eye and then, immediately afterwards, Arthur's stable had struck form. A steady flow of winners had begun to come from Farhaven. The successes had for the most part been at minor meetings, for Arthur had no really high-class horses in his stable that year, but those he had had been skilfully placed. A winner is a name in the frame wherever it is, Daddy told himself, and the constant appearance of his name in the papers leading the results had attracted the attention of owners and trainers who had all but forgotten him. His telephone had begun to ring again and his book to fill. Cash, too, was starting to come to the little house in Wolverhampton in quantities that now made small luxuries possible. The doubts about his survival in racing which had assailed him in the early part of the season had disappeared. He felt he was riding better than ever.

But he wished he could think the same thoughts about his personal life. Millie seemed to be out of sorts all the time now. She was irritable with the boys, scolding them constantly for offences many of which Daddy thought existed only in her imagination. Whenever he was there she snapped at him, too. He seemed unable, now, to establish any contact with the Millie he had once known. It was almost a relief, he thought guiltily, that he was away so much. At times he wondered if she was jealous of his sudden resurgence into success. He was more hers, after all, when he was at home, idle and a failure.

But it was not all jealousy, of that he felt sure. Once or twice he had seen cross her face that spasm of pain which he had first observed a few months back. It was becoming more frequent now and she was taking less trouble to hide it. Then, again, when she thought he was not looking he had seen her press her hand to her side immediately after the spasm came. She was not well, that was the truth of it. Several times he had asked her about it, and implored her to see a doctor, but she had snapped him into silence. Perhaps she had seen one, for he had found a bottle of little yellow pills in a drawer hidden under some dish cloths. All she would say was that sometimes she got a bit of a stitch and that it went away after a time. Perhaps it was not anything more than a stitch. But he really must persuade her to go to the doctor. The trouble was that she was so pig-headed and stubborn when she was unhappy, and having scenes with her only made things worse.

He turned into the gates of Farhaven and parked his car by the lower yard. The second lot had just come in. One of the junior lads who was sweeping the tarmac surface of the yard told him he thought the Major was in the house.

At his desk in his office Arthur was grappling with his accounts. Ruth's insistence on drawing his attention to every detail down to the last decimal was, as usual, making him ruffle his hair, twist his pencil and stamp his feet in tormented frustration. He was heartily glad to see Daddy. 'Come in, come in,' he said. 'Now then, Ruth, we've got work to do. Real work. Take those damned figurres and dots away from me. Anyway, why can't they use plain honest to God pounds, shillings and pence like they used to!'

'I've been over at Linsbury,' Daddy said as he sat down. 'Mr Bragdon asked me to school Form Book for him.'

'Oh, yes, I remember. He rang me. That has the makings of a fair horse if Miss Meredith doesn't persuade him to do something silly with him.'

'He's a nice horse. I wish we had him. But I'm afraid she has her mind set on running him in the National.'

'Good God. Well, I hope young Alastair stands up to her.'

'He asked me to ride him at Warwick next week. Will that be all right?'

'I expect so. Let's look at the engagements.' Arthur drew the book towards him and together they began to discuss their horses and what they would do with them. 'Watchmaker,' Arthur said. 'I want to talk to you about him. He's in at Fontwell. I don't think I'll run him there.'

Arthur was determined to take Watchmaker quietly along with the object of bringing him to his peak in early April when the National was to be run. He was being aimed at the National and Robert had given him a free hand. Robert, astonishingly,

205

had been home last week. He had said he was too busy to come down and see the horse but they had talked together on the telephone. Arthur could not for the life of him imagine what urgent, business had brought back Robert from the sunny shores of the Indian Ocean to the ice and snow of Britain. Indeed he never thought Robert had any urgent business. But during that telephone conversation he had confirmed that Arthur could do with Watchmaker just what he thought best. 'Get him to the gate sound and I'll have a bet,' he had said.

Arthur had already formed the opinion that Watchmaker would not carry any great weight successfully round Aintree. It was the class horses by and large that won or were placed in the National nowadays. On that long run-in blood told and Watchmaker had not quite the class to survive it with a big burden on his back. On the other hand that long run in also made the weight tell and brought the best and the worst, if not together, very nearly so. Arthur was of the opinion that, given the right weight, Watchmaker would run really well. His jumping was impeccable and he stayed forever. Daddy's hands and horsemanship should, given luck—and luck was the imponderable you always prayed for at Liverpool—have him handy at the finish.

It was perfectly feasible to try to secure a light-weight without cheating and this was what Arthur was doing. He was not chasing after the big prizes with Watchmaker so that a lucky win or a good run into a place would make him shoot up in the weights. Nor was he making extravagant statements to the press about Watchmaker being his National horse and sure to run well in it. What with Rob Roy back again and certain to head the handicap and Pirate Gold being an entry, too, or so they said, then when the weights for the National were published Watchmaker, along with a good many others, was sure to get in with a realistic handicap. Then they could set about getting him ready for the big one. Arthur did not believe in giving your National hope a hard season before Christmas though this was something that appeared to be becoming fashionable. He was lucky, he supposed, that, with the exception of Robert, and in this instance he hardly counted as one, he did not train for betting owners. He wondered again what on earth could have brought Robert back and whether it could be anything to do with Clayhampton. David had said nothing if it was, but then David and he had seemingly almost ceased to communicate.

'He should be well enough in when we see the weights,' Daddy said.

'Yes. Just what is the date?' Arthur turned the pages of his desk diary. 'February 13. We can really start preparing him then. Come along and have some lunch.'

Mary was waiting for them in the study where drinks were laid out. She was just putting down the telephone when they came in. 'That was Myles Aylward,' she said to Arthur.

'Myles? What did he want?'

'He said to tell you Jim Malvey thought he had located Henson if you are still interested.'

Three days after Form Book's set-back Alastair was standing watching his first lot pull out. He was feeling far more cheerful about things in general and Form Book in particular.

In the first place he had had his interview with Davies and the other lad the afternoon following the school, and the whole thing had passed off much more satisfactorily than he had hoped. In fact, he told himself, he had really handled the matter rather well. After some consideration he had decided to approach it rather in the manner of a pained parent or, as he said to his wife afterwards, to deal out avuncular guff. Davies especially had seemed anxious to talk things over and, within limits, to express his repentance. It had come out that Davies, who did Form Book, had indeed resented Daddy being brought down to school him. He had also stated that this was only the confirmation of his general and increasing dissatisfaction with his lot. He considered that his riding had progressed enough for him to be put up in public and he did not think Alastair was giving him the chances he deserved.

This was, Alastair knew, a frequent complaint of lads in stables but on thinking it over quickly while Davies was talking he recognised that in his case there might well be grounds. Davies's riding had improved enormously and he had not been given the opportunities to prove himself in public that perhaps he should have had. In his anxiety to get good riders from outside Alastair had overlooked the promise that lay under his eyes in his own yard. Giving Davies his chance might well solve both their problems. Old Credibility was in a chase at Warwick the same day as Form Book. He was just the thing for the boy to begin on. He had promised him the ride. Davies went away delighted. Since it also had transpired that the row between the two was really over a girl in the pub, who both had now decided was only interested in the travelling head lad from a neighbouring yard, that matter was happily resolved, too.

Then, and more important still, the heat had gone from Form Book's leg as quickly as it had come—or had it? Alastair was satisfied that the horse was ready to resume work; his head lad was not so sure. But Alastair was now determined that the horse was sound, would stay sound and would run next week. He had given instructions that they would canter him with the first lot today.

The lads pulled the five horses that comprised Alastair's first lot out of their boxes. They filed past him in the grey, cold light of early morning. Alastair blew on his fingers and put on his gloves. Then he mounted his hack and followed them.

Bill Anderson's lot passed him, making for another part of the Downs. He ran his eye over them, recognising one or two and making mental notes of their condition. The village was still shuttered and sleeping as they made their way down its only street, Davies on Form Book leading the string.

A twisting, narrow roadway led to the Downs where markers showed the area laid out for work that day. Everything was still and quiet. The silence was only broken by an occasional murmur of talk between the lads, a muttered curse or cajolement, the clink of shoes on the metalled road. As they turned on to the Downs, Alastair issued his instructions. Davies was to lead on Form Book. 'Canter, now, and I mean canter. Don't go pissing off.'

Davies looked back and grinned.

Alastair cantered back to the point where he would watch the work. The string sorted itself out into a line. Then they started to come towards him, Form Book leading.

The big novice was taking the hell of a hold, Alastair saw. He breathed a prayer that everything would go off all right. But Davies had him in his hands. The boy could ride. He had been right to give him his chance.

They were nearing him now. Form Book, hard held, was covering the ground with an easy loping stride, pulling away a little from the others despite all that Davies could do. But there

208

was no sign of the stride shortening or faltering, or even that he was feeling the ground. So he had been right, Alastair thought. The horse was sound. They'd run at Warwick and win.

There was a slight slope up to a ridge in front of where Alastair stood. The horses would breast this ridge, pass him and pull up.

As Form Book came over this ridge Alastair suddenly saw the big horse appear to check in his stride. He swayed, lost his action, tried to stride out again and failed. The near fore came to the ground and seemed almost to knuckle under him. Davies stopped him in an instant and slid off. Sick at heart, Alastair kicked his horse into a canter. He pulled up beside Form Book and jumped down.

Davies was already bending over the leg. He looked up at Alastair. 'He's gone, sir,' he almost sobbed. 'He's gone!'

It was only too true. Even in his short career Alastair had seen too many horses break down not to recognise this for what it was. 'Go down as quick as you can and get a box,' he said to one of the lads. Then he ran his hand over the tendon. It was already beginning to swell and the horse flinched from his touch. Now what was he to say to old Meg?

'When do you think I should ring the old dragon up?' he said to his wife after evening stables that day. 'Now, I suppose.'

'There isn't anything else for it, is there? The longer you look at it the less you'll like it as the old groom used to say who took us hunting.'

'Oh, Lord, well, yes, that's about it. Here goes the last of the Bragdons.' He picked up the telephone and began to dial.

When the telephone rang, Meg was at home, sitting in her library, sipping sherry and bitters and conferring with Joseph. Joseph picked up the antique receiver and put it to his ear. 'It's Mr Bragdon, miss,' he said.

'Is it, indeed. And what does he want?'

'I did not enquire, miss. I think he seems a little—er—troubled.'

'Troubled? I'm not surprised. That young man has the brains of an oyster. Oh, very well, give me the wretched thing.' She reached out her hand for the telephone. 'Has it ever occurred to you, Joseph, that this insufferable invention

209

has destroyed half the pleasure of writing and receiving letters? Besides which I can never hear what anyone says.' This last statement was a complete lie and Meg knew it for she could in fact hear perfectly well. But she put it about that she suffered from telephone deafness, using this as an excuse either to complicate conversations or to terminate them altogether. 'Well?' she shouted into the mouthpiece now. 'What is it, boy, what is it?'

There was a sort of gulp at the other end of the telephone. 'Aunt Meg,' Alastair's voice said. 'I'm afraid I have very bad news for you.'

'Speak up, boy, speak up. I can't hear you.'

'Bad news,' Alastair was now shouting in return so that Meg, making a face, was forced to hold the instrument away from her ear. 'I'm afraid Form Book . . .'

'What?' Meg sat up and replaced the telephone against her ear, her deafness now quite forgotten. 'What about Form Book? Is he dead?'

'No. No. It's not quite as bad as that.'

'What is it then? And don't scream so at me, boy.'

'He's broken down, Aunt Meg.'

'Broken down? What have you been doing with him? How bad is it?'

'Bad enough, I'm afraid. He'll be out for the season anyway.'

'So, when I give you a good horse to train you break him down. You were in too much of a hurry, that's what it is.'

Although in the circumstances this happened to be true it was also grossly unfair. 'Aunt Meg,' Alastair almost wailed into the telephone. 'You did tell me to get him qualified for the National.'

'I didn't tell you to break him down, did I?' This accusation leaving Alastair speechless at the other end, Meg continued: 'You've lost me the best horse I'm ever likely to have this side of the grave, which with these shocks and my old heart appears ever more imminent.' Meg had just been to her doctor who had told her she had the heart of an Olympic athlete and was good for ten more years at least.

'Oh dear, don't say that, Aunt Meg.'

'Why not? You don't expect me to go on for ever buying good horses for you to knock about, do you?'

'I'm only doing my best for you, Aunt Meg.'

'Then your best isn't very good, is it? I haven't been at all well lately. All that is left to me is to fulfill my ambition to have a good horse carry my colours at Aintree. Now you have destroyed that hope. I must think again about all sorts of things. Goodbye, Alastair.' She put down the telephone.

'I'm very sorry to hear you say you haven't been well, miss,' Joseph said.

'Nonsense. Nonsense. Never been better in my life. But that young man needs a lesson. He's in too much of a hurry. Just like his father. Well, Joseph, we'll have no runner in the National this year it seems.'

Joseph coughed. 'I wonder, miss, if perhaps we might not remedy that. If I may say so, miss, I find reading sales catalogues quite absorbing and I have taken the liberty of borrowing one or two from your desk recently. For some time previously I devoted my reading to Western or cowboy stories. Very exciting some of them are, too, though I cannot say much for the way they treat their horses. I also read detective stories but there I prefer the older school of the period known, I understand, as the Golden Age. These are increasingly difficult to obtain. I find the moderns filled too much with sex and violence. Miss Sayers, now . . .'

'I don't require your views on current literature, Joseph. I have my own. What are you trying to say?'

'I find the sales catalogues quite fascinating, miss.'

'Very good. You've made that point. What of it?'

'I read them in bed before I sleep. Last night I was perusing the catalogue of the coming sale at Doncaster. I set myself the exercise of finding a substitute for you in the event of some mishap or mischief such as in fact occurred. I also consulted the Book.' Here Joseph reverently laid his hand on the big brass-bound book which went everywhere with Meg and now lay on the desk between them.

'Did you, indeed? And what did the Book say?'

'It said the stars were opportune and appropriate.'

'Are you trying to tell me out of all this rigmarole that there is a horse coming up at the Doncaster sales you think I ought to buy?'

'Yes, miss.' Joseph opened the thick yellow catalogue. 'This horse ran fifth in the National last year. He is nine years old by Rodney out of Flying Pennant.'

211

'Joseph, once and for all, what is his name?'
'Admiral of the Blue, miss.'

14

The chauffeur-driven Silver Shadow bore Martin Barkley north on the eve of the Doncaster January sale. Encapsulated in its whispering silence he dictated several letters to tidy up some loose ends of his managing directorship, and then picked up the sales catalogue.

A paper marker indicated the entry for Admiral of the Blue. The tabulated breeding which stretched across the sheet to the right of the horse's name meant nothing to him and he disregarded it. The horse's performances were what interested him.

ADMIRAL OF THE BLUE (he read) *winner of five hurdle races and nine steeplechases. Placed fifth in the Grand National last year, and second in the Kirk and Kirk Steeplechase in November* . . .

The entry omitted to say that Admiral of the Blue had fallen last time out in the Hennessy. Martin reached for the fat, blackbound, loose-leaf form book that lay on the seat beside him. Opening it, he looked up the horse's name in the index and turned to the page bearing the last reference number. *Fell three out when well placed and making progress*, he read. A prickle of excitement ran through him. He was beginning to feel that this horse might bring him the big victory in racing which he so badly wanted.

Closing the catalogue he thought again how wonderful it would be to own a National winner. That would show those shellbacks in the Jockey Club that he could beat them at their own game. Visions of leading in Admiral of the Blue with Miriam at his side floated before his eyes and as they did so his thoughts came back to the subject they rarely left nowadays—that of his wife.

Miriam had not accompanied him on this trip. She was tired,

she said, and she did not see why she should spend the day staring at a lot of boring old horses all of which looked alike to her. Since his suspicions of her liaison with Colby had hardened into something approaching certainty he had tried to keep her closer to his side. This he had done as unobtrusively as possible, but even so he was aware that what he was doing had not gone unobserved. She had been irritable with him and several times he had caught her watching him speculatively as if wondering what lay behind his attitude and how much he knew. Always a steady drinker she now seemed to be having recourse to the bottle earlier and more frequently than before. He had never tried to check her drinking for hitherto alcohol had appeared to make her softer and more amorous but now it seemed to be having the opposite effect. She became silent and moody, making ever more frequent excuses for withholding her body from him.

That had been the state of affairs when he had had to fly to America to wind up some loose ends. It had taken him longer than he had expected for there had been a sudden slump on Wall Street and to liquidate his interests in a hurry would have meant a loss greater than he either wanted or could afford. He had been desperately busy during that time trying to place his shares in the subsidiary at the right price and with the right people. In the end it had all come out as he had planned but there had been no time for him to try to exercise long-distance surveillance over Miriam's movements. His pride had refused to allow him to employ private detectives and, in addition, he dreaded what would happen if she discovered him doing so. When he had returned she had once more been compliant and loving. Against all that his intelligence and judgment told him, this had almost lulled him into a sense of satisfaction and security. But her refusal to accompany him to Doncaster had reawakened his fears. At least, however, there he would have at hand the telephone with a comparatively short distance to span. It was a poor substitute for a chastity belt but it would have to do.

Martin dined that night in Punch's with Paul Cantrey.

'Miriam didn't come?' Paul said to him over the smoked salmon, and regretted it the moment he had said it.

Paul Cantrey was a gnarled little man who had been a leading jockey some years back. He was one of the few members of

214

his profession to survive its hard knocks with his physical and mental faculties unscathed and to make the change to training a successful and profitable one. He knew all the current racecourse gossip about Miriam and Pat Colby. Idly he wondered where it was all going to end but it was none of his business, which was training racehorses. If it ended in his losing Martin as an owner that meant nothing to him. Owners were queuing up for the privilege of having horses trained by him. He just wished he had not mentioned it.

Martin glanced quickly at him but the other's face was expressionless. 'No,' he said. 'She says she can't tell one horse from another so there wasn't much point. I'm to ring her later. Now, what about this horse?'

'Admiral of the Blue? He's worth buying if we can get him at the right price.'

'What would you think that would be?'

'Hard to say. Eighteen to twenty thousand. That's a guess of course. What had you in mind?'

'Twenty at the outside.'

'That should do it, but then you never know.'

'If we do get him, what will you do with him?'

'I've looked up his engagements. He's in a three mile chase at Wrayfield next week. I expect they put him into it with the National in mind. I'll run him there.' This was said with flat finality. Paul Cantrey did not expect his owners either to argue with him or to dispute his decisions. If they did they left the stable It was as simple as that. Owners, he had said once after watching a re-run of Laughton's *Bligh of the Bounty* on the box, were the same as the King's midshipmen then—the lowest form of animal life. He had only consented to come to the sales at all and spend a night away from his yard because he liked the sound of Admiral of the Blue; he had no real National horse this year and he thought he might well win it if he got him.

Over their brandies they arranged to meet in the paddocks next morning before the sales began and to look at the horse together. The trainer then stumped off to bed. Not for him the chat and the whiskies and the pre-sales castles in the air which dissolved all too quickly in the cold early morning of a Yorkshire January.

Martin nodded to an acquaintance or two in the lounge, refused several offers of drinks and then went up to his room.

215

There he put through a telephone call to Miriam.

'Yes, dah-ling,' Miriam cooed at the end of the line. 'I'm all right. Of course I'm all right, dah-ling. I was so tired, I came up early. What about you and that lovely horse?'

'Paul says we should buy him.'

'You do that, dah-ling, and I'll lead him in at Liverpool for you. By-ee, dah-ling.' Miriam put down the telephone and snuggled up to her partner in the big bed. 'Wasn't it lucky the staff are all out and even the housekeeper had to go to a sick aunt,' she said. 'There's no one to bother us at all. Love me again, Patsy, dearest, love me. Oh, you wonderful, wonderful boy.'

When Martin arrived at the sales paddocks the next morning Paul was there already talking to a hawk-faced Irish peer. He gestured a greeting to Martin with his catalogue and then walked over to meet him. He was wearing an old-fashioned, battered pork-pie hat and an equally old leather sheepskin coat worn and stained round the neck and shoulders. He looked like a vaguely malevolent gnome.

As they approached the box where Admiral of the Blue was stabled they met Meg Meredith coming out, followed by Joseph. 'Morning, Meg,' Paul said, lifting his hat. 'Buying or selling today?'

'Minding my own business, something I commend to you,' Meg said sweeping on and staring hard at Martin. 'Who is that?' she said to Joseph when they had passed. 'Is it Martin Barkley?'

'Yes, miss.'

'Hm. Where's his wife, I wonder?'

Paul stared at her retreating back. 'If she's interested we may have to pay a bit for this fellow,' he said as they entered the box. 'She's got those damn boots of hers on, too. That means she's up to something.'

Admiral of the Blue was a big, rangy bay. Paul stared at him at length in that disquietening, horse-coping silence that is born of a knowledge which the uninitiated can never acquire. Martin shuffled his feet, wished he could say something both wise and appropriate and, realising he could not, had the sense to hold his tongue. Here was an occasion, as he was compelled to admit, when those steeped in the lore of the horse had the advantage over him. But he instantly capped the admission by

216

telling himself that if you hadn't got it you paid people like Paul Cantrey to exercise it for you. It was just another instance of money and business acumen paying off in this sphere as everywhere else.

'Humph,' Paul said at length. 'All right, let's have him out.'

The boy opened the box and led the horse outside. There, at Paul's gesture, he walked and trotted the horse for them.

'He's got a good shoulder on him,' Paul muttered under his breath so that Martin could scarcely hear. 'Bit light of his loins perhaps.' Then he was silent again, staring at the horse through narrowed eyes. 'Very well. Put him back,' he said. He walked off, scowling slightly, his eyes on the ground.

Martin was consumed with anxiety. He had set his heart on this horse. And now here was his adviser, silent and seemingly unimpressed by him. 'What are we going to do?' he asked the trainer. 'Don't you like him? Will we buy him?'

'Buy him? Of course we'll buy him. That's not a bad sort of horse at all. There's a man I want to see.' The trainer looked at his catalogue, and then at his watch. He made a mental calculation. 'He should come up a little after twelve,' he said. 'Meet me here a few minutes before the hour.'

Left to himself Martin looked about him. Horses were everywhere, being brought in or out of stables, jogged or walked out for inspection, or led round the pre-sale rings. There was an all-pervading air of bustle and suppressed excitement. The loudspeakers crackled as the auctioneer went into his sales patter. Martin leant against the rails of one of the outside rings and watched the horses being led by him. He tried once more to divine what made the experts pick one out to praise or condemn, to find out what points or qualities separated the excellent from the good, the ones for a gamble, the moderates and the plain useless. After a bit he gave it up as a hopeless exercise. Twelve o'clock was approaching. Excitement gripped him. He went to the bar and ordered himself a large brandy and ginger ale.

Meg took up her position in the sales ring in good time. She entered, followed by Joseph bearing rugs, catalogues, form books, a king-size thermos flask and a foot-warmer. The seat which she considered her own, though she had not occupied it for over three years, was taken. After glaring forbiddingly at the unfortunate man she placed herself on the row beneath him and

217

motioned Joseph to her side. Handing him the catalogue—for he was to do the actual bidding for her—she spread herself and her belongings over the seats on her other side. Then she settled down to watch the proceedings.

Nothing of any great value was as yet on offer and the sales ring was sparsely occupied. One or two lots were sold quickly and cheaply; others were led out unsold. There was a flurry of interest when a recent hurdles winner, also a winner on the flat made eight thousand guineas. As the time approached when Admiral of the Blue was expected to come up the ring began to fill. Meg saw Martin Barkley and Paul Cantrey come in and take seats opposite to her. Instinctively she recognised them as the enemy.

A fresh and senior auctioneer came to the rostrum. 'Lot 109,' he read out. 'Admiral of the Blue. A nine year old gelding by Rodney out of Flying Pennant. Winner of five hurdle races and nine steeplechases, Admiral of the Blue was placed fifth in the Grand National last year. This gelding goes back to the famous Sheldrake family. He's sure to win good races. Who'll put him in? What shall I say, gentlemen? Ten thousand pounds to start me? Come along now, gentlemen, he must be worth—Five thousand, thank you, sir. Five thousand I have . . .'

Meg watched the two men opposite intently. The bidding was not coming from them.

'Six I have—thank you, sir. Seven? Seven it is. It's against you in front . . .'

The bidding went to nine thousand and then to ten. 'It's not enough, you know,' the auctioneer was saying. 'Ah, thank you, sir. Eleven I have.' His trained eyes had caught the minute flick of Paul's catalogue as he entered the bidding.

Both Joseph and Meg had seen it, too. 'Mr Cantrey's in, miss,' Joseph said to Meg.

'So I see. I'm not blind, am I? Go on, man, bid.'

Joseph raised his hand.

'Twelve. I have twelve. It's on my right. Thirteen, thank you. Thirteen on my left.'

At fifteen the other bidders had dropped out and it became a duel.

At eighteen Joseph hesitated only to receive a savage dig in the ribs from his employer. Meg was now leaning forward with the light of battle in her eyes.

218

'Nineteen.' The auctioneer took his bid. 'And twenty on the left.' Paul Cantrey had come again.

The auctioneer looked quickly behind him, and held a hurried consultation. Then he turned again to the ring. 'At twenty and I'm selling,' he said. 'At twenty thousand pounds and I am selling Admiral of the Blue.' He raised his hammer.

'Bid, man, bid,' Meg hissed at Joseph.

'Twenty-one thousand,' Joseph had raised his hand. 'Twenty-one thousand,' he looked towards where Martin and Paul Cantrey sat. 'I'm selling this time . . .'

Auction fever combined with the lust to acquire now had Martin fully in their possession. 'Buy this horse,' he said to Paul. 'Go on, buy him, whatever it costs.'

Paul flicked his catalogue.

Word of the contest had now gone round the sales paddocks. People were leaving horses, drinks and early lunches to crowd the tiers of seats and watch the action.

Meg ceremoniously opened her thermos, poured herself a mug of coffee laced with rum and drank it off. 'I'm selling on the left,' the auctioneer said now, looking at Joseph.

'Twenty-three thousand.'

Joseph had raised the bid again. He was immediately capped by a flick of Paul's catalogue. A little buzz of excitement ran around the ring.

When Joseph made it twenty-eight there was another pause. It looked for a moment as if Meg had won.

'I'm selling now on the right,' the auctioneer said.

Silence fell save for a cough somewhere and a shuffling of feet. All eyes and heads turned to where Martin and Paul sat. The auctioneer raised his hammer. 'Go to thirty straight,' Martin said to Paul.

The trainer flicked his catalogue and raised two fingers.

'Thirty thousand? Thirty, is it, sir? Yes, thirty thousand I have. Thirty on the left. It's against you on the right. Thirty I have.'

'Go on, man. Thirty-one.' Meg, fortified by the coffee and rum, hissed in Joseph's ear.

Joseph shook his head. 'No, miss, no, it won't do.'

'I'm selling now on the left.' The auctioneer's hand was raised as he looked to where Meg sat.

'What do you mean it won't do?' Meg demanded in an angry

whisper.

The pause had allowed the joy of battle slightly to subside in her. Thirty thousand guineas, she suddenly realised, was a sizeable sum of money. It would pay for the badly needed repairs to the roof and fabric of the tower block. At least she supposed they were badly needed. Joseph said so. She had not been there for years.

'The Book says stop, miss, the Book . . .'

Meg hesitated. If the stars were against her buying at this price then she'd never have any luck with Admiral of the Blue, that was for sure. 'Oh, well, if that's the case . . .'

'It is, miss, it is. I assure you.'

'I'm selling once. I'm selling twice—' The hammer came down with a bang. 'Sold at thirty thousand. Mr Paul Cantrey.'

Meg stood up shedding her belongings about her, walked to the gangway and left the ring. Despite the fact that common sense reinforced by the book told her the price was too high and she'd never have any luck had she gone on and bought, she was smarting over her defeat.

Outside several people came up to commiserate with her.

'That's the hell of a price for a gelding,' one of them said. 'Who was Cantrey buying for?'

'It must be Martin Barkley. He was sitting with him,' another answered.

This pin-pointing of Martin as the buyer combined with expressions of sympathy which she did not want added fuel to Meg's fury. She never liked being beaten and the more she thought about it the more her resentment was focussed on the man who had beaten her, especially since she now realised she considered him both a newcomer and a nincompoop. 'Martin Barkley,' she declared in tones that carried to the furthest confines of the paddocks. 'What's he doing here anyway? He'd be better employed at home putting an end to his wife's goings-on.'

Martin had also left the sales ring after his successful bid. The old fool of a woman had made him pay ten thousand pounds more than he had intended. He saw the group around her and hesitated on its fringes debating whether politeness required him to speak to her and express the hope that she was not too disappointed. Hearing the remark, as he could not fail to do, he turned on his heel and walked away, the taste of victory sour in his mouth and a cold bitter rage welling up inside him.

Joseph had remained in the ring gathering up Meg's belongings which were strewn around her seat. This done he watched one or two more lots go through the ring. As he did so he turned over the pages of the catalogue to see what would be coming up in the immediate future. Suddenly his attention concentrated on one entry. He read the details carefully, then, putting the opened catalogue on the seat beside him, referred to the form book. After that he consulted the Book of Stars. When he had finished with the omens, he looked at the indicator which showed the number of the lot then passing through the ring. On seeing this he bolted up the gangway and out into the sales paddocks looking for his mistress.

Catching sight of her he brandished the catalogue. 'Miss, miss,' he said. 'I've found a horse for you.'

'What is it?' Meg asked testily. 'You've just lost me one. Haven't you done enough?'

'He shouldn't be dear, miss. He's an eleven year old.'

'Eleven? Don't be ridiculous. He's as old as I am.'

'Eleven year olds win Nationals nowadays, miss. I've looked him up. He ran last year.'

'Well, what did he do?' Despite herself Meg began to be interested.

'Fell, miss. Baulked at the twelfth, the form book says. His name is right and the Book says he must be your lucky horse.'

'What *is* his name?'

'Starflight, miss.'

Twenty minutes later Meg was the owner of a chestnut gelding, eleven years old, Starflight, by Planetarium out of High Review, at the price of four thousand guineas.

Slightly abashed at his own temerity in buying him, Joseph coughed behind his hand. 'He's in training, miss,' he said. 'What do you wish done with him?'

They were standing in Starflight's box looking at him. Truth to tell Meg did not much like what she saw. To her eye Starflight was an angular brute with indifferent hocks and a badly set-on head. She had not given any thought at all to what she would do with him if she got him. Joseph was quite right, since he was in training she could not take him home. She could, she

221

supposed, leave him where he was. His pbesent trainer had a small string somewhere near Nottingham, but she knew nothing of him and the idea did not appeal to her. There was, of course, always Arthur if he would have him. But Arthur might well refuse. She recollected only too clearly their difference of opinion over the riding of the young hurdler. She had been worsted in that one. She was in no mood to risk another rebuff from Arthur, especially since he had been proved right about the hurdler whom he was now talking about for the Sun Alliance Hurdle at Cheltenham. Arthur was altogether too independent. It was entirely possible that he might laugh at both the horse and her. Suddenly she made up her mind. 'Send him to young Mr Bragdon,' she said. 'He's shown he can ruin a good horse. We'll see what he can do with a bad one.'

15

NATIONAL CANDIDATES ON VIEW AT WRAYFIELD
was the headline over the racing page of the *Daily Post* a week
later, and Myles Aylward, along with all the other major racing
correspondents, was there to see them perform.

Wrayfield Park was part of a new sports complex financed by
a syndicate of businessmen of whom Julius Marker was the
principal. The racecourse had been built in the park and land-
scaped into it. The mansion itself was a vast Palladian affair
whose last owner had been quite unable to maintain it.
Regarded as one of Hawksmoor's masterpieces, however, it
had been scheduled as a national monument. The syndicate
had restored and preserved the fabric, turning the main block
into a club-house, one wing into offices and the other into
changing rooms, saunas, squash courts and other appurten-
ances of modern leisure. Besides the racecourse there was an
Olympic swimming pool, a covered riding school, a show jumping arena and a golf course which approached championship
standards.

Rather to everyone's surprise save that of Julius, who had
costed the enterprise with some accuracy and decided that the
odds were in its favour, the venture had been a success. The
racecourse itself had two tracks, named for the sake of tradition
the old and the new courses. At Julius's insistence the old
course had been built so that three of the fences had drops on
the landing side, thus giving races there after Christmas or in
early spring claims to be called useful National trials. The pub-
licising of them as such trials had been greatly helped by the
fact that in the few years since the course had started these races
had provided one National winner and two placed horses.

Julius had sunk a considerable amount of money into Wrayfield Park. He was well aware that dividends in hard cash would be slow in coming but he calculated, rightly, that the intangible profit accruing to him could be far greater than any monetary one.

At a time when local authorities were looking hungrily at under-developed land occupied by racecourses near big towns, and property magnates planning take-overs were also casting eager eyes on them, the Jockey Club and other racing authorities were anxious to see courses securely held in hands that would preserve them for the sport. They also welcomed Julius's plan for making the racecourse part of a great sports complex so that criticism of wasteful use of land or of exclusiveness could be answered immediately.

Julius also took the opportunity of sponsoring a valuable race and providing a handsome trophy with additional prizes for everyone concerned from the winner down to the lad who did him and his breeder.

All this, Julius felt, could not fail to increase his standing with those in positions of power in the Jockey Club and further his ambition to be elected a member. He was made a steward of the meeting from its inception and, since he was far from ignorant about horses and racing, he performed his duties with sense and tact. This, as he intended, had not gone unnoticed.

Julius had a genuine passion for horses and racing. When dealing with either of them he was quite a different person from the hard and often brutal taskmaster of his business or family affairs. He longed to be known and recognised as a sportsman, and to be accepted as one by those whom Martin Barkley regarded as shellbacks. Where Martin rejected the ethos of those men, Julius accepted it wholeheartedly and now that the sands of his life were beginning to run out he coveted above all things the little silver badge with the words JOCKEY CLUB stamped on it, the possession of which would mark his acceptance into the ranks of the racing élite.

Thanks to Julius's acumen and attention to detail everything had been well planned at Wrayfield. He had brought over one of the best French racing architects to design the stands, and the general paddock lay-out. All these, therefore, were up to the minute, well-sited, comfortable and attractive to racegoers, whether for the flat or steeplechasing, and blended well with

224

the beauty of the park. Julius had also had the good sense and strength of will to resist, and persuade his fellow-directors to resist, the temptation to open the course to the public before everything was absolutely ready. Thus he had avoided the adverse criticism and comment that have come to many courses who have encountered teething troubles by unveiling their improvements too soon in the hope of a quick and early return on their money.

The car-parks, too, were well-placed, and it was in one of these that Myles sat that clear January afternoon eating his sandwiches, drinking his coffee and studying the form in *Sporting Life*.

The Julius Marker National Trial Stakes of three and a half miles was the chief race on the card. It was natural and inevitable that Alexander should be entered in it but so was Admiral of the Blue, Martin Barkley's recent expensive acquisition. In it also was a National outsider called Peter's Pence but Myles disregarded his chances and, in common with most of the other correspondents, made it a race between Alexander and Admiral of the Blue.

Myles had, of course, heard all about the excitement at Doncaster over the purchase of Admiral of the Blue. He was, however, interested to see that Meg's later purchase, Starflight, was down to run in an earlier two and a half mile chase and that Pat Colby's name appeared as his rider.

Alastair Bragdon would of course have taken over Starflight with his engagements. Even if he were aiming him at the National – and, since he was now Meg's property, Myles assumed that this must be Starflight's objective – it was not all that unusual to run him over two and a half miles instead of the longer distance. Short runners on park courses had been known to win the National before now. This race would, too, keep him away from the cracks, give Meg an opportunity to have a bet if she wanted one, and tell Alastair how he coped with the drops.

Myles checked his racecard to see that the extra blank pages for his notes were safely clipped into it, then he picked up his raceglasses and opened the door of his car.

The glasses were a new pair, a fact which he resented, for like most constant racegoers he regarded his raceglasses as an old friend worn into his ways and the focus of his eyes by constant usage. But his flat had been burgled a few nights before when he was out to dinner. This was, in fact, his second burglary, about par for the course in London these days, he supposed. The sense of outrage and intrusion of personal privacy which had come with the first had now vanished into a sort of distasteful acceptance of an unsavoury fact of modern life. After the previous visit he had seen to it that nothing much of value was left in the flat but he could hardly put his raceglasses in a bank. His three pairs had all been taken, later, he supposed, to adorn the shelves of some second-hand shop in East London. His locked filing cabinets, too, had been broken open, presumably in a search for valuables and just because they were locked. A gold wristwatch, bought long ago with the proceeds of the first set of racing articles he had sold to a glossy monthly and later reprinted in an American magazine, and which he had foolishly left beside his bed, had gone as well, but nothing else that he could see.

As he entered the course he met Arthur Malcolm. 'Yes,' Arthur said in answer to his query, 'I run one in the three mile chase. He has no chance against the top two. By the way, Myles, seeing you reminds me I should have done something about it but I've been so damn busy with all these runners after the thaw that I didn't. What happened about Henson? You said you'd found him.'

'We found him or rather Malvey did but we lost him again. He was living in Corby, a little village in the dales, under an assumed name, helping in a sort of riding and trekking school.'

'How the devil did you manage that?'

'Malvey went down to Clayhampton and asked questions. Then he went on digging. That's what they do, these chaps—they keep on digging. Don't ask me how they dig because I don't know a lot about it and what I do know I don't much like. Anyway they've lost him.'

'Lost him?'

'He's scarpered. He told his landlady he'd won a prize in the pools and was going on a holiday to Spain.'

'That's a bit odd, isn't it?'

'Jim Malvey thinks so. He's still digging. What is all this about, Arthur? Has it anything to do with the stud?'

Arthur hesitated. 'I suppose I should tell you. In a way its only supposition. However . . .' Very quickly Arthur recounted to Myles what he had already told his wife about his

226

speculations concerning Malifico and Burglar Alarm.

Myles whistled. 'That makes a nice nest of robins, doesn't it?' he said.

'It does indeed,' Arthur said grimly. 'And I'm worried about David being there. And here's more trouble. Look who's arriving now.'

They both turned to see Meg's Daimler making its stately way into the Members' Car Park.

'If she's got those damn boots of hers on I'm sorry for young Bragdon,' Arthur said. 'She's having a bad year.'

'I hear she was in good voice at Doncaster. She didn't send you that horse she did buy in the end?'

'No, and to tell the truth I'm not a bit sorry. He's running today, I see.'

'And she has Colby riding him.'

'Everyone wants Colby now. I must go and do my declarations. I'll see you later, Myles.' Arthur made his way towards the weighing-room.

Everyone did indeed want Colby now and Alastair had thought himself lucky to have got him. He had not been able to get in touch with Starflight's former trainer to find out anything about him but rather to his surprise the horse had worked much better than he had expected. The two and a half mile race at Wrayfield looked pretty moderate and Alastair began to think that Starflight could well have some sort of chance in it. Under cross-examination from his aunt on the telephone he had been misguided enough to tell her this and that he hoped to engage Daddy Rendall to ride him. The mention of Daddy's name had been rewarded by a screech of rage from the other end of the telephone and he had been directed in no uncertain terms to obtain Pat Colby's services for the horse and to make no mistake about it.

Pat had to be at Wrayfield anyway to ride Alexander. He was both piqued and annoyed that Chris had given the ride on a young hurdler in a later race to Steve Barrett who did him and he had no ride in the earlier chase. Looking at the entries when Alastair had rung him he had decided that it was unlikely he would be offered any other mount in it, and he had taken the ride on Starflight. Spurred on by a favourable report from the Book of Stars Meg had buttoned on her betting boots and came south in the Daimler, full of hope, enthusiasm and coffee laced

227

with rum.

'Now then, young man,' she said to Pat as they stood together in the parade ring before the race. 'I want you to win this for me.'

'Yes, ma'am,' Pat said, and smiled his little boy's smile. He was really rather good with old ladies, he thought. By and large they weren't much different from the other sort and he was really rather good with them, too.

Looking at him, Meg suddenly thought how much he reminded her of that other cavalier of her long past youth, Blaise Calverley whose bones had been bleaching the Western Desert for thirty years or more. He had the same boyish good looks, the same reckless shift of his head and the same quick, infinitely appealing smile. 'You must, you know,' she said. 'I've had a bet.'

Pat smiled at her again and old Meg, what with the excitement a runner always engendered in her and the total recall of long-past days and delights brought on by this boy, for an instant felt the racecourse swim and sway about her. All at once she was back forty years ago when she had stood beside Blaise at just such a moment as this, waiting for him to get up and go out and win her race for her.

Pat was on top of the world. He felt he had everything going for him. He was firmly convinced he would lead the jockeys' table when the season ended. He also had, he knew, a good chance of winning the both Gold Cup and the National in the same year on Pirate Gold and Alexander. The effect of the almighty rollicking that Chris had given him coming back from the court had stayed with him only for a day or so. After that, success and his own resilient spirit had banished it from his mind. For were there not available for the picking all the delights of life % excitement, adoration, public acclaim and, best of all perhaps, Miriam Barkley for his bed? He shifted a little on his feet. She was sure-fire all right; in fact she was all but enough for him, no wonder that old bugger Barkley looked a bit shaky at times.

There were only two small clouds hanging over Pat's satisfaction with things as they were. The first was that Evelyn Marker had not yet been to bed with him. Sexually this did not matter very much at the moment since Miriam was just about all he could manage with his other preoccupations, and the real

228

attack on Evelyn could wait until later. But, like many another successful swordsman, he felt it an insult to his virility that any woman upon whom he cast a favourable eye should not clamour to climb between the sheets with him. In fact he could not understand it and he had made the mistake, though he did not recognise it as such, of telling her so. When she had looked at him in that way of hers and laughed, he had been furious. But not so furious that he had abandoned their friendship. He was determined to conquer her but, quite apart from this, she was good company, and also she was a known personality with whom it flattered him to be seen about, and she was generous with her money.

Money – that was the other problem. He could never keep money however much he made. A hell of a lot of the stuff seemed to be coming his way now but as quickly as it came it went. That law case, with solicitor's and barrister's fees and the fine on top, had cost a bomb. He had always betted but recently because he was running short he had increased his stake and, as often happens when a constant better does this, he had struck a run of bad luck. He was not going to back this horse, though, whatever the old biddy of an owner who was beaming at him said. He was sure Tim Hanway would win it and he had had a goodish bet on him.

During this time Alastair was retailing his riding instructions. Alastair was one of those trainers who cannot refrain from issuing in the parade ring long, detailed and involved orders and advice as to how their horses should be ridden. Pat, whose private opinion was that Alastair could not train creeper to climb up a wall, paid no attention to him at all.

'Now is all that quite clear?' Alastair asked him.

'Absolutely,' Pat answered, having heard none of it save that Alastair considered the horse had worked at home much better than he had expected. If I were to carry out that lot, he thought, I'd need someone sitting behind me with a tape-recorder telling me what to do.

'Remember, now, I have had a bet, young man,' Meg said as he was put up. He touched his cap with his whip in a brief gesture and smiled at her again. He was quite happy. He'd get round, collect his riding fee and next time he'd win the big race on Alexander. That would please Chris and put him back in his good graces. Since the law case Chris had been giving more rides to young Steve Barrett, Pat had noticed, and he did not much like it.

Strictly speaking he could have protested about this since he held the first retainer, but he had just sense enough not to provoke a showdown with Chris at this stage of the season, what with Cheltenham and Aintree approaching and the many good rides coming at both places from Chris's powerful stable. Anyway he'd win on Alexander and all would be well. For once he was not really concentrating on the race ahead which he looked upon as a mere ride round. As he passed Miriam standing by the rail of the parade ring he gave her his infectious grin.

Beside Miriam, Martin saw that grin. It hit him like a blow in the stomach, shattering the slender illusion of security he had tried to build around him.

There were ten runners in the two and a half mile chase and two of them fell early. The course at Wrayfield Park is oval and left-handed. The last two jumps are plain fences and there is a slightly uphill finish of two furlongs. Designed as it had been by the most experienced of modern experts the view is excellent and everything can be seen from the stands. It was, too, a bright, clear January day with no fog or mist to obscure the view.

At the end of the first circuit Pat realised that Starflight was going far better than he had expected, and something of what Alastair had said in the ring about him working well came back to him. At the turn for home he was lying fifth and seemed full of running. But Tim Hanway's mount was a length or so in front of him, and Tim was sitting there with a double handful, just lobbing along. He was, too, a class above the rest of them. He had the winning of it all sewn up, Pat reckoned.

Landing over the third last, just after the turn, Pat was sure he could be placed. He was also convinced, now, that Starflight was going to win a race and quite soon, but not this one.

Starflight touched the top of the second last and made a slight mistake. It did not stop him but it gave Pat the opportunity he wanted. 'Next time,' he said to himself. 'Next time, old girl, and then we both can have a bet.' He dropped Starflight in behind two horses. Tim Hanway had by this time gone on.

Over the last Pat took out his whip and swung it. He gave the appearance of riding energetically home but he was not touching his horse. He finished fourth. He thought he had been rather clever. He did not realise that a pair of hot and jealous eyes had been following from the start every move he made.

Martin had watched the race with Paul Cantrey, having deliberately separated himself from Miriam in the crowd, for he did not want her beside him at that point. 'What did you think of young Bragdon's runner, Starflight?' he asked Cantrey.

'Didn't notice him much. I was watching my own. Now that you mention it he didn't seem all that busy.'

'Just what I thought too. They'll have to do something about it.' Martin went in search of someone in authority.

Meg came down from the stand with fury in her heart. Accompanied by Alastair she strode across the ring to where Pat was unsaddling Starflight. He looked up as she approached and gave her his most winning smile.

'I told you to win this race, young man,' Meg said.

'I'm sorry, ma'am,' he said. 'He hit the second last and it knocked the stuffing out of him.'

Meg, who had after all been racing since she was a girl and who was no fool when it came to reading a race, looked sternly at him. 'Tell me no tarradiddles, young man,' she said to him. 'That mistake didn't stop him. 'You stop . . .'

Alastair grabbed her arm. 'Aunt Meg, Aunt Meg,' he said. 'You're getting over-excited. Please, Aunt Meg . . .' It is one thing to think your jockey has been up to no good with your horse but quite another to tell him so at the top of your voice in the paddock and in the hearing of anyone who cares to listen.

Meg closed her mouth. Quite suddenly, Alastair noticed, she looked very old and very vulnerable. He wondered what could have happened. 'All right, boy,' she said to Pat. 'Go away and don't ever come near one of my horses again.' Opening her handbag she extracted from it an enormous handkerchief about the size of a small towel and took some time blowing her nose.

'Are you feeling bad, Aunt Meg?' Alastair asked. 'Your heart?'

'I'm quite well. It's just he reminded me of someone long ago, that's all.' She made her way slowly to one of the seats by the ring and sat down. 'Go and get me a brandy,' she commanded Alastair. 'And fetch Joseph. Tell him we're going home.'

When he left the stand Martin went in immediate search of a

231

stewards' secretary. As it happened the same young man whom he had sent with the message to Arthur some time back was on duty. At an important meeting such as this it is customary to have more than one stewards' secretary. But Wrayfield that day clashed with another meeting and two of the senior men were in bed with 'flu, so Mark Raynham was officiating alone. Martin met him as he left the stewards' stand and took him to one side. 'Did you see that?' he asked.

Mark's heart sank. Here was trouble.

'Er, just what did you mean, sir?' he said, backing slightly away.

'Mean? I mean Colby's riding in that race, of course. What else? He could certainly have been placed. I sincerely trust the stewards are having him in.'

'I don't think I heard them saying anything about it . . .'

'If they won't take action I shall have to see to it myself that something is done.'

'Perhaps you'd just wait a moment, sir,' Mark Raynham said and bolted for the stewards' room.

The stewards' room at Wrayfield was airy and comfortable, unlike the poky desolate cubicles that did duty on some country courses. Julius had seen to that. There was a carpet on the floor, a fireplace with a blazing fire in it, and deep chairs for comfort when the stewards were not actually at work. A video-screen stood in one corner with the equipment for running the tape beside it. In the centre of the room was a table for enquiries covered with green baize and with sheets of paper laid out on it in front of the stewards' placings. On one wall facing the windows was a row of pegs for the stewards' coats and hats. The names of the acting stewards of the day were typed on cards and slotted into keepers beneath these pegs. Off the main room was another, smaller one containing a bar, behind which was stored almost every conceivable drink a tired or thirsty steward could want on a winter day. Julius was nothing if not thorough.

The chairman of the stewards that day was Colonel Roicey. With him were George Spanner, a merchant banker who had been an amateur rider of some distinction in his time, and Julius Marker.

Colonel Roicey was warming his bottom in front of the fire and looking at the blank face of the video-screen when Mark came in. 'Where have you been?' he barked testily at Mark's entrance. 'We were waiting for you to run the picture.'

'I've been with Mr Barkley, sir. He's worried about Colby's riding in that race. I think he wants you to have him in.'

'Does he, indeed! Anyone else have any ideas on that point?' The chairman had no very high opinion of Martin Barkley's knowledge of racing. Martin, outside, consulting his racecard as to who the local stewards were, remembered his last encounter with Roicey, and it made him all the more determined that something should be done.

'He didn't seem to be doing very much, I must say,' George Spanner said.

'Very well. Let's have the picture.'

The curtains were drawn, the spools on the recorder spun and the race came suddenly to life and colour on the screen.

The three men sat forward and watched intently. The young secretary picked up the long pointer, indicated the various horses in the race and murmured a muted commentary. 'That's Colby in the white cap and sheepskin noseband .... the winner is there in red and black . . .'

They ran it twice and then sat back in their chairs.

'Doesn't look too good,' Colonel Roicey said.

'He did make that mistake,' Julius put in.

George Spanner extinguished a cigarette. 'It wasn't enough to stop him in my opinion,' he said. 'I don't think he could have won but he might have been placed. What was the betting?' He looked at Mark Raynham.

The secretary consulted the back of his racecard. For a moment he frowned over his hurried notes, struggling to make them out. Then: 'Started second favourite,' he said. 'He came in from sixes to fours.'

'That was old Meg's money you may be sure,' Colonel Roicey remarked. 'She'd better burn those boots.' He sighed. All he had wanted was peace and an easy afternoon. No one would have taken any notice of a little incident like this in his day. 'Better have them both in. Young Bragdon, too, to find out what his instructions were.'

'I wonder,' Julius said suddenly, 'if it's proper for me to sit. Colby's riding for me in the next.'

The chairman grunted. 'Of course you must sit, Julius,' he said. 'If every steward stood down just because the jockey rode for him we'd never have a panel at all. I appreciate your attitude, though. Bring them in, Raynham, please.'

The three men took their places at the table, Colonel Roicey in the middle, Julius and George Spanner on either side.

A moment or two later there was a knock on the door and Mark Raynham came in. 'Mr Bragdon and Colby are here now, sir,' he said.

Alastair Bragdon and Pat filed in and stood side by side in front of the green baize-covered table.

'Now,' Colonel Roicey said, clearing his throat. 'We're enquiring into the running and riding of—what's the horse's name?'

'Starflight, sir,' Raynham said.

'Of Starflight in the second race. Especially the riding, your riding, Colby. The stewards think you might have been placed, didn't make sufficient effort, in fact.' Colonel Roicey stared, probably more belligerently than he intended, at the young man who was destroying the even tenor of his afternoon.

Pat felt a rare tremor of unease run through him. He was up against reality here and no mistake and what was more the old boy looked remarkably tough. This was no susceptible chair-women to yield to his little-boy blandishments. By now he had convinced himself that he had done everything possible on the horse to have him placed and was running through in his head the arguments he could put forward to make the stewards share that conviction. He wondered if old Marker would be on his side but a rapid glance in that direction did little for these hopes since old Marker's features were set and grim.

'Well, Mr Bragdon,' the chairman was saying. 'What were your instructions?'

God, thought Alastair, what *were* my instructions? He knew he had said a lot but he could not remember just what he had said. And he was flustered. He did not understand why he should have been brought in. When he had asked Raynham why they wanted him, Raynham had replied that the stewards would tell him that. Did they think he had told Colby to stop the horse? And what was Aunt Meg going to say when she heard about this? He ran his tongue across his lips. 'I'd just got the horse,' he began nervously, 'I didn't know much about him. I thought he must be pretty moderate but he worked better than I expected . . .'

'We don't want the horse's history. What did you tell Colby?'

'I told him . . . I told him . . .' Alastair hesitated, making things worse for himself. He'd given Colby all sorts of instructions but the trouble was he could not remember just what they were. 'I told him I didn't know much about the horse but to win if he could,' he said at last in desperation.

'Was that all?'

Pat, observing his trainer's confusion, was beginning to regain much of his confidence, which took a considerable amount to shake in any event. He might get out of this if he could put the blame on Alastair. 'He told me not to be too hard on him, sir,' he said.

'Wait until you're asked before you speak. However, did you say that?'

Alastair was by now hopelessly confused. He hesitated again. 'I don't believe I did,' he said at length. 'No. I'm sure I didn't.'

'Humph. Now, Colby, what have you to say?'

Pat assumed his most innocent expression. 'He hit the second last, sir, and it knocked the stuffing out of him.'

'It didn't look much of a mistake to me,' George Spanner told him. 'You know you're obliged to ride your horse out for a place?'

'Oh, yes, sir. But I did. I always do. As soon as I had him going again I took out my whip.'

'You say you hit him?'

'Yes, sir, and he was hanging to the left after that mistake. I had a job keeping him straight.'

'I see. It didn't seem very much like that to me, Colby.'

The chairman coughed. 'Any more questions, gentlemen? No? Let's have the picture then.'

Again the room was darkened and the race appeared once more on the screen Mark Raynham took up the pointer.

'Take particular notice from the second last fence if you please,' Colonel Roicey said.

'There is the mistake,' the secretary's baton tapped the screen as it picked up Starflight. 'If you watch Starflight now, you'll see just what occurred. He's in the noseband.' As they landed over the last the horse unquestionably began to drift to the left behind two others. Colby could also be seen to take out his whip and begin to swing it. Then the horses were past the post and pulling up. The lights went on again.

'You say horse was hanging to the left?' George Spanner asked Pat.

'Yes, sir.'

'If that is the case why had you your whip in the right hand?'

'He swung so suddenly I hadn't time to change.'

'It looks to me as if you were only swinging your whip, not hitting him.'

'Oh, no, sir, I was hitting him. I was doing my best, sir.'

'You say you were told not to be too hard on him,' Colonel Roicey said.

'Yes, sir, but of course, sir, I would always try to be placed.'

'Very commendable, I'm sure,' the chairman said. 'Any more questions? No? Then wait outside, please.'

Trainer and jockey filed out and the door shut behind them.

'Now then, what do we do with them?' Colonel Roicey asked.

'He dropped him out. I haven't any doubt about that at all,' George Spanner said. 'And I don't believe he really hit him either.'

'Could he have been hanging?' Julius asked. 'They neither of them knew anything about the horse. Or that's what they say.'

'I expect that part of it's true. He's only just gone to Bragdon since last Doncaster sales.'

'Bragdon is a fool,' Colonel Roicey said. 'He doesn't know how to give instructions. I've heard he practically preaches a sermon at his jockeys. I suppose it's just possible he said not to be too hard on him, though personally I doubt it. But I agree with you, George. The horse wasn't hanging and what is more he made no real effort.'

'Barkely will want us to send him on to the Stewards of the Jockey Club.'

'It's that wife of his. She's the original jockey's mattress from all I hear, and she's making a set at Colby. I can't see why we should allow Barkley's private affairs to influence our decision.'

'Of course not. And we'd have had him in anyway once we'd seen the picture.'

Colonel Roicey turned to Julius. 'What do you think about sending him on, Julius?'

'Here is how I see it. I'm looking at it from a business point of view, but that's in a way what I'm here for. You two know the racing end of it. I don't know much about that.'

'You can read a race as well as the next fellow. But go on,

Julius.'

Julius purred slightly at the compliment. Things were going well. 'If we send him on they may take his licence away. If Barkley has anything to do with it, they will, and he's on the disciplinary committee. That means the loss of his livelihood. It seems to me much too severe.'

'I agree,' George Spanner said. 'I don't think he could have won. It's not a case of flagrant stopping. In a way it's a minor infringement.'

'But one which those gentlemen in Portman Square are getting very worked up about,' Colonel Roicey said. 'However . . .'

At that moment there was a knock on the door and Mark Raynham stood hesitating on the threshold. 'Excuse me, sir,' he said. 'I thought I should tell you. They're going out for the next race.'

'And I have a runner,' Julius said.

'We'll decide after this one, then. Thank you, Raynham.' The stewards made their way to the parade ring.

Pat had mounted Alexander and joined the file of runners circling the ring when Julius entered it and crossed to where Chris was standing.

For once in his life Pat Colby was worried. Beside Chris in the ring, waiting to be put up, he knew for the first time what suspense really meant. The stewards were taking the hell of a time making up their minds. Was this good or bad? He daren't ask Chris what he thought for Chris had glowered at him when he came in and then remained silent confining his riding instructions to the terse utterance: 'Don't hit the front too soon.'

If they sent him on Pat knew he was in dead trouble. That bastard Barkley was a member of the disciplinary committee and he'd make it hot for him, never fear. They might take his licence away and then what was he to do? How would he pay that bastard Buckner and the others he owed money to? Cheltenham and the National were coming up. He'd miss those rides. He might lose Miriam, too. Christ! Well, bugger her, she was the cause of it all and there were always other women. Why did that old bastard Barkley have to be so bloody uptight about his wife? He ought to be past it, now.

Pat knew he should be concentrating on the coming race but for once he found it all but impossible. He had too much in his

237

thoughts. What would the stewards do? They couldn't send him on for that —or could they? That George Spanner had ridden enough to know what he had been up to. Why the hell had he had to sit today? He might just have conned the others into believing him. Julius had never ridden at all and if old Roicey had it must have been back when Noah was a boy. Would old Marker stand by him? Perhaps he would if he won this race on Alexander.

By this time they were down at the start and he tried to collect his thoughts. He answered his name automatically to the starter's roll call and watched him move towards the rostrum. Then he brought the big horse into line as they were called up. Tim Hanway on Admiral of the Blue was on his left in the inside berth, his usual place if he could get it.

As he was being gradually brought to peak fitness for the National by Chris, Alexander was beginning to take a stronger hold. Pat could still place him as he wanted but it required more effort and jockeyship than had been required earlier in the season. Today after his long lay-off he was really anxious to get on with the job and Pat at first found it taking all his time to hold him and to obey Chris's injunction not to go to the front.

Approaching the fourth last Tim Hanway on Admiral of the Blue was in the lead. Arthur Malcolm's horse Bayview was beside Pat in second place but he was weakening. Pat thought he had better not let Admiral of the Blue get too far from him. He kicked on to close the gap. Alexander's response was electric. At the fence he stood back and jumped it with breathtaking speed, landing alongside Tim Hanway's girths. They galloped together towards the next.

The pundits looked like being right. It was developing into a two horse race between the cracks.

Out of the corner of his eye Pat could see Admiral of the Blue beside him. He was getting nine pounds from the other horse and he thought he was going the better. In fact Alexander was so full of running that now, Pat thought, was the time to go on. Then Chris's admonition not to hit the front too soon suddenly rang in his ears. Ordinarily he'd have ridden his own race and to hell with everyone including Chris, relying on his wits to explain why his tactics had differed from his instructions. But he remembered Chris's scowling face in the ring. With all his other troubles upon him he could not afford to fall out with

Chris at this juncture.

They were coming into the third fence from home now, going very fast indeed, with Alexander a fraction in front. He'd land a length ahead at this rate with no option but to go on, Pat thought. He pulled Alexander back, or tried to. It was a mistake. He unbalanced the big horse. Alexander hit the top of the fence with a crash. The third last was one of Julius's drop fences. Big and strong as he was Alexander might have got away with it but for that. With the ground disappearing beneath him he pitched forward on to his head. Pat suddenly saw nothing in front of him but empty air. He left the saddle and hit the ground, hard, with a sobbing curse on his lips. It was not his day.

Alexander, relieved of his weight, recovered and galloped on riderless. Admiral of the Blue won, pulling up by five lengths.

On the owners' and trainers' stand Julius lowered his glasses. 'Did he fall off?' he said to Chris with whom he had watched the race.

Whatever Chris said to his jockeys in private he was fiercely protective of them in public. 'No one could have stayed on,' he said. 'I hope to hell the horse is all right.' He was watching the riderless Alexander who had jumped the last fence by himself, then veered towards the rails. Deciding at the last moment not to jump he had then come galloping up the course. 'Ah, they've got him,' Chris said, relieved, and hurried from the stand.

Julius made his way towards the stewards' room. 'Bad luck,' George Spanner greeted him. 'He'd just about have won it.'

'That's racing, isn't it?'

'Perhaps. Good of you to take it that way, though.' Colonel Roicey was back in his accustomed position before the fire. 'We'd better make up our minds now what we are going to do with him. I suppose he's all right, is he?'

'Yes, sir,' Mark Raynham said from the door. 'He only came back in the ambulance for a lift. He's outside now. They both are.'

'Very well, gentlemen, are we agreed that we don't send him on? He's had a roughish day, today. It may teach him a lesson.'

'If it doesn't Chris will, if I know him,' George Spanner said. 'I agree, and I don't think we should suspend him, either.'

'Very well, then, a fine. It'll have to be enough to hurt. What would you say to a hundred pounds?'

'The maximum. It's a little high, I think. I would say seventy-five.'

'And you, Julius, apart from wanting to see him in perdition for losing your race for you?'

'I think seventy-five would meet the case. It's a little awkward for me . . .'

'Fiddlesticks, man, you're behaving very properly. If certain other people . . .' Colonel Roicey coughed. 'However, we'd better have them in.'

Once more Alastair and Pat stood arraigned before the stewards.

'Now then,' Colonel Roicey addressed them: 'We've discussed your case at some length, Colby. We find you did not make sufficient effort to be placed on, what is the name of the horse, yes, Starflight, in the second race. We therefore fine you seventy-five pounds. I may add that you should consider yourself very lucky we have not reported you to the Stewards of the Jockey Club. Very well, you may go.' When Pat had left, the senior steward turned to Alastair. 'Now, Mr Bragdon, the stewards are not at all satisfied with the adequacy of the instructions which you gave your jockey. Because of that we don't think you can be regarded as being completely blameless in this matter. We therefore warn you most severely that in future you must be more specific in your riding orders. Is that quite clear?'

'Nicely put, Dick, nicely put,' George Spanner said when Alastair had gone. 'Spoken like a Dutch uncle.'

'Thank you, George. I don't suppose Barkley will be pleased. And now, gentlemen, I think we've all earned a drink.'

In the press room Myles Aylward was wrestling with his conscience or, as he put it to himself, what was left of it after his years in the street. Against his inclinations he had written glowingly of Pat Colby earlier in the season because he felt he deserved it and that was what an unbiased man would write. Now he had both the opportunity and every justification for doing exactly the opposite. Pat had scarcely covered himself in glory that afternoon. In before the stewards for his riding of the second favourite in one race and falling off the favourite in another. With his usual luck the stewards had, too, in Myles's opinion, let him off bloody lightly. He wondered if Julius, leaning over backwards, had had anything to do with that. Julius,

240

he thought, was a strange mixture, savage in business and family matters, fair almost to a fault in sport. Of course that very fairness might be at least in part assumed in order to further his ambitions. In any case these thoughts were not helping him to write his piece. The fact that Pat had lost the race on Alexander, a horse in which Myles took an especial interest, did not make him any more disposed to kindness in what he wrote.

Pat Colby will not put down today's events at Wrayfield Park in red letters in his book of memories, he began. Then he paused and stared at the words, asking himself in his introspective way whether he was doing this because the events actually merited making it the lead story or because of his dislike for the jockey. As he did so he lifted his eyes from the page to see Hector Mallinson regarding him quizzically from across the table.

'Pat's nights of love have caught up with him at last,' Hector said. 'He fell off.' His cupid's bow mouth was moist with the satisfaction of seeing another human being in trouble.

'Did he fall off?' Myles was aware of the revulsion and desire to contradict the other man always caused in him. 'I thought that was a frightful mistake. No one could have stayed on.'

'You do defend the boys in the bright jerseys, don't you, Myles dear?' Mallinson said with malice in every syllable. 'You must have wanted to be one of them very badly. I've no such hang-ups, believe me. She's here, too, the gorgeous thing. And my spies tell me Barkley himself initiated that enquiry. It's all going to do me very nicely thank you for next Wednesday.' He sauntered from the room with a flick of his buttocks and the door closed behind him.

Myles tore the top sheet from his pad. Scrumpling it into a ball he threw it in the general direction of the wastebasket. Then he began again. Whether *Admiral of the Blue enhanced his prospects for Aintree at Wrayfield Park today is arguable*, he wrote, *for Alexander, normally a safe jumper from what we've seen of him, made a terrible hash of the second last and parted with his jockey. No one could have stayed on and Pat Colby did well to last as long as he did . . .*

When he had finished he decided to watch the last race from the car park so as to get early away. He was going to phone in his copy from a friend's house. If anything of vital importance happened in the last, which was unlikely, he could make the necessary addition there. As he left the course he met Steve Barrett, who was also off early, and they walked together towards their cars discussing the racing. At Myles's car they paused, and as they stood talking a man came up to them. He was wearing a long mackintosh, its collar turned up against the cold and a cap pulled down over his eyes. 'Mr Aylward?' he said.

'Yes,' Myles answered. 'What can I do for you?'

'I was told to give you this.' He pushed an envelope into Myles's hands and walked quickly away.

Myles looked at the envelope. It was a plain brown business type, thousands of which are used every day. There was no writing or address of any sort on it. 'That's an odd sort of thing,' he said to his companion. 'I wonder—' He broke off because Steve Barrett was staring fixedly at the retreating back of the man in the mackintosh.

'It's him,' he said excitedly. 'It's him! I know it is!'

'Who? What on earth?'

'The man on the moor. The man who flagged me down last year.'

'After him then. Come on!' Myles crammed the envelope into his pocket and began to run.

Turning, the man saw them. He dived between a line of cars and began to run himself.

They were hindered by their raceglasses and in Barrett's case his colour bag. He threw it down but the man gained on them.

'Go that way,' Myles panted to the jockey. 'Make for the entrance, try to head him off.' He himself followed the running figure as best he could. He saw him twist between another line of cars and then he lost him completely.

Myles ran towards the place he had last seen him. There was no one in sight when he got there. The fugitive had disappeared. None of the cars was moving so he was not making a getaway from anywhere near where Myles stood. He was either hiding in a car or had bent down below the line of sight and dodged away unseen. Myles swore. He went down a nearby line of cars looking into them and found nothing. It was hopeless. Disconsolately he began to make his way back to his own car. As he reached it he saw Steve Barrett running towards him.

'I lost him, I'm afraid,' he said as the jockey came up. 'Did you have any luck?'

'A bit, sir, I saw him getting into his car. It was parked just inside the entrance. I couldn't get up to him but I took his number.'

'Well done. Have you got it?'

'Here it is. I wrote it down.' He handed Myles the backsheet of the racecard on which the number was written. 'Can you trace him, sir?'

'I can't. But I know someone who will. That's if it isn't a stolen car. You're certain it was the same man?'

'Oh, yes, sir. I saw his face and that what do you call it on it.'

'Scar tissue. That's identification, anyway. Thanks, Steve. I'll get in touch with Mr Rokeby and tell him what's happening.'

Back in his car Myles remembered the envelope. He took it out of his pocket, put his thumb under the flap and opened it. There was only one enclosure. He slid it out and turned it over.

He was staring at the colour photograph he had taken that day, it seemed so long ago now, that they had bought Alexander from Barty Moriarty. It was of Evelyn, naked, laughing, breathtakingly lovely, coming out of the sea towards him.

16

'That ought to do the trick. Thank you, Sidney.'

The technician straightened up from Myles's phone, snapped his bag shut and left the flat. Jim Malvey took a cigarette packet from his pocket, opened it, muttered something about 'coffin nails' and put it back again. Then he turned to Myles. 'All you have to do,' he said, 'is to press that red tit. Then anyone who calls you is on the air. He's being recorded until you stop the works by pressing the green one. Got it?'

'It's simple enough if it works. You think they'll ring, not write?'

'They usually do. It's an even bet.' Malvey looked lugubriously at the black box beside the telephone. 'It seems to me that burglary was a sort of exploration. They struck lucky.'

'I was a bloody fool. I forgot all about the spool of film.' Myles had spent a restless night pondering his best course of action. It was obvious that the delivery of the photograph to him was some sort of threat and that there would be a follow-up. It was equally obvious that the photograph and the man who delivered it were connected and that the man had been involved in the assault on Steve Barrett. All this pointed directly to Larry Buckner being behind both. The only way of tracing the man lay through Malvey and his Private File organisation. Myles had been tempted to keep the subject of the photograph away from Malvey. His private life had always been his own and he wanted it to remain that way. Besides, he hated involving Evelyn, however marginally. Finally, though, he decided that this course was impossible and he had told Malvey the whole story.

Malvey had acted quickly. 'Everyone is a bloody fool

sometimes,' he said now, in answer to Myles. 'That's what we live on. I told you Buckner would make a mistake and a bloody silly one. Looks like he's done it.'

'By employing the same man who stopped Barrett on the moor to deliver the photograph?'

'That's it. And I'm willing to bet that car isn't stolen. He'll have used his own car either to fiddle his expenses or because he's just another amateur. We'll get him, never fear.'

'That reminds me, did you ever do anything further about Henson, the stud-groom at Clayhampton?'

'Not much. He went off to Benidorm or somewhere, didn't he? Is there anything in it?'

'There's more than I thought.' Quickly Myles recounted the story of Arthur's suspicions and deductions which he had heard at Wrayfield the previous day.

Malvey listened intently. When Myles had finished he rubbed his long nose. Then his nostrils twitched, rather, Myles thought, like a hound suddenly striking a scent. 'Systematic fraud,' he said. 'That'd be quite something to uncover. You say this stud is one of the most important in the country?'

'It was. It's running down.'

'Could there be a ring? Could the people there be in with others doing the same thing?'

'It's possible, I suppose. I never thought of that.'

'The bigger it is the better for us. The Men Who Ruin Our Bloodstock Industry sort of thing. It's worth another look, anyway. I'll have a word with Featherstone about it.'

'You'll have to find Henson first, won't you?'

'Perhaps. If we have to we'll do it. We find everyone from bank robbers to cabinet ministers on the run—if it's worth our while. And it might be. I'll tell you something—' he paused, frowning.

'What?'

'There's a wrong feeling about that place, Clayhampton. I could sort of smell something bent down there. It was all right on the surface but when I dug a bit there was fear about. Everyone was looking over their shoulders. Who did you say owns the place?'

'Lord Warminster. He's in Kenya now.'

'Another bloody refugee from bust and broke England. He's loaded, I suppose.'

'I've always heard so.'

Malvey belched, felt in his pocket, half withdrew the packet of cigarettes and then put it back again. Instead he took out a sheet of stomach pills, tore off one, put it in his mouth and began to chew. 'Bloody ulcer,' he said half to himself, and then went on to what Myles was beginning to realise was his favourite theme. 'I don't understand these people. I don't understand anything any more. Come to think of it I'm not dead sure I understand this business of your photograph yet. It's the permissive age or so we're told. Nude photographs aren't a smear any more. The best people's daughters are queuing up to get their full frontals on to centre-spreads.'

'That's not to say the best people themselves actually enjoy it.'

The telephone suddenly shrilled.

'Expecting that?' Malvey asked.

'No.'

'It might be our friend. Listen now, Myles, whatever happens, ask for time. He won't be wanting money. It'll be something else. So ask for time.'

A prickle of excitement running up his spine, Myles crossed the room and picked up the receiver. There was a pause. Myles looked at Malvey. 'He's calling from a box,' he said.

Malvey nodded. He took out a cigarette, and this time he put it in his mouth and lighted it. 'That's par for the course. It's him all right.'

Myles reached forward and pressed the red button. 'Mr Aylward?' The voice was as it had been described to him—late twentieth-century, classless and slightly highly pitched, whether from nerves, affectation or a desire to disguise, it was impossible to say.

'Yes. Who is it?'

'I have a message for you.'

'Who are you and what do you want?'

'It's quite simple. If the *Daily Post* do not stop their current sporting investigations an interesting photograph will be sent to Julius Marker.'

'Look—I'm only a racing reporter. How do you think I can stop them?'

'That's your problem. But my friends tell me there are plenty of ways you can. Think of them for yourself. And there's another thing.'

'What's that?'

'My friends say if you are in any doubt remember what happened to Steve Barrett.'

'I can't do this in a minute. You've got to give me time.'

There was a moment's hesitation at the end of the line. Then: 'Ten days to know you've made a start. We'll be back to you.' The line went dead. Myles pressed the green button. Then he sat down. His legs, he noticed, were distinctly shaky. He had just been threatened by the criminal world or the fringe of it and he did not care for the experience.

Malvey crossed to the box. He ran the tape back and pressed the 'play' switch. They listened in silence to the recorded conversation.

'Julius Marker,' Malvey said pensively. 'Owns all those horses. I've seen him racing. Tough-looking old cove. Maybe you're right and he isn't in the permissive age.'

'Where his daughter is concerned he isn't, believe me.'

'What about her?'

'Evelyn? She wouldn't give a damn or she'd pretend not to. But she isn't in this, Jim. They're enough people in it already.'

'Can he get at you?'

'Julius? He's ruthless where his own are concerned. I don't know how, but he'd find some way. He's a friend of the old Lord's. He might get my job.'

'Friend of the old Lord, is he? I didn't know that. Then he might get your job. The old Lord is rather that way himself. Francies himself as a guardian of the old morality bit. What's more he's been known to kill stories before. But Featherstone won't haul off until he has to. You're in a spot.'

'But why get at me?'

Malvey regarded him quizzically. 'Because you're in racing and they're in racing,' he said. 'I've been with you people now long enough to know that you insiders think no one knows racing but yourselves. And let me tell you something else . . .' Malvey pointed a long, prehensile finger towards Myles.

'What?'

'Mr Larry Buckner can't see beyond the end of his nose. Like I said before he's an amateur. There's someone behind him using that amateurism to do his dirty work for him, and to shelter behind if Larry's caught. It's him I aim to get. But first catch the sprat.' Malvey picked up the tape, came over and dropped it in Myles's lap. 'Play that to young Barrett and Errington and see if they recognise the voice,' he said.

'And then?'

'Come back to me. And don't be too long. I'll have found the owner of the car by that time.'

'That's him! That's him! I'd know the voice anywhere,' Steve Barrett said excitedly as he listened to the tape.

'You're on record now for saying it,' Myles said, smiling, as he pressed the stop button. 'You're quite sure?'

'No doubts at all. I think I sort of noticed it when he spoke to you at Wrayfield and that's what first put me on to him. You don't recognise him yourself, do you, sir?'

'No, I can't say I do. I was too surprised when he came up to pay much attention to how he spoke. Anyway that's another step in the right direction.'

'Have you found him yet?'

'No. But we will.'

They were sitting in Myles's car at the car park at Lingfield. Myles had arranged to meet Steve before racing and to play him the tape. Earlier that morning as he was preparing to leave he had telephoned Malvey to find out how the hunt was going. They had, Malvey said, got a name for the owner of the car and an address. The owner had moved from the address but they had got another lead which they were following up. It was only a question of time, now, he added.

When Steve had gone Myles sat on in the car. He had a busy day in front of him. The National weights had come out the day before. Both Arthur and Chris had runners at Lingfield and he wanted to discuss their reactions to the weights given to Watchmaker and Alexander. Watchmaker, in fact, was running today in the Manifesto Chase. Rob Roy, predictably enough, had been given the full penalty of twelve stone in the National. Chris had tried to ring Val Errington the night before both for a comment on this and to try to fix a time for running the tape for him. The trainer had not been available and, since he did not have a runner at Lingfield, both these things would have to wait.

Myles, at this juncture, was jumpy and he knew it. He hated the threat to his future implied in the blackmail over the photograph, for Malvey's remarks about the old Lord had convinced him that this could well be a real one. The prospect of physical

248

violence to himself, so easy to effect in the London of today as he well knew, was not an inviting one either, and he was worried sick about the trouble he might be bringing on Evelyn. He had lunched with Evelyn at the Ritz a day or so back and it had not gone well. The thought of the photograph uppermost in his mind, Myles had sounded her on her relations with Julius.

'No. I haven't seen the old monster and I don't want to,' she said in answer to his question, looking out of the tall window at the bare trees in Green Park.

'Why don't you try an approach yourself?' Myles said.

'Why?' she flared at him. 'Why? I'll tell you why. Because he doesn't give a damn about me and never has.'

'I think he does.'

'You're taking his side.'

Myles sighed. 'I'm not taking any sides,' he said. 'It just seems to me that perhaps you're both too alike, too proud, I suppose. If one of you gave an inch—'

'Well, it won't be me. And anyway he was bloody over that enquiry when they had Pat in and fined him. He did that because he didn't win with Alexander, I suppose.'

'You're wrong there. From all I hear Julius didn't want to sit on that enquiry. If you want to know who really started it all, it was Martin Barkley.'

'Oh.'

Their eyes met across the table and for once it was Evelyn who dropped hers first. Truth to tell she had not seen much of Pat lately. It was that Barkley bitch, she supposed, for she still had vivid recollections of the red Jensen whisking down the High Street after the court case. Julius had been right in a way when he surmised that the affair might have nearly run its course. But although Evelyn was never really sure just what her feelings for Pat were she did not like being either discarded or supplanted. In her book when it came to that it was she who took the first step. As a result of Myles's last remark Pat Colby was very much in her mind when she left him after lunch, went to the Arlington Street entrance and told the commissionaire to get her a taxi.

'I think we're in well enough,' was Arthur Malcolm's reply to Myles's question about the National weights. 'Ten stone, seven seems fair to me. You can say I'm satisfied.'

249

'You're running him today, I see.'

'Yes. I've been looking for a race for him since the thaw. I thought the class here might be too good but it's cut up a bit.' He was always open about his horses with those whom he liked and felt he could trust. 'He's well in here, too, and the ground .has come right for him. I think he must have a chance.' He chuckled then. 'If he does win it'll make no difference now. The weights are out.'

And, impeccably ridden by Daddy, he did win by a length and a half from one of Chris Rokeby's ridden by Pat. It was Pat's third second in five rides. Things seemed suddenly to have turned against him.

Chris's reaction to Myles's query about the National weights had been rather different from Arthur's. 'Eleven stone three, it's too fucking much!' he had exploded. 'Far too fucking much! Wait till I see that bloody handicapper.'

'It's a computer now, Chris.'

'Well, fuck the computer, then. Those bloody things can never get anything right. Not even my income tax demands.'

'I thought you were always one jump ahead of the tax man. How is Alexander?'

'He's bloody well in himself and that's enough from you, you miserable scribbler.'

But, as a matter of fact, Alexander was far from being bloody well in himself, and that was one of Chris's worries. Alexander had not worked well since he came home after the fall at Wrayfield, and Chris could find no reason for it. There was no trace of heat in his legs or joints, he had not the slightest sign of a temperature, he was eating up and his droppings were clear. It was one of those mysterious things that come to plague every trainer at times, but Chris could have wished it had happened at any other time and to any other horse. He now wanted to set about really preparing Alexander for the National, especially since his private opinion, unlike that 'so publicly and forceably expressed to Myles, was that the handicapper had not done too badly by him at all. Eleven three was a reasonable enough weight and a big horse like Alexander should shoulder it with ease. But only if he was right, which at that moment he was not. And Chris very much wanted to run him at Haydock in a fortnight's time to get his confidence back over the drops.

Chris's other worry was, of course, his jockey. He had driven back with Pat to the cottage after racing at Wrayfield. Going in with him, he had refused a drink and, as was his way, had come straight to the point. 'You're a bloody young fool,' he had said. 'I've warned you before. Give that woman up.'

Pat had attempted, rather feebly, to bluster. 'What do you mean?' he had said. 'And what right have you anyway . . .'

'You know damn well what I mean. If they'd sent you on you'd have been stood down. That could be you'd miss Cheltenham and Liverpool. And then, by God, I'd give *you* up.'

'You can't do that,' Pat said sulkily. 'I've got a retainer.'

'Can't I? Try me and see. Listen, my lad, everyone in racing knows you're banging that bitch. Barkley's a steward of the Jockey Club. He's on the disciplinary committee as well. Who'd give you rides if I throw you out? You think you're bloody good, don't you? I've seen better than you go right out of racing. They're forgotten in five minutes when they do. I can do what I like with you, and don't you forget it. If I say go, you'll go. And then you're out, finished, washed up. What'll you do— peddle vacuum cleaners?'

At that moment the telephone went and Pat picked it up. 'Pat,' the hucky, sexy voice at the other end, breathed into it. 'Pat, it's me, Miriam. I must see you.'

'No,' Pat said desperately. 'Not now. I can't talk, later . . .'

Chris reached over and plucked the receiver from Pat's hand. 'It's not Pat, Mrs Barkley,' he said. 'Pat won't be seeing you any more ever, Mrs Barkley.' And he slammed the receiver back on its rest.

They stood staring at each other for a moment after that, two angry men whose wills were clashing. Then Pat's eyes went involuntarily to where his bank sheets were strewn about on the floor and table. He had been looking through them before he left for racing and they did not make cheerful reading. Chris followed his glance and took in what he saw.

Because there was a kind core in Chris beneath all the toughness, because basically he liked Pat, admired his riding and divined in him something that could be saved and needed saving his voice softened and he said: 'Look, if you're in trouble with the books and want a loan I can help out.'

'I won't take your bloody money.'

'As you wish,' Chris said quietly. 'But sometime you may want it, and the offer won't remain open for ever. Just

251

remember what I said.'

But Chris had to admit that Pat had ridden a blinder on a moderate horse today against Watchmaker, even though he had been beaten. Chris knew better than the next man that the rider of the second, though he seldom gets the credit, has often ridden a better race than the winner. That didn't quite apply today for old man Rendall, Chris thought to himself, appeared to have taken a new lease of life and to be riding as if he were ten years younger. But still, to give weight to Watchmaker and only to be beaten a length and a half was something, Chris reckoned, for Watchmaker seemed to have improved too.

These sentiments were echoed by Daddy as he stripped the tack from the winner. 'He's coming good, just like we hoped,' he said to Arthur before hurrying into the weighing-room.

Daddy was anxious to get the formalities of weighing-in over as quickly as possible. He had no other ride that day and he wanted to get home. He had left Millie in tears and the boys terrified at the scene that had blown up between them. To this moment he could not say what had caused it. Seeing her put her hand to her side he had made some chance remark to her about her health and that, apparently, had touched off the storm. She had flown at him with a torrent of abuse, her voice high and shrill. This was utterly unlike Millie who, until very recently, however she felt about his racing, had always been quiet about it, suppressing her anxiety and accepting her lot. Now he had been subjected to a tirade about his selfishness in going on when he should have retired and his lack of sympathy with her throughout their married life. Every single sentence he had uttered during the last six months had, it seemed, been stored away in her mind and was now thrown back at him each one twisted to give it a meaning he had never intended.

On one thing Daddy was now quite determined and that was, when he returned home, to insist that she should see the doctor again and this time with him accompanying her.

Colonel Roicey met George Spanner as they were leaving the stand after the Manifesto Chase. 'Not working today, George?' he said.

'No. I'm not a steward here. That was a nice win for Arthur. He's having a good season though he told me at the beginning that his horses were very moderate.'

'Most of them are, but he's placed them well. He's no fool in

252

his own way, Arthur. That'll be his National horse, I suppose. He could go well in it.'

'So Barkley seems to think. I met him just now and he was muttering dark things about discrepancies in form.'

'What rubbish! What discrepancies? He beat that big horse of Rokeby's at Towcester in October, by a fluke or so I'm told. Rokeby's had spread a plate. Watchmaker ran well enough last time out to entitle him to win here. The man's becoming a nuisance.'

'He had some sort of run-in with Arthur at Cheltenham a while back, I believe. He doesn't forget, it seems.'

'Hm. Care for a drink, George?'

Over their whiskies in a secluded corner of the members' bar the two men resumed their conversation.

'It rather puzzles me,' George Spanner said, 'how Barkley ever got elected.'

'Blenkiron had a rush of liberalism to the head. Said it would show we weren't a self-perpetuating old-boy network or some such rubbish. It would please the press too, so he said, and demonstrate our broadmindedness. And Barkley was put about to be a great enthusiast and a tremendous worker, which he is, of course. His business brain would be a great help, so Blenkiron said. You know how it is, people don't like objecting—'

'If I'd known as much then as I do now I think I would have objected.'

'No one did. That's just the thing. Far better for the chap that's put up if we know too little about him rather than too much. He lay very low, too, after he was elected. Learning the job, I suppose. I must say he does know the rule book. And they tell me he was very good on that international committee thing. At least Blenkiron says so. Those were all the arguments he used when he put him in as steward. It's only since he was in that he's been showing his teeth. Anyway, George, that brings me to what I really wanted to talk to you about. Julius behaved very well at that enquiry.'

'I thought so. Good fellow, Julius, and he's always most helpful at Wrayfield.'

'He's always helpful everywhere. And his horses are run dead straight. I never heard a word against them, did you?'

'No, I didn't.'

'You know, I've given it a lot of thought. I think I'd like to put him up. Will you object?'

'Good Lord no. I'd support it.'

'Splendid. Have a talk with some of the others, will you, and sound out the ground. I'll do the same.'

'I shouldn't think there'll be any trouble, except possibly with these flat-racin' people.'

'I don't imagine so. Robert Warminster spoke quite warmly about him last summer.'

'Did he? He's abroad now, isn't he? Why doesn't he do something about Clayhampton. I don't think much of that chap Bradbury he has there, do you?'

'No. Clever fellow with horses, though, they tell me.' Colonel Roicey finished his whisky. 'Let's go and have a look at the Hunter Chase,' he said.

On their way to the ring they passed Tommy Pereira wearing his racing jersey and on his way to ride Cummerbund. Seeing them he gave a brief nod of recognition and passed on.

'Looks pretty green about the gills,' commented George Spanner.

'Not surprised. Don't care about the chap. Too much hair.'

'Rides like a tailor, too.'

'Trains on pot, they tell me.'

Tommy, in fact, was in the grip of nervous horrors and hating every minute of what he was doing. It was useless for him to tell himself that Cummerbund had never fallen, that he was far the safest jumper in the field and that he could ride him round in his own pace on the wide outside. The whole thing, he kept repeating over and over in his mind, was far safer than crossing Piccadilly in a hurry after lunch at his club. It didn't do him any good at all. Reason and sense had deserted him and nothing seemed to be able to still the shaking of his knees. When he glanced at the number board he saw that he was the only rider in the field who had lost the weight allowance given to those who have not ridden twenty-five winners. So far from reassuring him this made him, if anything, feel worse. Both George Spanner and Colonel Roicey might agree that he rode like a tailor but still he had had so many good horses of his own over the years since he began that twenty-seven winners had come his way. Looking about him he thought that all these inexperienced youngsters getting up with the light of enthusiasm in their faces would not

be able to keep their horses straight and would assuredly somehow contrive to knock him down.

At the start he kept to himself, determined to secure the outside if he could and plod round safely well out of danger. After
all, he consoled himself, if things got too bad he could always
pull up. He could do no one any harm by this. He was riding his
own horse and anyone sufficiently insane to have backed him
deserved no better reward.

Usually on these occasions he was accustomed to join heartily in such badinage and forced joking as went on while they
waited for the starter. Now he was silent and morose. 'What's
the matter, Tommy,' someone asked him. 'Sickening for something?'

'Could be,' he said slowly. 'Feels a bit like that, anyway.'

Then the tapes went up and they were off. All went well for
Tommy on the first circuit. No one tried to take the outside
from him. No one fell in front of him, and Cummerbund
jumped in his usual sedate and faultless way. In fact Cummerbund seemed to be enjoying himself and some of Tommy's
doubts and fears began to dissipate. At this rate he should at
least finish. There were a good many casualties amongst the enthusiastic young men. It was one of the early hunter chases and
this was to be expected. Also many of those that were left upright were making mistakes. At the second last fence in the
straight Tommy suddenly realised that he was lying third with
a good chance of winning.

All sorts of thoughts shot through Tommy's mind then. If he
won now surely he could hang up his boots with honour? He'd
go out with a win; no one could say he had lost his nerve or got
frightened and had chickened out of the National. Yes, by God,
if he won this he could go out at the top and leave behind forever
those sickening nerves that turned him into a jelly at the
thought of riding another race.

Tommy gave Cummerbund a kick and he responded immediately, forging past the second whose rider was rolling in
the saddle from exhaustion. He then began to close the gap between himself and the leader.

Had Tommy kept his head all might have been well. But,
excited beyond measure at the thought of putting an end to all
his nerves and fears, he proceeded to lose it. He was going to
win this race, by God he was. He kicked Cummerbund hard,

255

shook him up and, with the courage born of desperation, went at the last fence as if it was not there.

Up on the stand Colonel Roicey, looking through his glasses, growled under his breath: 'Sit still, you bloody young fool, sit still.'

Cummerbund was totally unaccustomed to the treatment he was suddenly and quite unexpectedly being subjected to. In all his races heretofore he had measured his fences and jumped them in his own way and in his own time without interference from the man on his back. Now he was thrown right out of his stride and, as a result, he met the fence all wrong. He did not fall. Cummerbund never fell, but he made a dreadful mistake. It was greatly to Tommy's credit that he did not come off. He shot up Cummerbund's neck. The horse was brought almost to a standstill and Tommy somehow scrambled back into the saddle. But he had lost all chance of winning. They galloped slowly past the winning post to finish fourth.

Coming in, Tommy passed a little group comprised of George Spanner, Arthur Malcolm and Colonel Roicey. They were eyeing him sagely and Tommy could just imagine what they were saying. Damn them anyway, he'd have to ride in the National now.

17

Exactly nine days later, Myles received an unexpected summons to see Featherstone. The sports editor was alone in his office when Myles came in. He looked, Myles thought, rather more shifty than usual.

'Sit down, Myles,' he said. 'That is if you can find anywhere with all this paper about. Heard anything from our friend, yet?'

Myles swept a bundle of galleys off the only chair and pulled it nearer the desk. 'No,' he said. 'And I have a feeling I won't until the full ten days are up.'

Featherstone took up a pencil and chewed the end of it meditatively. Then he pushed a box of cigarettes towards Myles. 'There have been some developments nevertheless,' he said. His eyes were wandering all around the room, Myles noticed, but they never seemed to meet his.

'Oh. What's been happening?'

Featherstone was now playing with a letter opener. He put it down and stood up. 'Time runs out tomorrow, doesn't it?' he said.

'Yes.'

'And I suppose they'll phone you.'

'I should imagine so.' Myles began to wonder where all this was leading and when Featherstone would come to the point.

'When they do,' Featherstone said suddenly and abruptly, 'tell them that you have done their job for them. We're closing down the investigation. It's all off. Kaput. Finish.'

'But—'

'Look, Myles. That's it. I can't say any more.'

Myles's first feeling, to his dismay, was one of relief.

Something of this must have shown on his face for Featherstone immediately went on: 'Aren't you pleased? Gets you off the hook, doesn't it?'

'It does that, all right. In a way, yes, I suppose I am pleased. But I don't like the thought of these bastards getting away with it. Racing is my life and this sort of thing isn't doing it any good. Wasn't Jim able to trace the chap?'

Featherstone made no direct answer and his eyes, as usual, went all over the room. 'Let's just say that the investigation has been closed down. That's as far as I can go with you at the moment, Myles. And, Myles—'

'Yes.'

'Stay close to the telephone all tomorrow, will you. We don't want you to miss him.'

'I'm supposed to be racing at Fontwell.'

'No problem. I'll arrange it with Vic.'

The call came through about six o'clock the following evening. Myles had spent the day alone in the flat writing up his notes, and catching up on his correspondence which entailed amongst other things turning down an offer from a publisher with a racing list to do a life of a leading trainer. He had done work for this firm before and had liked neither their editors nor their results. The terms, so his agent said, were fair but Myles wanted nothing further to do with them. Once again he thanked his stars for his financial independence and that he could afford to refuse the offer.

That brought his mind back to his pbesent position. It was indeed a stroke of luck that the investigation was being called off. Apart from the relief from physical danger, which was akin to that he had experienced all those years ago when the surgeon told him he could ride no more races and which he despised in himself, there was the possible loss of his job to be considered. Vic Ackroyd, who had been on the paper far longer than he had, had confirmed that one of his predecessors had left mysteriously and abruptly as a result, it was widely believed, of direct interference by the old Lord. He pondered again as to what could have happened to make them call it off and as he was doing so the telephone went. Pressing down the red button he picked up the receiver.

'Mr Aylward?'

'Yes.'

'Have you any news for us?' It was the same slightly high-pitched voice, classless, anonymous.

'I have,' Myles said flatly. 'The investigation is being called off.'

'What?' The voice seemed for a moment to come to life, to take on an expression of surprise. 'There will be nothing more done?'

'Nothing.'

'You seem to have managed very quickly. My friends say they hope this is genuine.'

'Of course it's genuine. What more do you expect me to do? And now what about my negative?'

There was a pause at the other end and then the voice came back. 'My friends say they always like to hold some collateral. They'll keep the negative just in case anyone gets ideas about changing his mind.'

'Why, you—' The line went dead and Myles was left staring at the receiver in his hand.

He did not spend a very restful night. He was far from being off the hook. If at any time he got up against Larry Buckner or the faceless people behind him they could always use the threat of the photograph against him. His thoughts ran riot as he twisted and turned. He should have told them to send it to Julius and be damned; he should have confided in Evelyn what was going on, though goodness only knew what she would have done if he had. If they had been successful in tracing the man in the car could they have done anything with him? At least there was plenty of identification now. Apart from himself and Steve Barrett he had confirmed with Val Errington that the voice was the same as that which had threatened him.

Errington had added a few succinct comments on the owner of the voice and what he would like to do with him and then went on to say in answer to Myles's further questions that he thought he might have been given a pound or two less in the National weights but he supposed that on the whole he couldn't complain.

Myles himself had also a few more than murderous thoughts about Larry Buckner running through his mind. It was not a pleasant prospect to know that the negative was still in hostile hands.

259

He was cooking his breakfast when Jim Malvey rang. 'Did our friend get in touch?' Malvey asked.

'Yes.'

'What did you tell him?'

'Just what Featherstone said. The investigation is off.'

'Good. I'll be round in half an hour. We're going to Exeter.'

'What?'

'Exeter, like I said. Half an hour, then.'

Myles ate his egg and toast with very little appetite. Then he drank two cups of very black, very hot coffee. What in hell was going on now, he wondered.

'Listen, Sherlock,' he said sourly to Malvey when he arrived. 'You'd better tell me what you're up to or I'll stay right here until you do. I thought this thing was all over.'

'On the contrary it's just beginning. We've found our friend.'

'Good on you,' Myles said sarcastically. 'And just what do you propose to do with him now you've told me it's all off?'

Malvey dropped his long body into an armchair. 'We just want to have a few, let's say, final words with him. You're to come down to confirm the identification.'

'And what if I don't?'

Malvey uncoiled himself, stood up and rested his long arms on the table which still had the remains of Myles's breakfast on it. 'Listen, Myles,' he said. 'I've come to like you since I've been on this job. I'm not supposed to tell you this but I will. Featherstone is using you as a fall guy or a sort of one. You must know he's been pushing the sports pages popularwise as far as he can. That being so he thinks you're expendable. You were told that we were pulling out because he wanted you to sound convincing. He's got a high idea about your morals. Thinks you mightn't make a good liar, see? He was determined that our friend would get the good news back to his immediate boss, Larry Buckner, and make it stick. Now you and I are to have a word with our friend whose name by the way is Scarman.'

'What are you going to do with him?'

'I'm going to frighten the living daylights out of him and you're going to help me. Come on.'

They drove down the M.4 mostly in silence and came to Exeter about 12.30.

Frobisher Avenue, where Scarman lived, proved to be a street of tiny red-brick Victorian houses all virtually identical

260

and set in a maze of other similar streets. Cars were parked in front of the houses on either side. Malvey found a space and squeezed his Morris Marina into it.

There was a short flagged path to the door of Number 117 which was the address Malvey had. He opened the wooden gate, walked up the path and pressed the bell. From a room on the right of the door Myles could hear the sound of a typewriter.

The door was opened by a woman with wispy hair. She had a worn worried look and a child was dragging out of one of her hands. The child was crying and whining. 'Be quiet, Bertie, can't you,' she snapped petulantly, and then, to Malvey: 'What do you want? I'm afraid we can't afford . . .'

'Social security, Mrs Scarman. We want to see your husband.' Myles noticed that his foot, quite unobtrusively, had slid across the doorstep to prevent a sudden slam.

'I'm afraid I don't understand . . .'

'You will.' Malvey brushed past her, pushing her and the child roughly against the wall. He threw open the door on the right and walked in. Myles, not liking any of this, followed him.

A man was sitting at a plain wooden trestle table in the window, typing. Sheets covered with figures were all around him on the table. There was a letter with the heading LARRY BUCKNER on it in bold letters; copies of *Sporting Life* and some form books were scattered about.

The man pushed his chair back and turned round as they came in.

'What—' he started to say.

Malvey kicked the door shut behind him. 'You're in dead trouble, mate,' he said.

Scarman half-rose from the chair. He was a man of medium height, aged around forty, Myles guessed, with the beginnings of a paunch. He saw, too, with a little thrill of recognition, the pucker of scar tissue on the jaw. When he began to speak Myles had no doubt that they had run their quarry to earth.

'What's the meaning of this?' he said and his voice had the same distinctive high quality of the voice on the telephone. 'How dare you come bursting into my house?'

Malvey took no notice of the protest at all. 'Do you know this gentleman?' he said nodding towards Myles.

'Of course not. I've never seen him before in my life.' But as his eyes met Myles's a flash of recognition came into them to be

261

followed immediately by naked fear.

'That's the first lie you've told this morning. It'd better be the last. Do you recognise him, Myles?'

'Yes,' Myles said shortly. 'It's the man who handed me the photograph at Wrayfield. And his voice is the same as whoever telephoned me.'

Scarman looked at Myles. Suddenly whatever resistance there was in him seemed to crumple and he almost cringed backwards in the chair. 'What do you want?' he said.

The door handle rattled behind Malvey, and Scarman's wife's voice came across from the hallway. 'Are you all right? Who are these men?'

'Tell her to go away,' Malvey said.

Scarman swallowed. When he spoke his voice seemed even higher than before. 'It's all right, Mavis, quite all right. They're friends.'

Malvey pointed a long finger at him. 'This gentleman identifies you,' he said. 'Blackmail. That's what you've tried on him. Errington, the letter-bomb, remember, has identified your voice on the tape. So has Steve Barrett. You'd remember him, I think. He got knocked on the head. He nearly died. G.B.H. Know what that is? Grievous Bodily Harm. You'd get four years for that.'

'I didn't touch him.' The voice was a frightened squeak.

'That doesn't matter, friend. You should learn some law. You were there with them when they did it. That's enough.'

Myles had by now crossed to the table. He picked up one of the sheets of paper with the figures and inspected it. The nature of Scarman's employment became immediately apparent to him. 'You're a part-time settler for Larry Buckner, aren't you?' he said. He also noticed something else as he put the sheet down.

Scarman swallowed and nodded. For the moment he seemed incapable of speech. 'Look,' Myles said not unkindly. 'You'd better tell us all about it. You're caught, you know.'

The other man nodded. He swallowed again several times and then the words came out. 'I had to do it,' he said. 'I had to. They made me.'

'That's no defence in law,' Malvey said brutally. 'We're ready to call in the coppers this instant unless you tell us the rest. If you do, I dunno, they say turning Queen's Evidence is

262

taken into account. You might get away scot free. It's your only chance.'

'What can I do—'

'You can make an affidavit. I'll draft it on that typewriter. There's a commissioner for oaths lined up to swear it. He'll be round as soon as I ring him.'

Scarman gave a sort of groan. 'Why did I ever let myself get mixed up in this thing? Oh, God.'

'You can call on him if you like but as of this moment we're the only people likely to help you.'

'They made me redundant . . .'

'Who did?'

'It was a company of Marker's, Amalgamated Oils, when he had that reorganisation. I was doing well. I thought I was se-cure—manager in the sales department, I thought nothing could ever happen to me. Then one morning I was called before the director of personnel. They were cutting down, he said. He'd no option, the orders came from the top, from old man Marker himself. I was one of the six to be chopped. I was out, finished. There was the mortgage, the children . . .'

'All right, so there was. I'm breaking into tears right now but this isn't getting us anywhere.'

'I'm trying to explain. I was always good at figures and I'd followed the horses a bit. I used to have a bet on old Marker's once in a while actually. I saw in *Sporting Life* an advertisement for bookmaker's settlers wanted. I applied and got taken on by Buckner's. Well, I was still in shock after the redundancy I sup-pose. I talked in the office about old Marker and what I'd like to do to him, if I got the chance. One night a man came here and asked me if I wanted to get something back on him. It was nothing much, he said, just a sort of practical joke on the lad who did Marker's horses. There'd be a hundred nicker on the side for me and no need to declare it for tax. I'd run up debts and got behind with the mortgage when I was out of a job. A hundred nicker was a godsend. I didn't allow myself to think about what I was getting into.'

'So you *were* on the moor?'

'What's the use of denying it now? You've got me, haven't you?'

'We've got you, never fear.' Malvey was making notes. 'Did anyone that night on the moor say anything to connect Buckner

263

with what was going on?'

Scarman hesitated and licked his lips.

'Did they?' persisted Malvey.

'When Barrett was hit,' Scarman said almost in a whisper, 'I heard one of them say "Larry won't like this," and he laughed when he said it. It was horrid.' He gave a little shudder at the recollection.

'What about the rest of the jobs? Who gave you your instructions?'

'The same man who visited me the first time. He seemed to know exactly what to say and do.'

'Very well. We'll get it all down on paper now. Ring this number for the commissioner, will you, Myles?' Malvey handed him a slip of paper with an Exeter number typed on it.

'Wait. What are you going to do? I haven't said I'd sign anything yet. I've been thinking. I can't. They'll kill me. Look what happened to Barrett . . .'

Malvey turned on him with sudden venom. 'You'll sign and like it,' he said. 'Otherwise the coppers come. Think what *they'll* do to you. How'd you like to be driven away from here in handcuffs? Nice for the neighbours, eh? Nice for the wife and kids you were thinking so much about when you took that hundred nicker in your hot little hands. And I'll tell you what else you'll do. I'm going to save your skin for you much as I hate doing it. You've told someone the heat is off Buckner, haven't you?'

Scarman nodded.

'Go on telling them that then and they'll leave you alone. I suppose you've sense enough not to mention our visit here. If you value your skin like you seem to you'll keep quiet about it. Now let me get on with this affidavit.'

'Just what are you and Featherstone up to?' Myles said in the car on the way back to London. 'You've double-crossed me and I suppose you'll do the same to that wretched creature.'

'Don't waste too much sympathy on him. He walked into crime pretty easy, didn't he?'

'He was pressured. That's the way modern life goes.'

'Pressured!' Malvey snorted. 'He has all the cut of a small-time crook, if you ask me. I expect he had his hand somewhere in that company's till if we only knew and that's why he was made redundant.'

264

'You may just be right. I thought I saw betting slips pushed away under a pile of papers on his table. Settlers are never permitted to take betting slips out of their bookmaker's offices. It's one of the easiest ways they can go on the fiddle.'

'There you are then.'

'What about the legal stuff you fired at him. Is it accurate?'

'Near enough, I expect. I've picked up a bit here and there. And it worked; it scared the shit out of him. And it got you off the hook, Myles. Don't forget that.'

'Buckner's still got the negative.'

'There's no point in his using it, now. Anyway I tell you Buckner's only a link.' He belched suddenly. 'Spanish cooking,' he went on. 'All oil. Played hell with me. There are pills in the glove box, Myles. Thanks.'

'Spanish cooking? Just what have you been doing, Jim?'

'I've been in Spain. Benidorm. Torremolinos. Very interesting out of season. Can't even get fish and chips. And we've been doing some digging in the Companies Office. Should have done it before. Very rewarding, too. We've got Scarman. We've found Henson. Told you we could find anyone if we put our minds to it.'

'When you've finished talking in riddles, Jim, perhaps you'd translate. Must be all that Spanish food you've been taking.'

Malvey belched again and swore. 'Buckner's head will roll all in good time,' he said. 'I told you we were after bigger game. It looks as if we've found it.' He pulled the car to the pavement outside Myles's flat. 'No thanks. I won't come up for a drink, my stomach wouldn't stand it. That business of the stud you told me about.'

'Yes?'

'Would it surprise you to know we think the two things are connected?'

'Connected? What on earth do you mean, Jim?'

'Bradbury's behind Buckner. The Companies Office put us on to that after a hell of a lot of digging and analysing. Bradbury switched those horses, too. Henson talked when I tackled him in Spain. He's frightened of Bradbury but he talked just the same. He tried to put the squeeze on Bradbury and Bradbury squeezed him back, telling him that it was only one man's word against another and that he, Bradbury, would be the one that would be believed. He put the breeze up Henson and Henson was glad enough to get out. He's been taking his cut, too, never fear. But the thing is, is there anyone behind Bradbury controlling him and Buckner?'

'Who's your candidate?'

'What about Lord Warminster himself?'

'Don't be ridiculous. Why should he be mixed up in this?'

'You said he's loaded, maybe he's not as loaded as you think. He's a gambler. His life style is expensive. It's a thought. We'll see.'

PART THREE

SPRING

18

March came in like a lion. Rain, gales and storms lashed the country. There was snow on high ground. Three racing days in succession were lost. Several training establishments were struck by the virus.

Admiral of the Blue won a three mile race at Sandown with tremendous authority. Hills and Ladbrokes cut his Grand National odds from twenty to one to sixteen to one.

Val Errington, gloomily contemplating the conditions underfoot and wondering where and when he would get the good ground he wanted to give Rob Roy his warming-up run before the National, announced that he had changed his mind about the handicap. He now thought he should have been given at least two pounds less and he could not understand why he was required to concede twenty-one pounds to Admiral of the Blue. Hills and Ladbrokes extended Rob Roy's price in the National betting from ten to one to twelve to one.

Chris Rokeby ran Alexander at Haydock. He coped with the drop fences adequately enough and completed the race without a mistake. His running, however, was listless throughout and he could do no better than finish sixth out of ten runners. Hills and Ladbrokes quoted him at thirty-five to one for the National. He did not eat up after the race and the following day he was coughing.

Pirate Gold won the Mandarin Chase at Newbury like a hero. In his work after it he pleased everyone including his trainer and jockey. Hills and Ladbrokes made him a four to one favourite for the Cheltenham Gold Cup.

Starflight, to the surprise of everyone including his trainer, won a three and a half mile chase at Warwick. His owner had taken to her bed after the débâcle at Wrayfield Park, announcing that she was suffering from 'flu. She was not present at Warwick to see her horse win, declaring herself unfit to face the weather. Having informed Alastair over the telephone that she did not care who rode her horse so long as it was not 'that young man', Starflight had been ridden by one W. Rendall who now stood high in the volatile estimation of Starflight's trainer.

Daddy Rendall went with Millie to the surgery of the overworked local doctor. Once there he succeeded in persuading him that Millie's sumptoms required further investigation. She was now undergoing tests.

Miriam Barkley did not cease from her pursuit of Pat Colby.

Pat Colby, his trainer's words still ringing in his ears, and with the prospect before him of riding the winner of both the Gold Cup and the Grand National in his first season as a professional, made half-hearted attempts to avoid her. One expedient was to try to see more of Evelyn Marker.

Larry Buckner became daily more pleased with his lot. His sanguine spirit told him that the weather and the weight would combine to prevent Rob Roy winning his second National. It was true that if Pirate Gold won the Gold Cup he would not have a good result on that race, but he had succeeded in laying off much of the money invested on Pirate Gold, and in any event the betting on the Gold Cup was only a fraction of that on the National. Best of all it appeared that the squeeze on Myles had been successful. Certainly the message he had received appeared to show that Myles had reacted as predicted. It had been a bit of luck finding that photograph, and better luck still that he had recognised who the bird in the water was—old Julius Marker's daughter, by God. Damn fine looking filly she was, too, Myles Aylward had something going for him there all right. It was true, Larry reflected, that he had not much cared about putting the photograph to the use that he had done. It was a shit's trick, if ever there was one, but, he consoled himself, needs must when the devil drove and at least it had avoided any necessity for physical violence.

Myles himself, with much on his mind, journeyed down to Farhaven to see Arthur Malcolm.

'Watchmaker?' Arthur answered his first question. 'He's never been better. I'm not running him at Cheltenham. He'll go in a chase at Ludlow in a couple of weeks' time. Come and see

270

him, Myles.'

He looked, Myles thought, in great shape, just as his trainer had said. Myles could see, too, that Arthur had left himself something to work on so as to bring the horse to cherry-ripe condition for the big day. 'I see they quote him at thirty-three to one,' he said.

Arthur smiled. 'If he goes along as I expect he'll shorten from that,' he said. 'Given luck I think he'll go well, though I suppose *you wouldn't say he's really a National horse—if there is such a thing.*'

'I've never thought there was,' Myles said. 'Not since the 1920s anyway, though Julius Marker wouldn't agree with me.'

'You're looking a bit peaked, Myles. Job getting you down? Must say I wouldn't care for it. Come up to the house and have something.'

Peaked, Myles thought, was not a bad way to describe how he felt these days. The knowledge of the existence of the photograph, and in whose hands it was, was a constant, nagging worry. In addition he had seen little of Evelyn and he had more than a suspicion that the affair with Colby was hotting up again. Then there was the feeling that there was something happening on the paper that he didn't know or was not being told about. This, coupled with Malvey's covert warnings concerning Featherstone's opinion that he was expendable, constituted another threat to his peace of mind. Just now he felt he owed it to Arthur, since Arthur after all had initiated the enquiry, to tell him at least something of what Malvey had uncovered concerning Clayhampton and what the journalist had disclosed to him. 'You remember those suspicions you told me you had about Bradbury and Clayhampton,' he said. 'I'm afraid I'm pretty sure you were right.'

'That doesn't surprise me,' Arthur said grimly.

Myles did not know quite how much he could tell without breaking either Malvey's or the paper's confidence. But he guessed that Arthur's chief concern in the matter was to protect David. He must therefore, he decided, tell him something more. 'Malvey found the stud-groom in Spain,' he said. 'Apparently he's talked. Bradbury has been playing the devil and all there for years.'

'Including switching Burglar Alarm?'

'So I gather.'

271

'Just what I thought. The fellow is too glib altogether. Never cared for him. Shouldn't have let David go there at all. Only did it because of Robert. He'll have to come out now. I only hope it's not too late.'

'You'll be seeing him?'

'He's coming to lunch tomorrow.'

'Are you going to say anything to Lord Warminster?'

'I think I must. You remember that at the outset it was he who asked me if I could suggest what was wrong with the stud?'

'Is it at all possible,' Myles said slowly, 'that he could in any way be mixed up in all this himself?'

Arthur looked up, startled. 'Robert? Good God no. What a thing to suggest, Myles. I'd stake my life on him. No. No. It can't be.'

'I just wondered. He's a gambler, you know. He may not be as rich as we all think. Look, this is confidential, in fact I'm pretty sure that I shouldn't be telling you it at all but the paper is after Larry Buckner.'

'That's no harm.'

'They think someone is behind Larry Buckner and as far as I can gather it is the same someone who has been manipulating the stud.'

'Good God!'

'We were pretty close on Buckner's tracks a month or so back. I heard that Warminster was home then. It struck me as unusual.'

'It's true he was home. He told me it was business. I couldn't think then what business had brought him back. But, no, it can't be. Robert Warminster is not a crook.'

After Myles had gone Arthur found his post waiting for him. Picking up a paper-knife he slit the letters open. 'Good God!' he said again as he read one of them.

'What is it, dear?' Mary had come in and was pouring his pre-lunch gin. 'Robert Warminster is on his way home. He's coming back early. What can that mean?'

Lunch at Farhaven the following day was not a particularly happy meal. Arthur was very conscious of the coming interview with his son and wondering how best he should conduct it. As a result he became positively monosyllabic. David, who had never shown much interest in his horses, now seemed anxious

272

to discuss Watchmaker's progress and his prospects in the National. After saying that the horse was very well, Arthur's further response to his son's enquiries was a series of grunts. When at length the meal was over, he suggested that they step along to his office for 'a bit of a chat'.

Once in the office Arthur seated himself behind his desk and stared out of the window. A weak sun had come out to brighten the bleak afternoon. Growth would soon begin, Arthur thought. He would have to get the grass cut and begin clipping hedges. Then he put these thoughts aside and turned back to the task in hand. 'Sit down, David,' he said. 'Care for a cigar? A cigarette? Didn't bring any drinks along I'm afraid. A brandy?'

'No, thank you, father.' David was wondering what this was all about. At first the whole thing seemed all too reminiscent of a summons to his housemaster's study. Now the old man appeared to be trying to be affable.

Arthur lighted a cigar with some fuss—making a major production out of it was David's mental comment. He shook out the match and dropped it into an ashtray. He did not know quite how to begin the interview. For years now he had never quite known how to tackle any discussion with David. At length, being Arthur, he plunged straight in. 'I want to talk to you about the stud,' he said.

David's hackles went up immediately. 'What about the stud?' he said.

'I think it better if you left Clayhampton as soon as possible.'

'Why? I like it there. I'm getting on all right, aren't I? Have there been any complaints?'

'No. No. It's not that at all. It's Bradbury. I fear he's in trouble.'

'What sort of trouble, father?'

'He's been, well, let's put it this way, he's been running the stud for himself, not for his owner.'

'You mean he's on the fiddle?'

Arthur fidgeted and brushed away a cloud of cigar smoke from around his face. 'Yes, well, yes, that is a way of saying it, I suppose,' he said.

David laughed. 'But, father, you don't think I'm all that innocent, do you?' he said. 'Of course he's on the fiddle. All of them are. They've all got their hands out. The take on the side is just one of those things in the bloodstock business. And, anyway, what does Lord Warminster expect? He never takes any interest in the place. I've seen him there just once since I went to the place and that was only for about ten minutes. An accountant comes down twice a year. That's all the supervision there is. It's his own fault.'

Arthur felt his irritation rising. Really, he did *not* understand this strange world in which he was now living. 'You don't seem to put much account to it, I must say,' he remarked icily. 'Well, let me tell you, it goes rather further than that.'

'Oh, where's that, then?'

Arthur was in a quandary. His annoyance at David's calm acceptance of the swindling at Clayhampton had led him to say rather more than he meant. Now he had to amplify what he had said or leave the whole conversation hopelessly in the air and, incidentally, retire defeated. 'I am given to understand from a reliable source that he's switched stallions, one at least of which has been sold abroad. That is a criminal offence.'

David stared across the big desk at his father. 'Look, father,' he said slowly. 'I don't care what Bill Bradbury has done. He has been a good friend to me. And anything he may have done to Lord Warminster, well, in my book Lord Warminster had it coming to him. Bradbury has had all the work and respon-sibility at Clayhampton for years without any advice or direc-tion from the top. They say in the stud that the pay he gets is lousy and he hasn't had an increase since he came just because Lord Warminster or the accountants or whoever runs it won't bother. What else can they expect but that he fiddles his bit?'

'They can expect at least a modicum of honesty or so I should imagine,' Arthur said sharply.

'Honesty? These days you get the honesty you pay for, father. Anyway why should old Warminster have all that money? He's never done a stroke of work in his life. I expect his ancestors fiddled or stole or robbed for it all or got it by some other bent way if we only knew. All he's done is lie about and enjoy it while others do the work for him.'

Arthur felt his rage steadily rising. Here was his own son ex-pressing the sentiments by which the present-day world, or so it seemed to him, ran its affairs, sentiments which he loathed and despised. Since it was David, however, he strove to master the anger which was threatening to consume him, and to speak quietly and steadily. 'Between the years 1939 and 1945,' he

274

said, 'Robert Warminster put his life on the line for you and your like and for Bradbury too for all I know. He was at Dunkirk, in Tunisia and up through Italy—at what they now call the sharp end pretty well all of that time. If he and others like him hadn't done just that, you and your friends wouldn't be enjoying the life they do now. And Bradbury, for that matter, wouldn't be free to do his fiddles as he chooses. He'd be up against a wall looking at a firing squad.'

'That old war,' David said scornfully. 'You and Warminster and the rest, you were only fighting to try and preserve privilege and power and class-consciousness. Up against a wall! You're talking like a crypto-fascist.'

'I don't know what that means but you're talking like a communist or whatever they call them nowadays.'

'If you and your lot had only done something after the war to try to make life fairer . . .'

Arthur sighed. 'That's something no one will ever do, as you will presently learn. Cancer isn't fair. Heart attacks aren't fair. Some horses run faster than others. That isn't fair.'

'Some horses aren't born with silver spoons in their mouths . . .'

'Aren't they, David, aren't they? You're on a stud, David. You ought to know better than that.'

'Father, I'm not leaving Clayhampton. Bill Bradbury has helped me and taught me. I'm of age. I can make my own life. I'm staying.'

'Then there doesn't seem to be anything more to say, does there?'

After Arthur and Mary had seen David drive off they went back into the house.

'It didn't go too well, did it?' Mary said.

'No,' Arthur told her. 'It didn't, I'm afraid, my dear. He won't leave Bradbury. He says Robert shouldn't have ever had any money, that we shouldn't have fought the war at all and that I'm a crypto-fascist whatever that may be.' He sighed heavily. 'Really, my dear, I don't understand them, do you?'

Mary put her hand on his shoulder. 'No,' she said. 'I don't. But perhaps our parents didn't understand us, either. And, remember, Arthur, he's loyal to a fault, just like you. I only hope as I said before that it doesn't all end in tears.'

On his way back to Clayhampton David called in to see Tommy Pereira who acted as a sort of friend and father confessor to David and his circle. He did not find Tommy in a particularly receptive or sympathetic mood. When David arrived he was studying the yellow-covered book of Programmes of Meetings Part II. If Cummerbund was to go in the National he must have another run before it. Tommy had entered him liberally all over the place and he was now poring over the various conditions of races, trying to decide what was the easiest course and most suitable article of the race for himself and Cummerbund to make their next appearance in public. The thought of riding another race almost made his stomach heave. That mistake at the last fence at Lingfield was still vivid in his memory. He could re-live every instant of it. Next time he might not be so lucky. He tried to analyse just why he was frightened and of what but this was unsuccessful and he gave it up. All he was quite sure of was that people who took up riding over fences for pleasure were bloody fools and those who persisted after the pleasure had gone were practically certifiable. One thing was certain and that was that after the National he was going to hang up his boots forever and no one then need know that it was fear which had made him do it.

'Just had lunch with the old man,' David said as he came into the room.

Tommy inserted a marker into the programmes book and put it aside. 'Progressed from Alamein to the Sangro, has he?' he said. 'And still going strong up the toe of Italy?'

'That's about it. He's been on again about the stud. Wants me to go. He says Bill Bradbury has been on the fiddle. Everyone in the bloodstock business has his hand in someone else's pocket. Why does he have to go on about it so?'

'Some odd people think having your hand in other people's pockets isn't such a good idea.'

'That's a load of crap. Why should old Warminster have all that money and Bill Bradbury have none? Why shouldn't Bill take his whack? Warminster will only spend it all at chemmy anyway.'

'Don't ask me to philosophise, young David, it's not my thing at all.'

'We had a master at my public school. He told us that he got into trouble at the University pinching books he needed and

276

couldn't pay for. A don who was a friend of his got him off by saying it wasn't stealing at all but a way of helping the under-privileged to better themselves when they couldn't pay for books.'

'So Bill Bradbury is okay so long as he robs the rich to pay the poor, that is, himself?'

'Something like that. I can't see why the old man is so uptight about it. And old Bill asked me to find out how he thought Watchmaker would go in the National. I did try at lunch. He was uptight about that, too.'

'I'm not surprised. He's Warminster's horse, isn't he? I suppose that was why Bradbury wanted to know his form.'

'The old man said something about a criminal prosecution for switching stallions. Do you think there could be anything in that?'

'Yes, if he says so. It looks as if Bradbury may be about to get his come-uppance at last. Remember I told you that if he fell the whole field would gallop over him.'

'You're not being much help, Tommy. What about Cummerbund? Are you going to ride him in the National?'

'Yes, why?'

'Someone said you were giving up.'

'Who said that?' Tommy asked, sharply for him. 'Of course I'm going to ride him in the National. I'm getting on a bit though. I may pack it in after that.'

'I wonder, should I warn old Bill?' David went on as if he had not heard Tommy's reply.

'You're a bloody fool if you do. Don't get mixed up in this, David. Bill Bradbury is well able to look after himself.'

'I know, but he's been damned decent to me.'

'For Christ's sake, David, sort yourself out and stop crying on my shoulder. If Bill Bradbury had been switching stallions and swindling Warminster I think he's a shit even if you and your schoolmaster chum who steals books don't. Either you go along with him or stay out of it. It's nearly six o'clock and I'm going out to dinner. If you want a drink you can have one now before I go and change.'

There was no comfort here for David. 'No. I don't think I do want a drink,' he said and took his leave.

Two days later Robert Warminster flew into Heathrow from Kenya. After seeing his solicitors and accountants, spending an

277

afternoon in the City and an evening at the Spades and Hearts Club, he went down to Farhaven to discuss Watchmaker with Arthur. On this visit he actually bestirred himself to see Watchmaker work. Having done so he expressed himself well pleased. He was justified in this for Watchmaker lost the two companions Arthur had put into the gallop to test him. The horse was working better and better every day and Daddy Rendall, who had ridden him in the gallop, said so to his owner.

'He's thirty-three to one in the market, I see,' Robert said when they were back at the house.

'That's how they quote him, yes.'

'Nice price. I can have a bet.'

'There are still some weeks to go, Robert.'

Robert laughed. 'Always cautious, aren't you, Arthur? If he wins at Ludlow he'll shorten, won't he?'

'Indeed he will. Considerably so, I imagine.'

'There you are then. It's time to move in.'

'Always provided he wins at Ludlow,' Arthur said and Robert laughed again. 'Robert,' Arthur went on. 'Do you remember last year before you went abroad you asked me about Clayhampton?'

Robert nodded. He sipped his coffee and sat waiting.

'I heard something more or less by chance,' Arthur continued, 'which led me to believe that there was in fact something that might be very wrong there. I made some enquiries and, well, Robert, there's something amiss, I'm afraid. I should perhaps make quite clear that the enquiries I made were not through David.'

Robert nodded again and put down his coffee cup. 'What you say does not come as a surprise,' he said. 'It's Bradbury, isn't it?'

Arthur looked at his friend closely. Suddenly it occurred to him that Robert was more alive, more awake than he had seen him in years. The man sitting opposite him now more nearly resembled the man with whom he had fought through the Kasserine Pass than the idle layabout of the last decade. 'I'm afraid so,' he said. 'In fact I have little doubt of it.'

'You know,' Robert said. 'After we talked in London last year I began seriously to think about Bradbury. Before I left I went down to Clayhampton and found that Henson had gone. No one seemed to know why or where. Bradbury's explanation was that he had been unwell and had simply demanded his cards and walked out. Henson had been there for years and I knew of him as a good and loyal servant. The explanation seemed lame to me. After I had been to Clayhampton I called on the accountants and got from them all the records and figures for the stud covering the past ten years. I took them abroad with me.'

'You were setting yourself quite a task,' Arthur said.

'It took me three months' hard slogging to analyse them. Jack Watherton with whom I stayed much of the time helped. He had a stud of his own in Wiltshire before he sold up and went to live abroad. Between us we found things, things which I suppose the accountants could scarcely have been expected to pick up.'

'They never do find the things you want them to and that's a fact. Was this why you came back after Christmas?'

'Yes. I was determined to have it out with Bradbury then but, do you know, the damn accountants and solicitors persuaded me not to.'

'Why on earth did they do that?'

'The accountants weren't too pleased at being caught out, I suppose, even though I made it clear I wasn't holding them liable. Solicitors, so far as I can see, always tell you the difficulties ahead; they're a defeatist lot of sods. At all events the two of them got at me and argued me out of it. I suppose in a way I was half-ready to be persuaded. It's a bloody business sacking old employees and Bradbury's such a persuasive bugger.'

'He certainly is all of that,' Arthur said thinking of David's reactions of a few days back.

'Anyway,' Robert went on, 'they said we'd have a desperate job making the figures stand up in court, that Bradbury was bound to sue for wrongful dismissal, that it would all cost a fortune, drag my name through the press and not do anyone any good. Then they pointed out that the stud season was about to begin, that if Bradbury went it would disrupt the whole stud programme, that he had everything in his head and the workforce under his thumb and could play merry hell with them. In the end they said to leave it to them, they'd ease Bradbury out in their own good time. Perhaps they were right. But I've been to see them both and they've done damn all so far.'

'It goes a little farther than that, though, Robert, if my information is right,' Arthur said. Quickly he told him about Burglar Alarm and the suspected switch and how Myles and the *Daily Post* had discovered Henson.

Robert sat quietly in thought for a moment, staring at his coffee cup, then he said quietly: 'They'd slap it on to the front pages, would they?'

'I'm afraid that's highly likely. I must take some responsibility for this, Robert, and I apologise. I never dreamt when I asked young Myles Aylward . . .'

'Nonsense, Arthur, you were trying to help me. But I can tell you it's not going to happen.'

'What?'

'There's never been a public scandal at Clayhampton or in our family yet and I'm not going to be the first to have one. It was the thought of publicity and of Bradbury taking an action that really stopped me a month or so back. Good God, if all this came out they'd probably have to re-write the stud-book.'

'Not quite, though I don't know just what they would do. This sort of switch has never been made public before. Put an addenda at the end perhaps.'

'It doesn't much matter about the Burglar Alarms, I suppose,' Robert went on as if thinking aloud. 'He's just about finished and they're ninety per cent of them geldings anyway. But what about the sire he sent to Chile?'

'He's dead,' Arthur said. 'I checked that. Died of colic soon after he arrived. Never acclimatised himself.'

'So that's that.'

'But if they break the story, Robert, what can you do?'

Robert smiled. 'I can say that there's no story to break, can't I?' he said. 'I saw others beside the accountants and solicitors when I was home after Christmas. I had a chap I know in the City make some enquiries for me. Bill Bradbury isn't getting any younger. He's had an end to his career of crime in view for some time now. For years he's been putting my money away in a Swiss bank. He's bought a property there, too, at Nyons outside Geneva to be precise. He's all set to cut and run if he has to. You've given me enough ammunition to make him. Without him there won't be any story. And if Henson thinks he's injuring me he won't talk either. It's Bill Bradbury he'll be after, not me. I'll see that that newspaper knows that if it lets out any

280

story about Clayhampton without firm evidence behind it they'll face the humdinger of a libel action.'

'Are you sure Bradbury will cut and run? They say he controls Larry Buckner. He may want to protect that investment.'

Robert smiled. 'My chap found out something about that, too,' he said. 'It's true. He is behind Buckner, through a series of holding companies set up with my money, too, I imagine. But he has now set Buckner up as a fall guy. Once the pressure is on he'll get out and let Buckner take the consequences.'

'You're playing this pretty ruthlessly, Robert.'

Robert stood up. 'It's a bit like the war, isn't it?' he said. 'Either the other fellow gets you or you get him. Do you know, I feel suddenly as if I was alive again.'

'I hope,' Arthur said, now, like many another man, wishing profoundly that he had not started something he could not stop, 'that this does not get Myles Aylward into trouble.'

'The newspaperman? That's just like the war, too, isn't it? He'll just have to take his chance.'

19

So they all, or most of them, came to the big March meeting at
Cheltenham, the National Hunt Meeting, the Ascot of Steeplechasing. The weather had relented and, with one of its sudden
quirks peculiar to March, had turned balmy and springlike.
The ground was drying rapidly and on the Tuesday Arthur
won the first race of the meeting. It was Division I of the Sun
Alliance Hurdle and the horse was Miss M. Meredith's Harnessed Lad ridden by W. Rendall.

Meg, revived bodily and spiritually by her week in bed, had
come down in slow stages in the Daimler. Stopping off at Long
Eaton the night before, she had spent some time in consultation
with Joseph and a close study of the Book of Stars. Through the
window of her suite they had taken sightings on the constella-
tions and done many mysterious sums and calculations. The
upshot of it all was that the omens were favourable. The following morning Joseph had given the betting boots an extra polish
and Meg had buttoned them on full of confidence and lust for
battle with the bookmakers.

When they reached the course Joseph was entrusted with
enormous bundles of notes of all denominations for Meg rarely
backed on credit. With these he went into attack on the ring,
especially Larry Buckner.

Her boots gleaming in the spring sunlight, Meg strode into
the parade ring and beamed on the once despised Daddy Rendall. 'Win this for me,' she said, 'and I'll see to it that it is worth
your while. Everything is right today. I feel it. I am about to
have a bet. What horse is that young man riding?' she suddenly
shot at Arthur.

'Who? Oh, yes,' Arthur said, putting two and two together

with remarkable swiftness for him. 'Pat Colby? He rides the favourite, Tell Me Again.'

'You will see to it that you beat him, please,' Meg said to Daddy.

'Someone is backing yours, Meg,' Arthur said looking at the indicator board. 'He's shortening all the time.'

'It is my money,' Meg said flatly and proudly. There was no doubt that she was on the top of her form. And when Harnessed Lad came storming up the hill leaving Tell Me Again toiling in his wake, she was all but ecstatic. Daddy, back with Millie and the boys that evening, confided to Millie that he thought she was going to kiss him and wondered what that would have been like. Millie, whose tests had not yet been finalised but who seemed to be in better humour, smiled and said that she hoped Meg's present would live up to her promises.

Later on the same day Chris had run Alexander in the National Hunt Chase. Alexander's cough had only lasted two days. It had gone as quickly as it had been slow to develop. Chris and his vet had decided that the cough must have been the culmination of the infection not its commencement. There were so many combinations and permutations of this virus that it was as difficult to prognosticate about as the common cold in humans. At all events Alexander had commenced immediately to eat up again and Chris had him back cantering within the week. He was in the National Hunt Chase and Chris wanted him to run in it. Although some trainers did not care for this race as a National trial Chris did not agree with them. This year, too, there were other National candidates in it so it would be useful to compare their running, and, besides, Chris wanted to see how Alexander dealt with the testing Cheltenham course. Alexander, ridden tenderly and exactly to instructions by Pat, had run a splendid race, coming up the hill like a hero to finish a close up third to Moonlight Sonata one of the National Candidates.

'Even Barkley can't say there's much wrong about that,' Chris remarked to Pat as they stood in the unsaddling stall. Martin Barkley, searching carefully through the form book in an attempt to try to justify a query on Alexander's running, reluctantly came to the same conclusion.

Pat was right back in the winning groove again. Now he was only five behind Tim Hanway in the championship table. On

283

the second day of the meeting he rode two winners to Tim's one and on the third he rode himself and Pirate Gold into glory by winning the Cheltenham Gold Cup. It was Tim Hanway he beat in this, too, after a terrific battle up the hill. He did not have by any means an easy ride in the Championship for Pirate Gold was just about at his worst on the first circuit, hardly meeting a fence right. Pat had had to coax him and nurse him all the way. Then, turning for home, he had sent him on down the hill, going with tremendous dash for the three final fences.

Tim Hanway closed on him at the last. A slight mistake made no difference to Pirate Gold. Fired by his rider's courage and driven by his strength he just held on in an epic struggle, to win by half a length.

On the same afternoon Tommy Pereira finished sixth out of seven runners in the Kim Muir Steeplechase for amateur riders. Although Cheltenham was far from the easiest of courses his pride had temporarily overcome his fears and persuaded him to make a last appearance there. 'Safely round at any rate,' he said to Cummerbund, slapping him gratefully on the neck as he dismounted, 'and do I only hope the National goes as well.'

Later the owner of Pirate Gold gave a party in his suite at the Queen's Hotel. Pat was the hero of the hour and he brought Evelyn with him to the party. It was, as was to be expected, something of a riot. Champagne came in magnums and the waiters could hardly keep pace with the consumption of every other kind of conceivable drink on the trays they whisked around. Tim Hanway proposed Pat's health and Pat proposed everyone else's health except Tim's, 'whom I have to beat in the championship'. Chris made a speech which no one heard, which was just as well, and the owner of Pirate Gold beamed affably at everyone from behind horn-rimmed glasses, hiccupped slightly and confined his public remarks to saying to the head-waiter: 'More champagne. See that they have more champagne.'

Chris had consumed vast quantities of whisky after the race with various cronies and other old racing hands who had come up to congratulate him. He was now, most unusually for him, very slightly drunk and was recounting to the owner's wife in some detail just what he and the Queen Mother had said to each other in the parade ring. Then, spotting Pat and Evelyn

talking together in a corner, he walked over to them. Taking
Evelyn by the arm he drew her slightly aside. 'By God,' he said
looking at Pat. 'He rode a race today if he's never to ride
another. He rode a hell of a race. Didn't he?'

'Yes, Chris,' Evelyn said, smiling.

'There aren't many like him, are there?'

'No, Chris, there aren't.'

Chris leant nearer to her and said very quietly and confid-
ingly in her ear: 'Keep him away from that Barkley bitch. She'll
ruin him if she can, you mark my words. I've seen 'em before
diggin' their graves—no, I shouldn't say that to you, should I?
Just you keep her off him for all our sakes, m'dear.' He swallowed a huge gulp from the glass in his hand and ambled off.

'What did he say?' Pat asked her suspiciously when Evelyn
rejoined him.

'He said you rode the hell of a race but you've heard that
before.'

'Not from him. Thanks.'

Evelyn saw Pat looking at her contemplatively and realised
that he was mentally undressing her—*oeil de dérober* as the man
at that finishing school at Vincennes had taught her to describe
it. Whether it was the champagne, the excitement of the occasion, the panache that went with him or the flattery of being
singled out by him in this crowd she did not know, but, with the
realisation, came the knowledge that she did not mind. Sensing
this he turned to her and said: 'Let's get out of here and have
dinner somewhere quiet together.'

They made their way through the crowd, Pat collecting more
slaps on the back and handshakes on the way. Seeing them go,
Chris helped himself to another whisky. At least, he thought,
he's out of the clutches of the Barkley woman for tonight.

Miriam Barkley had not enjoyed Gold Cup day. In the first
place the fickle weather had let her down. Expecting rain after
two days' sunshine and seeing the clouds low down when she
got up, she had worn the wrong clothes. Then she could
nowhere find Pat to have a word with him and arrange a meeting. She felt sure now that he was avoiding her and she was determined that he should not continue to do so. When she
glimpsed him at the very end he was with that insipid Marker
girl. If Pat thought he was going to cast her lightly aside at this

285

juncture he was very much mistaken. Besides, every fibre in her thrummed with desire, and she longed to share his triumph with him. She brooded and while she brooded she drank.

After racing she drove the Jensen into Cheltenham. When she had parked it she made her way into the Queen's. The hotel was thronged but there was no sign of Pat. In the bar she heard someone say there was a hell of a party going on upstairs given by the owner of Pirate Gold. That, she surmised, was where Pat was sure to be. She had not been asked but another voice nearer her announced that it seemed to be a pretty good free for all and why shouldn't they crash it? That seemed a good idea to her, too. She went up in the lift and entered the suite. No one tried to stop her. The first waiter she saw she sent in search of a large brandy. Such were her looks and the imperiousness of her command that he went meekly off and was back in a moment with a brimming glass on a salver. As she sipped it she surveyed the room or what she could see of it, but she could not find Pat.

Steadily working her way down the brandy, Miriam progressed through the crowd. When she had finished the drink she found the same waiter and told him to bring her another which he immediately did. As she lifted it to her lips she saw that Hector Mallinson was standing beside her.

'Looking for someone?' Hector said.

By now Miriam was becoming desperate. 'I was to meet Pat Colby here,' she said to him. 'Have you seen him?'

Mallinson's lips pursed into their most innocent and cherubic expression. 'Yes, indeed, my dear,' he said to her. 'He left just a minute ago with Evelyn Marker.'

Downstairs again Miriam went into the bar and drank and brooded. A drunken ex-jockey tried to pick her up and she pushed him away.

Tommy Pereira, talking to a group of people nearby, saw the incident and walked over to her. Tommy was feeling friendly and magnanimous towards the whole world. He had completed the course in one piece; the National was still ten days away so he could put all thought of it aside for the present; better still during the three days of the National Hunt meeting no one had offered him a ride so that he had not had to betray himself by refusing. It was true of course that nowadays he was seldom if ever offered rides on other people's horses. When he was younger this might have worried him though even then they did

286

not come his way all that frequently. Now he was delighted. So altogether it had been a good Cheltenham for him, espescially as he had had a nice bet on Pirate Gold and would collect some tax-free money when the cheque from his bookmaker came in. So when he saw Miriam alone and looking dispirited and coping with an oafish pick-up he felt he must offer to help.

'I'm all right, thank you,' she said to his enquiry. 'But you can get me another drink if you like.'

When the waiter had brought it Tommy, thinking again that she looked somehow stricken and lost said to her: 'If you're alone, why don't you join us?'

'Well, thanks. I was waiting for some people but they're so late they seem to have gone absent.'

'All too easy in this place. Come along.'

Later they went into dinner. Throughout the meal Miriam responded automatically to the remarks that were made to her for her thoughts were elsewhere and with Pat Colby. Where had he gone and what were he and the Marker girl doing now?

Outside after dinner she left her companions and went to the Jensen. She had continued drinking steadily through dinner but she found that she could walk quite well and she told herself she was fit to drive. Still Pat filled all her thoughts to the exclusion of everything else. Where was he? She looked at her watch. It was getting late. Probably by now he'd have gone back to the cottage. Yes, and that girl with him. Well, she'd give them both a surprise. She'd go to the cottage, too. She had a key and if they weren't there she'd wait for them. If they had arrived and were there together they'd find out just what she could do. She started the engine and swung into the emptying streets. Once outside the city she sent the red car savagely along.

Evelyn and Pat dined together in the pub near Pat's cottage where he had once thought to meet Miriam. It was full as everywhere was in Cheltenham week but at the appearance of Pat, the rider of the winner of the Gold Cup with a beautiful girl beside him, a table was immediately produced.

They talked quietly as they ate their steaks and sipped their wine. Pat was not boastful; he was relaxed after effort. They discussed the day's racing in a knowing, intimate way, Pat treating her as an equal, as one who knew as much of it as

287

himself. He was hardly inexperienced with women and he instinctively realised that this was the right approach with her. She felt herself warming more and more to him as the meal went on.

The place was crowded and tables were at a premium. They were asked to have their coffee in the lounge. Once more a table very quickly appeared vacant and ready for them and Pat ordered brandies. In a corner a man with a huge handlebar moustache was belting an upright piano and a group were singing mostly, it seemed, old wartime tunes which had recently been swept into popularity on a wave of nostalgia. The man with the moustache began to bang out 'Bless 'em All' and the whole room took it up.

Tim Hanway, who had come in before them with a party, pushed back his chair and walked over to them. 'Come on, Pat, a song from you now,' he said. 'Didn't know he was a songbird, did you, Miss Marker?' Then, laughing, he turned to the piano. 'Here's the winner!' he called holding up Pat's arm. 'He's going to give you a song!'

Never one to avoid the limelight, Pat walked to the piano. Evelyn wondered what would happen now. If he swung into some bawdiness she thought it would ruin the occasion and that she would hate him for it.

Leaning over the piano Pat spoke to the pianist and Evelyn saw the man nod.

'Give me a note,' Pat said.

The man with the moustache touched the keys.

'That'll do.' Pat turned to look directly across the room at Evelyn. Then he smiled. He leant an elbow negligently against the piano top and Evelyn was reminded how all his movements were infused with casual grace. His lips opened. The words came out strong and pure and true in a clear tenor voice. Evelyn was astonished and delighted.

> 'Take a pair of sparkling eyes,
>   Hidden ever and anon,'

Slowly silence fell on the crowded lounge. Drinks were put down and faces turned towards the singer.

> 'Take a figure trimly planned
>   Such as admiration whets

288

(Be particular in this);'

He was singing for her and at her now. She knew this. For them there was no one else in the room but each other.

    'Ah! Take all these, you lucky man—
    Take and keep them, if you can!'

He was coming to the end of the song his eyes still holding hers as if no one else existed.

    'Ah! Take my counsel, happy man;
    Act upon it, if you can!'

The last notes died away. Someone began to clap. Spontaneously everyone in the room joined in. The clapping went on and on.

Pat threw his head back and laughed. He waved an arm. Suddenly he was standing beside her. He took her by the hand and, still laughing, they ran out to the car. Once in it he sent it flying along the narrow roads.

'Where are we going?' she asked him.

'The cottage, of course.'

Almost a mile from the cottage was a cross-roads. Though none of their occupants knew it the Jaguar and the Jensen were approaching this cross on converging courses.

The road on which Miriam was travelling led her round a bend some fifty yards from the cross. High hedgerows masked the headlights of both cars. Driven by internal fires and furies she was driving fast, too fast. She took the bend at speed as the Jaguar came pelting down the short straight to the cross. The beams of their headlights suddenly converged.

Miriam threw up her hand to shield her eyes. Involuntarily her foot trod on the accelerator. The car leapt across the road.

The right-hand front wheel of the Jaguar took the right-hand rear panel of the Jensen. The two cars locked with a crash. There was the rattle and smash of splintering glass followed by the horrible sound of tearing metal. Then their speed tore them apart.

The Jensen slewed sideways, hit the hedge, lifted on two wheels and turned over. The Jaguar, its steering broken, went out of control immediately. It careered down the road, ploughed up the grass verge and spun into the road again. Still spinning it smashed a hole in the far hedge. Then its nearside wheel hit a tree. The windscreen disintegrated and the car came to a tearing, shuddering stop.

Evelyn's seat-belt saved her. It held her tight against the back of the seat during the car's wild gyrations. She hit her head against the door pillar at the outset of the impacts. This partly stunned her and the events of the next few seconds happened so quickly she had no time to feel anything. Gradually her head cleared and her mind began to work. She knew shock would be on her in a minute and she fought to keep it at bay. Slowly she moved her limbs to see if anything was broken. They seemed to act as they should. Her left shoulder hurt where it had hit the door pillar at the same time as her head and there was a small cut on her forehead from broken glass. That seemed to be the extent of the damage. She'd been lucky. Then she looked at Pat.

He was slumped over the broken wheel. Reckless as ever, he had not bothered to fasten his seat-belt. His head was wedged down between the remains of the wheel and the forepart of the broken fascia. She could not tell whether he was alive or dead. A slow, cold fear possessed her.

The catch of her belt was jammed and she was pinned in her seat. She struggled and tore at it. After a moment or two, while terrible thoughts raced through her mind, something gave and she was free. Bending over Pat she saw that he was breathing and a wave of relief swept over her. He was alive, but how badly was he hurt?

He groaned and his head moved. That was something. He could not do that if his neck was broken. 'Pat,' she said urgently. 'Pat, can you hear me?'

There was no answer. Then suddenly he opened his eyes, stared blankly at her and said: 'Tell the Guv'nor I'll be all right to ride the big fellow at Aintree for him.' Then he passed out again.

Despite their predicament Evelyn almost laughed. In his concussed condition he must have thought he had had a fall racing. His automatic reaction had been to think of the National and his ride on Alexander. Such were steeplechase jockeys. But perhaps it meant that he was not so badly hurt after all?

Then another thought came to her. With a sudden flash of recollection she remembered Madam Chairman's warning to

290

Pat at the end of the law case. She had said that if he ever became involved in further trouble over driving he could expect no mercy. And the barrister had echoed that warning.

Pat had not been drunk or anything like it but still she doubted if he would pass the breath test, and anyway with this crash he'd be bound to be in trouble with the law again. And in front of the same justices. He'd lose his driving licence. He might go to gaol. His life would be ruined. It mustn't happen.

With Evelyn, to think was to act. She never heeded the consequences. Now, in her shocked state, she was less likely than ever to take thought of them. All she knew was that she must save Pat. Seizing him by the shoulders she began to pull him towards her seat.

It was not an easy undertaking. Fortunately his seat had shifted a little on its supports so that there was some room between it and the shattered wheel. Gradually she began to work his inert body across the car. And then she found she could go no farther. The space available for what she wanted to do was too cramped. If she was to succeed she would have to open the door and work from outside. She pulled the catch. The door was jammed.

With Pat's weight lying against her she was unable to exert any leverage to free the door. Worse still, a sudden wave of nausea assailed her and she thought she was going to pass out. She fought it off and tugged again at the door handle. Nothing happened. She banged it with her shoulder and a wave of pain shot through her. Evelyn gasped and collapsed back into her seat.

When the pain had gone and her mind had cleared again she turned to a new attack. By twisting in her seat she found that she could exert pressure with her leg as well as her arm. Moreover this way she could brace herself against the seat back. The door protested, creaked and opened six inches. Two minutes later she had a wide enough gap to leave the car and stumble into the cold night air. Then she set about arranging Pat in her seat. One of his feet caught in the remains of the wheel and she thought for an instant that she would not have the strength to complete the task. Then she freed it and lifted his legs over the transmission tunnel. In a few seconds he was slumped in her seat in an untidy heap, still unconscious, still breathing heavily but at least not in the driver's position. For good measure she arranged the shattered remains of the seat-belt about him. As she finished she remembered the other car.

No one had come from it. There had been no sound beyond that first, initial, terrible crash. Again fear gripped her. Climbing down into the road she began to run towards it. The car lay on its back, one headlight defiantly blazing into the sky.

She was five yards from it when she recognised the red Jensen.

20

Myles did not enjoy Gold Cup day. It was true he had tipped Pirate Gold for the Championship but then so had almost everyone else, and the rest of his selections, such as they were, had proved unsuccessful. He had seen Evelyn in the distance but the crowds were so great and he had been so busy that he had not been able to find her and talk to her. Moreover he had more than a suspicion that she had come with Pat. Most unpleasant of all, however, was a strange interview which he had had with Jim Malvey.

Malvey had approached him near the Arkle statue looking even more lugubrious than ever.

'What are you doing here?' Myles asked him. 'I thought this part of the investigation was supposed to be over?'

'It's only just beginning thanks to you, you bastard,' Malvey said.

'What the devil do you mean?'

'You've killed the story.'

'You never will stop talking in riddles, Jim. What is all this?'

'You told someone about Bradbury and what we'd found.'

'I told Arthur Malcolm certainly. I had to. He started it all.'

'You're another bloody amateur. I should have known. You didn't have to.'

'It was between friends.'

'Friends? Yes, your bloody establishment friends. And he told a friend of his all on the old boy network. Do you know who it was?'

'No. Of course not.'

'Of course not, deah boy, of course not,' Malvey mimicked

him. 'I'll tell you who it was then. It was Lord Mucking Warminster and he's been too smart for us. Bradbury's gone.'

'Gone?'

'Yes, gone. And our story has gone with him. Henson has
gone back on everything he said. Says it was all forced out of
him and he'll deny it. We'll never get Warminster now.'

'That was all cock anyway, Jim. Warminster was never behind it.'

'That's the sort of thing you all say. He was at school with
me, deah boy. He acted pretty quick shipping Bradbury off and
turning Henson around, didn't he?'

'If he did it—perhaps Bradbury just bolted.'

'Anyway I think you're a bastard. I think you're all bastards.
So does Featherstone, by the way.'

'You still have Buckner cold, haven't you?'

'We've got him and we'll use him but like I said we were after
bigger game.'

'It only existed in your imagination, Jim.'

'Did it? Well, let me tell you something that doesn't exist
only in my imagination. We've got Buckner but he's got something else.'

'What?'

'That photograph of the Marker girl and all those pretty
prints.'

So it did not come as altogether a surprise when the following
day Myles received a summons to Featherstone's office. The
sports editor's eyes were, as usual, all over the place and he was
chewing the ends of his extraordinary moustache, but he
looked, Myles thought, very much as if he was in command of
the situation. In fact he looked, to Myles's eyes, like a man
about to play a poker hand knowing that he has all the high
cards and his opponent all the low ones. Myles's heart sank. He
had been expecting a telling off or a demand for an explanation.
Now it seemed that something worse might be coming. Featherstone's first words did little to reassure him. 'Myles,' he
said. 'I've asked for and been given leave to have a word with
you. This is unofficial. You'll be hearing it officially later this
morning. You know the paper has been going badly for some
time. We're losing circulation every day. The last figures were
terrible.'

294

'I heard something of the sort,' Myles said. 'But I'm mostly outside. I know very little of the business of the place.' Too little, he thought now. Why didn't I bother myself more with office politics or at least try to find out something that went on behind the sports pages?

'If we're to survive something drastic has to be done,' Featherstone went on. 'The old Lord has called for panic stations. There's no future in the paper as it is at present. We're catering for a non-existent public. We haven't kept up with the right readership demand. That's going to be changed.'

Featherstone was looking directly at him. His eyes, now that Myles could see them clearly for the first time, were deep-sunken and of a curious green colour. Also they held no message for Myles beyond, he thought, a certain satisfaction in what he was about to do.

'We're re-vamping the paper but especially the sports pages,' Featherstone was continuing. 'We can't afford two leading racing writers any more, Myles.'

It was then that Myles knew for certain what was coming, yet he could scarcely realise the enormity of the blow. He was going to lose his job. He felt as if he had been kicked in the stomach. All his vague fears came together and crystallised to form a horrid sickly knot inside him. He now knew what the wretched Scarman must have felt when he got the knock. And that bastard on the other side of the table looked as if he was enjoying it. So that's the way it happens, he thought, and I never really believed it could happen to me. 'I'm to be sacked—fired?' he said.

'No,' Featherstone said. 'It's not come to that yet. That's why I especially asked to be allowed to have this talk with you. I'd like to suggest to you that you resign, Myles.'

'So as to save the old Lord the trouble of firing me?'

Featherstone went on as if he had not heard. 'The old days of golden handshakes have gone, I'm afraid,' he said, 'since they became taxable. But still I think you'd find that the powers above us would be generous enough if you do resign. There'll be salary in lieu of notice, computation of holiday pay and pension entitlement plus, I gather, a solacium within the tax-free bracket. I don't know the details of course.'

The nightmare—was it a nightmare and would he wake up? he knew he wouldn't—was even worse than he thought. 'Am I to go immediately?'

Featherstone smiled in a way obviously intended to be sympathetic but the result came out as a sort of leer that was entangled with his moustache. 'Everyone realises that this is hard on you,' he said. 'We'd like you to stay to cover the National which is what I imagine you'd like too. That would give you something over a week, say a fortnight, to tidy things up.'

Myles was beginning to get over his shock and to become angry.

'What if I don't resign and fight this?' he said.

'The Industrial Court, do you mean?'

'Something like that.' Myles had only very hazy ideas of what means of contest lay to his hand but he had heard someone discussing redundancies recently and saying how hard they were to make stick.

'I wouldn't do that if I were you. In fact that is why I so much wanted to have this private discussion with you. In the first place the principle of last in first out applies in redundancy and you came here after Vic, but that's not all. There's something more.'

'What's that?'

'It seems that by talking to one of your establishment friends we may have lost just the story we were looking for.'

'Good heavens, you don't believe that bilge about Robert Warminster which Malvey was going on about, do you?'

'I don't believe anything without proof. We were very near to getting proof one way or another. Now we will not—through you.'

'But . . .'

For a moment Featherstone once more stared directly at him, his green eyes unfathomable. Then he said quietly: 'You would be wise to resign, Myles. You're an old-fashioned innocent. Innocents have no place on present-day papers.'

'Papers run by you and your sort,' Myles said hotly.

'I thought it would come to that in the end,' Featherstone said almost sadly. 'You have a few hours to think it over. But remember this: I and my sort, as you call us, it is we and people like us who run things now.'

Martin Barkley had been unable to be at Cheltenham on Gold Cup day. The loose ends in his business re-organisation,

296

after the manner of such loose ends, had required more tying up than he had expected. One of the last of them needed his urgent attention and he had missed all but the first day of the National Hunt Meeting. This had not prevented Miriam from going to it. Knowing that one horse looked much like another to her he had suspected that her motive for going was to seek out Colby. There was little he could do about it, however, save to get home as soon as possible and wait for her return.

As the hours passed and she did not arrive he grew more and more worried and perturbed. Surely she could not be openly flaunting him by staying away all night when she knew he was at home? At length he took two sleeping pills and went to bed.

In the small hours the jarring sound of the bedside telephone awoke him. At first hardly able to rouse himself from his drugged slumber, he could not take in what the voice on the other end of the line was saying. Then the import of the message cut like a knife through the drowsy fogs in his brain. 'An accident . . .' the voice said. 'Your wife . . . severe injuries. You should come at once . . .'

'Yes,' he said. 'Yes. Where?' His hand reached for a pad and pencil which were on a bedside table. 'I see. Thank you. How bad is she?'

There was a silence, then the voice said, 'It's an emergency. The surgeon is operating now.'

'Can you tell me what happened?' he said desperately.

'It was a motor accident.'

'Oh, God. I'll come; of course I'll come. Immediately.'

Throwing on some clothes Martin ran downstairs and out to the Rolls. And all the way as the big car sliced through the night he prayed to a God in whom he thought he did not believe to save the life of his injured wife.

The hospital waiting room was bare and antiseptic. The walls were pale green. Some stiff modern chairs were beside a table. There was a bench with a long cushion on it. Nothing else. The nurse who brought him there was sympathetic. She offered him coffee which he refused. After ten interminable minutes the door opened and a man in a white coat came in.

'Mr Barkley?'

Martin sprang to his feet. 'Yes.'

'My name is Hornsby. You know by now, I'm sure, that your wife has been in a motor accident. She suffered severe injuries,

297

I'm afraid.'

'How . . . how bad is she?'

'She is gravely ill, Mr Barkley. There were crushing injuries to the abdomen and she ruptured her spleen.'

The room seemed to tilt about Martin. He swallowed, and clutched the edge of the table for support. 'Can you tell me what her chances are?'

'The next forty-eight hours will be vital. If she survives those she should have at least an equal chance of complete recovery. I need scarcely tell you she is in intensive care and being given every attention.'

'Thank you, thank you,' Martin murmured. 'Can I see her?'

'It would be inadvisable just now, I'm afraid. There is one other thing I must tell you.'

'Yes,' Martin said, dreading what further terror was to come.

'Much of the glass in the car must have been smashed. It would seem that it came into the car on impact. Your wife must have been struck by this flying glass. If she survives she will be badly scarred about the face. There is little we can do about that now but, today, of course, facial surgery can work wonders.'

When the surgeon had gone Martin put his face in his hands and wept. He had just realised how much he truly loved his worthless wife.

21

The news of the accident was not in the morning papers but it made minor headlines in the early editions of the evenings. These were brought to Julius as they came out and it was his habit to leaf through them, paying special attention only to the racing results and the financial pages. But the headline RACING PERSONALITIES IN ACCIDENT could not fail to catch his eye. At first he only glanced at it; then his own name, Marker, caught his attention. He looked more closely. Evelyn! Thank God, anyway, she was not seriously hurt. She had been discharged after an hour or so. Pat was said to be comfortable. Miriam Barkley's condition was stated to be critical.

Julius read the report again. Almost immediately something struck him as odd. Evelyn was mentioned as the driver of the Jaguar. Evelyn did not own a Jaguar. That must be a mistake. If so it should be rectified immediately. But whatever had happened she would need help and advice. He pressed the switch on the office phone and told the operator to ring Evelyn's flat. But she was not there nor was she at her cottage and it was the following morning before he found her.

In the intervening twenty-four hours Julius gave the matter much thought. His first feeling of anxiety for his daughter had been replaced by one of puzzlement and rising irritation. What damn fool affair had she got herself mixed up in now, he wondered? And with Colby, too. And the third party had been Barkley's wife whom the morning papers showed as still on the critical list. It all added up to pretty juicy pickings for the press to get hold of. The morning papers had been comparatively restrained partly, he supposed, because of the gravity of the Barkley woman's injuries, but Hector Mallinson had not avoided throwing a few titillating hints into his report.

As well as that aspect of the matter there was, too, the business of Evelyn being reported as the driver. Could this be true? If so, why had she been driving? She was, he knew, a skilful and reliable driver. It was unlikely she would have precipitated an accident like this. Could it have been that Colby was drunk and she was taking him home? He read the reports again and as he did so suddenly remembered the driving case Colby had been involved in a month or so back. The press had gone to town on that one. Hadn't Colby been warned not to get into trouble again? Indeed he had, Julius remembered it quite clearly now, and, knowing his daughter, he was able to make a shrewd guess at the real reason why she had been reported as the driver of the car. Whatever the truth was, she was in trouble; she would need help and Julius would not refuse it to her. He told the operator to ring his solicitors.

Evelyn was fortunate in being able to spend the remainder of the night after the accident with friends. The hospital had wanted to detain her but since she had not disclosed that she had been knocked out for a moment and since her injuries were minor they could not insist. She had signed the necessary document and discharged herself. The next morning she had been interviewed by the police and had made a statement. She could recollect very little of the facts of the actual accident but she had confirmed to them that she was the driver of the car. When she heard that Miriam Barkley was still on the critical list she began to realise something of the enormity of what she was getting herself into. On reaching her flat she felt very lost and alone. There was no one she could turn to for the advice she felt she needed. It was almost a relief when the telephone rang and she picked it up to hear Julius's voice. She agreed with surprising meekness to come round to his office.

'You've had a lucky escape,' Julius said once he had satisfied himself that she was in fact unhurt. 'What I don't understand,' he went on quietly enough for him, for there was in his voice nothing of the hectoring tone he often adopted on these occasions, especially with his daughter, 'is why you are said to have been driving the car. That's wrong surely?'

'No,' Evelyn said flatly. 'It's not wrong. I was driving.'

'It's not like you to drive other people's cars without a reason.

300

Was he drunk?'

'No,' Evelyn said. 'He wasn't drunk.'

'I see. I don't understand it. The driver usually gets the more serious injuries. Here it seems the other way round. How bad is he?'

'He's not very bad. Concussion, cuts and bruises. The hospital say he'll be out soon.'

'But the woman. She's badly hurt, I understand.'

'Yes, Julius,' Evelyn said quietly. 'I'm afraid so.'

'And you still say you were driving?'

'Yes. What is this, Julius? Why are you badgering me?' Evelyn felt her temper rising. She had wanted help and sympathy. She might have known it would be like this.

'Because I'm trying to help you, my girl, that's why. Do you realise that if that woman dies you'll be facing a charge of manslaughter? You can go to prison for three years. Now, were you driving that car?'

Evelyn felt her father's eyes go right through her, boring into her brain. She thought she almost recoiled physically. Her mouth went dry with fear. Prison! She had never thought of that. As she met her father's eyes again she knew that he had read her own and that he knew she was lying. But what could she do? She had told the police. She had to go through with it now. Besides, although her father might know she was lying he could never prove it. 'I was driving that car, Julius,' she said. 'Can't we leave it now?'

'No. We can't leave it. You're lying. You're lying to protect that worthless Colby. What are you doing, girl, ruining your life for that dross?'

'He's not dross,' Evelyn said hotly.

'We'll see about that when he comes out of hospital and if he's man enough to say who was driving and take what's coming to him.'

'Don't you go near him, Julius. If you do I'll never speak to you again.'

'Don't threaten me, my girl. You need my help. How are you going to defend yourself if you persist in this ridiculous lie? They'll bring charges, no doubt about that.'

'I have my own money. I can find my own lawyers,' she flared at him. 'You made me independent. You're forgetting that.'

'That I'm not,' Julius said. 'I warned you once not to count too much on that independence.'

'You can't take it back.'

'That's just what I can do.' Julius flipped a key on the desk box. 'Ask Mr Daunt to come in,' he said.

The door opened and a thin-faced man with a flat briefcase under his arm entered.

'This is John Daunt from my solicitors,' Julius said. 'You remember him from the time I made the settlement.'

Evelyn nodded without speaking.

'Daunt,' Julius said. 'I don't think my daughter will quite believe me if I tell her I have a power of revocation under those settlements. Perhaps you would explain.'

The solicitor cleared his throat. 'When your father settled the money and the place in Sussex on you, Miss Marker,' he said, 'you were, of course, very young. He was anxious to give you some independence and yet retain a measure of control if, for instance, you should—er—contract an undesirable alliance . . .'

'Which seems to have happened,' Julius put in grimly.

'To that end therefore,' the solicitor continued, 'he instructed us to put a revocation clause into the deed. Which means, in effect, that he can cancel all the settlements at any time.'

'It's not fair!' Evelyn exclaimed. 'How could you? I'll fight it!'

Daunt coughed. 'That is, of course, a matter for you, Miss Marker,' he said. 'But I think you would be ill-advised to do so. We took the precaution of having you independently advised by another solicitor. I have no doubt that he will be able to give evidence that he explained the contents of the deeds very thoroughly to you before you executed them.'

'I didn't listen to him.'

'Listen to me, now, then,' Julius put in. 'She says she was driving the car, Daunt, in this accident.' He tapped the newspaper report which was in front of him. 'What will happen to her?'

'She will certainly face charges of dangerous driving.'

'And manslaughter?'

'If the lady who was involved and who is, I understand, critically ill, dies, then, very probably, yes.'

'Thank you, Daunt.'

When the solicitor had gone Julius looked at his daughter

and sighed. Suddenly he felt very old. He knew beyond thinking or talking that she had not been driving that car. But she sat there denying it and staring defiantly back at him. Nothing now, it seemed, would make her tell the truth. And all on account of that young whelp Colby. He sighed again. Tough and hard as he was this was his daughter. He must give her another chance. 'You're in trouble,' he said. 'I want to help. You've heard what Daunt said. You face a trial, possibly gaol. You want the best that can be got to defend you. Think it over.'

Outside his office Evelyn felt her legs trembling beneath her. She had met her father at his most elemental and the experience had shaken her. For the first time for as long as she could remember she felt tears welling behind her eyes. She knew now that she had behaved like a fool. It had been an impulsive act which had seemed the right thing to do at the moment of its inception. She had never even dreamt of these consequences. But how could she now go back on what she had said? She'd even told the police. And what about the consequences to Pat if she did? What was she going to do?

She badly needed someone to confide in, someone to advise her. Her father had only made things far worse. But who could she turn to? It was then that she thought of Myles. He was always there to come back to. He was kind, thoughtful and understanding. Myles would know what to do. Myles would never refuse to help.

She crossed the road to Claridges and rang Myles's flat.

Alone in his office Julius stared again at the paper on his desk with the report of the accident in it. Then he told the telephone operator to get him Chris Rokeby on the line.

'Yes,' Chris said, he knew all about the accident. He was glad to hear that Evelyn had not been injured. He had been to the hospital to see Colby. He, too, was not badly hurt. The concussion had cleared. The X-ray had shown no damage. He would be out the following day.

'Did he say anything about the accident?' Julius asked.

'He can't remember a thing after they left the hotel,' Chris answered. 'That happens, you know, in concussion cases. They've no memory of what went on immediately before the impact. He's just blank.'

'Very convenient,' Julius commented grimly. 'So he didn't

303

say who was driving the car?'

'No,' Chris said, surprised. 'As I said, he's a complete blank.'

'Does he remember who was driving when they got into the car?'

'I didn't ask him. But I shouldn't think so. Says he can't remember a thing after singing a song in the pub. I understood, Julius, that your daughter made it clear she was the driver.'

'That's what she says, but I'm not satisfied. I think he was.' In that moment all Julius's pent-up rage and anger became fused and concentrated on Pat Colby. He had an occasional capacity for sudden savage decisions, much of which his daughter had inherited and not all of which had served him well. He made one now. 'Look here, Chris,' he said. 'I won't have Colby riding Alexander in the National. I won't have him ride any of my horses again, ever.'

'But, Julius, he must ride. He's ridden him through the season. He's the stable jockey.'

'I don't care what he is, he doesn't ride Alexander.'

'Look, Julius, can't we talk this over?'

'Do you want to lose my horses and that goes for Alexander, too?' Julius said, dangerously.

Ordinarily Chris might have been expected to flare up at this moment, his temper matching Julius's. With another man and on another occasion he might well have told him to take his horses out of his yard and to hell with him and them. But he recognised the steel in Julius's voice and he had dealt with him too long not to know that all the danger signals were out. It was the thought of losing Alexander that deterred him. With that staring him in the face he recognised how much Alexander meant to him. He had liked the horse from the start. He had placed him and nursed him through a long and difficult season when luck and injuries by and large had run against them. Now he thought that he had him right and ready to run for his life in the big one.

Chris had not by his standards had a good season. His horses had been plagued by injuries and illness. When he had had a bet mostly some malign fate had come along to upset the few good things he had expected to come up. Expenses, too, were running higher every day and one couldn't increase training fees anything like fast enough to keep pace with them. Julius was a good owner. The plain fact was that just at this moment

304

he could not afford to let him go. But it was above all the possibility of losing Alexander that compelled him to keep his temper. That horse! There was something about him he had liked from the first moment he had seen him. That was why he had taken so much trouble with him. Myles Aylward, he had to admit, had been right about him when he bought him. For a moment he thought of calling in Myles to help in this situation and immediately discarded the idea. Myles was in some way mixed up with Julius's daughter. It might only make things worse. But he had one more try at temporising. 'Give me three days, Julius, will you,' he said.

'I'll give you three minutes,' was Julius's reply.

Chris swore under his breath. His ready temper almost mastered him. It was on the tip of his tongue to let fly a storm of abuse and bad language back at his best owner. Then he thought once more of Alexander and fought down his anger. 'Very well, Julius, just as you say,' he said. 'What am I to tell the press?'

'Damn the press,' Julius said.

As Chris replaced the telephone he saw his wife standing at the door of the room watching him. 'That was Julius,' he said.

'What was it all about? You look savage.'

'I feel savage. Of all the—' Chris exploded into obscenity.

'Now that you've got that off your chest,' his wife said as he finished. 'What has he done?'

'He's jocked Pat Colby off Alexander.'

'Good heavens. It's that car crash, I suppose.'

'He seems to think his daughter wasn't driving.'

'Could that be true?'

'She says she was. Pat doesn't remember anything. Damn Pat Colby anyway. He's more trouble than he's worth. One thing is certain and that is I'm not renewing his retainer next year.'

'Who will ride Alexander now?'

'Steve Barrett. I suppose Julius will agree to that. He's ridden him in his work. And he's come on a lot this year.'

'What a wonderful chance for Steve.'

'I only hope he makes the most of it.'

When Evelyn rang, Myles was sitting staring at the empty fireplace in his flat and striving not to give way to self-pity. He

305

was surprised to hear her voice and concerned to note an uncharacteristic tremor in it. 'I must see you, Myles,' she said.

'Come on round then, but you won't find me a very cheerful companion.'

As he waited for her Myles picked up the paper and read again the report of the accident. Like Julius he had divined that there was more in the matter than had been revealed but, especially with his own worries upon him, he was not disposed to be particularly sympathetic towards Evelyn. She had been with Colby, she had got herself into this mess and she and Colby could get themselves out of it. Just where Miriam Barkley and the other car came into it was a mystery but it was one which, he told himself, was none of his concern. He had troubles of his own.

At the sight of Evelyn, however, all these resolutions disappeared. She seemed stricken. 'Myles,' she said. 'Something terrible has happened.'

Looking at her sitting on the edge of one of his chairs, twisting a handkerchief between her fingers, her face drawn and grey, Myles felt his heart turn over. For the first time since he had known her she appeared lost and vulnerable. It was better to learn the worst immediately. He spoke the thought which had been uppermost in his mind since she had rung him. 'Is Miriam Barkley dead?' he asked her.

'No. No. She's still on the critical list but she's alive. It is about that accident, though.'

'What happened to you? It's not like you.'

'You might as well know I'd been out with Pat. I suppose it's in the papers anyway. It's awful. It's like a nightmare. I have to tell someone. I wasn't driving the car.'

'But, good Lord, the papers said . . .'

'Myles, Myles, what am I to do? Julius says I'll go to prison for three years. Oh, Myles!' Then the tears came. In a storm of sudden weeping she threw herself into his arms and sobbed her heart out.

Her defences were down. He had never seen her like this before. As the tears ceased Myles shook her gently and led her to a chair. 'The first thing you need is a large drink,' he said. 'Brandy?' She nodded without speaking as she searched for a handkerchief. Myles brought the drink over to her. 'I've made it neat,' he said. 'That's my best brandy so don't murder it. It

306

may be the last I have for some time.'

'Thanks.' She took the glass. 'Christ, I did go all missish, didn't I? I never thought I'd do that. I must be in a bad way. Sorry.'

'Not to worry. I like it. Makes a nice change.'

She laughed at that. 'Belt up, Myles,' she said. She sipped her drink and its warmth steadied her and began to send her strength.

'Let's begin at the beginning,' Myles said. 'Just what did happen?'

'We'd been at that pub, the Red Red Rose, after the Gold Cup, Pat and I. Then we got into his car. We were going along, fairly fast, I think. The other car suddenly shot across in front of us and we hit it.'

'This was Miriam Barkley's car. How did she come to be there?'

'Don't ask me. It's a mystery. I didn't know who it was, of course. Anyway I wasn't much knocked about and I suddenly remembered Pat's law case. He was unconscious. I pulled him into my seat and said I was driving.'

'But there's no problem. The bloody fellow will have to tell the truth as soon as he comes out of hospital. It's as simple as that.'

'It isn't, Myles. That's just it. He can't. He's had concussion. He doesn't remember anything. I've told the police I was driving. Even if he were to say he was the driver no one would believe him. And to make matters worse I've had a flaming row with Julius over it all.'

'Julius? Where does he come into it?'

'He read the reports in the paper. He asked me to come round. He was trying to help in his own way, I suppose. He has a sort of uncanny instinct where I am concerned. He guessed I wasn't driving. I wouldn't tell him the truth. I didn't even tell him Pat's memory had gone I was so furious. He's cut me off with a shilling or whatever you do nowadays, because of it all. Or he says he is going to.'

'But I thought all that money was settled on you.'

'So did I but it seems the cunning old monster put something into the small print that means he can take everything back. He says he'll do it unless I tell the truth to the police. How can I?'

'It's bad all right. I suppose it is true that Pat can't remember

307

anything?'

'Of course it is. It often happens, doesn't it?'

'Look at it another way, though. Perhaps a court or the police or someone would decide that you or rather Pat, or the driver anyway, wasn't to blame. The other car, you say, shot across the road?'

Evelyn brightened a little. 'I never thought of that,' she said. 'Is there any way of finding out?'

'I imagine so. I could ask ehe legal staff on the paper.' Myles checked himself. The paper. The paper was always there to help. But it wasn't any more, or wouldn't be in a few days.

Evelyn noticed his hesitation. She looked at him as if she was seeing him for the first time. 'You're a bit grey round the edges, yourself, Myles, this morning. I've been so busy pouring out my own troubles I didn't notice. Is there anything wrong?'

Myles drew a deep breath. 'Since we're playing truth together,' he said. 'I might as well tell you. I've been fired.'

'Fired? But you can't be.'

'I've made an ass of myself. I've been asked to resign. I'm redundant. It's the same thing.'

'So I've been walled up as we said that time in Ireland, or its modern equivalent, and you've been made redundant. We seem to be in it together. But they can't do this to you. Could Julius help?'

Myles smiled wryly. 'No, above all, Julius can't help.'

'What do you mean? Did he have a hand in it?'

'No, but he might have done.'

'What is this mystery, Myles? Hadn't you better tell me?'

'I suppose I had.' Quickly he recounted the whole story beginning with the interview with Featherstone.

'So,' Evelyn said, 'in a way I'm responsible for your troubles, too. If you hadn't taken the photograph you wouldn't be in this mess.'

'Not so. The photograph is only a part of it.'

'Have you got a print? I might as well see if I was worth it.'

Myles unlocked the drawer, took out the envelope and handed it to her. She looked at it for a moment and then laughed. 'Very nice too,' she said. 'And all in gorgeous colour. Now I know how I look full frontal. I suppose if all else fails I could go for a stripper.'

'That'd be something for Hector's column.'

308

'And for Julius. At least he doesn't matter now. He can't do anything more to either of us.'

'He might. Don't forget Buckner still has the negative.'

'What will you do, Myles?'

'Go freelance, I suppose. There doesn't seem much else. I was happy on the old *Post* but maybe it was bound to come anyway. Featherstone was changing the sports pages. There wasn't room for me in the set-up that was coming.'

'I won't have any money, Myles. We're both in the same boat.'

'As long as we're in it together it won't matter much to me,' Myles said.

22

When Pat came out of hospital Chris drove to the cottage to see him. It seemed to him that what he had to say had better be said personally than over the telephone.

Despite his repeated assurances that he was perfectly all right Pat, in fact, did not look well. Used to hard knocks though he was this one had been of a different sort and harder than most. Chris thought him still shaken. His cheeks were colourless and had a drawn look about them. This did not alter Chris's determination to have the matter of his driving and indeed of his riding out with him once and for all.

'There's something I must say to you,' he told Pat after he had enquired about his health.

'What's that?'

'Were you or were you not driving the car on the night of the accident?'

Pat looked at him, startled. 'Why do you ask that? I can't remember a thing about it at all. It's a blank.'

'Are you sure?'

'Of course I'm sure. What is this?'

'It's not like you to surrender the wheel to anyone. You didn't to Tommy when you had that other crash.'

'They found me in the passenger's seat, didn't they?'

'That's true,' Chris said, frowning uncertainly.

'Evelyn said she was driving. Would she have said it if she wasn't?' Even as Pat finished speaking something stirred at the back of his mind. His memory was not quite as blank as he had thought at first. Glimpses of recollection were creeping back. He recalled singing his song; he remembered running out to the car with Evelyn beside him. A vague sort of film-like flicker

310

showed himself getting into the driving seat. But was this memory or mental reconstruction? Whatever it was it must be wrong. She had claimed to be the driver. He brushed the doubts away.

'Mr Marker thinks she's shielding you,' Chris said grimly.

'Shielding me? What for?'

'You were warned in that law case that you'd be for the high jump if you ever got into car trouble again. She was there. I saw her. She heard it all. Maybe she did switch seats. She was unhurt or damn nearly. Can't you remember anything, Pat?'

'No,' Pat said sulkily. 'Of course I can't.' But that faint recollection slipped into the back of his mind just the same.

'Mr Marker is a bad man to get across. He believes you were driving and nothing will shake him.'

'What can the old fool do?'

'I'll tell you what the old fool can do. He's already done it. You're not going to ride Alexander in the National.'

'You must be joking.'

'I'm not and neither is he.'

'Why didn't you stop him? You're his trainer, aren't you? You could have told him where to put it.'

'If I had he'd have taken all his horses away. Then you couldn't have ridden Alexander anyway. That wouldn't have done anyone any good.'

'You've let me be jocked off,' Pat said hotly.

'That's as maybe.' Chris's ready temper was rising now. 'But let me tell you this. You've brought this trouble on yourself. You're nothing but trouble. You're more trouble than you're worth. I'm not renewing your contract.'

'Think I care? I can get another anywhere. I can go freelance. And I'm going to ride Alexander in the National. I can sue old Marker. Tommy Pereira will get me a lawyer.'

'Don't be a fool. You're not suing anyone. They'd tear you in pieces. What did happen about that accident, anyway? It all looks bloody odd to me. The Barkley woman is still on the critical list. What was she doing there?'

'How should I know? I was having dinner with Evelyn.'

'Were you drunk?'

'No.'

'Why did you let her drive, then?'

'I don't know. Ask her.'

311

'Her father's doing that right now, I imagine.'

'What about my riding fee and the present if he wins?'

'I'll have to see Mr Marker about that. You'll be damn lucky to get anything.'

'Who rides Alexander if I don't.'

'Steve Barrett.'

'Little Steve! He couldn't ride one side of him.'

'He's as good a jockey as you are now. He has a head on his shoulders. He'll be five times the man you are in a year's time.'

'Oh, go and stuff yourself, Chris, and old man Marker, too.'

Ten minutes after Chris had gone the telephone rang. Pat was sitding in an armchair glowering at a picture on the opposite wall. Immediately the door had closed on Chris he had set upon an unoffending leather-covered pouffe and all but kicked it to pieces. That had relieved some but not all of his frustrations. For a few moments he let the ringing continue then, lunging at the instrument, he picked it up. At first he did not recognise the voice at the other end. Then he heard the name. It was Hector Mallinson.

The journalist was at his most unctuous. He had rung, he said, to enquire about Pat's fitness. Would he be taking any rides before the National?

Pat growled back that he didn't know, he expected so, he was quite well now.

'No ill-effects from that awful crash?' Hector's voice was like treacle.

'No. None. None at all, I tell you. Except that I can't remember anything,' Pat added hastily.

'I see. So you can't tell us details. And this Mrs Barkley, poor lady, she's still very ill, I understand.'

'So it seems.'

'But you'll be well enough anyway, to do Alexander justice in the National?'

'I don't know whether I will or not. I'm not riding him in the National. I've been jocked off.'

At the other end of the line Mallinson sat up with a jerk. He pulled a pencil and writing-pad towards him. He was excited. His column for tomorrow was pretty tame. He had rung Pat on the pure chance of picking up something. The fly he had cast seemed to have hooked a big fish. Here was a story and just

312

what he was looking for. His smoothness deserted him for an instant. 'You've been what?' he exclaimed.

'I've been jocked off like I said.'

'Because of your injuries? They don't think you'll be well enough . . .'

'I'm perfectly fit, I tell you,' Pat almost shouted into the telephone. 'All I know is that Mr Marker has jocked me off. I don't even know if I'll get my riding fee.'

'Ah. Mr Marker, I see. You were with his daughter in the car, of course.'

'What's that got to do with it?'

A purring sound came through Mallinson's pursed lips. 'Perhaps everything, perhaps nothing. It raises interesting areas of speculation. When did this happen?'

'About half an hour ago.'

'So no one else knows it yet?'

'No.'

'Do me a favour, dear boy. Keep it that way. I'll see you don't lose by it.'

Mallinson put down the telephone and started to write. His tongue protruded slightly between his lips and he made a faint hissing sound as his pen crossed the paper. This was dynamite; this was something special. And if only luck held and Pat kept quiet it was all his. Moreover it tied in with that law case and with the hints he had been dropping, cleaned from his own observations and racecourse gossip. He'd have to avoid libel, of course, Julius Marker was a tough nut, but he was used to skating on thin ice. That was what he was paid for. He stretched out a hand and, picking up the telephone, rang the paper. 'You've got my story,' he said to the sports editor.

'We're setting it up.'

'Kill it. I've got a better one. Here it is.'

Val Errington stood at the door of Rob Roy's box, his hands thrust deep into the pockets of his short mackintosh, and stared lugubriously at his horse. The horse looked a picture. There was nothing wrong there. He had him ready or almost so. Rob Roy's preparation had gone just as he had wanted without interruption from illness or injury. If the luck held he could go to Aintree full of confidence that he was bringing with him the third horse in living memory to win the National in successive

313

years.

But as he stood and stared the rain was beating on his shoulders in a steady downpour. Grey clouds were sweeping in over the coast from the Atlantic. It was raining as if it was never going to stop. And the weather at Liverpool, so he was told, was even worse. A little rain would not have worried him. Rob Roy was not really a firm ground specialist. He liked the ground good enough to suit his long stride; it did not have to be the next thing to concrete the way some of them wanted it. But the one thing he could not cope with was heavy going. In that he lost his action and floundered.

But the state of the going was far from being the worst of Val's worries. His sanguine nature told him this weather could not go on for ever and anyway Liverpool dried very quickly. On thinking back it was years, he told himself, since the ground there had been really heavy. On anything else his old hero would be fit and fancied to win again—that was if he could find a suitable jockey. It was lack of a rider that was bringing the worried scowl to his features as he watched Rob Roy placidly consuming his second feed.

Chick Manton who had ridden and won on him last year had been claimed elsewhere. He had kept reassuring Val that everything would be all right, and that he would be free to ride Rob Roy again since his present Guv'nor's entry would not run. The horse, so Chick had said, was useless. He was quoted at a hundred to one and it might as well be five hundred. He was certain to be struck out. But at the last forfeit stage he had been left in, his owner taking the view that hundred to one chances had won the National before and he wanted to have a run for his money. He had also insisted that the claim on Manton should be enforced and that he would ride him.

By then all of the leading jockeys had made their arrangements and Val had had to look around him in a hurry. He had heard good reports of Ginger Arkwright, Paul Cantrey's second jockey, and had gone to Taunton to see him ride. Paul was a great trainer of jockeys and, impressed with the boy's performance, Val had engaged him there and then.

Paul had had a runner in a novice chase at Hereford a few days later. He had no intention of risking Tim Hanway's valuable bones on a chancy jumper in a novice chase so soon before the National. Ginger Arkwright had had the ride. The horse had turned over at the open ditch and broken Ginger's right arm at the elbow. He would be out for most of the season. Val had no jockey and was at his wits' end to find one.

It was not the riding fee, he told himself, though there had been times not so long ago when he had been hard put to it to find it. Running a horse in the National was an expensive business. It always had been but now, of course, it had increased like everything else. You paid twenty pounds to enter, sixty more unless you struck the horse out by a date in February, another thirty if you left him in at the last forfeit stage and a further forty if you declared him to run. That made a hundred and fifty and there was the jockey's riding fee on top of it all. The ordinary riding fee for a jockey was seventeen pounds twenty-five pence, but by an old custom the going rate for riding in the National was a hundred pounds and this had recently been doubled. Some of the leading jockeys wanted even more. So that in entries and fees you were out of pocket at least three hundred and fifty nicker before you came under starter's orders and then, Val told himself, the bugger would as like as not get knocked over at the first fence.

In Val's bad days it had been hard enough to find the money to meet these expenses. The prize, though was enormous, far bigger than anything else in chasing. Last year he had pocketed nearly twenty thousand for his win and that was after expenses as well as presents to the jockey and everyone else in the yard had been paid. So now he was in the position that he did not have to worry what it cost him. But he still had not got a jockey.

His head lad joined him and together they stared through the rain, over the half-door, at the horse.

'Seen Hector Mallinson's column today?' the head lad asked him.

'No,' Val answered without moving his head. 'I never read that trash.'

'I think you'd be interested in this all the same,' the head lad said, taking the paper from his pocket and handing it to Val. It was folded open at Hector's piece. The rain dropped from the peak of Val's cap as he read it.

JOCKED OFF!

The National is not the National without sensations, and

315

they started yesterday. Pat Colby has been jocked off Alexander, Chris Rokeby's runner in the big race. There is no question of unfitness. Colby assures me he has completely recovered from injuries received in the recent motor accident and is one hundred per cent fit now. No reason has been given. Chris Rokeby, when I made contact with him last night, confined himself to saying that the decision was the owner's not his. Mr Marker was not available for comment. However, as readers of this column will know, Colby has recently been seen racing and elsewhere much in the company of Mr Marker's daughter, Evelyn, the three day event rider. They were together in Colby's car when it collided with one driven by Mrs Miriam Barkley, wife of another racing personality and a steward of the Jockey Club. Mrs Barkley is, I understand, still critically ill. Thus private lives of prominent people have public repercussions. Mention of the public leads to another thought. Alexander is presently quoted at 25–1 in the ante-post lists. No runner in the National from Rokeby's powerful string can ever be ignored. The public have backed Alexander. It cannot assist his chances to be deprived of Colby's services at this juncture. Colby is currently second in the jockey's list, has recently won the Gold Cup on Pirate Gold and is riding as well as anyone in England today. This is not the way the public or their money ought to be treated. Nor is it in the best interests of racing. In the absence of an explanation one can only speculate on the reasons behind Mr Marker's precipitate action and some of the speculations must verge on the scandalous. Owners as much if not more than anyone else in racing owe a duty to the public. Mr Marker should think again.

Val read the piece twice. Then he pushed the paper into the head lad's hands and ran across the yard to the house. Throwing the door open he shouted: 'Where is the Turf Directory? What is Pat Colby's telephone number?'

Pat was at home staring alternatively at his bank sheets and the rain which was pouring down his window panes. He was still raging inwardly at Chris's treatment of him, cursing his financial position and struggling with a small voice which was saying somewhere in the depths of his consciousness that perhaps he had been driving the car.

The phone had been ringing constantly since the news broke of his removal from riding Alexander. He had been so pestered by it that when it rang again he was in two minds whether or not to lift it off the hook. Finally he did so, thinking that when he put it down he would leave it off altogether.

'Val Errington here,' a voice said. 'I've just read Hector Mallinson's column. Is it true?'

'True? What do you mean true? That I've been jocked off?'

'Have you?'

'Yes, it's that fucking Marker. He . . .'

'Will you ride Rob Roy for me in the National?'

Pat drew a deep breath. Would he ride Rob Roy! This was like a fairy story. Would he not ride Rob Roy and show those . . . Then his eye fell on the bank sheets. It would not do to be too keen. If Errington wanted him, he wanted him badly. 'I've got offers already,' he said. This was true, he had, and neither of them was to his liking. They were both for outsiders, one of whom to his certain knowledge was a hundred to one against his getting beyond Becher's first time round. 'I'll ride him for you,' he said. 'If the fee is right.'

'What do you want?'

'A thousand pounds.'

Val drew a deep breath. 'That's a lot of money,' he said. 'I could get Piggott for that.'

'Not in the National you couldn't. But I'll do for you what Piggott would on the flat. What more do you want?'

'You'll take seven-fifty?'

'No. A thousand.'

'Very well then, if I must, I must. It's yours. When can you come down and get the feel of him?'

'I'll ring you this afternoon when I've looked at my book.'

Putting the phone down Pat glanced again at the bank sheets. A thousand nicker! That'd be a help. And the present if he won. Damn it, he'd forgotten to tie that one up. It had to be at least ten per cent of the stake. When he went down to Val's to ride Rob Roy he'd make certain it was a damn sight more. Then he could thumb his nose at bank managers, owners, trainers, the whole bloody lot, for a bit anyway.

Back in Somerset Val went out to the yard and walked across

317

to Rob Roy's box. He looked in at the horse and the horse looked placidly back at him. 'I've got a jockey for you, me old hero,' he said. 'He'll give you a ride, too, even if I do think he's a right bastard.'

Colonel Richard Roicey was having breakfast with his wife when the paper with Mallinson's piece on it arrived. He always read Mallinson's column. He read it with distaste, but still he read it. That was why Mallinson commanded one of the highest fees in racing journalism. Opening the paper he wondered what mischief Mallinson was up to now. As he read he choked slightly. Then he put down his coffee cup with a bang. 'Good God!' he said. 'Good God!'

'What is it, Richard?' his wife enquired. 'It's not that wretched man Mallinson again, is it? Really, dear, if you go on reading him sooner or later you'll have a stroke. It's inevitable.'

'Julius Marker has jocked off—hateful expression by the way—young Colby in the National.'

'Why?'

'Why? I don't know why. Mallinson hints that it has something to do with that motor accident. I must ring George Spanner immediately.' He pushed back his chair and left the room.

'Richard, you haven't finished your breakfast,' his wife called after him. Then she picked up the paper and looked at it. 'What a *horrid* man,' she murmured as she read.

'George,' Colonel Roicey bellowed into the phone. 'Seen Mallinson's column this morning?'

'Just finished reading it, Dick, as a matter of fact. Is it correct? Has to be, I suppose. Julius must be mad.'

'Taken leave of his senses. But, look here, George, that matter we were talking about—putting him up, y'know. Won't do now. Bound to be objections.'

'I'm afraid so. And it would look very badly in the press if he was elected just after this. You know there's something in what Mallinson says though it's not the way I'd have said it. Pity.'

'Great pity. Must be that daughter of his and Colby. He's very fond of her, I believe.'

'Mallinson certainly hints that something like that is behind it.'

'Terrible fellow, but he usually knows what is going on. Bad luck on Chris Rokeby.'

318

'Yes. He'll scarcely win it now. Not that I think he would have anyway. That horse has been difficult to train, I believe.'

'Well, pass the word around, will you, George, that we're not going on with putting him up, for the present anyway. I'll do the same.'

So Hector Mallinson in his own way had cooked yet another man's goose, an achievement in which he always took considerable pride.

23

The days before the National bring tension with them to every-one remotely concerned with it. The Gold Cup may be the racing man's steeplechase but the Grand National is everyman's. It is followed all over the world and is the greatest event in the steeplechasing calendar. The fences may have changed and the class of horse that contests it diminished but nothing can alter the tightening of nerves as the day ap-proaches. It is still the big one, the winning of which stamps the seal of success on the racing careers of both horse and man.

Jockeys are infused with the sense of coming occasion. It is heightened by the fact that most trainers instruct their National riders not to take mounts in novice chases or on uncertain jum-pers for at least a week before the day. This is to ensure that they preserve themselves intact for the coming Saturday when they will put themselves at risk over thirty of the biggest fences in the world.

Perhaps trainers find their nerves stretching more than anyone. One hint of illness or an injury however slight may bring the work of months to naught. And there is the constant worry as to whether they have correctly timed their charges' preparation to bring them to the highest peak of fitness on the day. Have they, in fact, put one gallop too many or one too few into them?

For the Grand National is incalculable, 'a law unto itself' as the old timers used to say. No one can tell the type of horse that will win it. The winner's enclosure has been occupied by a horse who started his career between the shafts of a dray, by old-fashioned 'National types', by flat race weeds, by favour-ites, by long shots, by geldings, mares and entires, by horses that could not jump park courses, and by horses that could not stay two and a half miles over the same park courses. There is therefore no yardstick for owner, trainer or jockey to tell him how his horse is likely to perform over the four miles, eight hundred and fifty-six yards of level Liverpool ground.

Even if there was it would not take in the greatest imponderable of them all—luck. Given everything human care and skill can do in preparing a horse for the National, given, too, the utmost in equine ability and courage coupled with the ultimate in jockeyship, no horse can win at Aintree without having luck on his side—luck to avoid fallen horses, luck to save one from interference or being knocked off or knocked over, luck to protect from the hazard of loose horses plunging, weaving and running wild. And no one has a lease on luck in racing. So it is no wonder that nerves begin to stretch and twang.

Even Robert Warminster caught the infection. He took to telephoning every day to enquire about his horse. He was backing Watchmaker as if defeat was out of the question. Arthur dreaded to think the amount he stood to lose. Mentally and not for the first time he damned all betting owners whose activities only served to increase the general strain of preparing horses for the National. Robert, too, insisted on coming down to see Watchmaker in his work and would not accept any of the excuses Arthur rather lamely made in an effort to put him off.

Watchmaker had not, in fact, won at Ludlow. He had finished second. But since he had only been beaten half a length by a young and promising horse of Paul Cantrey's who was getting weight and who was not in the National and since he had still left himself something to work on, Arthur was satisfied enough. He could improve him a pound or two before the race, Arthur thought.

Daddy, too, was happy with the horse and more happy with his home life than he had been for some time. The results of her tests had not yet come to hand but Millie seemed calmer and easier in her mind. So things were better between them. He had not again mentioned to her his thoughts about the little farm and she had not nagged him about his retirement. But Daddy had begun to think that he should pack it in anyway. He was nearly thirty-eight; he had had a good season and he could go out on top. If he wanted to get horses to do on that little farm it would help that his name had been back in the news again. He had, this year, succeeded in putting by some of the money which had come in. He thought he could get a mortgage and he was sure the Guv'nor would do what he could to help. If only he could win the National with Watchmaker! He would be certain of getting at least three thousand and, since his Lordship was betting, so he was told, as if it was going out of fashion, he'd probably be good for considerably more.

For Daddy could not disguise from himself that since Christmas things had been telling on him more than they had done. When he had a fall nowadays he felt it more than he used to. That fall at Worcester last week, for instance, had seemed to go right through him and had left him shaken for days even though nothing had been broken. And now that the season was coming to its climax the mental and physical strain were both beginning to get to him. He was tired, that's what it was, more tired than he should have been, more tired than he had ever been before. He had been hard at it now for twenty years. Come to that he'd been hard at it since August of this year, riding more than he'd been for years back. Racehorses got rests on and off through the season but their jockeys didn't. It was time to go—if only he could win the big one and secure his future!

Meg Meredith pored over the Book of Stars and pondered her dreams which, such of them as she could remember, were becoming more and more confused as the day approached. She consulted the book, the firmament and Joseph. The one person that she did not consult was her trainer, Alastair Bragdon.

Alastair was puzzled about Starflight. He had won that race at Warwick and won it well. Alastair had backed him at tens and that was very satisfactory. But since then he had seemed to work in snatches, one day being impressive and raising hopes and the next listless, uninterested and virtually doing nothing. Alastair had asked his former trainer about him but had learnt very little save the opinion that the horse ran his best races when he was fresh. Suspecting heart trouble Alastair had called in his vet. They had galloped Starflight and jumped him. Afterwards the vet had placed his stethoscope on Starflight and declared that as far as he could see the horse's heart was better than his own. Could it, Alastair wondered, be the virus, or a blood complaint or was it just sheer equine cussedness and bloody-mindedness? Like Val he, too, had jockey problems. He had no experienced jockey to ride Starflight and no hope of getting one. He had asked Tim Hanway if he could recommend anyone and to his surprise Tim had suggested that he should put up his own boy, Dixon. 'He rode that old horse of yours, Credibility, right well at Nottingham,' Tim said. 'I watched him. You could have the makings of something good there.'

Alastair had rung his aunt and when she found that she could not obtain Rendall's services she had rather surprisingly agreed to Alastair's putting the boy up. 'I'm puzzled about the omens,' she said in all seriousness. 'The Book says something unusual is about to happen. Perhaps this is it.'

So Dicky Dixon to his unabashed delight secured his first ride in the National and the riding fee of two hundred pounds for doing it.

Chris grew every day more silent and morose which was the way things took him. He kept telling himself that young Steve would give the big horse every bit as good a ride as Pat would have done but in his heart of hearts he doubted it. Steve was a damn good little jockey but he had neither the strength nor the experience of Pat. He could do nothing about the former but in order to go some way toward remedying the latter he hired a camera projector and the films of the last six Nationals. The projector and its screen were set up in his drawing-room and here in the evenings he and Steve spent hours running and re-running the films, analysing the tactics of the successful jockeys, discussing the fallers and the failures and the reasons for them and thrashing out their tactics for the big day.

Chris worried, too, over Alexander and his preparation. He had not been able really to learn as much about him as he would have liked. There had been that first lay-off early in the season owing to the spread plate and then the virus infection—if virus it had really been, for Chris was now inclined to doubt it. It was true he had come to hand very quickly on both occasions and run good races after them. That run at Cheltenham had been excellent but the horse had not been pressed and it had really told him very little beyond that he appeared to have made a complete recovery. But when he was asked the ultimate question would they find that the mysterious virus had left its mark? How much work should he shove into him now before the race, bearing in mind the possible effects of the virus and the risk of over-doing it, if, as he believed, the horse required a comparatively gentle preparation to bring him to his peak? He believed that but he had no proof of it as he would have done if the horse had been with him longer or if he had had an uninterrupted preparation. Either way, if he gave him one gallop too much or one too little there was the risk of leaving the race behind him here on the training gallops. It was, Chris told himself, one hell of a problem. It was, too, as he knew, Julius's greatest ambition to win this race. He would not thank Chris for a blatant failure, even if much of the reason for it could be laid at his own door for losing his jockey.

The weather was improving, the forecast was good, Val Errington's ebullient spirits were on the upgrade and he was cramming all the work he could into his hero on the springy turf of Cloutsworthy Golf course. He, at least, had no problems about not knowing his horse. He knew every minutest detail of Rob Roy's habits, necessities and needs, and could detect any change in his condition almost before it had happened. He knew that to bring him to supreme fitness what Rob Roy needed in the last few days before the race was work, work and again work. And he saw to it that he got it.

He was, too, delighted with his jockey. Every spare moment he had Pat drove to Cloutsworthy and either rode Rob Roy out or discussed the coming race with his trainer. They, also, had a film; in their case it was of last year's race which Rob Roy had won. Together they ran it through and studied it. 'Tim Hanway'll have the inside, that's the way he likes to go,' Errington said. 'But my money's on the middle. That's where I used to go when I rode and that's where we were last year.'

'It's more of a race, remember, nowadays, even the first time round,' Pat said.

'Doesn't matter, me lad. It's still as true as ever that you just let him go round the first time especially with that weight on his back. Then you can start riding your race. Let those light-weights burst themselves bollicking about first time round. You stay upright; that's the thing to keep your mind on, boy. They'll have thinned out by the time you reach the water and then you can begin to go.'

Pat nodded. He was beginning to think that the rotund, cheerful man, whom up till now he had regarded as a lucky fool

324

of a permit holder, might know a thing or two after all. Val for his part felt his respect for Pat's professionalism and riding abilities increasing every day. Against his inclinations he also found himself beginning to like Pat even if he had driven the devil's own hard bargain over the riding fee and the present. As well as his percentage of the winning stake Pat had stipulated, and got, a slice of the place money if they were placed but did not win. Admittedly the place money was huge—something like ten thousand for second and over five for third so Val supposed he could afford it. Apart from that he had no fault to find with his jockey. Pat had charm when he wanted to use it and he wanted to use it now. He was desperately anxious to win this race and nothing else in the days before it mattered to him at all save learning about the horse and the best way to go about riding him and winning. No pains were too great for him to take. He lived quietly, talked and laughed with Val and the lads and charmed Val's wife.

Paul Cantrey and Tim Hanway knew each other and their methods and plans so well that they did not discuss the race between them very much. Paul was not a talkative type even with his intimates. Admiral of the Blue was well; he had pleased him both in his preparation and in his races. Tim would get the inside where, he held, though the drops were steeper and the fences stiffer there was less chance of interference, go round the shortest way and win if he could and the horse was good enough. That was all there was to it. But Tim had one peculiarity regarding the National. It was the only event in the year when he allowed any pre-race tension to get to him. He hated both the build-up and the waiting. So he always liked to ride in an earlier race which made the time pass and shortened the waiting period. Paul therefore had to look for a safe jumper for him to ride in the first race, a handicap hurdle, and the one jumping race on the card before the National.

Tommy Pereira began to get the shakes really badly three days before the race. He was determined, however, not to pull out or stand down. Ride in this race he would, come what may. But he began to have ever more frequent recourse to the bizarre little room off his dressing-room where he sought nirvana and found solace for his fears.

Martin Barkley took a suite in a hotel in Cheltenham and drove daily to the hospital to enquire for his wife. She was putting up a tremendous struggle for her life and each day there seemed to be a slight improvement though she was still very seriously ill. He had been allowed to see her though as yet she scarcely recognised him. He put all thoughts of everything else, even the coming race, out of his mind. Nothing mattered to him now beyond Miriam's recovery.

Myles was affected by the build-up and the tension but in a different way. He hated the thought that this was the last time he would cover the race for the *Post*. That was bad enough but even worse was the constant worry as to what use Larry Buckner might put the photograph. For Featherstone had commenced the campaign which was, Myles knew, to culminate in the undoing of Larry Buckner. The lead-up was a series of attacks on bookmakers in general terms. This began with a comparison of the racing finances in England and France, pointing out the enormous gain to racing in a pari-mutuel monopoly, and drawing attention to the fact that there had been an opportunity of abolishing bookmakers altogether when racing restarted after the war which had not been seized. Gradually the articles moved from the general to the particular, alleging that bookmakers, or some of them, besides damaging the finances of the Turf, damaged the interests and threatened the integrity of all those connected with it owing to the opportunities offered them for malpractice. There were references to the doping of Derby favourites in the not too distant past and the promise of revelations to come.

The campaign attracted attention. Shoals of readers' letters, always a gauge of the success or failure of a press controversy, poured in. There was, too, a middle article contributed by a hard-hitting, hard-headed crusading racing writer who often appeared on TV, commending the *Post* for its efforts to clean-up 'one of the last Augean stables in racing'.

Myles wondered once more what Larry's reaction to all this would be.

Even before the articles appeared Larry was beginning to run scared, for his luck which had seemed to be going so well, was

326

turning and turning badly. The first thing to happen was the realisation of every bookmaker's nightmare during the run-up to the National. The favourite, Cottontail, won the Lincoln at ten to one. The 'Spring Double' for bets on the Lincoln and the National, coupling Cottontail and Rob Roy, seemed wide open for the winning. In Larry's book the amount of money going forward on to Rob Roy in doubles and accumulative bets was enormous. And the flood of money for Rob Roy in single bets increased. Larry cut his price below that offered by other leading firms but that did not stem the flow. If Rob Roy won he would be facing ruin.

In his dilemma he tried to get in touch with Bradbury for advice and guidance and failed. The number with the answering service which had been arranged as their method of communication merely said and went on saying that Colonel Bradbury was not available. Nor did he appear on the racecourse.

Then the news broke of Pat Colby's 'jocking off' and his engagement to ride Rob Roy.

In desperation Larry rang Clayhampton which he had been strictly instructed he must never do. But he got no comfort there either. The stud merely told him that Colonel Bradbury was away. When pressed, they had answered that his absence might be a long one. Larry began to suspect that the leading rat had left the sinking ship. After that panic took hold of him.

He had so much on his mind that he paid little attention to the articles in the *Post*. In any event they were in general terms and did not appear to be aimed at him specifically. The main thing, in fact the only thing, was somehow to stop Rob Roy winning. If Pat could be prevented riding him that would enormously decrease his chances. At this late hour Val would have difficulty getting any jockey let alone one of the leaders.

The obvious way of preventing Pat riding was the application of physical violence and for this the Benn brothers and their henchmen lay ready to his hand. But the thought of physical violence revolted Larry. The beating up of Steve Barrett and the sleepless nights of worry that had caused him were only too vivid in his mind. And God only knew what they'd do to Pat if he passed the word along. You couldn't control them, that was the trouble. They enjoyed injuring and hurting and destroying people. They might even kill him. They would almost certainly

327

end his riding career for ever. Larry shuddered.

Then something else occurred to him. Jockeys were not allowed to bet and the most condign penalties were handed out by the stewards to those who were proved to have infringed this rule. Nevertheless everyone knew that jockeys did bet though they took the precaution of betting in other people's names, to avoid placing themselves directly in the power of their bookmaker.

Larry knew all this as well as the next man and he also knew that Pat betted, and betted heavily at times. In addition he knew that Pat and Tommy Pereira were close friends. Tommy had an account with Larry, but he also had accounts with two other leading bookmakers. In common with most other members of the ring Larry had acquired a sort of sixth sense where certain accounts were concerned and he had for some time felt there was something strange about this account of Tommy's. He sent for it now and when it arrived began to examine it.

When scrutinised this account was indeed revealing for it disclosed that an unusually high proportion of the bets were on horses ridden by Pat. The heavier bets, too, were on Pat's fancied horses. Tommy was not a big gambler and, although he and Pat were close friends, it still looked odd especially as the account now showed a substantial loss. At least it showed that someone with special knowledge or what he thought to be special knowledge was operating the account. On enquiry Larry found that the bets were phoned in, generally on the morning of the race. The caller had given the account number, and no one had ever thought of querying the bets. They were within the credit limit, which was substantial, and the account had been settled promptly until very recently when it had begun to run on. There was now quite an amount outstanding. The recent losses corresponded almost exactly with Pat's long run of seconds.

Larry was as sure as he could be of anything that this was Pat's own account. By now Larry was losing his nerve completely. He was desperate. Physical violence was out; he wouldn't go through all that again. But he had to do something. What he was about to do was a bluff, but it might work. He told his telephone operator to get him an outside line. Then he dialled Scarman's number. 'Ring Pat Colby,' he said when the settler came on the line. 'And tell him if he rides Rob Roy in the

National evidence of his betting will be sent to the stewards.'

It was unfortunate for him the *Daily Post* was still monitoring all Scarman's calls.

The *Post* broke the story on Friday, the day before the National.

The only paper Larry looked at that morning was *Sporting Life*. He searched it in vain for a report that Pat would not ride Rob Roy. When he did not find it he knew that his gamble had failed. His heart sank. As he extended his hand to pick a letter from his desk he saw that it was shaking. He knew that ruin stared him in the face. Then he told himself not to be a fool. If Rob Roy was beaten, and a thousand things could combine to defeat him, he might just get by. A victory for Admiral of the Blue whose odds were shortening every day would not, it was true, do him any good either but it would not be as disastrous as if Rob Roy won again. And what about a hundred to one outsider winning? This had happened often before. Something like that thing of Miss Meredith's, Starflight, for instance, or even for that matter Tommy Pererira's Cummerbund, presently quoted at a hundred to one, though, as Larry told himself with a faint grin, those odds might just as well have been five hundred or five thousand.

In a slightly more cheerful frame of mind he went upstairs to his lunch. The daily papers were stacked on the table beside his chair. He commenced to skim through them, paying attention chiefly to the sporting pages. When he came to the *Post* the headline PROOF CONCLUSIVE! caught his eye and the name JAMES MALVEY on the by-line stirred an uneasy recollection. He began to read: *The Post can now show by a concrete example that its allegations concerning interference by a bookmaker with racing and those concerned in it are well-founded. The* Post's *Private File team have uncovered evidence of interference with a jockey, of threats and attempted violence to a trainer and of intimidation offered to punters who have brought up large winning bets. The story is told by* Post's *reporter JAMES MALVEY.*

It was all there—the assault on Steve Barret, the letter bomb, the various acts of blackmail and intimidation on those who had winning Yankees and Canadians, ending with the recent threat to disclose to the stewards the betting of 'a leading jockey' who was, of course, unnamed. Larry Buckner was not

329

named either. But the last sence read: *The* Post *is in possession of a sworn affidavit offering conclusive proof of these facts. This affidavit has been handed to the police.*

When Larry put the paper down his face was white and his hands were trembling. He knew beyond any shadow of doubt that he was the man referred to. So the Steve Barrett affair had not been dead and buried after all. It had been traced to him, just as he had always dreaded, and brought home with a vengeance.

Then the last paragraph with its mention of the police leapt up at him. Scarman. It must have been Scarman. They had got to him somehow. But—the police! He would be arrested and charged. He'd be taken out of his own home and, he supposed, to the police station with a coat thrown over his head as he had seen on TV screens. Brought from his father's house to the police station—what would old Gentleman Joe say to that?

Larry stood at the big bow window of the dining-room and looked at the garden below. Only part of it was kept up now. There was an orchard at the far end where grass and weeds grew at will under the trees. The paths down there, too, were overgrown; what would his father have said to *that*? There had been three gardeners in old Joe's day and a weed found on a path brought a storm down on their heads.

Picking up the paper again, Larry read the article once more and then threw it away. He had made up his mind. No one was going to take him out of his father's house unless he wanted to go. He wondered how much time he had. If the affidavit had been sent to the police—and he assumed it must have been since the *Post* said so—then probably they'd move pretty quickly. Crossing to a door in the far wall he opened it and went into his study. There, pulling a chair to his desk, he took a pad of writing paper and began to write, covering the pages at speed in his small neat hand-writing. When he had finished he addressed and sealed the envelopes. Ringing a bell he sent them down for posting.

There was a gun-rack in the corner of the room. His father in a typically extravagant gesture had had two pairs of Purdeys made for him. Larry had sold one but the other was still there though he had little time for shooting nowadays. Taking his keys from his pocket he unlocked the glass-fronted doors and took down one of the guns. As he put it under his arm he admired yet again its balance and the craftsmanship that had gone into its making. Like his father he loved splendid things. They both loved them too well, he thought, that was the root of their troubles. Then he opened a drawer beneath the rack and, taking two twelve bore cartridges from a box, dropped them into his pocket.

Back in the dining-room he saw the bottle of liqueur brandy on the sideboard. Making a wry grimace he poured himself a measure and sipped it slowly, savouring its warm smoothness. 'Nothing but the best for the Buckners,' he murmured looking at the label on the bottle. Then he replaced the cap and put down the empty glass.

Downstairs he let himself out of the house by a side door. Friarsford was built against a hill. Facing Larry, a gate gave on to a path that led to its crest. Below him and to his right lay the tumbled mass of the Friarsford woods. He remembered how his father had enjoyed bringing down the high pheasants that had soared out of those woods. Larry knew every inch of them since boyhood. They would take some time to find him in their depths, he thought.

It was a spring-like day. The flowers were pushing their way up, the birds were singing. He looked at the sweep of country going down to the valley below him in a patchwork of little fields and, beyond the valley the farther fields that stretched away to the faint golden brown of the moor. It was his country; he had grown up here; it was hard to leave it. Then he turned and took the path that led to the woods.

Hardly had he entered them when a low black car drew up at his father's ornate portico. Two men, one in uniform, got out. They went up the steps and banged on the brass knocker. When the door was opened for them they went into the house.

24

As was its wont, Aintree woke early—somewhere around six o'clock—on Grand National morning. The usual faint haze hung over the course as the lads made their way towards the grim, fortress-like stables to start preparing their charges for the afternoon's great event. Above the haze the sky was a faint steel-like blue. Sea-fog had kept away and the course seemed it. There was the promise of heat in the air and of the sun breaking through later on.

The weather had see-sawed in typical March fashion all the month but it now looked as if Val Errington's luck had held and that he was going to get for his hero the drying ground he needed.

Val had despatched Rob Roy the day before in a specially hired horse-box whose driver had been given explicit instructions to lock himself in and to stop for nothing and nobody on the road. As an extra precaution against unlawful interference Val had sent along the biggest and toughest of his lads and an ex-pugilist from the village to travel with the horses. These he had equipped with pick-helves and given them orders to hit first and ask questions afterwards should any suspicious characters attempt to hold them up. 'I'll see to any damage money, don't you worry,' he said. 'The stake will look after that!'

Both Chris and Arthur had their own horse-boxes. Alastair employed a firm from Yorkshire, from whom his aunt had chartered a box at the lasd moment and at great expense. Tommy shared transport with a friend who lived some miles away and was sending a horse to run in another race at the meeting.

Tommy himself had made up his mind to arrive at the course

as late as possible so as to cut down the interminable period of waiting and he was, unlike the others, determined not to work Cummerbund at early morning exercise on the day of the race.

Soon a considerable number of people had gathered on the course as trainers had their horses brought out to exercise and spectators gathered to watch them.

Chris gave Alexander a pipe opener. When the horse blew clear as he pulled up he breathed a sigh of relief. Then he and Steve set out to walk the course. Although Chris had never been in the top flight of steeplechase jockeys he had been at his best round Liverpool. As well as winning the Sefton he had been placed twice in the National, and he had his own ideas about how to ride the race. 'Some say this and some say that,' he said as they walked down to the first fence. 'But *I* say you'll start between the middle and the outside. And don't go too fucking fast into this first bunker, young Steve.'

They stood for a moment looking at it, a formidable green wall, four feet six inches high, faced with gorse. Unlike fences on other courses National fences are constructed on a foundation of truncated, natural thorn trees. The gorse or fir covering is built around these. The recent addition of an 'apron' of gorse built out from the bottom of the fence to make the horses stand back at it gave it a barely less formidable appearance. Steve, whose first visit to Aintree this was, gazed at it with some awe. Looking back to the start he saw the long run down of nearly five hundred yards, and was not quite sure whether to be glad or sorry for it. The considerable distance from the starting gate, far longer than on park courses, gave an opportunity for the field to sort itself out but it also meant that you had more time to think about the exceptional size and strength of the approaching obstacle.

'See that drop?' Chris pointed to the slight fall on the landing side. 'That's what brings 'em down at this one, especially the buggers who haven't been here before and are going too fast. They're not expecting it and they come on to their heads. Sit tight here and don't go too fast into it. D'ye hear me?'

Steve nodded. 'Tim Hanway told me never to push on first time round,' he said as they trudged on to the third where Chris paused for a moment.

'He's right. Tim usually is right. Take a look at this one now. It's the biggest, they say. It isn't but early on it seems as if it is.

It's all but five foot and it looks bloody big coming into it. Anyway watch for it. Some of 'em will still be going too fast and it'll catch 'em out.'

'What about Becher's?' Steve said as they walked on.

'Becher's is just another fence, Steve boy. Don't get a bogey about it.'

Looking at the mighty drop on landing and the pennant with the white B on it fluttering like a battle flag in the breeze, Steve swallowed hard and said he supposed so. Privately he was thinking that these bunkers looked even bigger in reality than when you saw them on the screen.

'It's the fence after it that really counts,' Chris was striding on, talking as he went. 'You've got to get into it right. Look at it. It's not all that big, but it's on the turn. Go into it wrong and you'll lose lengths. That big bugger Alexander may take a bit of balancing, too. But have him right here and you're dead safe for the Canal Turn and can go on down to Valentine's enjoying yourself.'

'I hope so.'

'Frightened, young Steve?' Chris asked as they came back on to the racecourse again.

'Bloody terrified.'

'That's the way to be. You need to be frightened before you get up here. I always pissed myself for three solid days. But as soon as you're over the first you'll know there's nothing like it. You can't describe it; you've got to do it to know. But you'll enjoy yourself my lucky lad. And don't forget, when you get there—' Chris pointed to the water. 'It's then that you can start riding a race.'

'If I get there,' Steve said under his breath, as he made his way towards the weighing-room.

Other riders were beginning to drift towards it, too, though there were still long hours of waiting to be filled. Soon the whole place began to be crowded. There were thirty-seven starters that year—a far greater number than in any ordinary steeple-chase, which in itself meant that the changing room was more thronged than usual. This led to the jockeys' valets being badgered and overworked as they tried to fit out their charges for the earlier races as well as prepare them for the big one. Added to that, trainers, officials and others were bustling in and out all the time, and members of the TV crew setting up and testing their equipment all increased the general air of nervous confusion. People talked in jerky monosyllables or became uncharacteristically voluble. The atmosphere of suppressed tension permeating the whole confined area soon became almost palpable.

Tim Hanway, wearing the colours in which he would ride the first race, sat on a bench turning a whip between his fingers and staring grimly at the ground. Hearing someone come to the peg beside him he looked up. It was Daddy Rendall. This was Daddy's nineteenth ride in the National. He was one of the few whom pre-race nerves on National day completely passed by. And today he had a special reason for feeling good. He was humming beneath his breath.

'What are you feeling so bloody cheerful about?' Tim asked him sourly.

'It's the missus,' Daddy said.

'Oh, what's it with Millie then?'

'She's been sick on and off all winter. Pain in her side, she said she had. I was worried something dreadful about her.'

'Tough. I didn't know that. You kept very quiet about it.'

Daddy sat down beside Tim and commenced to pull off his tie. 'You know how frightened you get about something like that,' he said. 'You always think it's the worst and it seems to be everywhere nowadays.'

Tim nodded. 'That and heart attacks,' he said. 'Looks like a toss-up which gets you.'

'The doctor did tests. She wouldn't go at first but then I persuaded her. Bit of a time I had with her, too, I can tell you. Seemed like the results would never come. Yesterday they did.'

Tim glanced at the other's smiling face. 'The news was good, then?'

'Couldn't be much better. It's nothing much at all. It's a thing called diverticulitis.'

'Sounds terrible but it can't be if you say so.'

'The doctor says it's common enough and those that have it always think they have cancer. Once he's spotted it he'll have it right in no time.'

'Telegram for you, Daddy,' someone said.

The board was becoming crowded with letters, telegrams, and messages from friends, relations and others who merely wanted to wish their favourite jockeys or fancied runners a clear run and the best of luck.

Daddy took his and opened it. *Good luck to the old man from a has been who could have given you a couple of years*, he read. It was signed by a jockey who had won the race a couple of years back when older than Daddy. Then someone handed him another. *Best of luck dear Daddy from Millie and the boys* this one ran. Daddy read it twice, smiled happily, folded it and put it into the pocket of his jacket.

Tim Hanway rode in the first race, finished third and came back to the changing room to put on his National jersey. He broke the rubber band he was rolling on to secure the sleeve at the wrist and snapped at the valet when he failed to replace it immediately. Then, having weighed out and handed the saddle to Paul Cantrey's head lad, he returned to his seat on the bench and stared morosely at the ground.

The tension mounted. Nerves began to display themselves in all sorts of ways. Shin-guards would not go on properly; pieces of clothing or equipment were mysteriously mislaid and equally mysteriously immediately found; knots on cap-strings would not tie; favourite whips were carefully put aside and then, their hiding place forgotten, had to be feverishly searched for.

Steve Barrett found that he was almost literally pissing himself. He paid frequent visits to the lavatory and offered up a silent prayer that his nerves would not get him in the bowels, too.

Pat grew more and more silent. The conditions were right for Rob Roy or as near right as he could ever have hoped. He *must* win this race. Nothing else mattered at all. He had to win in order to set the seal on his reputation and secure his future and to show those bastards what they had done to themselves by jocking him off. He was encapsulated in his own concentration. He had no time for nerves. All he had time for was thinking out his tactics and repeating to himself his determination to win. He changed slowly, tying his cap with great care and fitting his shin-guards and boots meticulously to his legs so that there could be no possibility of their causing him the slightest discomfort and therefore distraction from the task in hand. He considered the question of wearing gloves. He weighed it in his mind as if it was the most important matter in the world and finally came down against it. It was not going to rain; he would not need them. All these things, though he did not recognise them as such, were signs that the tension was getting to him, too.

Tommy Pereira had the most extraordinary hangover imaginable. He had spent longer than usual last evening in the room off the dressing-room and his recollections of just what he had done or how many he had smoked were more than a little blurred. He had, however, succeeded in waking up in good time to meet his friend and be driven to Aintree. Some time ago he had resolved that nothing in the world would persuade him to walk the course since the sight of those ghastly obstacles would frighten him out of his mind. Besides he had ridden round—or part of the way round—twice before. At the moment, though, his fears seemed temporarily at least to have vanished into a sort of misty limbo that hovered somewhere on the edge of his consciousness. He felt rather as if another man, a replica of himself, was standing beside him and that in some peculiar way he occupied both bodies. The other man appeared to have absorbed all his fears and to be looking at him sardonically and telling him he was a bloody fool. The one that was himself did not therefore suffer from either fear or nerves but drifted along as if he was walking on cushions, as if nothing mattered and everything was fixed and pre-ordained. It was all really rather remarkable and very reassuring.

But outside the tension mounted too. Even Robert Warminster felt it. He looked at his watch for the tenth time in five minutes. 'When does this damn race start?' he said to Arthur.

'Three-fifteen,' Arthur said calmly. 'Over an hour to go yet, Robert. Remind you of anything?'

'Moving up to the start line?'

'Bit like that. It's worse if you're riding. Good afternoon, Meg.'

Both men took off their hats.

'Not wearin' me boots today, Arthur,' Meg said. 'Book doesn't seem to know what to tell me about this one. Haven't been able to see the stars for two nights either. The stake will have to do today.'

'I hope you win if we don't,' Arthur said, smiling at her.

Meg, in fact, was looking rather smart and dashing. She was

337

wearing a blue hat with a wide brim and a tailormade blue suit that showed off her tall figure. In the revers of her coat was a brooch consisting of a huge sapphire circled with diamonds. It had been the last present Blaise Calverly had given her before he sailed for the Western Desert and his death. He had, however, omitted to pay for it and she herself had settled the bill at Asprey's. It must have been the hurry of his departure that had made him forget. She had told herself this so often that she almost believed it, and ever afterwards had fondly treasured the present as a special memory.

Alastair pondered over what instructions he was to give to his jockey. The lecture he had received from Colonel Roicey had gone home. He knew now that he did always try to tell them too much and ended up by telling them nothing. But what the hell was he to say about this horse with his in-and-out way of running to an inexperienced jockey who had never ridden here before?

Again and again Chris turned over in his mind the problem of Alexander. Had he given him one gallop too much or one too little? Had he left his race behind him or failed to bring it with him? And young Steve—could he hold that big horse together and ride him out at the end of four miles of the most testing country in the world? Once more he wished he had Pat riding him. But Pat was on Rob Roy and if he had found any weaknesses in Alexander he would know well how to exploit them. And on top of all this there was Julius and his ambitions.

Julius had not again brought up or mentioned the matter of his jocking Pat off and the storm of adverse criticism he had encountered from the press. Outwardly he appeared unmoved by it all. He preserved an unruffled exterior, puffing on a Corona and commenting that the big 'oss looked right well. Chris noticed, however, that he did not appear to be on speaking terms with his daughter. Horses, Chris thought, were difficult enough to deal with but when humans mixed their problems up with them as well. . . .

Myles wondered if this would be the last National he would cover for a Daily. He had done nothing about looking for another job. He could still scarcely realise what had hit him, and had let the days slip by in a sort of haze. Now, on the course, he thought to himself that next year if he was a freelance he might not even get a press pass. He had not seen much of

338

Evelyn in the few days that had gone by since their talk in the flat, but they had arranged to meet after the press conference that ended the day's proceedings and to travel home together. He had been desperately anxious to tip the winner of this race as his swan song on the *Post*. All his instincts told him to go for Alexander. After all he had bought him and had watched him come along and surmount his difficulties and, whatever way you looked at it, he had close links with his connections. But reason told him that on the book Alexander had little hope of beating either Rob Roy or Admiral of the Blue. And the substitution of Steve for Pat would not help the horse either. After poring over his charts and the form books for hours he had come down in favour of Admiral of the Blue.

Back in the changing room the minutes were crawling by. A talkative Irish jockey had been giving his opinion on everything under the sun including the fact that the third looked bigger than ever until he was told forcibly by his neighbours to belt up. He then began to hum 'Mother Macree' untunefully in a low clef which caused more profanity. Those chosen to appear before the TV cameras for interviews and prospects of the race had done their pieces and returned. The senior steward came in and gave his little address about not going too fast at the first. 'There's a hell of a long way to go, lads, take it steady, don't let's have a pile up, good luck,' which had sunk in perhaps to a few of the younger riders. The old hands had heard it all often before. The TV commentator came down too. In his hand was the big racecard with the colours painted in beside the names. He wanted a last-minute check, for some of the colours were unfamiliar even to him. It was necessary for him, too, to find out the Christian names and ages and number of times some of the more unfamiliar riders had ridden in the race. This was for his commentary during the parade. There were always in this race a few riders, mostly gallant and enthusiastic amateurs riding for the thrill of it, who were seldom seen on the racecourse otherwise.

Then at last came the long-awaited call: 'Jockeys out, please!'

Somehow the thirty-seven riders sorted themselves into a long file that wound its way through the crowd to the parade ring. In the centre the yellow and green of the daffodil bed made

339

a blaze of colour. The horses with their name sheets on them paraded round the outside while the jockeys identified their owners and trainers and made their way towards them. The sun had broken through and sparkled on the silks and jerseys.

Now began for the riders what was perhaps the most agonising period of waiting of them all—the final few minutes before they were put up and got to grips with it.

Steve wondered wildly if his guts really *were* going to dissolve and what he would do if they did. Tim Hanway, tight-lipped, snapped at Paul Cantbey: 'Why the hell do they always keep us hanging around here? Where's the owner anyway?'

'In Cheltenham. His wife is still bad,' Paul said.

Daddy beamed at everyone and told Arthur all about Millie. Pat screwed his concentration on what he had to do tighter than ever, and Tommy still felt as if he was about two feet off the ground, levitating, a sort of spectator and actor too.

Strained jokes were exchanged and last-minute instructions given. Alastair, after much thought, uttered about the only co-herent and sensible instructions he had ever given a jockey since he started training. 'You know as much about this fellow as I do,' he said. 'Ride him as you find him.'

The bell rang for the jockeys to mount. Rugs and namesheets came off. Horses and riders began to sort themselves into the order they appeared on the racecard before filing out on to the course for the parade.

'Rob Roy,' the commentator said. 'Last year's winner and favourite this year to win again. Carries 12 stone. Ridden by Pat Colby, twenty-four years of age riding in his third Grand National, Pat has had a wonderful first season as a professional, winning the Gold Cup a week or so back at Cheltenham and hoping to complete a Gold Cup and Grand National double which so few jockeys have done . . . Admiral of the Blue, the mount of Tim Hanway, the present champion jockey. Twenty-seven years of age riding in his eighth Grand National . . .' And so it went on as the horses crossed the thick carpet of green grass in front of the stands to parade in a long line down the far rails.

At the end of the parade they turned, and the lads slipped the leading reins. The jockeys caught hold of their heads as the horses jumped into their stride to canter once more past the stands and turn left towards the start.

Feeling the sudden surge and thrust of Alexander's powerful

340

quarters underneath him, seeing the shake of his head and hearing the sudden snort of enjoyment the big horse gave as he laid himself down to go, Steve felt all his nervous dreads drop away from him like the shedding of a cloak. His bowels weren't going to dissolve. This big fellow was as well in himself as he could be. Whatever happened, the horse was right and so was he. They'd have one bloody good go together.

After final and last minute adjustments to girths and equipment had been made, the starter, bowler-hatted and in breeches and boots, called the roll and mounted the rostrum.

There was always a good deal of pushing and scrummaging at the National start as jockeys sought the places they wanted.

Tim Hanway found that one of the young and inexperienced amateurs had forestalled him in the extreme inner berth. 'My place,' he said firmly. The young man, who was an accountant in private life, seeing the champion's grim features glaring at him hastily pulled out and looked elsewhere for his starting position. Pat, equally determined, got just where he wanted to be in the middle. 'Can't you take that bloody great brute somewhere else?' a voice snarled at Steve as they wheeled for position. He kept his ground and it was the other who pulled out.

Tommy had no problems. Smiling happily to himself he took Cummerbund to the extreme outside and stayed there. No one appeared to dispute his chosen position and he told himself that neither now nor at any time during the race would he yield the outside to anyone. Daddy quietly brought Watchmaker into the place he had so often occupied before. Dicky Dixon, unused to it all, was edged out and finally found himself towards the outside not far from Tommy.

The wheeling line straightened. Down the course the white flag went up.

'They're under starter's orders,' the race-reader said over the loud-speakers.

Silence fell on the packed stands. Glasses were raised and focussed.

Julius exhaled a cloud of cigar-smoke, picked out his colours and stared stonily at them. Alastair felt his stomach muscles tighten. Would this bloody horse give the old girl a good run? Chris thought about that last gallop and Evelyn Marker, gripped with the excitement of the moment, wished she was out there riding herself.

341

The long line swayed, held steady and moved up towards the single-strand starting gate.

'It looks like a first timer,' the TV commentator said. 'It is—and they're away!'

The bright colours broke up and went thundering down to the first fence.

25

They were over the Melling Road where it crosses the track on the way to the first in, it seemed to Steve, a mere instant after the start. The thunder of hooves was all about him and, despite the long run up to it, they were facing the fence almost before he had time to think. Automatically he had reacted as Chris had instructed him; he was not going too fast; he was taking it at a good steady gallop, almost a hunting pace.

Then they were in the air. Beside him and a little in front of him, someone went down, caught out by the drop and turning over just as Chris had said. Steve did not know who it was nor did he care for he was safely clear. The big horse landed lightly as a ballet dancer and strode on towards the next which he lifted himself over with scarcely an effort.

Then they were approaching the third. This was the one which every rider, facing that great grim wall with its ditch before it early in the race, wanted above all to have safely behind him.

By now the field was spread right across the course. Alexander had plenty of daylight in front of him to see the fence and to measure it. As the guard-rail came up Steve kicked him. An instant later he wished he hadn't. Alexander stood back and jumped. The power and thrust of those great quarters, answering the question he had been really asked for the first time over these big fences, nearly had him out of the saddle. He gasped as he gathered in his reins on the far side. But the big horse had dealt with the drop just as he should. He was galloping on without pause or check. This was an Aintree horse all right.

Steve risked a quick look round him. Daddy on Watchmaker was to his right. On his left, almost beside him, were Pat and

Rob Roy. Tim was beyond them glued to the rails.

All those with years of experience behind them were taking it steady, concentrating on jumping their fences cleanly and safely and keeping out of trouble. Next time, if they got there, it would be different; next time they would be racing.

Already the field had begun to sort itself out. Those on front runners or hard pullers or who were anxious to make the most of a light weight, had gone on. Behind them came the middle division, the old-timers, who knew too much to hurry at the start or those such as Steve into whom experienced Aintree riders had hammered similar instructions. At the rear were the slow beginners, the few who could not cope with the fences at all and who were already out-faced and out-classed, and most of those who were having a bump around for the fun of it.

Starflight was amongst the leaders. Dicky Dixon had been told to ride him as he found him. He found him full of himself, ready and eager to go, and he let him go. Besides, he had not much liked being pushed around at the start. Out in front he thought he would be clear of all that sort of thing. And he was. What was more, Starflight was definitely having one of his going and jumping days. He was enjoying himself, bowling along at the head of affairs, flipping over the big fences as if he did this every day before breakfast, as his rider said afterwards.

Tommy Pereira was bringing up the rear. He sat on old Cummerbund with a happy smile on his face and a haze inside his head. The whole scene being enacted all around him appeared to him rather like figures dancing on a screen. Since he had the wide outside he was more or less alone with no one very near him. He felt as if he was riding a ghost horse in a dream. Had he but known it this was the best thing he could have done. He was completely relaxed and Cummerbund, his head free and his mouth suffering no interference from a frightened pair of hands, was galloping on at one pace, sedately measuring his fences and jumping them perfectly.

And then they were approaching Becher's. 'Here it comes, lads,' the Irish jockey sang out. The breeze whipped the little red flag. The field stormed into it.

Pat, Steve and Daddy took it almost abreast. In front and on their right two horses came crashing down. Beside Steve, as they jumped, someone hit the top and turned over. The next instant as Alexander went out over the drop he felt as if he was

344

floating, weightless, poised in the air. Then the big horse touched down and was instantly into his stride away from the rolling carnage of riderless horses and fallen men.

On Steve's right Watchmaker nodded slightly as he landed, the drop almost catching him out. Daddy sat still, giving him time and rein to recover and, when he did, nursed him along towards the next.

Quick as lightning Pat had Rob Roy just where he wanted him at this next fence which was the one on the turn, set at an angle from Becher's. Once over the Canal Turn, having lost no ground at all, he was veering in towards Tim on the rails with time, effort and distance all saved for the favourite. Every second and every yard meant something when you had the top weight on your back.

Steve followed him as best he could. He too came over the Canal Turn on the right leg and out of trouble, and he was tracking Pat going down to Valentine's. But it was not all that easy for Steve. Alexander had not made a mistake; he was fit and full of running. He wanted to go and Steve had his work cut out restraining him. 'Wait,' he murmured to the big horse as, even at this stage, his arms and thighs began to ache. 'Wait. Next time but not now. Next time you can begin to go.'

Along the far side, coming back towards the racecourse, all the fancied horses, so far as Steve could see, were still there. The fences seemed nothing to Alexander. But, Holy Jesus! he was taking a hold! He wanted to get on with it and here, somehow, he did not seem to like the idea of others being in front of him. Yet hold him, and hold him up he must, Steve knew. The ache in his legs and arms grew worse.

It was at this period that the presence of loose horses began to add to the general perils of the race. They wove in and out amongst the leaders or galloped, nostrils flaring, alongside them. Unless they ran out, they were going to cause trouble, Daddy thought, as the field converged towards the Chair.

The Chair fence—so-called from the little iron chair placed beside it no one knew how many years before—is the highest and biggest open ditch in England. The ditch itself is six feet wide and two and a half feet deep. It is bounded by an unbreakable baulk of timber that is its guard-rail. The fence is a huge solid upright, over five feet high and nearly four feet wide.

Approaching it down the railed-off portion of the course by

345

the stands, for it and the water are only jumped once, was, Daddy always thought, like going down a funnel with a huge obstacle at the end. But he himself, unlike many riders, did not dread the Chair. He had never fallen there and he saw no reason why he should do so now. Apart from that nod at Becher's and a swerve to avoid a faller at the twelfth, Watchmaker had not given him a moment's worry.

The loose horses did not run out.

Two of them jumped it in front. The third swerved across it in mid-air and brought three other runners with him in a crashing pile-up.

Starflight took it immediately behind the first two loose horses, thus avoiding the mêlée. As a result he was left in the lead, and, going down to the water, was ten lengths clear.

Pat and Steve were far enough back to steer away from trouble as was Daddy, but Tim Hanway, on the inside, was almost brought down by one of the fallers. Starflight skimmed over the fifteen feet of water without the slightest trouble and went sailing on.

'I suppose that fellow will come back to us,' Daddy thought. 'He's been up there since the start. All the same . . .' He began to move Watchmaker up a place or two.

'They're going out into the country for the second time,' the commentator said. 'It's Starflight well clear now. He's all of twelve lengths in front. Then come Moonlight Sonata and Nasturtium. Then Rob Roy, Alexander and Watchmaker all in a bunch. Admiral of the Blue met with some interference at the Chair . . .'

In his hotel room at Cheltenham Martin Barkley, his eyes glued to the television set, groaned and tried to pick out his colours from the shifting, striving mass on the screen.

'They're across the Melling Road. Starflight the leader. He's still clear. Rob Roy is well there, so is Watchmaker . . .' the commentator went on.

By now those with a chance were all beginning to close on the leaders. There were seventeen of the original thirty-five starters still standing but some of these were already hopelessly out of it. Cummerbund, to his rider's faintly bemused surprise, had remained upright and was in touch with the middle division.

Once the Melling Road was behind them, they were jumping the fences for the second time. Their tops were ragged and torn, showing where horses had hit them and ploughed through the gorse covering. One or two had holes in them where they had been well and truly smashed into and had exacted their penalty. Wise jockeys avoided these holes. A horse, by now accustomed to the size and span of the intact fence, if pointed at a gap almost invariably either made a mistake or came down.

Steve's arms and thighs were one long continuous ache. He had thought himself fit but this race demanded fitness above and beyond the calls of ordinary steeplechasing. Other races would be all but over by now. Here they had hardly started the second circuit.

The twentieth was a plain fence. There was a bit of a drop but Alexander had dealt with the drops so far without any trouble at all. Surely he'd do this one all right. Steve relaxed for an instant.

Alexander got too close to it, bucked over it and came to the drop in a sprawling heap.

He did not fall; his strength and balance saved him. He staggered, lurched and heaved himself upright again. Steve went out on to his neck.

'I'm gone! I'm gone!' Steve almost sobbed to himself. The grass was racing by underneath his eyes. His arms were round the horse's neck. Desperately, he grabbed at the plaited mane and entwined his fingers in it. 'I won't fall off. I won't fall off,' he muttered through clenched teeth.

Inch by inch he fought his way back. Somehow, with one last heave he clawed himself into the saddle. He was only just in time for they were facing the next. With one iron swinging loose, he never knew how he stayed there over it. Then, miraculously, his foot found the stirrup. He was back in control again. And then Becher's was looming up for the second time.

As the fence approached he heard a laugh. Pat on Rob Roy came up on his left. 'Told you you couldn't ride one side of him,' Pat jeered. 'He needs a man on his back!'

Both horses jumped Becher's perfectly. Pat was very close to him. Too close, Steve thought. He was all but leaning on him. He would have to go wider than he wanted at the one on the turn. They were over it and Pat was still there. Steve glanced at him. Pat was smiling. Then Steve realised what Pat was doing.

He was pushing him out, slowly, inexorably. He would have no chance now of taking the Canal Turn where he had been told to go. Pat had only a few seconds to do it in. But Pat could do it; Pat was a superb rider; he could edge Alexander out and keep his own place, too.

The big horse was galloping strongly, going straight on, pointing at the board fence that bordered the canal. 'You bastard!' Steve shouted.

But Pat had left him, edging away to take the turn just where he wanted on his own line, ready to set sail for Valentine's and home.

Another horse came up inside Steve. Once over the fence he had to wrench Alexander's head round and struggle with him to get him balanced again. He had lost lengths.

Starflight was still jumping merrily along in front. Tim had Admiral of the Blue back on the inside and was very much in the race. Rob Roy was closing on him and Daddy on Watchmaker was not far behind.

'This is a murderous pace for this stage of the race,' the commentator said. 'It seems now as if the winner must come from this group—Starflight, Rob Roy, Admiral of the Blue or Watchmaker. Rob Roy is running a tremendous race under his big weight. It looks very much as if he may do it again. But Admiral of the Blue is there with him . . .'

In his Cheltenham room Martin Barkley's teeth clenched so fiercely on the stem of his pipe that he almost bit it in two.

'How are you going?' Tim called to Pat.

'Better than you,' Pat shouted back. But was he? He thought the weight might be beginning to tell. Rob Roy did not seem quite so fluent as he had been. But they must all be tiring too. This was the National. The others should surely be feeling it now. If only that bugger in front with a mere ten stone on him would come back to them.

Over Valentine's with its drop they pounded, all the leaders landing safely. Crossing the next there was no change in the order.

Then Pat sensed that Starflight was beginning to stop. He'd run his race, he thought, he was probably no danger now. But that bloody Admiral with Tim on him was beside him and

348

going ominously well. And getting a stone and a half from him too.

Rob Roy did not do the second fence after Valentine's, the last open ditch, all that well. He reached for it and the big drop on landing almost caught him out. But Rob Roy had been here before; he was an Aintree horse; he knew all about drops and had the strength and balance to cope with them. He also had the heart and courage to survive mistakes. He shook his head and went striding on. 'This *is* one hell of a horse,' thought Pat.

Admiral of the Blue was a length ahead now and going well. And that bloody Starflight was still there even if not so far ahead as before. One more fence and they'd be on the racecourse again. He'd have to move then but not until then.

They were approaching the fence. Starflight was at it; he was taking off. And in that instant the whole race changed dramatically.

Starflight had shot his bolt. He hardly rose at the fence at all. He hit it half way up, turned over with a crash and lay, winded, on the far side. Admiral of the Blue may have been distracted by the sight of the leader falling or he, too, may have been tiring. For whatever reason he misjudged the fence, brushed through the top and came down.

'Christ! Am I glad to see you go!' Pat thought and immediately afterwards: 'I'm left in front! I've got it won!'

Three lengths behind him Daddy thought so, too. For Watchmaker was stopping with every stride. The brutal fact was that they had all been wrong, Aintree had found Watchmaker out as it had found out so many horses over the years. Watchmaker did not truly stay the four miles. But Daddy knew that much could still happen in the race. There were two more fences to be jumped. Rob Roy must be tiring and he was carrying twelve stone. Rob Roy could fall or the weight could stop him. Watchmaker might find from somewhere some unknown reserve of strength and energy. There was still hope. He must drive Watchmaker on. Daddy was tired; he was aching; his breath was going. But while there was hope Daddy would drive and drive and drive until he dropped.

Unknown to them both Steve had got Alexander balanced and going again. And the big horse was eating into their lead.

At the turn Alexander had collared Daddy and passed him. But Rob Roy had increased his lead over Watchmaker. He was six lengths ahead and going strongly for home. Both Alexander and Rob Roy cleared the second last without trouble or mistake but Alexander was closing the gap between them. Then they were at the last. It had been hammered into a shapeless mass of tattered gorse by horses hitting it earlier. It was one of the smaller fences on the course. It looked nothing much but it was here that Nationals were often lost and won.

Rob Roy was still striding out confidently. He was over safely, he had first run. Pat kicked on for home.

'He won't be caught now,' Val Errington said to himself on the stands. The commentator echoed his words. 'It looks as if it is Rob Roy's second National,' he said. 'They're beginning to cheer him home already . . .' Only Pat knew how tired the favourite was.

Steve saw the tattered remains of the last in front of him. He was aching all over; his wind was running out on him; he had thought he might fall off over the last two from sheer exhaustion. Suddenly all these things were forgotten. To hell with what he'd been told about taking the last carefully, that there was plenty of time on the run in. He drove Alexander into it.

Up on the stands Chris turned to Julius. 'If you have tears to shed, shed them now,' he said. 'He's going too fast on a tired horse. He'll fall.'

Myles's hands were shaking so much he could not hold his glasses steady. He shut his eyes. Evelyn leant forward, tense. 'Good boy, Steve,' she said. Julius drew fiercely on his cigar which had long since gone out. The fulfilment of his life's ambition, he told himself, lay in that boy and that jump.

Alexander met the fence just right, jumped it as if it was not there and gained two lengths in his leap. Steve took out his whip and sat down to ride.

But Pat had smelt danger. He knew someone was coming at him. He had his whip out, too.

The long sward of brilliant green grass that is Aintree's finishing straight stretched out in front of the riders, almost, it seemed to them, to infinity.

Alexander quickened as Chris had always said he would. His great relentless stride cut into the favourite's lead. At the elbow his head was at Rob Roy's quarters. Every man and woman on the stands were now on their feet shouting and roaring. A storm of excited cheering rolled across the racecourse. 'He's left it too late,' Chris said. 'The little bugger has left it too late.' No one heard him.

But it looked as though Chris was right. Although Pat could feel his great weight pegging him down with every stride Rob Roy was fighting back with all that heart and courage could give.

Half way to the post Alexander was at Rob Roy's girths.

Both horses were giving everything they had. Alexander's head was down. The speed of his burst had gone. It was a question of courage and guts now. His head crept closer.

The finishing post loomed large. It was only a few strides away. The jockeys, heads down, driving, whips singing, hardly saw it. Then it towered above them. As if he knew it, Alexander surged forward in one last effort. Locked together they swept past it.

As they pulled up, panting and sobbing for breath, both riders looked at each other. Neither of them knew which had won. There is no photograph at Aintree so they would not have long to wait. Both horses' heads hung down as they grabbed for air after their efforts. Rob Roy was rolling with fatigue; he had given all he had and more; he could scarcely stay on his feet.

Then the loudspeakers crackled. A hush fell over the racecourse. Steve and Pat sat quite still, turning their heads towards the enclosures.

'Here is the result,' the tinny, impersonal voice said. 'First number Twelve. Second Number One. Third Number Thirty-three. Distances—a short head, twenty lengths.'

'I've won!' Steve shouted. 'I've won it!'

Pat, to his eternal credit, reached over and stretched out his hand. 'Well done, little Steve,' he said. 'I didn't think you had it in you.'

Julius and Chris, Myles and Evelyn, each in their separate ways, pushed a path through the crowds that were beginning to stream towards the unsaddling enclosure.

In all the excitement none of them saw what happened to the third of the three leaders as they came to the last. Watchmaker and his rider were both desperately tired. Watchmaker struggled to rise to it, hit the top and turned over with Daddy underneath him. Nasturtium, an unconsidered outsider at thirty-six to one, jumped past the faller to be third. Another outsider, Cummerbund, ridden by his owner, who finished

351

with a beaming smile on his face, passed the post fourth, apparently full of running.

The two mounted policemen were waiting for Steve. Between them he came back in triumph through the milling crowds.

Chris was standing underneath the glass roof of the winner's enclosure. 'You left it bloody late,' were his first words as Steve slid to the ground.

'Well, I won it, didn't I?' Steve said. He could still hardly believe it had happened to him.

'The weight beat him,' Pat said tersely to Val as he stripped the saddle from Rob Roy's heaving flanks.

'You gave him a great ride, boy,' Val said. 'Game to the last, me old hero. Went down with all his guns firing, didn't he?'

'He did all of that and a bit more.' Pat went into the weighing room to receive the sympathy and commiserations he did not want. At any rate, he told himself, I should get about a thousand out of the second stake, that'll be something.

For almost the first time in his life Julius was speechless. He had waited over thirty years for this moment when he would stand in this winner's enclosure looking at the horse who had won the greatest steeplechase in the world for him. Now it had all come true. Whatever happened in the years that were left to him he would have this to look back on. This wonderful moment of fulfilment, triumph and happiness would be with him always. He reached over and slapped Alexander's sweat-stained neck. 'That's an 'oss. That's an 'ell of an 'oss,' he said. 'I always knew he was.'

'Congratulations, Julius.' Evelyn, looking, for once, shy and unsure of herself, was beside him.

He gripped her arm. 'You were there when he was bought,' he said. 'It's all in the family. I wish your mother was here.'

Looking at him for a second Evelyn saw his eyes film with the emotion of the moment. Then it had gone and he was himself again. 'Where's young Myles?' he shouted. 'Where is he? He'll have to share in this!'

Myles had been pushed into a corner by Barty Moriarty. Mr Moriarty was pressing upon him a tumbler that appeared to contain at least four double measures of Irish whiskey. 'Didn't I tell ye this big fellow would lep a town,' Mr Moriarty was saying. 'I gev him away to ye, that's what I did, so I did. Gev him away! What's he worth now? But, be God, Mr Aylward,

352

sir, d'ye know what it is, ye're a great judge. De minit I set me eyes on ye I said to meself if der's a National winner in it dis gentleman will find him! Isn't that right, Sean?' He turned to his acolyte, a little man with a puce complexion wearing a blue Melton coat.

The little man hiccuped slightly. 'I t'ink we'll have another drink, now, Barty,' he said.

Arthur Malcolm went by a few feet away. 'There is someone I must see,' Myles said, extricating himself. 'Arthur! One moment.'

Arthur checked and turned. 'Oh, it's you, Myles. Congratulations. You must be delighted.'

'Yes, of course. But how is Daddy Rendall?'

'I've just been in the ambulance room. They've taken him to hospital but it seems as if it's not as bad as they thought, though it's bad enough. A broken thigh and a bang on the head.'

'Is it a bad break?'

'I'm afraid so. It looks like the end of the road for him.'

'Bad luck and he was having such a good season.'

'Well, perhaps it was time. He should be all right financially. I'll see to that.'

'How is Warminster taking it all? Bit of a change from the flat.'

'Delighted. Never got such a thrill in his life, he says. Thinks Rendall gave him a great ride. He'll do something for him, too. Says he's hooked on it now. Wants me to buy him one to win next year!'

As Tommy was entering the weighing room he was stopped by one of the press association reporters whose job it was to compile an accurate record of the race with details of each horse's performance. 'Where did you fall?' the reporter asked him.

'Fall? What do you mean, fall?' Tommy said with great dignity. 'I'd have you know I'm told I finished fourth and I'm on my way to weigh in.'

Inside the changing room he began to pull off his boots. 'Fred,' he said to the valet. 'Send out immediately for a magnum of champagne. And as for these boots, take them away. Don't hang them up or do anything else with them—*Boil* them!' He smiled happily and began to tell his neighbour, who had fallen at the first, how much he had enjoyed his last, his very last ride over fences at Aintree or anywhere else.

After the TV interviews had finished the ground-floor press-room next door to the weighing-room was cleared for the usual ceremony of the Grand National Press Conference. All the press, including gossip writers and local reporters who had nothing to do with racing, crowded in. Myles took a place at the back and found himself beside Hector Mallinson.

The door opened and the Chief Constable entered followed by Julius and Evelyn with Chris and Steve Barrett behind them. They made their way to the head of the big table.

'His daughter is with him, I see,' Hector commented. 'The old man must be handing out general forgiveness all round.' Myles marvelled again at the accuracy of his information. How did he know about the quarrel? 'Heard about Larry Buckner?' Hector was going on.

'No. What now?'

'Shot himself. It just came through. They found the body about the time the race was starting. Symbolic in a way, isn't it?'

'Good God.'

'He never did quite measure up, did he?'

'I didn't think it would come to that.' Myles paused and then added under his breath. 'I hope Featherstone is pleased with his handiwork.'

'What did you say?'

'Nothing, Hector.'

By now the barrage of questions had started. Steve was going over his story of the race yet again for the benefit of those present. Evelyn, looking faintly surprised to be there, was sitting beside her father. Myles wondered what was going on in her mind. He had news to tell her and he wanted to see her. In common with most of the purely racing reporters he disliked having to appear at this conference and thought of it as a waste of time.

Evelyn's mind was far away from the events taking place in front of her. For the first time in her life during the days leading up to the National she had faced reality without the cushion of money and influence between her and it. With all her supports suddenly swept from under her she had come to realise how much she depended on them—and on Myles. More so on

354

Myles now than ever before. She had also decided that she did not care for Pat as much as she had thought or pretended to herself that she did. She had, she told herself once she was seeing things with a new clarity, deceived herself about Pat. It was clear to her now that Pat had wanted her above all as another scalp to hang at his belt and nothing more. Since the accident she had not seen him, nor had he made any attempt to get in touch with her. The fact that he had not written was excusable for, like many of his kind, he was not too good with his pen. But he could have rung her or at least done something. Perhaps, she told herself, he had rung and not found her. He had been desperately busy, she knew, what with getting the ride on Rob Roy unexpectedly and taking every other ride he could in an effort to catch Tim in the Championship. Perhaps, too, he somehow associated her with Julius and his being jocked off Alexander. But he still owed her something even if he did not know how much.

Despite herself, too, doubts about his loss of memory were beginning to seep in. Was it as absolute as he was leading everyone to believe? His concussion had not been all that severe. Could it be that he was hiding behind her? Was that why he was avoiding her? She did not care to contemplate that issue but, as was her way, she would have been happier had she been given the opportunity to ask him face to face if he remembered anything.

The sound of someone asking a question broke into her thoughts.

'Are you going to give Pat Colby his share of the stake, Mr Marker?' It was Hector Mallinson.

'That's my affair. No comment,' Julius said.

'Can you tell us why you changed jockeys?'

'Same answer. No comment. It worked, didn't it? We won. I think Steve Barrett gave my horse a wonderful ride. I've nothing but praise for him. I hope he'll ride all my horses in future. You can quote me on that.' Julius looked straight at Hector and gave him one of his savage grins that was somewhere between a snarl and a scowl and intended to contain elements of both. In the days leading up to the National it was Hector who had contributed most to his roasting in the press.

'What were your thoughts when you waited for the result, Mr Marker?' It was one of the gossip boys.

'I'm not sure. I think I was praying.'

355

Myles had heard enough. This was a lot of cods-wallop, anyway. There was nothing to add to his story here. He edged towards the entrance.

'Message for you, Myles.' Someone pushed a folded piece of paper into his hand. He opened it and his heart leapt as he read it. This was good news indeed.

'Myles,' another voice was saying. 'Could I have a word with you?' It was Andrew Mostyn his former senior colleague on the *World*.

Ten minutes later Myles met Evelyn outside the weighing-room as the Marker entourage left the press conference. 'The champagne bar,' he said. 'I've got good news for you.'

The old-fashioned Victorian bar was crowded but they found a corner and Myles filled their glasses.

Evelyn smiled at him. 'What is this good news, Myles?'

'I went to Cheltenham a day or so back. I knew how worried you were about Miriam Barkley. I got one of the attendants in the hospital to phone a message through to me the moment it happened. It's just come in. She's off the danger list.'

'Myles, how wonderful. That poor woman. And him, Myles?'

'He didn't come here. He's been pretty marvellous considering what she is, and he must know by now. He's never left her bedside. But, that's not all.'

'What else is there?'

'When I was there I got Tommy Pereira to put me in touch with the solicitor chap who defended Pat that time. I made enquiries through him about what the police would do over your accident.'

'Did you find out anything?'

'I did or rather he did. He seems a pretty efficient sort of customer. Obviously there will be no manslaughter charge now. But as well as that they may not go ahead with the dangerous driving part of it, either.'

'Oh, my God, that would be something. But why, Myles?'

'I'm not great on the law but it seems that if you hadn't made a statement at all they couldn't have done anything because there wouldn't have been any evidence against you. You see Pat can't remember anything or he says he can't and it's very doubtful if Miriam will either. There is precious little even in

356

your own statement or so Ordway, the solicitor, says from what he can find out. Apparently you said that she shot across in front of you and the measurements such as they are seem to bear this out. Even if they do prosecute, and it's unlikely, Ordway seems to think that they won't make it stick, that there's very little case against you.'

Evelyn felt as if a great weight had been suddenly lifted from her. 'Oh, Myles,' she said. 'And you did this in the middle of all your own troubles.'

'I've had plenty of time.'

'There's something I want to tell you, Myles. I don't think I'm going to see anything more of Pat, again, ever.'

'That's perhaps the best news I've heard today and today has been a good day.'

'Why? You do look happy now I come to think of it.'

'Alexander won the National. You know, just down the road here a few minutes ago in case you've forgotten.'

'Don't be an ass, Myles. There must be something else.'

'Andrew Mostyn stopped me just now. He hasn't been well for some time, he told me. He's retiring at the end of this season. He has been asked to recommend someone to take his place. He asked me if I'd like it.'

Evelyn smiled. 'And would you?'

'Would I hell! And I'll be away from that bloody Featherstone and his investigative journalism. Back to real racing again. And that's not all.'

'It should be nearly enough. What else?'

'Julius is buying more horses. He's talking about going on to the flat, too, though I don't believe that. He's asked me to buy them for him and I'm to be his racing manager.'

'He *is* handing out favours all round. I'm back in his good books too. I wonder how long it'll last.'

'That's just what's bothering me.'

'Why you for heaven's sake?'

'That bloody photograph or have you forgotten it? If that gets into his hands I'm scuppered and so are you. This walking on air will wear off soon enough. He's still the same Julius. Did you see the grin he gave Mallinson at the press conference? Hector deserves everything that's coming to him but I'd be almost sorry for him if Julius ever gets anything on him. But about that photograph. God knows what he'll do if it ever—'

Myles broke off as he saw someone pushing through the throng towards them. 'Scarman!' he exclaimed. 'What are you doing here?'

The settler paused beside their table. His face was a sick grey colour and his hands were shaking. 'Heard about Mr Buckner?' he said.

Myles nodded.

Scarman put his hand into his mackintosh pocket and pulled out an envelope. 'He wrote to me,' he said. 'He told me to find you today and to be sure to give you this.' He dropped the envelope on to the table in front of Myles, turned away quickly and disappeared into the crowd.

Myles tore open the envelope. A negative and two prints fell on to the table. It was the picture of Evelyn, naked, laughing, that stared up at them. Beside the prints was a folded piece of writing paper. Myles picked it up. On it was written: *I won't need these any more. My father always said I was nearly but not quite a bastard. Good luck. L.Bb.*

Without speaking Myles handed the sheet of paper to Evelyn. When she had read it their eyes met and they both raised their glasses.